The Adorations

Roger Boylan

The Adorations
A Novel

DALKEY ARCHIVE PRESS

McLean / Dublin.

Library of Congress Cataloging Number: 2018026163

McLean (Illinois) / Dublin (Ireland)

Dalkey Archive Press's mission is to publish and preserve literary works from around the world.

Printed on permanent/durable acid-free paper.

www.dalkeyarchive.com

Ce qui est terrible dans la vie, c'est que tout le monde a ses raisons.
What's terrible in life is that everyone has his reasons.

—Jean Renoir

Gustave
One

AROUND CHRISTMASTIME IN 1557 John Calvin was beset by visions, but if they were signs of a special Christmas gift it was a gift (judging by his comments in *Little Reformer, Big Reform*, the unpublishable sequel to his unreadable *Institutes*) that he wished were returnable, like an ill-fitting pair of trousers; and if his visions were the symptoms of illness it was an illness he dreaded more than any other, one he called *Dementia Romana*, the madness of Rome.

"God preserve me from the haggard hand of the hag of Rome," raves John in *Little Reforme*r, Vol. 2, throwing in Satan for good measure: "And around the waistline [sic?] of their works build ye a ring of fire that none may cross." Decidedly, having visions was much too Papist a pastime for the great Reformer's liking, but had it not been for their Romanist associations he might have just sat back and enjoyed the show, for his visions were of a variety and everydayness not often found in the mystical literature—actually, it may have been this very everydayness that he most resented, as few of his visions, oddly, were remotely Christian, or even religious, in theme. Stefanie von Rothenberg and I were far more orthodox in our visionary material. In fact, what Calvin saw more closely resembles the futuristic gibbering of Nostradamus or Madame Soleil than the luxuriant God-insights of the ladies of Ávila, Lisieux and Salzburg (or me). Ironically, Calvin's little mental one-reelers seemed to get going around the New Year, as if in sympathy with the general (if clandestine, in his Geneva) intoxication of the season. To me, one of his visions in particular, stands out. Recounted to his wife, Idelette, and recorded by her with her customary precision in a journal entry for January 2, 1558—immediately following an account of a visit to the family home in Noyon and an evocative, even poetic, description of her mother-in-law's goiter ("like a rotting, porous sea-barge moored to the crumbling jetty of her neck the thing is, unsteady, grayish, and moist to the touch")—this one hit old John as he was crossing Place St. Pierre on his way home from a hard day's fire-and-brimstone at the eponymous cathedral. Before him he beheld, "as in a trance, a herd of noisome beast-carriages with eyes of sulphur and gleaming carapaces as of monstrous insects," huddled at St. Pierre's very steps, up and down which swarmed spectral human figures "caparisoned in diabolical colors of red, yellow and green"; two of these wretches, a "grossly ill-fashioned male with whiskers" and "a red-clad female, clearly a harlot," seemed (to reeling, head-shaking Calvin) to be taken into the maw of one of the dreadful machine-creatures, "a squatting, malodorous rubicund brute" which then departed, snarling and exuding noxious vapors, thus expressing to our man "all the sins and lusts of Beelzebub." "Hell itself is at the very gates of my church," gasped stricken John, faithfully quoted by Idelette (Saturday, January 3). "These are visions, if true visions they be, of Gehenna, of the final days: the damned in Hell! I must speak of it to my congregation in terms of warning: *Caveat, Homo*! Tomorrow, thou art damned! Idelette, my sermon must be of these things, vision or no." Oddly, the reluctant visionary himself recorded and dated a memento of his vision, a sketch in the margin of said sermon ("Sermon on the Imperishable Glory of Our Lord And the Undying Malevolence of the Fiend": *Little Reformer*, Vol. 1, Folio II): Depicted above the poignant inscription "Seen or dreamed? 2 jan. 1558" are two vertically aligned chevrons in a shaky ellipse, a four-and-a-half-century-old doodle, really, an emblem meaningless in itself even to the ever-suspicious Calvin (he appended a curlicued question mark of most un-Protestant elegance), but which looked, to me, like the emblem of the French automobile manufacturer

Citroën: two chevrons in an oval. Yes, an exact replica, no emen-
dation necessary. *Reductio ad absurdum*, then: Could Calvin,
cursed by the visionary gift he didn't want, have briefly wandered across time and the Place St. Pierre simultaneously, say,
to the early twenty-first century? Might his vision have been of
nothing more diabolical than the parked and departing cars of
church- and (mostly) café-goers (those colors: too bright for earlier times)? Pushing this interpretation to very edge of reason, the
"squatting red brute" could well have been, given my frequent
nocturnal visits in the vicinity of St. Pierre, my very own car, the
one that sits in my garage even now, the Maranello-red, restored
(by my own loving hands) 1975 Citroën-Maserati SM coupe
with the three-liter V6 engine, power windows, black leather
seats, Bosch automatic, and no damned air bags—not a car, by
the way, that one would imagine appealing to the austere tastes
of the Genevan Ayatollah. How irresistible to imagine that a
glimpse of me getting into my car put the wind up John Calvin
at a distance of four and a half centuries! And the red-clad harlot? Could *she* have been . . . ? Well, let us remember that God
moves in mysterious ways.

Mind you, Calvin's reaction to the car (assuming that is what
he saw, or fantasized) could have been scripted by my ex-fiancée.
"Get rid of that damned ugly thing, Gustave!" Françoise had so
often said upon coming upon me hovering sudsily over it, cloth
and bucket in hand, Sunday mornings as she set out on her
lonely way to church (not Calvin's, by the way, no, Françoise was
Catholic, despite her eagerness to embrace celibacy rather than
me) . . . and how did the rest of that diatribe usually go? "You're
a professor, for God's sake, not a rally driver. You care more for
that damned old car than you do for me or my friends. Mad!
You're mad!" Or words to that effect. She was partly right about
the car versus herself, at least, and absolutely right about her
friends (smug, Leftish, overanalytical). Finally she left, after four
years of bickering and deepening mutual incomprehension. She
now runs a social relief agency in Lausanne and belongs to some
association of neo-Left activists or other; as for my and Calvin's
Citroën—I'm thinking of naming it John, in honor—it sits in

the communal garage of my apartment building, and I still drive it some days to and from Farel College, where I, mad or sane as ever, still ply my trade, that of teaching, or rather professing, history to the young (History, Alpine, 11B; History, Italo-Balkan, Modern, 12C; History, History of, 005A) and not so young (one of my students last year was seventy-nine) . . .

Question: Could the great Reformer have been mad? Certainly. Madness strikes in the loftiest places, said Galileo, himself deemed mad by lesser men. Anyway, it all comes down to genetics, like so much else, so the odds that I might have a screw loose were good from the start: Papa was clearly *pazzo*, Mamma clearly not. At least, that was how they appeared to me, back then. Could it have been the other way around? In his own way, after all, Papa was a kind of pocket Calvin, not perhaps so much an out-and-out nutter as a frustrated reformer, burning with an eternally frustrated zeal stemming from his orthodox Marxism that in turn grew out of his hatred of (in order of no importance), his parents Tancredo and Adua Termi, winegrowers, of Custoza in the Veneto (Custoza, by the way, is the only Italian town without a duplicated *z* in its name, its sole claim to distinction except for the fine grappa that originates there), snobs and prime saboteurs of his career as a car mechanic (and a damned fine one, once he'd moved to Switzerland); the Church; oddly, Russians; less oddly (he was Italian, after all), the British and French; Japanese cars, therefore, the Japanese themselves, as well as their racial cousins the Chinese, despite Maoism; homosexuals, consequently hippies, ballet dancers, actors, beauticians, and their ilk; and others of a racial, sexual, and professional stamp more conventionally abhorred by your narrower mind. His likes? The standard Italian communist's roll call, e.g., the Juventus Turin football team; the wines of Piedmont; Antonio Gramsci and Palmiro Togliatti; Fidel Castro; Sacco & Vanzetti; Lenin (a god); Stalin (demi-); Anna Magnani; Dario Fo; and even Mussolini, up to a point ("But only the YOUNG Benito, ey? The YOUNG Benito. Did you know E was a socialist? Ey? EY?").

Mamma, on the other hand, gave every impression of being

serene and above the fray, but I've realized in the intervening decades that still waters run deep, and I wonder how deep when I remember her wry smile in the face of Papa's (and later my) storms of passion, her defiant attendance of Mass, and the long solitary drives she used to take into the countryside at the wheel of our old Fiat 1800. The love she lavished on animals, too, a love that demanded no suffering or hard labor in return— this, too, was odd, and quite un-Italian. But her family, the Caldicottos, had only been Italian since the Caldecotts arrived in Turin from Midlothian around the turn of the twentieth century and Italianized themselves to the point of absurdity: Great-grandfather Joe—a man so polite, according to family lore, that he raised his hat to horses and beggars—in halting, Scots-befogged Italian, would give his name as Giuseppe Battista Caldicotto, the "Battista" being mere Italianate adornment . . . Anyhow, King Tut, our Siamese cat, was the main beneficiary of this atavistic animal love of hers, for on the other, more Italian, hand, Papa's dialogue with the cat was limited to abrasive shouts of "Fuck off, cat" or "cat, shut up" or, like a line from a Goldoni farce, "Go from me now, swine of misery!"

Befitting a true Italian wife and mother, as long as Papa was alive Mamma's mood changes were mercurial but brief, allegro to andante and back to allegro again, like a Mozart concerto, brief shadows passing over smiling uplands. Of course, the postpartum rupture of her uterus and subsequent life-and-death operations had something to do with her moodiness, no doubt. Humiliatingly for an Italian woman, the extinction of her womb meant she would have no more children after she had me—I, hefty even then (something, I imagine, like a huge pinkish grub with the face of a compressed Genghis Khan), requiring, for my existence to get going, eighteen hours of her labor and, ultimately, a nearly botched Caesarean, all this at the pristine Clinique Beau-Séjour in the placid Malagnou district of our fine city.

So I was off to the races that fourteenth day of June in the year of our Lord (and I say that advisedly) 1950, screaming and kicking and, as we have seen, nearly killing my mother in the

process, but nevertheless growing up confident in her love for
me. Papa, then as later, was ambivalent. Yes, he had a son, *un
figlio*, but one was all he would have, and one was not enough,
only one of a dream-brood of sons to educate, indoctrinate in
Marxist groupthink, drill, and raise into collective manhood: one
for the unions, one for the newspapers, one for the university,
one for the family business, all four or five (he was the youngest
of six) married by twenty-five (in Papa's Geneva, as in Calvin's,
there was no fucking around), fathers themselves of sons, of
course, before their thirtieth birthdays. But *chez nous* there was
just me, christened Gustavo (for an antifascist uncle) Antonio
(for Gramsci) Ilyich (for . . . well, it's obvious) at the Notre-
Dame cathedral under the aegis of Father Benedetto Sanzio, a
Left-leaning worker's priest Papa grudgingly allowed across his
threshold for the odd glass of wine and ideological squabble (and
who was a close confidant of my mother's and, later, mine). I
continued to be called Gustavo until I took matters into my
own ten-year-old hands and informed Papa, in the proud tones
of the first generation, that I was Swiss, that my native language
was French (English came later), and that my name was Gustave.
He put down his *Humanité* or *Unità* and raised his hand to me
in intended chastisement, but the threatened blow wilted into
a shrug of indifference and the single syllable "*Bé*," short for
"*Bene*," and he returned to his armchair and perusal of the proletarian gossip columns wherein he would delightedly chew over
such tidbits as "Comrade Thorez today inaugurated Phase One of
his ultimate struggle against the democratic imperialists by laying
the inexorable steps to be taken by the working classes of France
toward final victory" or "It was with great pleasure and deep solidarity that Comrade Togliatti welcomed to Italy Comrade Kim Il
Sung, representative of the Korean people's heroic class struggle."
Ah, the peerless fustian of pinkoes! O Golden Age of perpetual
revolution! *Aux barricades*! How bracing it was (what bliss to
be alive!) to revile what others revered: the Church, the USA,
aristocrats, material goods, free enterprise! Another installment
of the *Us versus Them* soap opera, and by the way you can bury
all that nonsense about peace and harmony. What the world

yearns for is a stark division between good and evil. Simply put, we need enemies. This Papa understood, and even called himself on occasion "a heretical Christian," substituting, blasphemously, his cardboard icons—Gramsci, Lenin, Fidel—for the gilded variety; and he carried that flame all his short life long. Suffering Mamma only shook her head when, after an extra grappa or so, he'd rant about his beliefs in the god Marx. *Magari, Tadzio*, she always said: If only it were true.

But Marxist or not, Papa insisted on sending me to the best school in the city, the World Academy, where, he reasoned, my exposure to the conventions of the resident satraps of society's upper crust would at best gently ease me into his footsteps, and if worst came to worst I would at least learn from the experts the skills wherewith to support my aged parents. Alas, he only lived to learn of my laziness. He died at fifty-six one warm August afternoon in 1968, on the balcony of our little rented chalet below La Faucille with in his dying eyes the cerulean sky against which Mont Blanc was incarnadined in the westering light. His last word was no word, but an orotund mouth fart blown in my direction as I rushed onto the balcony waving that day's *Tribune de Genève*, upon the front page of which headlines blared news from Prague: the stifling of Dubček's spring, Russian tanks circling Wenceslas Square, simian Brezhnev lying fluently to the world. Violent infarction followed Papa's valedictorian raspberry, and lo! he and Czech democracy were dead the same day, victims both (of Marx, of life, of lies). The funeral was at the Plainpalais Cemetery. Coincidentally, the tombstone inscribed

Tadzio Termi
1912–1968
È finita la commedia

lies not ten meters from a humbler, much older tombstone, bearing the initials "JC" (but no dates), beneath which lies the dust of a certain Reformer, Humanist, and secret seer.

Mamma mourned; then, recovering, she flourished, all in six months or less. She lost weight, dressed up, took vacations, and sold Papa's car business for a subpar but comfortable sum. We were, briefly, well-off. I, then a student at Occhetto University in Milan, affected fashionable disdain (it was, after all, '68 or '69, years of insolence) for the tweeds, scarves, and Dunhill cigarettes worn by others of the bourgeoisie. I briefly went the scruffy proletarian way, with beret and heavy corduroys, into the twilight of the sub-revolutionary era, emerging into the dawn of another age, that of Aquarius and my own burgeoning maturity. I returned from Milan a *laureato*, educated yet deeply ignorant, better-dressed-than but overly bookish and underexperienced, and arrogant in the way of all youth.

*

Mystics mystify me, as I suppose they do most ordinary mortals, so when I became one myself I was quite shocked, as if two distinct, opposing personalities had taken up residence behind my bluff, unremarkable exterior. One personality, the normal one, ate and drank and taught classes at Farel College, wrote the odd poem, worried sporadically about heart palpitations, acid indigestion, joint aches, eye inflammations, bronchitis, etc., and taught his students, sometimes indifferently, sometimes well. This fellow could be found most Wednesdays and every Saturday at his customary table in the Café Lyrique, working his way through a *demi* of Fendant and the latest *London Book Review* or *TéléGuide* or *Le Monde Littéraire*.

The other chap was the newcomer, the seer of visions, and he was above, or beyond, the merely physical. He, or rather his vision, manifested himself one breezy September night on the Corraterie, Geneva's Bond Street or Faubourg Saint-Honoré. I (containing both these personalities) was on my way to visit Giulia in her charming garret room in the bohemian district of Carouge, in the south of the city. Giulia was a law student at the University. She was from Parma, a lithe Emilian with limbs of ivory and an apple-round bum to die for. Trust fate or the Almighty, then, to interject the sacred into my profane life, that evening; for not only was I in a state of erotic eagerness, I was well wined and dined within the butter-yellow walls of the dear

old Café Lyrique (once, by the way, the watering hole of, allit-
eratively if not chronologically, Lamartine, Lenin, and Liszt),
a favored eatery of mine on weekdays when the yearning took
hold for *mignons de bœuf* or *magret de canard*. Memory serves
up perch from that night, along with a side of sweet *pommes
d'Argovie* and bitter Guy Gax, the novelist, a friend—or enemy,
I'd never figured out which (I know now)— since the third
year at World Academy, where we met during an arm-wrestling
match in the lunchroom. We went to England together in '69
and did our military service together in the Engadine, back in
'74—when one inebriated summer's day he and I, mere corporals, aimed a bazooka at the wrong barn, flushing out chickens
and an irate cow, and that night dressed as captains and celebrated the survival of the livestock with a slap-up dinner at the
Süsswinkel restaurant in Chur and charged it all to the Federal
Armed Services. Upshot: ten days in the cooler and demotion to
soldat. My military career, for which I never cared a fig anyway,
suffered greatly, and I was given an invalid's dispensation in '78
(chronic flatfeet) . . .

Anyway, the subject at hand that night was a resolutely
unmystical one, nothing more elevated than the latest shenani-
gans of a) Katia, Guy's ex-wife and b) Guy's publisher La Maison
de l'Herbe (none of these proceedings excessively oiled, maybe
an open carafe of your standard Fendant de Sion)—and BANG,
there was the Archangel Michael, awash in shimmering light,
hovering inside two concentric luminous circles of gold and
trailed by sparkles like Tinkerbell right there on the Corraterie.
I (or should I say the other Gustave, newly arrived?) recognized
him at once. He was unmistakably the same chap Pope Gregory
had seen atop Castel Sant'Angelo: his sword, which he held up,
then slowly sheathed; his bright blue shield; his halo, discreet
but penetrating, like the dome light in a Mercedes; and cinematic, California-lifeguard good looks. He was smiling blandly.
The wings, too, were a dead giveaway. He folded them neatly.
He was formal and reasonably polite; I, likewise. The exchange
went, approximately, thus:

"Good evening, Gustave Termi. Do not be afraid." His voice

was mellifluous yet mechanical, with a hint of the robotic; his speech unaccented, as if he'd learned the language from Linguaphone tapes.

"Ah, good evening. I am not afraid."

"You are a man."

"That I can hardly deny."

"With bestial lusts and the soul of a *hazzan*." (His Hebrew was better than his French. This means "cantor" in the ancient language of the Jews.)

"Rather, with the soul of a man, a mere mortal, a thinking reed." I was in good Pascalian form, although I didn't care for that reference to bestial lusts.

"But room for God therein."

"Oh, yes, room for God. And the other one, alas."

"To whom we refer, allusively, as the Adversary," and here he made an extraordinary putty-face, widening his eyes and lengthening his nose and cheeks into a vulpine muzzle, a touch of the werewolf chilling even to a lifelong fan of horror flicks—"but never by any other name." I was duly warned, and vowed never to practice in my shaving mirror.

"No, never," said I.

His face collapsed into bland Rivieran handsomeness.

"This is the first visit, Gustave," he intoned, like Marley's Ghost to Ebenezer, or Ezekiel to William Blake. "There will be more. Be prepared." With that Boy Scout exhortation, he vanished—or, to be more precise, he rose off the ground a little higher (he'd been floating about a half meter above) then dissolved into a white cloud, like Mr. Tidy in the detergent commercial. All the while, by the way, people were strolling along the street, a drunk was bawling, cars and tramcars were going by, a mild breeze (it was June) was wafting scents of an early summer city night (tree blossoms, *frites*, car exhaust, the river nearby); clearly, nobody else had heard or seen a middle-aged man conversing with an armed and hovering archangel, nor even that same middle-aged man gabbling at the empty air . . . well, I've read enough theology and sci-fi, good and bad, to have a stab at the reason. It's something to do with Time, our master, being

Their slave, and a little zone of non-Time being created around the angel and me, muddling everybody else's receptors for the nonce. (It muddled mine. For the duration of the encounter I felt on the verge of a momentous stammer, with a touch of nightmarish immobility.)

I worked out that Time theory on my way home, and let me add that I was in no mood for further lucubrations on the subject, not until I'd had a couple of stiff Ricards and watched a reassuringly boring political program on FR3 during the course of which no mention was made of archangels, visions or anything remotely otherworldly (or interesting).

I called Giulia, to apologize.

"Is OK."

"I'll make it up to you next time."

"A-o, *professore*. Is OK."

"Dinner? At the Boeuf Rouge?"

"A-o. Forget it. See you next week."

I drank more, then called Gax.

"It's too late," he mumbled. "Are you drunk?"

"Never mind that. Something happened to me on the way home. It's incredible."

I explained.

"And how do you know he was an archangel, my dear fellow?"

"The sword, the halo. The gilded circles surrounding him. The hair. Like the statue at the Castel Sant'Angelo depicting the vision Gregory the Great had during the plague. Straight out of one of those Victorian mezzotints. Or a Renaissance painting."

"Well, this is it, Termi."

Of course, he didn't mean "This is it, alert the media," or "This is it, it's the proof all mankind has been waiting two thousand years for," or even "This is it, what a story": no, no. Gax was bilious, as usual.

"You've gone off your rocker at last," he snapped. "After years of expert apprenticeship. Perhaps your imagination is underutilized, Termi? Stop watching so damn much television. Write more. Get married. Go around the world. If you need a psychiatrist, try LeCluyse, he's just down the block from you on the

Boulevard des Philosophes. He got me off heroin, you know. But if you want my honest opinion, it's our friends at Al-Anon you're more in need of." He concluded his insolent advice with a yawn. "And so to bed. Sleep it off, Termi."

I was outraged but unsurprised. I might well have reacted the same way, had our roles been reversed. I, too, reverted to banality (we all chant the everyday jingles, while in the shadows lurk demons), fearing as much the effort required to adjust to a blinding revelation of faith as the revelation itself—and the nagging doubts about my own sanity? Brazenly, my initial reaction was: Let them nag. As long as astrology and Islam and communism find followers, who's to say a mere mystic's mad? Then I wondered, too, if I weren't losing my mind—or at least paying a long-overdue debt to alcohol, not that I was an alcoholic (aha! the alcoholic's instinctive protest!), nor even a daily drinker, nor, certainly, an epileptic; but at age fifty-three, in as bibulous a city as Geneva, with the assistance of temperament (artistic) and profession (liberal, easy access to cafés), I probably drank more in a week than entire families in, say, Aleppo, do in a lifetime . . . but no more than most of my acquaintances, and less than some. Moreover, alcohol played no role in the visions of the great mystics of the past, as far as I knew. I mean to say, consider the dissonance in this composition:

St. John of the Cross;
Bernadette of Lourdes;
Sister Elisabeth of Schönau;
Sister Lúcia dos Santos;
Sister Hildegard of Bingen;
St. Thérèse of Lisieux;
Professor Gustave Termi, history department, Farel College.

This jarring note rang harshly in my ears. It upset my digestion. Worse, it took over the dream space formerly occupied by women, art, cars, and memory. It finally drove me to spend my free hours researching my new avocation, or curse. My inquiries began at the top, or as near as mere mortal ever got, with the only Teresa d'Ávila work that I owned: *The Way of Perfection*.

My perusal was brief, not only because of the profound boredom religious enthusiasm inspires in me, but also because of a
sneaking suspicion that I was unworthy to be, however remotely,
of the same company as the sweet madwoman of Ávila, who
believed in utter denial and gut-wrenching austerity as the means
to God, her whole life spent divided between the worldly (10%)
and the divine (90%). Her travails, and those of her chum John
of the Cross, although not as physically horrible as those of, say,
Miguel Servetus—burned at the stake here in Geneva (but now
honored in the name of our Second League football team, F. C.
Servette), courtesy of Big John Calvin, for farting on Sunday,
or something equally offensive in the eyes of Papa John—elevated mysticism to the rank of pure spirit, a saintly pastime far
out of the reach of a workaday sinner such as I. Anyway, such
transports were substitutes for, or successors to, Art, for which
I had no need of substitutes, thanks very much. They were akin
also, as visions of God, to the music of Palestrina or J. S. Bach,
i.e. sublime transcendence, a white liqueous light illuminating
the way ahead, immortality just around the bend (hard on the
heels of your average mystic)—and I always preferred Mozart
and Mahler and Wagner's *Parsifal*. But the visions of Teresa were
certainly not just phantoms of, say, a too-hastily consumed pork
chop, or bottle of acidic Gamay (although come to think of it,
the plonk I had that night at dinner with Gax *had* tasted a trifle
corked); no, nothing so mundane, and here was the crux of my
dilemma, sensuality being the essence of my life. I'm no Picasso,
but I love the first bite of a morning smoke, the soft stroke of a
spring breeze, the smoothness of a woman's thigh, the muffled
purr of a well-tuned engine, etc., etc. . . . . ah, but all these things
are of God, too, you will say, if you are the sage I take you for.
Yes, but that God is the humanist's God, and these things are
primarily of the world, and no mystic I'd ever read about had
ever been a man, or woman, of the world, or a humanist. All
were austere, self-denying, abstemious, in a word, crazy; or, at
least, so devotedly antiphysical that craziness came naturally, as
a result of no food or drink or sex for years on end. Their love of
a God of the spirit was absolute, fanatical, uncompromising. My

love of God? Awe, perhaps, at one remove, as deep as anyone's, but I stress that remove, through the prism of art and science and the works of Man . . . perhaps "love" never entered into it, now that I have all this under the magnifying glass. Who, post-Auschwitz, loves God? Love was for calmer times, when news of horrors never traveled, or could be dismissed as myth or the outlandish behavior of heathens . . . no, in my approach to the Almighty I was more of a Hebrew, fearful, respectful, admiring, humble before His works, yet detached and skeptical to the core, spiritually closer to Abraham, God's questioner, than to Aquinas, His unquestioning servant: Dr. Aquinas, consummate theologian, sage Doctor of the Church and heavyweight levitator. No, Aquinas was no example for me. His spirituality was beyond a layman's reach, and a layman can't have visions of the Almighty and His minions . . . or can he? What of Blake? Here indeed was a precedent: secular mystic, poet and visionary, man of the world (printer, sensualist, rebel) who above all yearned for God, the Divine, Infinity, the Universe, the Great Fuck, or something: "If the doors of perception were cleansed everything would appear to man as it is: infinite." Why, yes! Cleanse those doors, I say! You there! You, too, can rub elbows with infinity! At the mere age of ten didn't wee Willie see angels clustering in a tree? What of his encounter with Ezekiel in a field? Tea and scones with Jesus? O Brother mine! O great prophet of Orc, of Los, of Urizen! Full many a week had I slavered over his work back in my Edinburgh days—and it was there, too, now that I come to think of it, that I had what one might call my first mystical experience.

*

Edinburgh! Well matched to Geneva, Knoxian Avignon to my Calvinist Rome, both stern and crenellated windswept citadels of the past; both, in the episodic sunlight of their hilly realms, as coyly beautiful as their mercurial skies; both solid, too, and stolid, and deeply alcoholic. I'd arrived from Milan as an assistant lecturer in French and Italian, with doctoral ambitions. I found rooms on Balcarres Street, a semi-suburban stretch of Victorian highway bound on one side by a cemetery, on the other by long-disused, weed-grown railway tracks leading straight into that rank and silent place where Romance and Horror embrace. Balcarres Street was remote and unfashionable, which suited me. Also, I had a view, beyond the graveyard, of the Pentland Hills, yellowish-blue in the sun. On rainy days the winding paths up the hillsides glistened wetly like the mucal trails of giant snails. I roomed in a ground-floor bedsit for two years of my Edinburgh sojourn, sharing the rent with guitarists and language teachers and a ne'er-do-well named Willie, a linguist from Glasgow with whom I found instant companionship. My love of solitude and select debauchery coincided with his; my need of occasional outbursts, too, found a ready response in the high jinks that came so naturally to the Calvinist-born rebel he was. For instance (and here my digression returns, more or less, to its point), it was in Willie's company that the veil was first lifted and I saw, one Halloween . . . a spook? A stain on my eyeglasses? A mirage? An angel's harbinger? No angel, at least, not then. Willie and I were drunk, and in a cemetery at midnight on Halloween, it being common in the Scotland of Willie's childhood to spend All Hallows in a graveyard on a dare. As we had a graveyard handy, and were Dutch-courageous after an evening's drink, why, Willie and Swiss Gus were game, *och aye*! So there we sat, with our beer, on a broad new tombstone near the main gate, across from a small mourners' pavilion. As one a.m. tolled and rolled away, in that pavilion—as if responding, on cue, to the simultaneous pops of our beer can ring-tabs—something gathered itself mistily into existence and rose and limped, rather than walked, in our direction; something fog-like and pale and vague, yet with discernable features like a much-erased Identikit drawing; not the features of an archangel, nor a demon, either, but not quite your standard ghost, no mere spectral passerby . . . anyway, whatever it was or wasn't, it was invisible to Willie—"a spook, och aye, away yourself, fer Gawd's sake"—but THAT FACE a haunting severe enough to linger in my mind for days afterward, a visitant (or revenant) from deep within the spidery undergrowth of M. R. James, or the clammy vaults of Poe, and maybe, for

all I know, no more or less than a direct, digestive consequence
of that evening's vindaloo and dozen or more beers. I yelled,
pointed, bolted, caught my foot on a railing, went down face-
first, endured Willie's jibes, returned to the flat, took in an aria
or two (Puccini? Verdi?) and slept, to dream of who knows what.
Gravely, I reconnoitered the graveyard on the following day, hungover, ashamed, and doubtful. The best I could come up with,
anywhere near the pavilion, was the tomb of a deacon deceased
since 1890 or so. Oddly, the tomb was surmounted by an inor-
dinately spectacular, Neapolitan-style of the Archangel Michael,
somewhat militant in stance; downright prescient, if you credit
Memory with recording, rather than inventing, abilities.

Back home, I never made much of my encounter in the cemetery. It was just a dinner-table yarn that first amused, then worried, my colleagues at the College, skeptics and freethinkers all.
But if I'm a mystic, then Edinburgh was the crucible, and not
just because of the ghaistie in the boneyard. The city itself sim-
mers with long-suppressed magic that no amount of artistry, or
art, can disguise. As does Geneva, beneath its bland facade of
international do-goodery.

So, all those years later, I found myself mentally revisiting,
with the clarity of long-disused memory, the bonnie braes of the
Pentlands, where I'd often strolled (or "rambled," to keep the
Romantic spirit), innocent at heart, *Innocence* in hand: "To see
a World in a Grain of Sand/ And a Heaven in a Wild Flower,
/ Hold Infinity in the palm of your hand/ And Eternity in an
hour." I'd returned hopefully to the works of Blake, the great
mad polymath, and spent most of one Saturday morning (the
howling wintry bise cooperating to make the outdoors inhospita-
ble) rereading "Jerusalem," an intense exposure to quirky genius
that, in the end, tired me out: Ah, Brother William. Alas. *Già
basta*. Did He who made me make thee? The man was brilliant,
yes, visionary, quite possibly, and mad, beyond doubt, all these
in an entirely English way that was appealing mainly in short
doses or from a distance. He utterly lacked, however, that skepticism, that detachment, that touch of world-weariness that is
the stamp of my kind, my song of experience—that is, let me

say it plainly, so Italian. (Swiss that I proudly am, I am also, dear Papa, as Italian as Venetian grappa, or the bordellos of Pompeii.) Blake always reminded me of one of those bicycle-riding, ruddy-cheeked, half-a-pint-a-night Sunny Jims in corduroy trousers who sing in Gilbert and Sullivan societies at British universities and who, frequently, belong to political clubs or religious groups: too earnest by half, our William. But a crank, a genius? Oh yes. Those, if nothing else.

Post-"Jerusalem," and running short of other sources at home, I braved the Bise and made a visit to the eminent Central Library on the Boulevard Helvétique. (This would have been, let me see, a week or so after my run-in with the Archangel.)

"Have you mystics?"

"Beg pardon, monsieur?"

"I seek mystics. Their memoirs. Biographies. Et cetera."

"Ah. Ávila and company?"

"Yes. And/or Lisieux. And others."

Well, they had some such, yes. See under "Religion," which section was in a dusty, little-used corner of the library, adjacent to the heavier traffic of the "Mysteries" section—tsk, tsk! what an eloquent commentary on our Godless age!—dimly illuminated by flickering fluorescent strips. On the bookshelves, under the rubric "Religious Works," I first investigated Michael. I knew, of course, that he was the mightiest of angels, a great favorite of Jews, Muslims, and the Orthodox; and sure enough, there in the *Lex Vaticana*, Vol. III, was a photo of the effigy atop the Castel Sant'Angelo, sheathing or drawing his sword. "St. Michael is one of the principal angels," I read. "His name was the war-cry of the good angels in the battle fought in Heaven against the enemy and his followers." Well, we all know who *that* is, don't we? I remembered the archangel's blood-chilling imitation and shivered—I am tempted to add, in good literary style, "although it was a warm day," but in fact it was quite chilly. "Four times his name is recorded in Scripture," lectured the *Lex*. "Following these Scriptural passages, Christian tradition gives to St. Michael four offices:

• To fight against Satan.

• To rescue the souls of the faithful from the power of the enemy, especially at the hour of death.

• To be the champion of God's people, the Jews in the Old Law, the Christians in the New Testament; therefore he was the patron of the Church, and of the orders of knights during the Middle Ages.

• To call away from earth and bring men's souls to judgment (*signifer S. Michael repraesentet eas in lucam sanctam*, Offert. Miss Defunct. *Constituit eum principem super animas suscipiendas*, Antiph. off. Cf. Hermas, Pastor, I, 3, Simil. VIII, 3).

"Archangel Michael," gushed the *Lex*, "is known for his great powers of protection. His mighty sword cuts away anything which no longer serves: cords and bonds, astral energies, etc. He is associated with the color electric blue. His feast day is September 29."

Brrrr, indeed. According to my rough mental calculations, as it was now mid-October, I'd seen him in late September sometime, very likely on the twenty-ninth . . . And by the way, I quite like electric blue, but I didn't like that part about bringing men's souls to judgment, or rescuing the soul at the hour of death. Perhaps I was a secret Jew and he'd found time in his busy schedule to prepare me for the news?

(Or an even more secret Christian?)

Or about to die?

But he'd told me nothing, really. And—for God's sake! (As it were.) Enough of archangels. I turned for light relief to the short shelf of Mystics and found, as expected, Teresas three, those superstars of piety Ávila, Lisieux, and (completing the trinity of Teresas) Saint T. of Calcutta, this last a biography by a Vatican groupie and correspondent for *Einstein* magazine. Bored, I was on my way out. Then, like the close of an office workday, came release from tedium: a slim volume red with the gilt lettering of a Douai Bible, or a cardinal's robes. Its title was *Adoration: A Life of Stefanie Von Rothenberg*. A composite gold logo formed by a cross and a swastika adorned the spine. The author was one Martine Jeanrenaud, a TV journalist whose doctoral dissertation this book had originally been. Intrigued, I took it down, then hesitated; if this Martine Jeanrenaud was to guide me I needed to know more about her. I wanted no Leftish exegesis, no post-modern propaganda, no ideological havering. On the Table of Contents verso page, I came upon a short bio, with accompanying photograph of a pretty woman in her late thirties or so with shaggy hair and round glasses. Martine Jeanrenaud was, according to the blurb, a master's graduate of Geneva University and a doctor ex-Sorbonne-Paris II, with studies at Princeton also to her credit. (Aha! I sensed Career Woman at best, Feminist Scholar at worst.) Furthermore, she was the author of, apart from the present volume, *James Fazy: Radical Bourgeois*, and currently a TV reporter at Télé Suisse 1, known for her work on the "popular documentary series" *Priests of the People: Wholesome Rebels* (featuring among others Father Leonardo Boff and the Abbé Pierre) and producer of something called *Land Beyond the Yaks: Bhutan, Modern Shangri-La* . . . so, this Jeanrenaud person had a notch or two on her belt, that was clear. Her qualifications to write history were less so, but these days any journalist deems him- or herself qualified to craft the great book of life in all its forms, fictional, dramatic, historical, autobiographical, sexual, and we have only Time the great winnower to fall back on in our quest for culture.

I borrowed the volume, hurried home, and settled myself deep in my armchair. With a cigarette and an espresso at my side I embarked on Page One, reserving the right to resume at any moment my browsing elsewhere.

*

Adoration: A Life of Stefanie von Rothenberg
by Martine Jeanrenaud

Linz

Linz on the Danube; Linz, third city of Austria; Linz, placid, contented, aloof; Linz, June 28, 1907. The city simmered in the heat of the summer morning. It was ten o'clock by the bells of the Martinskirche. After dutifully noting the hour, the bells started pealing their joy, in unison with the bells of the Pfarrkirche, the Minoritenkirche, and the Cathedral: The Archduke was coming! Which archduke? Why, the Heir Apparent, Franz Ferdinand, of course. He and his lady, the Duchess Sophie, were coming down from their Bohemian retreat at Konopiště to celebrate their seventh wedding anniversary by dining and regiment-reviewing and paying a visit to Leonding stables, just outside the city, where His Imperial Highness kept fine Lipizzaners. Among the populace few knew and fewer cared, Linz being a pro-German town and the Archduke not being the popular idol his cousin Rudolf, darling of Mayerling, had been, despite which the joy broadcast by the pealing bells was quite genuinely felt by the townsfolk, at least in part. Truth to tell, as far as most Linzers were concerned it might as well have been Michaelmas, or St. Jude's, or the birthday of the Sultan in Constantinople. No matter. Like all Linz holidays, it would be a day of slow strolling along the riverside promenade of the Donaulände; of the gentle clown-music of tubas by the Holy Trinity pillar on the Hauptplatz; of foamy steins in the beer gardens of Urfahr; of grilled *Bergsteiger wurst* and *pläcke* potato cakes; and *Linzer torte*, and the coarse *Nusszopf* bread of the provinces; of laughter, and forlorn hopes, and piercing desire, and once-prim gazes suddenly burning with the unnameable. Only the carriage horses would hate the day, but even for them there would be extra feed, and a good rubdown under the linden trees. As for the humans— well, there was time enough, tomorrow, to nurse the hangover and stammer apologies to earn the deeper opprobrium of Herr Direktor, or Herr Doktor, or Vater Unser im Himmel. Today, a holiday, was made to enjoy. Relax! Drink deep! Work has made you free (for a day) . . . !

At ten ten the joyous pealing rippled into silence. The air was still. Along the Donaulände a few family groups were taking the air, working hard, in their Austrian way, at having a good time, and any one of them could have been any one of the others, all typically consisting of heavily whiskered Pappi in his Sunday best, a Franz Josef in miniature striding ahead and making pontifical comments on the blindingly obvious while Mamma was leading, or carrying, the young ones, oblivious to Pappi's dull discourse.

"The boat to Vienna, *Mutti*," he said. "Fifteen minutes late."

He paused, raised an expectant forefinger: the bell of the Pfarrkirche, newly returned to yeoman service, announced the quarter hour. The Vienna mailboat steamed by, downstream, under the Urfahr bridge.

"Get along, Pappi," said Mutti. "We'll be late for church."

On the bridge, looking down at the now-swift mail boat, a young man in artistic garb—floppy hat, neckerchief, ivory-tipped cane—consulted his pocket watch and, turning to the young woman beside him, he (being Austrian too) made the same predictable remark as our *bürgerlich* Pappi, but in his voice was a slight tremor, as if what he was saying were merely a salve to the nerves of a young man on a date.

"Look at that. It's nearly quarter of an hour late today."

She ignored the remark, admired the watch.

"Oh, how pretty. Is it new?"

"No, no. My father's. Twenty years of service in the Habsburg civil service." He said this sarcastically, yet with a hint of pride.

"May I see?"

She took the watch, turned it over. It was as big as an onion, gleamingly gold, or (more probably) gold-plated, with a smooth Swiss moonface (Audemars Piguet, Geneva) and Roman numerals. On the back was an inscription: *For Esteemed Colleague and Friend Alois Hitler! With Respect and Best Wishes, Office of the Royal and Imperial Customs, Braunau am Inn, the twenty-seventh of May, 1895.*

"It's very fine, Adolf. It suits you, especially today." She handed it back. "And that suit! Such respect for the Archduke!"

"The Archduke, pah! But I have the greatest respect, ah, er, for." He paused, wound the watch-stem once, and tucked the watch back into his vest pocket. "For certain distinguished young ladies." Then, the Austrian-male reflex: rapid coordination of heel-clicking and head-dip, hardly a bow, more a ritual tic. But Adolf, daringly, went further: "I mean, of course, for certain distinguished young ladies, in particular, ah, for you, Fräulein

Stefanie." Then, racked with nerves, he made sure the moment had passed, he hurried it on its way by abruptly raising the ivory-topped cane (a recent affectation) and pointing it, while uttering a hoarse bark of a laugh, at a straw-hatted cyclist passing them on the Donaulände.

"Ha! My goodness, look. I believe it's Gustl. Now him I can talk to. He respects me, I think. He agrees with me, anyway."

The cyclist waved, wobbled, nearly collided with the *bürgerlich* family in duck procession (or another one just like it), regained his balance, waved again, laughed. Adolf frowned.

"I wonder if he knows who you are," he said. "I'm sure he'll have many questions. Where is she from? How old is she? Is she rich?" He chuckled. "It's his main fault, he's too curious. I had to tell him more than once that the business he was inquiring about was mine, not his. Of course, I would never intrude on *your* business, Fräulein Stefanie." Again the half bow, the moment of peerless awkwardness that was, however, not unusual, neither with young Hitler nor in most Austrian middle-class circles, where formality generally forestalled grace. As the daughter of minor provincial nobility, Stefanie was used to it, but she sought release from it whenever possible, this time from a plume of smoke drifting skyward.

"Look," she said. "Isn't that the Vienna train?"

Adolf stiffened to attention.

"Yes," he said. "Ah yes, yes. The 10:20 express. I will be taking that train. Actually, I took that very train last year when I went up to Vienna. Our imperial capital, ha! In fact, it is a splendid city, Fräulein Stefanie, a splendid city. The buildings! The music! The coffeecakes! A bit dirty, and there are human dregs everywhere, even in the most elegant neighborhoods, but Paris is like that, too, I hear, and London, of course, and even Berlin. Shall we walk on?"

They did so. Anyway, it was a command rather than a suggestion. Adolf strode ahead, swinging his cane. Stefanie hurried after him like a meek *hausfrau*, somewhat resenting this (but he was a man, he was an Austrian . . .). He was talking over his shoulder as they descended the stairs from the bridge and came onto the Donaulände. Stefanie caught the tail end of his peroration.

". . . Vienna in October, you know, to study at the Academy. Perhaps sooner, except I will be sitting the admittance exam then. In any case, after I pass the exam I plan to keep a studio there and maintain my residence here, in Urfahr, with my mother. My mother is not well, these days. Too much worrying about her children, but this is so typical of mothers, *ja*? Or perhaps I will take an apartment on the Graben, depending on the extent of my artistic success." He slowed down, again aware of her. "You must come to visit me, Fräulein Stefanie!"

"Yes. I'd like to."

Vienna! She'd been to Munich, a nice town and more worldly than Linz, certainly; but Vienna, she knew from her reading, and letters from her Kahane cousins, was on another scale entirely: Habsburgs and the Hofburg! glamor! the theater! the arts! *Herrn* Klimt, Schnitzler and Mahler! The Opera! Lehár!

"Everything absolutely respectable, of course. Absolutely. Yes, I am an artist," a dreamy I-am-an-artist expression wafting across Adolf's features, "above all I am an artist, God be thanked, but please don't think that because of that I have no morals, no, no, I have the utmost respect, believe me. Not that I . . ."

He slowed down to interrupt himself, gave her a sidelong glance, slyly. True to prim form, Stefanie smiled, placidly awaiting resumption of the monologue. Inwardly she was assessing him, responding to his peacock-display: almost handsome, with those blue eyes, that mobile mouth, but not quite, with that beak of a nose, that oddly weak chin; but he was hardly ugly, and by no means stupid, a bit self-important, in fact pompous in the extreme when he started on his ideas, like so many men she knew, but he was passionate, at least, unlike most men, and so utterly courteous when he was paying attention to her that he was almost like a character in the theater, as if he'd only rehearsed his good manners, never practiced them. Most of all, he was an artist, and a good one, judging by the watercolors he'd shown her with that same odd combination of self-effacement and arrogance: Pah, it's nothing, only genius! He was a real artist, anyway, not just a talker, although a talker he certainly was, too . . . of course this was all part of the artistic personality, or so she'd heard.

"Not that I am incapable, or unaware," he resumed, standing with his hands behind his back, wagging the cane gently from side to side like a headmaster about to administer punishment, "of shall we say, oh I don't know, deeper feelings? As in, as with— have you seen *Tristan and Isolde*, Fräulein Stefanie? I saw it last year in Vienna. Magnificent! But perhaps you are too young . . . ?"

(Another quality he had was that of conveying his own nervous energy, almost to a fault: She felt slightly giddy, unsure yet elated at the same time, as if a great wonderment awaited.)

"No. No, I haven't seen it, but not because I'm too young, Adolf. My father wouldn't let me."

Young she was, barely eighteen, but eighteen, in that day and age, was young no longer; girls were mothers by then, and farmwives, and courtesans. Naivety was for the spoiled, ignorance for the extremes of rich and poor. Stefanie was neither especially naive nor ignorant, and, although spoiled, as is normal with an only child, she had sufficient grace and spiritual wherewithal to temper the effects. The worst that could be said of her was that she was, perhaps, overly hopeful and determined, but these were, for the most part, qualities derived from her solid stock, the von Rothenbergs of Salzburg and environs. Her father, Herr Doktor Hermann, physician and part-time church organist, claimed descent from the same minor nobility as the great poet and dramatist Hans von Rothenberg; yet "minor" was hardly apt in view of the way he carried on in all of Salzburg's best salons, for all the world as if his name were Habsburg. It was arrogance, but it imbued his daughter with a self-confidence and assuredness well beyond her years, qualities that normally come, if at all, only in opposition to life's unremitting tests. That self-confidence had enabled her to accept young Herr Hitler's invitation. It hadn't deserted her yet, but she felt it wavering at his mention of *Tristan and Isolde*, undermined by the suspicion that Adolf was, in his clumsy way, coming around to a declaration of some kind. Certainly mentioning that opera was a sign of unusual, not to say cosmopolitan, interests. *Tristan and Isolde* was still frowned upon in certain formal family circles like her own: Her father was wont to call Wagner "that Italian," implying not the glories of that nationality but the perceived over-amorousness, the lack of restraint, emotional extravagance . . . in brief, she knew the story, the great sweep of romantic passion, Nordic sensibilities allied to universal demands of the flesh.

Foolishly, her heart raced.

"Of course I know what it's about," she said, lowering her gaze.

"The great hymn of nationhood," said Adolf. He relaxed his stance, resumed walking, swung his cane. Over his shoulder he shot her intermittent glances, as if to make sure she was still following him. "German culture. In opposition to French. Do you understand? It is the greatest art ever created. I cannot begin to tell you of the esteem in which I hold Wagner. I would give anything for a chance to visit Bayreuth. Actually, I wrote a letter last month to Frau Winifred Wagner, wife of the Master's son Siegfried. Such a lady, ah, she is a lady of distinction. I have not received a reply, but I am hopeful. Of course, she has many correspondents. So, Fräulein Stefanie. May I invite you?"

Another pause, a direct blue gaze, for once hoping to elicit a response. Oh, he is an artist, she said to herself. Unpredictable, moody, passionate. A difficult man, but his good manners will keep him in check.

"Well, invite me where?"

"To the opera, of course! Next week the State Opera performs Wagner here. Kubizek is going, you can meet him." (As if his friend Kubizek's presence were an added attraction, the clincher, Adolf's company by itself not being enough of a draw.) "They will be performing *Rienzi*, a truly magnificent work of art. Do you know it?" He paused just long enough to draw breath. "The story of a noble Roman senator who led the people against stupidity and tyranny. It's not merely a great opera, Fräulein Stefanie. It's a cause, a manifesto, a declaration! But most people don't pay attention, you know. They think it should be all vulgar entertainment, like the music hall. Unless you point it out to them."

They were walking again. As they approached the nearby

Hofgasse, the sounds of thumping drums and burbling tubas could be heard coming from the Hauptplatz, the main square. A loudmouthed party of soldiers in leopard-skin waistcoats and green-white-and-red regimental plumes headed past them in a disorganized way, intent upon the music and beer tents and ready— as suggested by their sly glances at Stefanie (and brief, loud sniggering at the sight of her dashing companion)—for recreation.

"I thought *Tristan and Isolde* was about love," said Stefanie suddenly.

"Ah yes, yes. Did you see those soldiers? Hungarians, pah. What kind of country is this? One wonders what business they could possibly have here in Upper Austria. Doesn't Budapest need defending? Against gypsies, for example?"

This was evidently a joke, to judge by Adolf's subsequent cough of laughter. Stefanie ignored it and repeated her question.

"Love?" said Adolf. "But many things are about love. Most works of art are about love. But you must ask yourself, is that all they are about? Do they not have secondary purposes, meanings for the intellect? Is Goethe about love? Is, ah. Schiller?" Startled, he turned. She was speaking; indeed, she had interrupted.

"Oh yes," she said, firmly. "Goethe is about love, Adolf. Read *Elective Affinities*! The love of man for woman, woman for man. 'Eternal Womanhood Leads us on High,' as he said." At the Realschule, as Adolf would hardly know, having left the year before (a no doubt touchy point which she forbore to bring up), they had just finished with *Elective Affinities*. Amorous, intellectual, generous, oft-despairing yet ever hopeful, the Sage of Weimar was for Stefanie the summit of male perfection, a classical genius with Romantic panache, spirit and flesh co-existing in classical harmony.

"His love for Friederike of Sessenheim, Charlotte Buff, Maximiliane, Charlotte von Stein? Ach, Adolf, he was a great lover."

Adolf sensed her sincerity, even knowledge. *Von Rothenberg*, after all. The name, when brooded upon, implied a world of formality and letters and breeding foreign to the young Hitler, customs-man's son of woodsman stock, from tight little Braunau and the deep wild weald of the *Waldviertel*. He turned sullen and uncommunicative, feeling spurned in favor of the glamorous dead, Goethe especially. *Concerning German Nature and Art* was the only Goethe piece he'd ever read in its entirety, hoping for a screed; in fact, he'd found it a bore, and parts of it decidedly un-German. As for *Young Werther, The Wandering Jew, Wilhelm Meister, Faust*—yes, he'd dabbled, but the rigidity, the classicism, the wigs and silk stockings . . . he needed more. He needed paganism, but not Goethe's genteel Hellenismus; Germanic paganism, brute force, kicking down the doors of the past; he longed for the purity of passion (blonde women like Stefanie), mountaintop bonfires, Nietzsche (except for the Frenchified later Nietzsche, gaga from syphilis anyway), Beethoven, Wagner. Especially Wagner. Adolf's exposure to the great music-dramatist was of recent vintage, and his obsession had become quite dictatorial. In the absence of God, the ex-aspirant to the priesthood needed a God, and he'd found Wagner, who, in his opinion (however unfairly to Wagner), had it right, bringing together the pagan and the romantic, with a nod to Germanic Christendom: the Teutonic Knights, Parsifal the Conqueror, the Grail-Seeker, the Avenger, the Hermann of Teutoburger Forest, Frederick Redbeard, Frederick the Great, Walpurgisnacht, every woman's dream, every man's inspiration, purity and manliness personified. *Tristan?* A masterpiece, undoubtedly, but Tristan himself was a bit too French, too languid, too much the sexual athlete. Typical of a woman to go for that one and overlook *Parsifal* and *Rienzi*, the real masterpieces . . . but this was no time, Adolf Hitler reminded himself, to tell her how wrong she was, she, Stefanie of his waking and sleeping dreams, his Minerva; she, Stefanie, glimpsed from afar on morning walks; Stefanie, whom his friend Kubizek had so often heard called "My lady" or "The goddess" (of course Kubizek must have recognized her on the bridge, how could he not, after weeks of hearing about her!) or even, with dubious jocularity, "My future missus"; incredibly, she'd responded, a month previously, when he'd approached her on the Kaiserplatz, more nervous than he'd ever been in his life but somehow carried along by that intoxicating confidence that came over him at odd times . . . and when Adolf had telephoned a week later she—instantly recognizing his guttural accent over the telephone at her aunt's—had agreed to go out with him, without a chaperone even! Well, she'd made inquiries, of course, and her Aunt Marie was acquainted, distantly, with Frau Hitler, through mutual relatives in Linz and Leonding, and of course the late Herr Alois had been a civil servant of unimpeachable probity and standing . . . young Adolf's reputation was more uneven, however, and essentially came out as one of rebellious bohemianism which Stefanie, aspiring actress-playwright-dancer-poet and general woman of letters, found sorely lacking in placid Linz and dull Leonding.

So she'd lied to her aunt, or they'd have a chaperone now.

"Kitty's meeting me and we're going to the Getreidegasse Theater."

Kitty would be apprised. Stefanie hated the deception, but she knew there were some things beyond the moral compass of her family. She was certain that meeting Adolf was one of them.

They left the riverbank, crossed the nearby Hofgasse, and made their way to the Hauptplatz, the bustling heart of Linz. It was a little before eleven, and preparations were underway for the great day ahead. Banners stirred feebly in the muggy riverine air. Standing about were groups of soldiers from different regiments, Austrian mostly, with a sprinkling of Serbs and Moravians, and German-speakers from the marches of Bessarabia, and Slovenes from Capo d'Istria, and the already-noted Magyars; most were laughing coarsely and smoking, ogling the women and not so gently mocking their escorts. One such escort, a student to judge by his general dress and demeanor (plumed hat, lace shirt, swagger) turned on them and screamed obscenities. Adolf, too, screamed briefly, then fell silent, intimidated by the sight of a regiment of strapping lancers strolling in his general direction.

"You got something you want to discuss?" one of them shouted. "Herr Wandervogel?"

"Careful," said another. "Maybe that's a swordstick Herr Doktor Professor Artist is carrying."

Stefanie was nervous, but elated. There was something of the larger world in it all: the soldiers, the bantering, the undercurrent of male rivalry, the pervasiveness of sex. Almost, she thought, as if they weren't in Linz at all. Her breath caught in her throat; her heart skipped a beat, as if in fear, or great excitement. She had a familiar swooning sensation of elevation, a passing giddiness, and a mist floated before her eyes, then yielded to an equally abnormal, almost painful, clarity, limning distant things. A moment later she felt calm, lucid, ready for anything.

"There must be scenes like this in Vienna all the time," she said, as they walked away from the defenders of the Empire.

But Adolf seemed to have no further interest in Vienna. He rankled yet, over Goethe. Thoughts of stark Germanness had taken over. There was a faint throbbing in his temples. He felt thwarted, pent-up, unmanned.

"Let's go over here," he said, and abruptly changed course. They were just behind the reviewing stand, which faced a famous old drinking establishment, the *Alte Welt*. Grandees had fought duels in the Alte Welt; artists had cried over spilt wine in its cavernous cellars. In 1889 a Triestine count had, à la Prince Rudolf, shot himself and his mistress in a discreet room upstairs, and Anton Bruckner's ghost had been seen draping itself humbly around a beer. Today the Alte Welt was filling up with soldiers and members of the archducal entourage: hussars, grenadiers, dragoons. Adolf, suddenly self-conscious, had no desire to engage in an exchange of witticisms or abuse with men twice his size. He might get beaten up. Also, he was in the (for him) unusual position of having a lady's feelings, and impressions, to consider. Momentarily, he was at a loss; his hands kneaded the air; he was sweating. His hat was askew, revealing the pink line made by the hatband.

"Shall we?" he began, interrupted (again) by a sudden flurry of activity. Soldiers stopped lounging and assumed the rigid pose of review. Mounted units cantered in. An open carriage appeared in the distance. "Shall we," mumbled Adolf again; then he cleared his throat and fell silent, yielding reluctantly to external events utterly indifferent to him . . . and Stefanie had eyes only for the arriving palanquins of the archducal parade. (And anyway, there were people about, pushing and shoving. Adolf's walking stick, intended as an adornment, was rapidly becoming a liability.)

"Oh, look!" Stefanie exclaimed. Two soldiers of the Leibregiment, the royal guard, mounted on chestnut bays; hussars in leopard-skin and bandoliers, riding sturdy Andalusians; two dragoons, plumes nodding, breastplates afire, atop solid Lipizzaners; a brace of Arab-mounted Bukovinans (red, green, and gold uniforms, shakos shaking, swords shining) from the Archduke's favorite hunting grounds in the Empire's easternmost marches; a couple of Linz policemen in uniforms so disproportionately extravagant—silver piping, polished jackboots, braided epaulettes—that they nearly outshone their charge, His Imperial Highness himself, the Archduke Franz Ferdinand, heir to the twin thrones of the Dual Monarchy, seated ramrod-straight in the rear of the carriage next to his morganatic wife, the poor duchess Sophie, both unsmiling, neither waving, His Imperial Highness rather acknowledging the existence of the crowd by giving a series of curt nods beneath the lowering plumes of his archducal helmet, he and his Sophie fading adornments on the frothy Sachertorte that was the Austrian Empire.

"Anybody could shoot him, with him sitting there like that," said Adolf, momentarily restored at the thought. A veteran of the Cowboy-and-Indian wars of Old Shatterhand, fought in the sagebrush and chaparral of Braunau and environs, he mimed a gun, pointed, fired. "Pow!" As if in synchronism (or premonition) the Archduke glanced around. His eyes met Adolf's for a fraction of a second; he frowned, and was borne away. Stefanie nudged Adolf impatiently.

"Show some respect," she said, herself showing (he thought) none for him. "The Archduke! He's your future Emperor."

"Pah," said Adolf. "Emperor? Yours, maybe. Not mine." He said this sotto voce, aware of most of the crowd's adulation of Habsburgs (the fools). Not everyone was charmed, not in pro-German Linz. Cries of "*Heil*," the Germanists' salutation, vied with the pro-Habsburg "Hoch!" Cheers and jeers and comments adulatory and scornful were made. Franz Ferdinand and Sophie appeared oblivious to them all.

"Oh, look! She's so pretty."

"If only he'd smile more."

"Yes, but they say he's quite nice."

"They didn't bring the children."

"How many *do* they have? Three?"

"Four, I think."

"Get rid of the lot, I say."

"God save the Archduke!"

"Ach, piss on them."

"Germany forever!"

"Heil!"

"Hoch!"

The imperial procession had passed, slowed, and come to a halt at the Rathaus, farther up the Hauptplatz. The bürgermeister and other notables bustled forth and proceeded to fawn over His Imperially Bored Highness in their best professional manner. Fortunately for Franz Ferdinand, at the end of the speeches there was lunch and a gallop around the stables and a cruise down the Danube, just His Imperial Self and his Sophie (and a retainer or two, or ten) . . . Stefanie was excited, even thrilled, and deemed the day a success, if only for this. And Adolf—well, Adolf was an artist, and you'd expect an artist to be grumpy and cynical, in this kind of situation. Still, there was artistry in the pomp and circumstance, and Stefanie, for all her longing for a *vie de Bohème*, had a deep reverence within her for the settled order, and family, and God; and she was Austrian enough to love it all. Momentarily, she waxed patriotic.

"God save the Archduke!"

"I'm hungry. Why don't we, um."

Plaintively, Adolf pleaded. He was hungry, and tired, and fed up. It was getting on for noon, and he wasn't used to this kind of excitement and attention to another person not his mother. He was also sweating, and found himself almost (but not quite) longing for his quiet room in the flat in Urfahr (that attic window, those rooftops, the forested Pöstlingberg beyond). Not that Stefanie was any less alluring—somewhat more so, even, with a high color in her cheek and her blue eyes glistening with the emotion of having seen a genuine Imperial; and yet there were moments, and they were becoming more frequent, when he found himself damning all this man-woman rigmarole, the niceties of social life, the insincerity.

"Monchskeller," said Stefanie.

"Begging your pardon, what?"

"The Monchskeller, on the Badgasse. It shouldn't be too crowded, and they do a wonderful Linzer torte."

Now, this appealed to Adolf. He perked up, even gave his cane a swing. Things were better now, with Linzer torte on the menu! An excellent idea. Few things got his juices flowing like a slice of pie in a restaurant and the concomitant opportunity to sit across from someone and expound on subjects of his choice. Inspired in advance, he offered Stefanie his elbow. She accepted, and arm-in-arm like Biedermeiers they crossed the square again against the melodious background of bells tolling twelve. The crowd was breaking up, with clumps of people gravitating mindlessly toward the Rathaus entrance from which, in an hour or so, the Archduke must emerge. The archducal phaeton sat outside, manned by the postern who had periodically to rouse himself and swat away curious boys. Adolf glanced back.

"What a fine carriage," he said. "Someday I would like to ride in a carriage like that."

The expression of this desire was in itself sufficient token of his improving mood; but when they arrived in the Monchskeller, and discovered an astonishing dearth of customers, with plenty of room next to the tall garden windows, Adolf was nearly euphoric. The long tables gleamed in the leafy green light from outside. Flags adorned the low ceiling beams, and in the corner behind the bar counter stood a souvenir of past campaigns, the military standard of the owner's old regiment, the Styrian Jaegers. The owner himself, Herr Herzl, met them with a toothy grin and *Esteemed ladys* and *Fine gentlemans* galore. Adolf, responding in kind—good Austrian lad that he was—bowed and heel-clicked; masterfully, he selected the middle table of the row nearest the back, adjacent to the trellises of the as-yet empty wine garden; swashbucklingly, he tossed his cane, with a clatter, into the corner. His hat landed on the table. Stefanie settled herself, smoothed her skirts, and gazed into the garden, beyond which a blue patch of the blue Danube was visible between the neighboring houses and a spreading elm tree.

"Look," she said. "The river."

"Ah yes?"

Stefanie watched her companion as he finger-combed his hair, rapidly and nervously, adjusted his collar, cracked his knuckles, and arranged himself in what for him was an informal pose: torso forward, arms folded, a hearty scoutmaster on the verge of laughter, or anecdote. Both: he chuckled, then waxed expansive.

"Ah yes, the river. The beautiful blue Danube, *ja*? Haha? Our glorious Austrian heritage. Do you like the music of Strauss? I, too, but a genius, our beloved Herr Johann? Well, frankly, no. Too much the musical *pâtissier*, too many fancy confections— not that I have anything against fancy confections, quite the contrary! I'm looking forward to this torte, you can believe that! But I'm sure you know what I mean. The Austrian character? The soul of old Vienna? All cosmetics, no substance! Now, as to the Habsburgs, the Archduke, *ja*, I was less than enthusiastic, earlier. Should I apologize? Not at all! Of course, I understand your need for some kind of higher power to adulate," he said, chortling. "Many people feel that way, hence religion, not so? And of course when one's gods are also one's leaders, and gaily caparisoned they are in fancy uniforms and plumed helmets, with a thousand years of aristocracy behind them—well! It's appealing, I don't deny it! Like a permanent fancy-dress ball. But their day is done, their time has come, it's all over with, they should be booted out. No more kings and emperors and queens and archdukes. Ousted, I say!"

Stefanie reclaimed a small corner of the conversation.

"Altogether, I don't entirely disagree with you, Adolf, but I wanted to express my admiration for His Imperial Highness. I think he's the best of the lot. And he has handsome mustaches." She smiled, signifying flippancy, but Adolf had the unfortunate habit, born of literal-mindedness, of marrying high spirits and magisterial contempt for others. He waved a dismissive hand, as if to a servant.

"Handsome mustaches? Best of the lot? That bunch of

syphilitic fops? Pah. Look at 'em. Half Jewish, half Hungarian, and entirely Habsburg."

"Jewish? The Archduke?"

"Oh yes, yes. Jewish! Well, you know. Not literally. In the way they use the term Jewish in Vienna, the way Herr Lueger uses it, it's more of an idea than a fact . . . "

"However Herr Lueger uses it, it's a fact in my family. We have Jewish cousins by marriage. In Vienna."

Adolf was nonplussed. Herr Lueger, the Mayor of Vienna, was one of his heroes—a lesser presence in his personal empyrean than, say, Wagner, or Karl May, but a beacon in the ambient darkness, nonetheless. (And once again Stefanie had shown spirit, forthrightness, even insolence: contradicting him, dethroning Herr Lueger, enshrining Goethe, revealing Jewish links by marriage . . . where was it going to end?)

"Ah! So? Jewish in Vienna, eh? Well, of course. There are, I know, many Jews there. But your, ah, connection is by marriage, you say?"

"By marriage, yes. A wealthy industrialist, knighted by the Emperor. Ernst von Kahane, Baron Ottoheinz. He married let me see my aunt Liesl, so. Yes. Cousins, but not by blood. I've heard their house is something grand indeed. You should visit them when you're next in Vienna."

"Ah. I don't think so. Well, who knows. Perhaps, although I was planning to stay with my godparents, Herr und Frau Prinz. Distinguished folk, you know. Tell me, are these Jewish relatives of yours wealthy patrons of the arts? Or artists?"

"No. Well, they're wealthy, of course. And they go to concerts and the opera and they have chamber music recitals at home, yes, and chess tournaments, Baron Ernst is a keen chess player. But art? No, I don't think so."

"Jews are very good at chamber music and chess."

"Well, that's very Austrian also, isn't it? I mean, you can't . . . "

Adolf narrowed his eyes. Their torte arrived. Initially courteous to the publican to the point of obsequiousness, Adolf now ignored him, so intense was his concentration within himself on topics dear to his heart. He stuffed his mouth with torte, chewed vigorously, swallowed, laid aside his fork. His eyes darted; his mouth worked; he blurted his thoughts.

"My mother is not well, you know. She has a cancer. She has a new doctor, a certain Bloch. He is Jewish, by the way. I would prefer she found someone else. I have no faith in his competence. Not because he is Jewish, incidentally, but because I have heard so-so reports from others. Well, I even looked here in Linz for another doctor, but nobody wants to make the trip out to Leonding, and they didn't take to me, I could tell that straightaway, they thought I was too much the artist, or the outsider, or something, snobs, petty bourgeois in such a typical Austrian way . . . anyway, to get back to our subject, why am I using the term Austrian in the first place? What does Austrian really mean? Austrian, Austrian. I ask you to consider what that means. Germans of the Eastern Empire. Actually, it means nothing. The only distinction between the Germans of the Eastern Empire—Austrians—us—and the others, the Germans of the Greater Empire, is that conferred by us being ruled by that gang of overdressed syphilitic gypsy barons you seem to admire so much. Their fine mustaches, ha! I'd clip their fine mustaches, I can tell you! Not that I have much more use for the ruling clique of Prussia, I hasten to add. The Kaiser and his crowd, no, thank you very much! Red-faced Junkers with the brains of insects. They're even worse than our lot, if that's possible. Now. Allow me to describe to you my ideal form of government."

The thought passed through Stefanie's mind, otherwise aswim with pro-Adolf (or at least pro-artist) feelings (or at the very least responding favorably to the mating dance of the eager male), that young Herr Hitler could on occasion be quite overbearing, when the mood took him, as the mood seemed to take him now—well, perhaps overbearing wasn't quite the right word: importunate? Yes, but with such enthusiasm that he was hard to resist. The very opposite of monotonous, anyway. With his gestures he parried, feinted, and thrust; his face and hands were constantly on the go; he stared, lip-licked, and finger-fiddled. He demanded one's attention, which almost guaranteed that he wouldn't get Stefanie's. Such self-confidence, she thought, would be apt, no doubt, in the presence of worshippers, but she worshipped him not, and couldn't imagine anyone else doing so . . . he was an artist, after all! No one took the political ravings of artists seriously. Such palaver was for late nights in the smoky confines of a small garret eave-secreted in some great city's bohemian quarter (she dreamed, for a second, of herself in just such a garret: Life, Love, and Art, the blessed triumvirate of youth's empire!). No, no one would ever beg him to repeat himself. No one would dream of designing society along his lines. No one would restructure his or her life according to the ravings of Adolf the Artist! She felt pity (constant companion of her future life), pity for the intensity and seriousness and probable future failure of a bright but muddled young man. Only eighteen she might be, but she'd already seen, in her own family, in her own father and uncles and cousin and various distant relatives, enough shortcomings and fallings-short and half measures and life-imposed compromises to recognize failure in the making. Poor Adolf. And yet! The intensity was rare.

A shiver passed through her, heralding another of her spells. Migraine, the doctor had said. Nonsense, had been Stefanie's reply. She rubbed her eyes.

Adolf didn't notice. He had moved from the specific, his audience of one, to the general, an abstract, celestial audience of Hermanns and Frederick Redbeards and dumb but willing German yeomen. Talking all the while, he was gazing through the window at the sliver of blue Danube and the wooded Pöstlingberg beyond, momentarily indifferent to ambient banalities. He appeared to ignore, for instance, a mild metallic burning odor that caught in Stefanie's nose right away.

"Ugh."

The smell seeped faintly into the air, as if a frying pan had been left on the fire in the kitchen; then, suddenly, it was gone. Stefanie took a deep breath. She blinked away the rosettes of eyestrain. Specks of light danced before her eyes, then disappeared. In the distance there was a low screech, as of a chair being dragged across the floor. A warm breeze played over her neck.

"German ideals, of course," Adolf was saying. "We Germans

have never had much luck with the parliamentary style of government. We have our own needs, our own dictates. Why should
we try to imitate countries that after all are decaying from within?
These liberal and socialistic parties speak constantly of importing
the French, or the English, or the American, system . . . "

Adolf's ideal form of government, however tedious to
Stefanie, seemed to be arousing interest in other quarters, which
was hardly surprising, she thought, as Adolf had developed a very
audible, indeed hectoring, tone of voice; however, she had not
been aware of other customers sitting down nearby, but one or
two must have, behind their backs. Anyway, she was definitely
having another of those attacks, longer than usual. She wondered if something obvious triggered them: strain, anticipation,
excitement? Such attacks in a girl her age were quite absurd and
irritating, like an insistently recurring bout of heart palpitations
or some other ailment she associated with nervous old people
who spent most of their lives taking their pulses and sipping
muddy water at thermal spas . . . a violent throb in her temples
was followed by a swiftly dissipating mist that yielded to prism-
like clarity with a hint, too, of prism-like distortion, or refraction, around the edges, like a shimmering gilded frame. On this
particular occasion, while Adolf spoke of his ideals, through the
dissolving blur and subsequent lens-sharpness Stefanie discerned
the hard-edged profile of a stranger sitting in part-shadow at
an adjoining table, smoke rising from an invisible pipe or cigar
(odorless? perhaps it was a cigarette), his hands cupped in front
of him, his legs crossed in somewhat grotesque fashion, as if he
were seated sidesaddle on a horse. Was he a cripple? An athlete? Another artist, or agent provocateur? Stefanie idly shifted
her full attention from her haranguing companion to this new
arrival. Adolf seemed not to notice. The man's face, apart from
its profile—whose aquiline nose, weak chin, and high sloping
forehead were as sharp as if they had been etched in glass—was
oddly vague and imprecise, like a much-erased drawing. His
shoulders, or what Stefanie could see of them, seemed to be
shaking, as in silent laughter, although there was no corresponding mirth reflected on his features: perhaps he was ill? His eyes

seemed to be closed, or deep in shadow. Stefanie's attention was drawn again to his legs, which were as imprecise in outline as his face was in feature, as if heavy clouds were blotting out the sun (but they weren't, because she could see through the window into the cheerful sunlit world beyond), yet in some way those legs were grotesque, incomplete—not that she could see at all clearly under the neighboring table . . .

" . . . I firmly believe, and I'm aware that I probably offend you, I know some educated young ladies of liberal conscience would be quite shocked at my words, *ja, ja,* but I must say it, I do believe in the importance of maintaining national characteristics, that is to say: No foreigners! Now of course—before you say how shocked you are, before you remind me how Goethe would disagree, and so on—when you think about it, this is precisely the Greco-Roman ideal. Have you read Chamberlain? One of the most eminent English authors, I only recently discovered him, and I must say I am finding him very stimulating . . . but I see you are shocked."

Stefanie was indeed shocked, but not at Adolf's theorizing. She had found a precise comparison for the mental image evoked by the spasmodic shifting, or uncrossing (with hoof-like clattering of feet), of her neighbor's legs: the stables at her Uncle Karl's farm in the Salzkammergut, specifically (she remembered the acrid mingling of the smells, hay-urine-manure) the momentary loss of balance of a cow being milked. Or a horse stung by a fly. Or—and she squarely faced the final, diabolical image—a goat, startled, stumbling . . . the image was absurd, then terrifying for a second, then absurd *and* terrifying; then, as soon as the image began to fade, so did the mysterious stranger at the neighboring table, gathering up him- or itself (what was the appropriate pronoun for an angel, fallen or not?) and heading for the door in the corner (what door? there was no door there), but on his or its way out—moving in an ataxic, jerky, pantomime-horse kind of way—turning to look back, as Stefanie thought, not at her but at Adolf, and in an unaccountably intimate, devouring way, like a lover, or long-lost family member, enormous eyes flaming with a hideous immortality, a misshapen head that seemed to culminate—yes, she could have predicted it (*had* predicted it)—in an odd, stiff little coiffure that resembled horns . . . *were* horns. Of course.

Then, thank God, he, or it, was gone, fading into a small whirlwind of shadow. The smell that lingered was one that had earned its place in folklore.

Stefanie shook her head violently.

"My God! I have seen the devil," she murmured, head in hands.

"Ah," said Adolf. "You are ill?" There was a touch of impatience in his voice at this further sign of the unpredictability of this young woman, or women in general; indeed, his mind reluctantly filled with images of horrible illness setting in, unseemly dashing to and fro, a cab commandeered for the hospital, encounters with family members, feeble explanations offered and instantly dismissed, himself made to feel inferior again . . .

"No, I'm quite all right," she said. "But I will go home now, I think."

"But." He was confused, nonplussed, surprised. "It's not even two o'clock."

"And it was this morning we met! Already we've spent four hours together. It's enough, Herr Adolf. It was enjoyable, yes, but it's enough. My Aunt Marie will be wondering what has become of me. And I need to rest."

With a firmness of demeanor that impressed Adolf, while simultaneously pushing him to the brink of despair, Stefanie made preparations to leave. Sensing departure, their host Herr Herzl appeared, hovered, allowed a touch of hand-wringing impatience to show at Adolf's laborious (because reluctant) counting-out of coins that nonetheless ended with a surprisingly large gratuity being tossed disdainfully onto the table (thus restoring the landlord to the state of bluff groveling that was his trademark).

"Many thanks, esteemed young gentleman. Your servant, Fräulein."

Adolf retrieved his cane, clapped his artist's cap on his head, and bowingly gestured for Stefanie to precede him. They went through the door into the burning sunlight of the Hauptplatz.

"I would be most grateful"—oh, now he reminded himself

how lovely she was, with her hazel eyes, golden hair and honey brown skin, his longed-for Stefanie, dream companion of his haunted nighttime hours!—"if you would consent to accompany me again, Fräulein Stefanie, perhaps to the opera performance I mentioned?"

"*Ja*. Perhaps, Herr Adolf."

"And now? May I? Escort you, perhaps?"

"I have a visit to make. Thank you, but no."

"I kiss your hand, dear young lady."

Adolf Hitler did so, and bowed, relief and disappointment struggling within him: Relief, that he no longer had to play the courtier (not that he did so very well), pay attention, laugh at jokes, agree with the nonsensical opinions of another, flutter about, think of banalities, spend money; and disappointment, of course, at leaving the current object of his desire, who might now be on her way elsewhere for good, outraged or shocked or disappointed or disgusted—yes, he could all too easily imagine the type of smooth-talking middle-class or aristocratic Hungarian and/or Jewish skirt-chaser who might win her heart, a man with a box at the opera, a yacht at Fiume, a house in the Vienna Woods, and a well-rehearsed line of seductive patter; exactly the kind of suave Romeo, in fact, he had disapprovingly taken note of in Vienna. Just the type, he was sure, who would eagerly engage in silken chit-chat about Goethe and with supreme confidence offer his arm on the dance floor; raise a cape-cloaked arm to summon a cab out of nowhere on a rainy night; airily speak French, and Italian, and English, and say "old chap," and order expensive aperitifs; the kind of devious, disloyal, untrustworthy cosmopolite, in short, who would undermine Adolf's very notion of nationhood, i.e., civilization itself. Through his confusion he glimpsed, as he often did, salvation, with himself as Wagner reborn, successfully manning the barricades in a great social and cultural revolution, a French Revolution for Germany . . . and Austria, too . . . anyway, Stefanie was too young, that was it. Deeply as he desired her, he knew himself to be too mature, too seasoned, too steeped in learning and philosophy, too elevated by the fates and ambition to waste time on a girl, or girls. Some day one would heed the call and join him in his quest; but she would be more pliable, more understanding, more loyal, than the temperamental, if beautiful, Stefanie. The thought of the future and what it would hold reassured him, as it always did. He gave his cane a flourish and took out his pocket-watch. (Faintly, regret trembled, prompted by the fresh memory of Stefanie's awe; then it vanished, vanquished.) Two fifteen. That would give him a good three hours or so in the library. He was halfway through Chamberlain, and wanted to finish the book before going home to Leonding. He would tell Mamma he had shared a torte with Stefanie von Rothenberg. She would be impressed.

As for Stefanie, deeply shaken, she tried to explain her experience to the statues and altar and immanent God at the Mariakirche, a dark, chilly place dimly illuminated by red-flickering candles honoring the forgotten dead. But for a priest, the church was empty, yet it was full of the vast echoes of a living silence: footfalls; a creaking beam; a door closing; a scuffling churchmouse . . . dear God, said Stefanie to God, make me normal again. If what I saw was real, make me blind; if a vision, make me see as others see.

There was, of course, no reply. Then the priest shuffled by.

"Father."

"Yes, my child?"

"I want to make my confession, Father."

She confessed, but Father Rupprecht was an old priest who'd been in Linz since the days of Metternich and wanted only an easeful slide into dotage and death, with no sudden intrusions of mysticism and hallucinations to upset his nice parish and tear open his neatly wrapped package of a remote Christ triumphant and remoter God serene. Grudgingly (he had an appointment with an osteopath, then a game of chess at Meinherr Schmitz the barber's) he heard Stefanie's confession, which she watered down accordingly; then, paternally, impatiently, indifferently, he extended the benediction.

"Go in peace, my child."

In turmoil she went.

Gustave
Two

MY READING OF the Jeanrenaud book had been interrupted by sudden sleep yielding to unsettled dreams of little Hitlers here and bigger Hitlers there. A busy morning followed; then halfway through the afternoon I had an appointment with Gax's shrink, the aforementioned Dr. LeCluyse. I was kept waiting for half an hour before being ushered into the presence. A spidery corolla of hairs played around the doctor's bald head in the faint light from the half-shuttered window. Hunched forward, not looking at me directly, he fidgeted with a glass paperweight containing edelweiss, "Souvenir of Zermatt." A mingled stench of mothballs and deodorants roared out of his oversized suit when he raised an arm and bade me take a seat.

"You have seen an angel, you say, Mr. Termi?"

The psychiatrist was unctuous, yet patronizing, in the way of his kind.

"Yes. Actually, it's doctor, doctor. Doctor Termi."

"Of course. A doctor of . . . letters?"

"Yes." I almost apologized.

"And you were recommended by Mr. Gax, the, ah, journalist?"

"Yes, yes."

I was tiring of this interrogation. I had begun to regret my decision to consult a psychiatrist, even (or especially) one recommended by Guy Gax, the moment I walked through the door of Dr. LeCluyse's richly appointed surgery and realized that at that instant, even if I promptly turned on my heel and left, I would be seven hundred and fifty francs the poorer.

He deposited the paperweight on the table and spoke, smilingly.

"Ah yes. Well. What a coincidence, sir. Angels. Tsk-tsk. Tell me: Do you suffer from the migraine?"

"No."

"Ah. Sometimes what we call migraine aura can cause hallucinations, you see . . . well, then. Oh, such visions—angels, devils, monadian entities, and so on—are not unknown, in fact they're quite popular these days. Angels are definitely in the wind. You know, one of my patients maintains that she came upon a naked angel hunkering on his hams in her bathtub."

"Ah yes? What bullshit."

"Precisely. Wishful thinking, eh? But note I use the masculine pronoun, whereas angels are traditionally presumed to be neuter. Not in this case, oh no. The naked male figure, the fetal position, the bathtub . . . need one pursue it any further? I think not. Besides which, the lady has always claimed to have visions of nude males. Once, as I recall, while she was watching the skiing silver-medal contests on the television she had a vision of Johnny Hallyday, the singer, dressed in a very louche tutu, making suggestive gestures astride her sofa. No, no, I think we know only too well what lies down that road. By the way, she is now an outpatient at the Bel-Air clinic, and sings in a choir in one of the suburban churches."

"Doctor, the lady in question can be a deep-sea diver or a rugby champion for all I care. I hardly see the relevance. My vision was in no way sexual, I assure you."

"Ah, you assure me, do you? And yet, sir. And yet you say—I have my notes right here—the vision presented itself as a kind of 'Aryan poster boy'; a 'blond youth'; a 'young man with long blond hair'; . . . now I wonder, Mr. Termi, I truly wonder, if such terminology could be described as not containing a sexual element." The wretch leaned forward, clearing his throat in an exaggerated, cinematic way. "I understand you are unmarried?"

"Yes. However, it may interest you to know that I was on my way to visit a lady friend when I had the vision," I said, cravenly.

"A lady friend I visit on a weekly basis."

"How instructive. A forlorn journey of abandoned heterosexuality interrupted by a sudden vision of the poignantly homosexual truth. The old story, ah, I've heard it told a hundred times in a hundred different ways. Although, admittedly, the angel adds a, shall I say, distinctive touch. Incidentally, Mr. Termo, when you were younger, did you have any especially close friendships with other boys?"

"Yes, indeed. One of them was with Guy Gax, who recommended you, and whom I'm going to kill, as soon as I leave here."

I rose and departed stonily, preserving I hoped some small shred of dignity; after all, it was my money. As I passed through the waiting room on my way out I overheard the secretary, a porcelain *allumeuse* of a certain age, call out the name of LeCluyse's next victim over the speakerphone:

"Mademoiselle Jeanrenaud is here, Doctor. If you're through with Mr., um."

I stopped, turned. A lady, laterally lighted by the desk lamp, was sitting on a sofa on the far side of the waiting room. A couple seconds' scrutiny confirmed a resemblance to my memory of the photograph on the back flap of *Adoration*, the photograph from which I had been, in an idle moment, trying to tease an identity: sociable? sapphic? atheistic? good-time gal? bluestocking?

Mademoiselle, at least.

I stepped forward, impressive (I hoped) in my Burberry, elegant leather gloves held limply in my left hand.

"Mademoiselle Martine Jeanrenaud?"

"Yes."

"Ah!" I exclaimed. "Aha! It is you, then!"

"It is I, monsieur. And I see it is you, also, whoever you are."

Not totally unused to being accosted by strange men, then, attractive as she was, holding her own well: I'd give her, I thought, forty or so, maybe just this side thereof. She was cool and appraising, with a half smile of anticipation, face cocked slightly to one side like a curious dog; and of course her face in life had the odd wrinkle that was charitably absent from the photographed, airbrushed version. She was subtly clad in maroon tweed that went well with her (as I had surmised) russet hair, hair a bit fuller than in the photograph. Only in translating to celluloid her round, owlish glasses had the camera been entirely faithful to the original.

"Gustave Termi. *Dr.* Termi," I amended, with the pomposity of the forlorn. "I'm reading your book *Adoration*."

We shook hands.

"Oh? You're in a very small minority, then. Do you like it?"

"Very much. I'm intrigued. Very intrigued. Not only for reasons of history—I'm a professor of history, by the way, at the College . . . "

Dr. LeCluyse appeared at the door of his office. He looked back and forth, disapproval chasing obsequiousness across his face like a pair of battling lizards.

"Mademoiselle Jeanrenaud?"

"Sorry, doctor."

"Never mind him," I said. "The best he could do was tell me I was homosexual, which I most emphatically am not. Utter waste of time, Mademoiselle. You'd be better off having a coffee with me."

"I think not, Monsieur . . . Termi? This is a long-standing appointment."

"Later, then? There are serious points of history I would like to discuss."

"Oh, dear. What did I get wrong?"

"No, no, it's not that. It's more the mystical angle. May I call you, then?"

Flustered, under Dr. LeCluyse's gimlet eye, she confessed to being "in the book."

"Thank you, mademoiselle."

I bowed slightly, tipped an imaginary hat. And called her that evening, after first canceling—again—with Giulia.

"Giulia, I'm terribly sorry."

"Is all right, *dottore*."

"But this is two weeks in a row, my dear Giulietta. I feel I must make it up to you in some way."

"A-o, *professore*. You want me, you gimme a call."

Fair enough. It was all too characteristic of me—so professorial, some would say— to sentimentalize a purely economic (and sexual) relationship; yet I did, for Giulia was an honest, spirited girl of my blood, *paesana mia*, a kissing cousin in all but name. Then I called Martine. Oddly, in an age of infernal answering machines, she answered in person.

"Mademoiselle Jeanrenaud?" It's, etc.

"Ah, my sole reader! I thought I recognized your voice, monsieur."

Oh, but you underestimate the significance of your work . . . blah blah blah. Standard banalities after that (weather, cost of living, cost of psychoanalysts)—with the brief exception of, from my end, a barrage of animus directed at Dr. LeCluyse, on whose behalf she said, "Now, now, he's helped me through a couple of rough patches"—and in closing the expected invitation *à la danse*, or a drink, or at the very least a cup of coffee or tea, say mid-afternoon the next day (a Monday)? Mid-afternoon was less compromising and more businesslike, and there was scant likelihood of awkward advances amid financial magazines and the thunderous cigarette-coughing of the Ovaltine-sipping elderly and the brisk comings and goings of office workers.

Almost as soon as I hung up, the phone rang again and Guy Gax's aggressive baritone barged down the wire.

"Meet me for dinner," he said, peremptorily. "Lyrique at eight."

"Now, you're not going to . . . "

"Not at all," he said, with an attempt to inject geniality into his tone of voice. "No mockery of celestial visions, I promise you. Although I might ask a couple of questions, purely out of scientific interest. No, I have just a good old-fashioned litany of complaints, mostly about my ex-wife."

I had an Italo-Balkan History class at one o'clock and planned to be seated immediately afterward, or as fast as my bulbous legs could carry me, at a marble table in the corner next to the newspaper rack at the Café de Rive, with in front of me hot tea in a glass, Russian style. The Rive district is, or was, Geneva's Little

Russia, with such accents of the Motherland as said tea in a glass, and Slatkine's bookstore, and the gilt-domed Russian church on the Rue Beauvais, just up the way in a quiet neighborhood of handsome two-story town houses that has something about it even to this day of Saltykov-Shchedrin's Saratov-on-the-Volga, or Tolstoy's dusty Kazan. All this was Geneva's legacy from that doughty bunch of Russian expats (one named Lenin, another Plekhanov, and a third, Bukharin, who saluted Geneva as "the Holy City of Russian thought") when the world's worst horror seemed to be inequality, and serfdom, and starvation, and the Tsar's Cossacks on horseback. Then those who'd fled returned in '17 and got to work on horrors beyond all imagining, yielding the stage only, and not much, to Stefanie von Rothenberg's boyfriend, once he got going . . .

I arrived early at the café and filled the time waiting for Martine with another visit to the Europe of her gods and devils.

Vienna

In the autumn of 1909, by dint of hard work and perseverance, Stefanie von Rothenberg became the only girl from the Salzburg-Altstadt *Kreis* to matriculate in theology at the noble and ancient University of Vienna, in spite of prolonged arguments with her father, who wanted her to go to Paris to study dressmaking with Chanel, or at the very least music with his old friend Bénoit Lévy, the pianist.

"Theology, for the love of God?" her father had exclaimed.

"In a manner of speaking, Pappi."

"God, God, God," her Pappi had muttered. "Leave Him to the priests. Young ladies should study piano, dressmaking, the culinary arts. Perhaps psychology. In Paris, it's the capital of Europe. I mean, you already speak French. But theology? Unless it's a nun you want to be?"

"Oh no, Pappi," said young Stefanie. "I have no desire to be a nun. And I would love to see Paris, but that will come. You see, much of what we believe has been misunderstood. Half of Christianity's based on false interpretation. Women see these things. Men only want to impress each other."

"I'm very happy for you, *gans*," Stefanie's mutti said on the day of her daughter's departure. The Vienna express stood panting in Salzburg station. The Hohensalzburg castle stood out as clearly as a lithograph against the blinding white of the freshly snow-covered Salzkammergut range. Mother and daughter embraced affectionately. Pappi kissed Stefanie's cheek, then stood back to light a cigar and pollute the crisp early autumn air.

"Come on! Let's get on the train," said Stefanie's cousin Fritzl. He was accompanying her as a chaperon, as eager to show her the Imperial capital as she was to see it; in Salzburg, Munich was closer, and from there it seemed no effort to continue to Frankfurt, Berlin, or Paris, but Vienna lay in the other, eastern direction, and a mist of the exotic hung over it, as if it still were the westernmost outpost of the Turkish East: "Asia begins at the Landstrasse," in the words of Metternich. Capital of Empire, den of iniquity, high place of all art and culture.

The train ride took three hours. On the way they passed through Linz.

"Old Linz again," observed Fritzl, as the train pulled in. A red-faced and sweating Jewish family of parents and two children, the father heavily bearded, all four dressed in black, battled its way on board and tumbled, parents grumbling and shouting, into Stefanie's and Fritzl's compartment.

"Vienna?" the father inquired.

"No," said Fritzl. "This train terminates at Melk."

More Yiddish grumbling, and confused perusal of tickets, followed.

"This ticket says Vienna, this train," said the father, frowning.

"The Vienna train leaves from across the platform," lied Fritzl smoothly. "You'd better hurry if you want to catch it."

Husband and wife conferred. The two children, a boy and a girl between four and six, stared at Stefanie. The boy smiled. Stefanie was already in some discomfort over Fritzl's brazenness, yet she was deeply reluctant to share the compartment with anybody else, let alone a somewhat malodorous (wurst or boiled beef or something worse) family of four, let alone Jews, with their bizarre ways and incessant muttering . . . the boy was still staring at her. He was winsome, pale, black-haired, huge-eyed.

"Hello," he said. Stefanie smiled.

"Let's go, let's go," said the boy's father. "Thank you, mein Herr. Thank you, meine Frau." He bowed to Fritzl and Stefanie and shepherded his brood out of the compartment. Seconds later they were on the station platform again, arguing loudly. Fritzl snorted.

"Bloody Jews. I wasn't about to let them stink up our compartment, believe me."

"Ach, Fritzl. You're half a Jew, after all."

"Ach, Stefanie. You know what I mean. Papa's not a Jew, he's." Fritzl struggled with the concept. "He was born Jewish, *ja*, but he's not a *Jew*. Like them. You know what I mean," he repeated, petulantly.

Stefanie knew exactly what he meant. It was common coin in the Austria of those days. With a shrug, she endorsed her cousin's deception, and his hair-splitting distinctions. At least they had the compartment to themselves! (But she thought guiltily of the kids, too young to comprehend grownups' maneuvering . . . *ach, himmeldonnerwetter*. Sometimes you have to deceive to live, *ja*?)

The train resumed its journey. On one side the broad Danube stroked by, on the other the city of Linz dealt itself out like a deck of cards, dealing out, too, with the rapid dexterity of a croupier, Stefanie's memories of her years at the Linz Real-Gymnasium, years that had come to an end so recently . . . and friends, including one or two she was hoping to see in Vienna . . . and Adolf, awkward suitor, now fully an orphan, poor boy, so she'd heard, not having seen him since that day two years ago when she'd also seen something she'd rather forget. She'd had no repetition of the hallucinations, and wished for none. She wished, on the contrary, like all nineteen-year-old girls, for a semblance of normality, fun, success, and happiness. And what she wished for most of all, these days, was Vienna.

Two hours later, after glimpses of the monasteries of Melk and St. Pölten, and grim Schloss Dirnstein mirrored in the placid Danube, she got the latter part of her wish.

"Wien," boomed the conductor, a florid gentleman with Franz-Josefine dundrearies. "Wien Westbahnhof, next and final stop."

"Here we are, dear cousin," said Fritzl. "Now the adventure begins."

Stefanie hesitantly followed her cousin out of the echoing Westbahnhof into the bustle of the Bahnhofplatz. The autumn sun filled the hazy air with pale gold motes of light. It was mild, almost warm, a different climate entirely from Salzburg's knife-edged Alpine air. This was the plain, the mighty Danube, the first march of the steppes to the Black Sea, the first city of the Balkans: Mitteleuropa with a vengeance!

Fritzl raised a hand.

"I can get us a cab if you just give me a minute," he said.

The bustle was intense. Landaus, barouches, and hackney cabs; grocer's carts, coal wagons, and motor cars; a Royal and Imperial carriage; the country smell of manure and the city-scent of petrol fumes; well-dressed people in gray and black; scruffy people in a grubbier spectrum of reds, browns, beiges, and blues; people tall, short, and of medium height; dark-skinned people, yellow-skinned people, people pinkish-gray; an organ grinder, complete with performing monkey, playing "Rimini, My Rimini"; a police sergeant quite majestic atop a muscular bay . . .

"Vienna," sighed Stefanie.

"Maybe we should take one of those cabs," said Fritzl.

"I'll just follow my nose," said Stefanie.

"Forget your nose. Look! A motorbus."

They mounted, were borne away, past the Gürtel, down the busy Mariahilfer Strasse, into the center of the metropolis. Stefanie gawked at the shops, the teeming crowds, the traffic. Another bus, and a short walk across the Ringstrasse ("Look! The Opera!"), brought them to the Johannesgasse near the Stadtpark residence of Fritzl's parents the Baron and Baroness Ottoheinz, a restrained mansion, an urban *palais*.

"Stefanie!"

"Hello, Aunt Liesl. Uncle Ernst."

"Good evening, young lady."

"My heavens!" exclaimed the Baron. "Quite the young lady indeed! And the last time I saw you, you were so, um. Small!"

And so began Stefanie's life as a Viennese. Vienna, emotionally, became her deepest home, no matter where else she might reside: *Wien, Wien, noch du allein*! For the first four years she lived in the cozy mansion at No. 101 Johannesgasse, in a third-floor attic room with a mansard window and a view over the Stadtpark, famous for its autumn roses, a view that took on an indefinable melancholy on winter evenings when the lamps came on and the strollers were shades in a misty neverland. Throughout her sojourn Stefanie got along surprisingly well with her aunt and uncle, the parvenu nobles—riding on a fortune created from wood pulp and newsprint—and even did quite well with cheeky cousin Fritzl. Of course, cousin Fritzl was three years older than she, and he was engaged to the daughter of a wealthy Bavarian landowner. These facts kept flirtation and cousinly teasing to a minimum; moreover, Fritzl was a harmless youth whose ambitions were circumscribed by average intelligence and total lack of malice. Both of these would become irrelevant when he married his rich Catholic princess from Bavaria and thereby furthered the process of assimilation, not that Fritzl, blond and blue-eyed as he was, had very far to go. His father the Baron had Austrianized, or de-Judaized, himself to such an extent as to be quite unrecognizable as a Son of Israel (except, as Fritzl would point out at moments of ire, for his nose); bluff and grandiose, an aficionado of the opera and the hunt, an admirer of fine brandies and (when Aunt Liesl was elsewhere) of pretty women, Baron Ernst, né Isidor Kahane in Kalischt, Bohemia, was much like Stefanie's father, indeed much like a dozen Austrian pappis she could name. As with those others, ostentatious civility reigned, and the Baron was never less than courteous in his dealings with his niece. With others he could be less accommodating, as befit a man of business and wood pulp millionaire. He remained a dandy, but over the four years of Stefanie's sojourn his neck turned ropy, his hearing deteriorated, and the once-silken tones of his voice aged into a husky blare made huskier by

his incessant smoking of Egyptian cigarettes and loud prolonged
sinus-clearing hoots.

"I must move out of this city," he was wont to say, in spurious
despair. "How can anyone live in such a climate?"

"You'll never move, Uncle," Stefanie would reply, in a kind of
pantomime argument. "And the climate isn't so bad."

For her, the climate was perfect; she loved the damp chill of
the alluvial plain, the frosty breath on the cheek on an autumn
morning (in Vienna even well into late spring a melancholy wisp
of winter lurks), the billowing steam-clouds emanating from the
kitchens and laundries in the still morning when the tramcars
rattled down the Ringstrasse and the delivery horses clip-clopped
by, billowing tusks of nose-vapor, and students trudged their
thoughtful (or fearful or lovelorn or hungover) way through the
city, in Stefanie's case briskly walking the length of Johannesgasse
as far as the Kärntner Strasse and the glorious baroque pile of
the Augustiner Church, passing by the somber gray enigma of
the Hofburg (where one morning she saw the Archduke again,
this time driving himself in an open motorcar, no Sophie at
his side) and so down the Herrengasse to the Schottentor and
past the slender linden trees of the Schottenring to the entrance
to the University, where thirty-two statues of great men of the
ages dominated, with a fustian air of venerable masculinity, the
main courtyard, as at a gentleman's club. Although women were
admitted, just (she was once asked at high volume by a steely-
eyed veteran doorman for her papers and "a telephone number
where your father can be reached"), life in the distaff column was
rigorous in the theology faculty, most masculine sanctum sancto-
rum of the great institution's venerable departments. In fact, in
the first trimester, Stefanie's ambition to qualify as a Doctor of
Theology was thwarted by mockery and *double entendre*—and,
on one or two occasions, hostility ("A girl should be a wife or a
cabaret dancer, nothing else"; "As if we hadn't enough whores in
this town already!"; "Did you make the coffee yet, *meine kleine
Schmetterling?*")—but Stefanie von Rothenberg was of the mold
of greatness, and greatness wavers not. The study of God and His
relations with His creatures was Stefanie's passport to wisdom.

In her first trimestrial exams she scored three 10s, top marks grudgingly but respectfully given by the two Ancients, Herrn Doktoren Professoren von Schnitzl and Braun. Indeed, Herr Professor Braun succumbed to the ailment common to aging men: the need, with or without sexual undertones (with, in the professor's case), to take under their wings female fledglings. Fortunately, confusingly allied as they were with strong feelings of fatherhood, Professor Braun's urges led nowhere more daring than the Café Landtmann, once, for a *Kaffee mit Schlagobers* and a slice of *Indianer* cake.

"Fräulein von Rothenberg, your point concerning the ineluctability of the Wittenberg Principles was exceedingly well taken," said Professor Braun, no dab hand at the niceties of polite conversation (unsurprising, after forty-three years at the Faculty). "But I question your interest in the mystical experiences of Martin Luther. As far as I know, he had none. But on the other hand, he may have had. Who am I, ah, to judge? Another cognac?"

"No."

Not that Stefanie, at age twenty, was by any means a fledgling: She was poised, elegant, more worldly by the day, and could be mordant in her humor. Other men younger than Professor Braun were attracted, and were invariably turned away. One made it through the front door of the Palais Ottoheinz long enough to sample Aunt Liesl's Kaffee Maria Theresia and Braun Apfel at one of the family's monthly *jours*, or at-homes.

"Delicious," he said, but was ignored, and fell silent, chewing. Stefanie took note of this, and of the lad's reluctance to proclaim his existence any more loudly, and, unforgivingly, she affixed a note to her mental ledger reading NO beside his name (Baldur). She despised the timid, the ignorant, the pusillanimous, the conformist; she had all the confident, even brassy determination of an intelligent young woman of her class who had been well loved as a child. Few men, indeed, matched her demands, or aroused her desires. One who briefly did was a Polish violinist named Tadeusz Banaczynski, who performed Tchaikovsky, Clementi, and Josef Strauss one night at her aunt and uncle's, and who conversed with her, politely and quietly, after the performance. His prematurely graying beard, and the touch of aspersion in his humor, bid fair to win her over completely, but one night a week later the Royal and Imperial police forestalled any further amorousness by removing Tadeusz from the concert stage at the Musikverein; the second violinist in the Krakow Salon Ensemble had, it seemed, implicated the violinist in a plot to assassinate the Austrian Governor of Galicia.

"I believe our Stefanie had her eye on him," murmured the Baroness one evening after supper.

"Hmmm," replied the Baron, fishing for his matches.

"Banaczynski? The Polish violinist turned mad bomber? Dear?"

"Bomber? Ah yes. That *schleimer*." The Baron slewed around and, magically conjuring a handkerchief, uttered a long low sinus-clearing hoot. *Hüüüüümmm*.

"How perceptive of you, Aunt," said Stefanie, from the doorway. "I found him sensitive, intelligent, and original. I was as surprised as anyone to learn that he was . . . "

"An agent provocateur?" interjected the Baroness.

"Such a fine violinist."

Nodding sagely, the Baron lit his Egyptian cigarette and smoothly exhaled a stream of pungent Levantine smoke.

Happily, Tadeusz Banaczynski's life and accomplishments were by no means over. He was recruited to the Habsburg Secret Service by the not-yet-notorious Colonel Redl; arrested by Marshal Pilsudski's security forces in the 1920s; and rescued from the Krakow jail by a devoted female admirer with whom he spent nine years in Paris, finishing his life as a violin tutor in Greenpoint, Brooklyn, New York, USA, where, one morning in 1954, he read of Stefanie in the Gazeta Wyborcza *and remembered, suddenly, that evening at the Palais Ottoheinz in long-ago Vienna, the girl with the shining eyes, another age, another world, as if Tadeusz himself had lived from medieval times clear through to the Nuclear Age . . . then he died.*

Gustave
Three

I'D BEEN HALF an hour or so in the Café de Rive, at a marble table in the corner, tea and a sugar cube in front of me, *à la russe*, waiting for the lady, and feeling that spasmodic stirring of stomach butterflies that most men my age have long since consigned to distant youthful memories of courtship. I gazed meditatively through the veil of my cigarette smoke like the ulcer-ridden hero of an expressionist novel. In between jags of worrying about how my date would go, I thought about Stefanie and her Adolf—or rather, mostly about Adolf, and how even a repulsive scrap of human misanthropy like that had a childhood, a boyhood, a youth, and how even he tried to impress the girls, in his cockeyed wanker's way, very much as I had done, in my precollege days, with similar sartorial absurdities, right down to a silver-topped cane, my version of which had been leaning against the corner of one of Mamma's closets for about thirty years. Too, in the meandering of my thoughts there was Stefanie's vision of he who called to mind the stables of the Salzkammergut, quite clearly the cloven one, or someone cleverly disguised as him, or a hallucination . . . what did I mean, *or*? If it wasn't a hallucination, it was the real thing, and if it was the real thing all that religious rubbish—everything my rational, Italo-Swiss mind had excluded over the years—was all true. Yes: true. It was as simple as that. This line of thinking disturbed me, and I told her so when she arrived within thirty seconds of absolute punctuality (a good sign).

"Oh I don't know," she said. It was a breezy day, and her hair was in slight disarray, and there were blushes on her cheekbones. She sat down and patted her hair into place and adjusted her glasses and coolly looked me over with that slight head-tilt of hers, wondering perhaps if my precipitate launch into deep matters was a sign of endearing seriousness or dangerous eccentricity. "An espresso," to the waiter, then: "I feel quite certain that von Rothenberg saw what she said she saw. I'm just not sure that anyone else could have seen it."

"And thus we have the foundation of all religions," I said. "How convenient for them." (I decided against bringing up my vision, such as it was, for at that early stage few things, I imagined, could be better calculated to scare off a lady of evident breeding than an aging self-described poet telling her in all seriousness that he'd just seen the Archangel Michael.) "They all think they see what they say they see, don't they? Muhammad the illiterate camel trader taking dictation from the Angel Gabriel. Peter on his way out of Rome, then HOP, there's the Lord Himself: '*Quo vadis, Domine?*' '*Eo Romam iterum crucifigi,*' wasn't that it? And the rest of Peter's story, told from an upside-down cross. And St. Francis and his visions of the Virgin and Child; and Teresa of Ávila and John of the Cross . . . "

"I see you've done your research. Are you a theologian as well?"

"Like your heroine Stefanie? Perish the thought. A humble historian and occasional versifier, no more."

Her espresso came; she eyed the ashtray with a certain wistfulness. I responded to the signal like Pavlov's dog to the dinner bell.

"Cigarette?"

"Oh, may I? I'm trying to quit. Last week was my fortieth birthday, and I thought it would be a good way to celebrate."

I shrugged.

"If it makes you feel better. If not, it's really just giving in to social pressure. But that's just my opinion," I added, aware that I'd already jeopardized our relationship by in effect accusing her of having no convictions of her own. But she smiled and inhaled gratefully after I passed her my Bic.

"You're right. And it was ill-health, as a matter of fact. I had a touch of bronchitis. The Geneva climate," she said. "Not social pressure. I try to resist that, not that one always can. Well, take my book for example, as long as you've been so kind as to mention it." She was animated, and ready to talk, once she'd assessed me as being (I hoped) essentially harmless, even interesting, if bizarre—anyway, a woman of a certain age should like a man with his own opinions on things, or she's learned little from life. And if a man my age doesn't have his own opinions on things, he's learned nothing. I sat back.

"It was an uphill battle getting funding for the research, I can tell you," she told me. "Nothing about the project appealed to the trendies at the station . . . I work for the TSR1 TV channel, by the way."

I nodded knowingly.

"Yes, so it says on the jacket of your book."

"Oh so it does. Anyway, they wouldn't hear of any of it. A book on mysticism? Hitler? An Austrian aristocrat? I tried to make a feeble case that von Rothenberg was an inspiration to feminists, living in sin with a man like . . . "

I held up a restraining hand.

"Please. I've only read the first two chapters. Don't give anything away."

"Oh, sorry. Well, anyway, that line of argument led nowhere, so in the end I had to refinance my apartment just in order to take time off the job and spend a few weeks poking around in Austria and Germany."

This led down an agreeable byway of chitchat about Geneva's surfeited and corrupt real estate market, one in which we agreed we were both lucky to own our apartments—a deft way, by the way, of learning where she lived, and how. Alone, it turned out, except for a poodle, in an apartment in the Parc de Budé, that elegant enclave of sixties-modern comfort, a stone's throw from the United Nations, in the quiet, leafy heart of that other Geneva we natives regarded with disdain and envy in equal measure, and which is the only Geneva the world knows. I knew it from my affianced days; Françoise, my ex, had taught the autistic son of a South American diplomat there, and, young and filled with sap and vigor as I'd been, I'd made numerous clandestine late-night visits for amorous purposes, taking the service lift up to the South Americans' (Argentinians, I think) so as not to run into the concierge . . . Anyway, Martine, as the elder of two sisters, had acquired the flat from her mountain-climbing father after his death in a blizzard on the Aiguilles du Midi in 1995. Her mother, remarried a couple of years previously, lived in Pakistan with her Pakistani husband, whom she'd met at the Curry Pot on the Rue du Mont-Blanc. She had severed nearly all connections with home, allegedly on the insistence of her new Muslim in-laws.

"My sister, who lives in Paris, refuses to say a word to her, but she still talks to me, reluctantly. 'Have you married again?' she asks. 'Are you still drinking wine?' 'Are you still an unbeliever?' Very boring. Very sad."

A lost cause, I agreed. But as for Jeanrenaud *père*, well now he must have been quite the dynamo, I said.

"Mountains and precipices and sheer rock faces? Dramatic stuff, I mean."

"It always terrified me. I once watched him rappel down the face of El Capitan, in California. Sheer rock face, hundreds of meters high . . . I had nightmares for months after. I still do, in fact. That experience alone did me in. I don't even like to take the *téléférique* up the Salève."

"Awkward, being Swiss and not liking mountains."

"Oh, but I'm Genevese, not *Swiss*. Anyway, I love mountains, but from a distance. Like Jean-Jacques Rousseau."

"Ah, Rousseau."

Ah, indeed. Now we were getting somewhere. We had laid the essential groundwork, and the systole and diastole of a bur-geoning human relationship could begin: the sudden swells and slow diminutions, the anxiety of a moment of silence and its inevitable termination in simultaneous outbursts of speech; the lingering gaze not lingering too long lest it degenerate into ogling and the whole thing turn into a boy's (or girl's) one-night stand; the avoidance, in the early stages, of too much reminiscence. But we were on firm ground with Rousseau, I felt, and thought, accurately as it turned out, that to Martine he was more than just the name on a few plaques around town. Indeed, she had read all his work, and had in the end rejected his humid ramblings in favor of the crisper, drier climate of Voltaire.

"All our modern ills stem from Rousseau," she said. "He invented modern totalitarianism. You can't have an effective dictatorship without some high-minded ideology to justify it, and there was never a higher-minded ideologue than our precious Jean-Jacques. And what he did with his children doesn't bear thinking of! I'm having another espresso. More tea?"

I assented. We'd been talking for an hour and a half, and the awkward intermissions were fewer and fewer. It was half five when we left, she to meet a colleague at the TV building, I to do some late afternoon exam-marking in my office before meeting Gax for a no-doubt fractious dinner at eight.

After a desultory hour's work in restraining the worst excesses of my students' ignorance, I sat at my desk and smoked and gazed out at the rooftops and the sky from which the gray dusk was leeching the blue, and thought with a pleasant little upjump of the heart of Martine Jeanrenaud, and said thinking led me on the narrow track of my thoughts to Stefanie von Rothenberg; so, with an hour or more to go before my dinner engagement, I settled back, poured a Fendant from the half-empty bottle under my desk, and went on with the life of a Nazi mystic and her fearful gift (and her even more fearful beau).

Tristan

In 1912 Stefanie was in her third year at the University of Vienna. Her Index, or matriculation book, made mention of Church History, Theology I, Theology II, and Religious Literature. Her exams were the best. She had studied the early Church Fathers, misanthropes all (Jerome, Augustine, Ambrose); the first schisms and the Council of Nicaea; the struggle between kings and popes; Pope Leo IX, who revealingly said (c. 1450): "This myth of Christ has served us well," thus justifying Martin Luther and the Reformation, which in turn justified Ignacio Loyola and the Counter-Reformation . . . some of it was tedious stuff, yet her struggle to overcome the massed forces of arrogance and hierarchy had succeeded to the point of her becoming well known enough in limited circles to have acquired the (inevitable) nickname "The Lady Scholar."

It was a bright day in October. A new skirmish in the Balkans was kicking up mighty waves of *schadenfreude* in the normally calm waters of the Viennese press. Stefanie, books (Luther, Helmsen, von Barth) cradled to her bosom, was crossing the Schottenring, just down from the University. A voice brayed from behind.

"My dear Stefanie." It was Helmuth Meinl, rabbi's son, doctoral candidate, lackadaisical suitor: red-haired, pigeon-toed, a good fellow but gangling, and a watcher, not a doer, but good-natured as a sheepdog. "I say. I have free tickets to the opera. Saturday next. The matinee."

"Ah yes? How did you manage that?"

"My brother-in-law, you know. The stage manager? It's *Tristan*, you know. Bruno Walter's conducting."

Well, then.

(It was Stefanie's first official sortie with young Meinl, so she made sure not to broadcast any encouragement beyond simple courtesy. In any case, she wanted to take advantage of the free opera ticket, a rare commodity in Vienna.)

On the Saturday, they met at Landtmanns at one.

"We shouldn't have too much coffee," said Helmuth, with a dip of the head and a clownish smile. "It's a long opera."

"I'll have a *mélange*."

"Oh, good idea. Herr Ober!"

As if on cue, an abhorrence of mediocrity swooned through Stefanie's soul and she longed for passion, expression, art, even revelation. She thought of Goethe, Luther, Wagner, and lesser men, some of whom (the much lesser ones) she knew.

Tristan always attracted a crowd, even at the matinee performance, and the conductor, young Bruno Walter, the late great Mahler's understudy and second-in-command, was himself a powerful attraction, ramrod-straight, lithe, and—paradoxically, in a mostly cloudy climate—deeply tanned. In a city given to ranking its artists as another city might categorize sports figures or military heroes, Walter was nearing the top of the list for sheer enigma value, but the Klimt brothers and Oskar Kokoschka had the advantage, for the time being. Indeed, on that Saturday the eminent (or insignificant, depending on the degree of your modernism) Kokoschka was in the Mahler family box—"Look, isn't that Alma?" whispered Helmuth, and of course it was indeed the Maestro's widow—and a rumor made its way around the parterre to the effect that a Royal and Imperial personage would be, might be, WAS in attendance . . . yes! There he was, once again! His Imperial Highness Franz Ferdinand, in full Habsburg splendor, with his dutiful Sophie sitting a suitably morganatic distance behind him. Applause greeted their appearance. He bowed, she inclined her head. Stefanie looked away. She cared less for such personages than she had once.

"The Archduke," murmured Helmuth. "Never has he been seen at a performance of a Wagner opera. Why is he here? It's well known the man has no culture. Did you hear what he said about Kokoschka? 'I'd like to break every bone in his body.' Well, here's his chance, eh? Imagine the headlines!"

"Oh, forget him," said Stefanie, impatient at her own past awe, as well as irritated by Helmuth's moist, darting eyes and overuse of the word *culture* . . . then, with a truly fine congruity of sentiment and event, she saw Adolf Hitler, watching her, and at that moment the lights dimmed and Tristan's musical foreplay began. It was, of course, glorious. In the intervening three years Stefanie had evolved, in her all-or-nothing way, into a devotee of Wagner. Oh, she revered Mozart, as befit a Salzburger; Mahler, too, of the modernists, she adored (*oh see! how like a silver ship above his widow sails, on the blue Kokoschka-sea!*); and Bruckner, and, yes, stodgy old Brahms, photographs of whom reminded her of her pappi; but as she said to Cousin Fritzl a while back, a propos of nothing (in her spontaneous, girlish way) "You can have all the other music in the world if I could just keep the "Good Friday Music" from *Parsifal*." Hearty Fritzl obligingly said she was welcome to it, but Fritzl was a philistine, and knew nothing of art. And now she was in the company of another philistine, Helmuth, whose real interest in the opera, as became apparent after his third or fourth cavernous yawn, was primarily social (did she not see, in response to a slight hand gesture, a flirtatious twinkle of opera glasses, from a silk-brocaded feminine blur on the mezzanine?), not that he differed in this from the majority of his fellow Viennese. After all, no city can be as genuinely interested in culture as Vienna pretends to be, but any city can be as interested in dalliance and sex as Vienna really is. Yet there were exceptions: Stefanie, although enraptured by the overture and the stark Cornish blue-and-silver decor of the first act (*So frisch der Wind / Der Heimat zu*), stole a glance toward Adolf Hitler, sitting two rows forward to her right. Yes, unlike most of his side-glancing, flirting neighbors, he sat open-mouthed, staring, enraptured, a true and genuine worshipper in the act of worshipping. This decided Stefanie. At the first interval . . . !

She waited impatiently, torn between art and opportunity. At the first interval the lights went up, she excused herself. They met again, in the main aisle of the parterre. He was correctly, if shabbily, dressed like a junior government minister in an evening coat and striped trousers.

"Fräulein von Rothenberg, is it not? Dear God! How fortunate to find you here, at this fine performance of *Tristan*! Although the conductor . . . " He took himself in hand, with a visible effort (hard swallowing, a quick frisson). "How are you? And how is your estimable family?"

"Very well, Herr Hitler. Very well. I was sorry to hear about your mother."

"Ah! Ah. Yes. Thank you." He bowed slightly and clasped his hands in front of his crotch. Well, thought Stefanie, this is awkward, and likely to become more so. "Herr *Adolf*," she said, thereby half dispensing with such formalities, recovering something of the coy jocularity of the schoolyard. "Where are you living now? Are you studying at the Art Academy?"

"Ah," he said, eyes downcast. "No, not at the Art Academy."

"At the University, then? You know, I've been at the University for three years now, but I haven't seen you at all."

Adolf looked up, emotion twisting his features, on the verge of reply; then he glanced sidelong, surprised, taken aback by the nasal hallooing of Helmuth, who gangled through groups of people parting for his passage.

"My dear Stefanie, you do have this tendency to just up and go, don't you. Hello, who's this?"

"Adolf, this is Herr Dozent Helmuth Meinl."

"Meinl? Hitler." Adolf heel-clicked, bowed. Helmuth, sizing up the social inequality, was condescending in his brief acknowledgment: a dip of the head.

"Adolf," said Stefanie, "I'm living with my relatives. The Palais Ottoheinz, Johannesgasse."

"And I at the Heim für Männer, in the Inner City," said Adolf, with a hoarse laugh. "With my colleagues the mice."

"Oh dear."

"*Ja.* I'm afraid I must carry the smell with me. Some jumped-up little gypsy of an usher wouldn't let me in at first, not until I pointed out I was a citizen and that I had paid my admission with my hard-earned . . . well! There's the bell."

They did no more than exchange glances during the second interval and by the end of the opera, with the Love-Death haunting the air, Adolf had disappeared into the discretion of the night.

As Stefanie and Helmuth walked to the Café Central for a nightcap (bohemians all: young Klimt, Stiele, and in the corner, behind his thick round spectacles and a Kaffee mit Schlagsobers: the enigmatic Russian emigré "Trotsky," *né* Bronstein), Helmuth inquired, "Who was that sad-looking specimen you introduced to me?"

"Adolf Hitler. An old friend from my Linz days."

"He looked a little down on his luck. But not so far down as to not be able to afford the opera, eh? Ah, we Viennese."

Stefanie's cheeks burned. She had sensed the same unruliness of response in Adolf as she had all those years before. They knew each other not at all, they had met a mere two or three times, but something trembled in the air . . . as the moth to the flame, she was drawn to her memory of his magnetism, his passion, his perverse individuality, yet she held back, she acknowledged the faint something that was more akin to revulsion than to anything else. She recalled her vision of the devil, and shuddered, although among the many explanations she'd come up with, while firmly separating it from her actual memory of Adolf, had been one anchored firmly in the physical, viz., feminine problems, pre-menstrual stress, poor digestion, and other banalities that went only so far in explaining it; yet she felt the faint hot caress of that ominous half-forgotten fever, a memory made physical by the fresh stimulus of her recent, operatic encounter. Pity undoubt-edly played a part in her feelings for Adolf, as well, for Stefanie saw in him one, like her, who aimed for higher things; an artist, one of the chosen (or despised) few; and her ever-growing pity knew no bounds, pity for the abject, the scorned, the down-trodden, the pleading, even the arrogant when they were beaten down, for crushed pride is a pitiable sight.

Conversely, pride unchecked inspired nothing in her but contempt, and her contempt burned most of the young men of Vienna.

Der Heim für Männer

Not far from the Palais Ottoheinz, in the Inner City, First District, in the Heim für Männer on the Meldemannstrasse, Adolf nursed his growing madness. Outwardly meek, except when moved to diatribe by his reading, and the long chilly ennui of the evenings at the Heim für Männer (or by the dull wits of his housemates, most of them older and feebler than he), he was little known except as a journeyman artist, but an artist he was indeed, whatever the Academy said; in truth he was more of a professional than those old academicians, who never painted, or drew, or sold a sketch. In fact, young Hitler claimed that he lived off the slender proceeds of his art and therefore earned far too little to make any contribution to the Royal and Imperial Tax Authority (who remained unaware of Adolf's substantial pension, inherited from his father, and legacies from his mother and his aunt, that enabled him to straddle the line between *rentier* and tramp: hence the Heim für Männer, demesne of the underprivileged, an address never visited by the Tax Authority).

Adolf's artistic work was of the sub-Biedermeier school, nothing risqué or avant-garde, mostly charming views in aquarelle of
the Prater, the *heuriger* in Grinzing, and the Opernring at dusk
(actually, that one was quite evocative, with un-Hitlerian hints of
pointillism in the light-and-shadow effects, and an impressionis-
tic glimmer in the streetlamps). He painted *in situ*, or at home,
in the Heim für Männer's reading room, or in his own untidy
corner (his "atelier," as he ironically referred to it), a bohemian
congeries of easels, watercolors, palettes, drawing paper, xeno-
phobic monographs, magazines of Hollywood, the Wild West,
and German nationalism (*Blick, Karl May im Bild, Ostara*), the
collected works of Karl May, Houston Stewart Chamberlain,
Lanz von Liebenfels, and the Count Gobineau, a few delicate
china gewgaws from home, and a framed photograph of their
former owner, his dear dead mother. No ashtrays piled high
with the cigarette butts of an artist's late nights, for Adolf did
not smoke; no half-empty bottles of Algerian red, for Adolf, a
one-time drunk (kicked humiliatingly awake in a ditch by a surly
milkman), drank no more, bar the odd near-beer. He hardly
needed to: his dreams intoxicated him and occupied his days as
well as his nights. Was there ever such a dreamer? He dreamed
of so many things: of refashioning Vienna by slicing a great
gleaming East-West Axis through the dank medieval Hofburg
huddle; of building Linz into Vienna's rival, with proud factories and sweeping avenues; of mounting the decisive produc-
tion of *Parsifal* in Bayreuth, under the very eyes of Herr und
Frau Siegfried and Winifred Wagner; of adorning the Rathaus of
Braunau with a great mural twenty feet high, depicting the anni-
hilation of the three Roman legions in the Teutoburger Wald;
of erecting memorials to his mother in all the capitals of the
Greater German Empire of which, too, he dreamed, drawing its
borders, provisionally, at the Vosges Mountains in the west, the
Tannenberg Forest in the east, the Kattegat in the north, and
the Tirol in the south; of crafting a great work combining art,
drama, philosophy, and politics; and, even, in idle moments, of
women. Women were, of course, multitudinous in Vienna, but
few caught his fancy, and his one sexual encounter to date, with

an artist's model named Mitzi, had indeed been consummated but in a febrile, hasty fashion that left Mitzi, for one, wondering precisely what had happened. Friends had he none; acquaintances, few. Kubizek, his best friend from Linz days, had, ultimately, disappointed by going on to study at the Conservatory and turning into a boring up-at-six-home-at-five kind of grind; well! Adolf had put an end to that friendship by quite simply moving out, sleeping rough for a while before arriving in the depth of midwinter at the Heim für Männer, cloister of hacking coughs and brisk nocturnal scrubbing sounds, reminiscent at first of that horrible clinic where his mother had suffered so long, so needlessly . . . but now things were better. Things were taking shape, in a way. He was making a reasonable wage from his postcards; people were listening to what he had to say; and, oddly, his health was rather good. He was sleeping well, for a change. All kinds of ideas were forming in his brain. There were moments of clear-eyed and absolute triumph, when he was walking along (say) the Hoher Markt, or the Graben, and a Baroque or even Rococo cloud formation would catch his eye and a ray of light would pick out some distant cupola or attic window as if God Himself were plucking at his sleeve; and at such moments he knew beyond any doubt that his destiny was to . . . that he had a destiny, anyway, whether in the sweet, decaying capital of the Habsburgs or elsewhere, abroad, or in the vast marches of Pomerania or Prussia, as a Napoleon of great armies, a King Frederick of philosophy, a Goethe of art and romance. The irony, of course, was his current station in life, and the concomitant contempt with which he found himself treated by café managers, paint salesmen, policemen, theater ushers (like that nitwit at the Opera the other night) and their kind. Sometimes it was too much to bear, and he turned on people in the street, screaming obscenities, fits of anger that left him feeling drained and self-defiled. Still, these diatribes jolted his housemates into paying attention, and no one disturbed him behind his corner partition unless invited. Truth to tell, there was a coziness to the Heim für Männer, with its nooks and crannies, and the sense of being hidden away among multitudes, that a flat could never provide, flats being much lonelier places. Adolf was a solitary young man, and although he despised humanity he simultaneously longed for its approval; indeed, when he found himself spending too much time alone, he would drop in at one of the cafés, the Central or Landtmanns, and have a slice of torte and a cup of tea and read the *Wiener Zeitung*, disdaining the world while obscurely hoping for the ideal companion, the perfect acolyte and helpmate, Sieglinde to his Siegfried, to suddenly appear before him, so they could rise from the table and go together into a sunlit golden age of straight lines and magnificent boulevards and impeccable order.

Then he ran into Stefanie von Rothenberg at the Opera and disorder blew through his dreamworld like a gale through the gardens of Schönbrunn. He brooded on this the next day.

"Damn," he said, rocking back and forth on his chair. He stared out the window with a stony fixation. Autumn leaves wafted past the window, and the statue of Prince Eugene across the street was covered in what seemed, romantically, to be snow, but was really pigeon shit. The old street sweeper whom he'd once, foolishly, engaged in conversation and who now, irritatingly, greeted him without fail, shuffled past, pushing his broom. He looked up; Adolf looked away. When Adolf looked back the moment, and the old sweep, had passed.

He resumed thinking of Stefanie.

"Damn," he repeated. Their operatic encounter threatened the meticulous torpor of his existence, in which everything gravitated around his own inertia. Women! Women meant excursions, excuses, dinner dates, families. On the other hand, she did look beautiful, more radiant then she had been back in Linz (and he'd seen her once there from a distance, unseen by her, as he'd spied on her in the street) and back in Linz already he'd thought her the most desirable creature on earth—not that he was fully conscious of desiring her, for sexual satyrs played coy catch with innocent imps in the playground of Adolf's mind (and looming over them all, as in an opera stage set, was the stern Greco-Germanic visage of his Destiny).

A Portrait

Then Stefanie came to the Heim für Männer. She found the place without difficulty. It was a dingy ex-palace of the Metternich era, formerly and briefly the home of the Montenegrin Resident, of whose tenure it still bore traces: a coat-of-arms above the front door; a flagpole mount on the second-floor balcony; on the wall, the faded stain where a plaque had been. But the two broken windows on the second floor, and the sharp scent of ammonia, and the muffled sound of coughing, and the rheumy scrutiny of the two old Jews behind the front desk, contrived for a moment to make Stefanie reconsider the wisdom of her mission. This doubt spawned others: Why was the daughter of Herr Doktor Hermann von Rothenberg of Getreidegasse, Salzburg, calling on the denizen of a dosshouse? What kind of man, artist or not, would choose to live in such a place? And what did she really know about Adolf Hitler, anyway? That he painted; that he expostulated; that he'd loved his mother, once; that his eyes shone with a great belief in Art, or himself; that he'd obviously gone nowhere in life, save directly downhill . . . and yet! Few were those whose devotion to Art of any kind was as great as his! In fact, she knew of none, and half of Adolf's appeal (along with a certain nostalgia for the dear cozy days of Linz) was precisely this, the more so in light of the disdain in which the theologians with whom she associated held Art, poor cousin of Theology.

(After all, hadn't she seen that expression on his face last night at the opera? While others flirted, he adored.)

She inquired for him of the old Jews at the front desk, one of whom detached himself from his post, eyes bulging like pigeon eggs.

"Hiddler? *Ja*, he should be here. I'll geddim for ya."

She stood in the doorway, amid the softly susurrating leaves. The other old Jew stared at her.

"Cold," he said.

"Yes," she said, politely. "It's . . . "

"*Ja*, bud id'll be a lot colder soon," he interrupted, taking her aback with the insolence of it: an old Jew in a flophouse, interrupting a lady, and not for anything of significance, but for the tritest of banalities!

She heard Adolf's hoarse voice and turned.

"*Ja, ja*, Neumann, I'm not blind, I can see her and I can manage with my things quite well, thank you very much."

"Bah," said the old Jew thus addressed. "Hiddler, you can be a real *putzkopf*. Well, here he is, lady."

Adolf was dressed as he had been at the opera, in a white shirt with high collar and tie and pinstriped trousers with shining knees; wasn't he, thought Stefanie (herself conservative in brown and gray), the very picture of genteel hard times, *la vie de bohème* in person? Under his arm he carried the tools of his trade: easel, palette, paint box, and a triage of paintbrushes wagging through bony fingers.

"Such a surprise to see you at the door of this shithouse. I beg your pardon, but I must say so."

"It's not so bad. Anyway, I warned you I'd be coming."

(Suddenly she saw herself sweeping onstage, an overdressed *grande dame*, a patroness of artists taking a condescending shine to a scruffy nobody.)

"Hiddler, ya want the key?" shouted Neumann, as Adolf and Stefanie walked out the door. "You gedding back before curfew?"

"*Ja, ja*, Neumann," said Adolf, crossly. "I'll be back."

They stepped out. With his overburdened arm, Adolf motioned for Stefanie to precede him. The gesture was excessive: things spilled to the ground. Adolf and Stefanie spent the next two or three minutes picking up the tools of an artist's trade. Stefanie offered to ease his burden by carrying, at least, the paintbrushes, but Adolf angrily declined.

"No, no, a lady does not carry things in the street, good God I may have degraded socially but," his voice rose, raucous, "I'm not a moral degenerate yet, if you don't mind!"

"Of course," said Stefanie. Awkwardness hovered over them like a vulture. Adolf was breathing hard, with a shallow whistling sound. With his free hand, he repetitively brushed aside an overhanging forelock. When passersby turned to look, he began muttering. They came to the Ringstrasse by the Rathaus, and

Stefanie realized that she had no plan, no intention, no goal at all. The day suddenly loomed emptier than a Sunday in Linz.

A propos of which: since his days in that city Adolf had turned tougher, turned inward, developed mannerisms. For a moment Stefanie longed to leave, to forget him, to return to the security of her own kind (acknowledging to herself that he wasn't one of *her* kind after all); then, as will happen at crucial moments, a word made all the difference:

"Sorry," said Adolf.

"Oh, that's all right."

"I live alone now, or rather I live with fools, tramps and Jews, which amounts to the same thing. Did you see any of them, by the way? Apart from the old Yids at the front door? The Yiddischer Cerberus twins, ah?"

Stefanie, buoyed by his sudden bonhomie, responded with tentative good humor of her own.

"Yes, they're a pair of beauties, aren't they? Listen, Adolf, we're not far from my uncle and aunt's house. If you've nothing planned, you could drop in and do my portrait. On commission, of course."

He stared, frowned, looked away. He was thinking of Isolde.

"I don't do portraits," he said. "Not very well, anyway."

"Oh come on."

"I have a commission in the Stadtpark. The statue of the Emperor Joseph?"

"But that's right next door."

Adolf's commission was a lie. In truth, he was in a bind, a woman-bind, just as he feared (politeness vs. desire vs. freedom); but there was a small challenge in doing a portrait, and a portrait of a society lady like Stefanie von Rothenberg might lead to other commissions, and her people were well-off . . .

"*Ja*," he said. "But don't expect a masterpiece."

At the house, they ran into the Baron.

"Steffi," he said. "*Hüüüümmm*. Whom have we here?"

"Uncle, this is a painter friend of mine who is here to do my portrait. Our families were slightly acquainted, in Linz. Herr Adolf Hitler, Baron Ottoheinz."

"Hitler, Hitler. From Salzburg?"

Adolf bowed, clicked his heels, shifted paints and brushes clumsily about.

"From Linz, Herr Baron."

"Ah, Linz. Dreary little town, if you don't mind my saying so. You'll find yourself much better off here in Vienna."

"Just so, Herr Baron. A dreary little town, as you say. And Vienna of course, well . . . !" Stefanie was amused to behold pure Austrian *bürgerlich* groveling: Adolf was standing quite rigidly at attention, like a soldier. An obsequious smile played over his lips, rabbiting forward his not-insubstantial teeth; with his art supplies tucked under his arm, his hands were stiffly folded across his crotch, and from his mouth there issued banalities of a peerlessness impressive even to long-time observers of middle-class manners like Stefanie, daughter of the von Rothenberg of that ilk.

"Of course, Herr Baron. You are quite right, Herr Baron. Herr Baron, how true. Ah, the climate, *ja, ja*. Oh, for the moment, I have artist's digs across the Innere Stadt, in the former Montenegran Residenz. A bit of this, a bit of that, you know, Herr Baron. One does what one must."

"He seems all right, your painter friend, if a bit on edge," said the Baron a moment later, after Adolf had disappeared into the little salon to set up his easel. "Perhaps I should ask him to do my portrait, too."

"Wait until we see how he does with me," said Stefanie.

Despite the abruptness of the event, things got underway. The appropriate flesh tints were found, and crisp new drawing paper, and Adolf's brushes and palette were brand-new, as the result of a particularly good commission (the Plague Column on the Graben, always a favorite with tourists) from one of the Jewish souvenir shops on the Hoher Markt; his abilities as a portraitist, however, as he was the first to admit, were severely compromised by the stiffness and rigidity of his style, which lent itself to landscape and city-scene. His last attempt at a portrait had been one of Kubizek's sister: frankly, an utter failure, as Kubizek had stated with uncommon boldness, thereby causing a rupture in their friendship . . . yes, the subtleties and shades of the human face represented quite another topography, one he'd always been reluctant to explore, and one which had cost him admission to the Art Academy, the second time around, when a decent portrait *plus* his landscapes might well have earned him entrée.

The chosen room was a small salon, off the main hallway, reserved for such events as military anniversaries, the Wattmen's Ball, and Fritzl's wedding reception. Light from the French windows gleamed on the flagstones of the uncarpeted floor, suitable for paint spillage. Adolf sweated over disposition of easel and paints while, on a standard Biedermeier settee, Stefanie reposed unerotically, cheek upon hand, capturing the very essence of middle-class Austrian art.

"More to the left." Adolf was pale and strained, crouching like a troll behind his easel, muttering half remembered phrases from Seelebach's *Self-Taught Draughtsman*, the amateur artist's bible. "The planes—the contours—above all, the shadows, which themselves can evoke form more precisely than a line . . . "

His brushes clicked; he grunted, shooting glances around the corner of his easel at Stefanie. Time slowed to a crawl. Shadows slowly gathered. Stefanie rubbed her forehead. She felt warm.

"Hands down, please." Adolf painted and painted. The room was close, or so thought Stefanie, and birds or heavy clouds episodically blotted out the daylight; there was no breeze, and the stuffiness was increasing. Adolf's face shone waxen, like a beacon on a midnight strand. The daylight brightened, dimmed, brightened, dimmed, and finally simply faded away completely. It felt too early for darkness. Stefanie, sure she was sweating, touched her forehead. It was still dry, but warmer than the room, if not by much. There wasn't even a fire in the grate.

"DON'T MOVE!" snapped Adolf, temperamentally every inch the portraitist, even if the whole undertaking was a wild gamble for him (but he thought it was going quite well).

"Sorry," said Stefanie.

She blinked. A faint blurry mist disappeared, except around the edges of her vision: clear was her focus on what she was increasingly reluctant to see, Adolf, for instance, who suddenly appeared to be wearing a black pullover (although Stefanie clearly recalled noticing that he was wearing the same white shirt he'd worn at the opera the night before), from which his pallid face emerged, wan and haggard, forehead cleft by a frown of concentration. Moreover, his trousers appeared to be turning black, too, as did the easel, and one by one most of the furnishings in the room, as if Stefanie, trading in the common currency of dreams, were alone on a stage peering into a darkened theater in which a single pale face, Adolf's, peered back at her.

Time stuttered, slowed, stalled; then Time and everything else seemed to coagulate and swell up like a gigantic boil.

"*Himmeldonnerwetter*," said Stefanie. "I feel a little bit sick." Sick was the word: A wave of nausea swept over her. Perversely, she felt pregnant. She touched her forehead again. This time she was sweating. Uncle Ernst was right, with his incessant complaining: Damn this Viennese climate! She must have picked up a chill, walking over to that dingy dosshouse . . . her heart paused, poised, dropped, hammered.

"Nonsense, there is nothing the matter with you, nothing at all," roared Adolf—or rather, roared a voice from Adolf's direction, a voice, now that Stefanie thought about it, as unlike Adolf's as her own; and unlike the Baron's, too, or any of the servants, except maybe that new chauffeur from Moravia . . . to make matters worse, somebody had definitely switched off the lights. It was as dark as midnight.

"Adolf?" she cried.

Silence, then laughter; laughter, perfectly articulated, basso profundo and operatic, and utterly chilling to the blood.

"Ha. Ha. Ha. Ha-ha-ha. Ha."

Then Stefanie allowed herself to remember, that other time, that vision.

"Oh God."

This seemed to upset The Voice, which boomed,

"Say it not!"

Eyes, enormous and forever hungry; a shape, bent, twisted yet powerful, like an enormous dwarf's; a smell . . . yes! How had she missed the smell? It filled the room, a pungent, acrid, farmyard smell, with an overlay of scorched metal; then, as it had that other time, it dissipated, vanished, leaving behind only that all-devouring physical presence.

Those giant's eyes that were windows into hot pools of lust and greed.

"How very like an opera," thought Stefanie, in an oddly detached way. Gounod's *Faust* and Boito's *Mefistofele* passed through her mind; then she could bear it no longer, but clapped her hands over her eyes and screamed. Moments later, the awakening, the solicitous faces: Uncle Ernst, Aunt Liesl . . .

"It has turned noticeably chilly in here."

"We'll get a fire lit."

"Ach, poor Steffi!"

And all was normal once again, or reassuringly abnormal in a quotidian way.

"Look," said the Baron. "Young Hitler finished the portrait, my dear."

He held up a picture.

"Is that me?" Stefanie sat up, dabbed at her (for some reason) teary eyes. The picture, flattering, was only a touch awkward in the slightly too simian bulk of the jaw, but otherwise it was unmistakably Stefanie, and even the body was rendered quite gracefully, with none of the squareness typical of amateurs, or landscape artists.

"We'll hang it in the hallway," said the Baron. "Damned if I might not ask him to do mine, too."

It had all taken, as it transpired, nearly three hours, and if it seemed dark it was simply because five o'clock had struck, and it was a Vienna October evening. In the street outside, the streetlamps were lit and their yellowish light shimmered through the drizzle.

"Yes, yes. Odd chap, that young Hitler. He left, you know, after telling me you'd had a bit of a turn. Said he had an urgent appointment in the Stadtpark, of all places."

"You must have caught a chill, *Liebling*, or is it your time of month?" murmured Aunt Liesl.

"Neither," said Stefanie.

Gustave
Four

THE CAR STAYED garaged on my boozy nights with Gax, and my sluggish blood needed circulating; anyway, the Lyrique was only a kilometre or so from my office. I consciously took a different route and avoided the Corraterie, now more the stage setting for uninvited archangels than the banal shopping street it was.

Gax was already at our usual table under the newspaper racks, nursing a *kyr*, smoking his pipe, and looking like that bilious bloke in Degas's *L'Absinthe*.

"Ay, Termi," he called out, "there you are, you old visionary. Seen any archangels lately? By the by, did you know that Mallarmé had visions too? Once when he was down on his luck and hadn't eaten for days he awoke from a fevered doze to see on his bedside table a fine baked ham with capers, onions, asparagus, and roast potatoes, just the way Maman Mallarmé used to make it. In his frenzy he grabbed at it, only to fall out of his bed and sprain his hand, which en route to being sprained clutched at nothing more appetizing than an overflowing ashtray."

"Better for him than an archangel, roast or raw. At least no one would accuse him of being a religious loony."

"Just a loony, eh? But that's all right. He was a poet. Which explains why he smelled it, too. He said the vision kept him going for days, and anyway the pain of the sprained hand eased that of his unfulfilled stomach. So tell me more, Termi. What was he wearing?"

He was in bitter form, the old cynic. After I'd satsified his curiosity about the Archangel's wardrobe we went on to empty a pair of bottles of Fendant de Sion over our respective *poule des Dombes* and *lapin rôti à la mode du Valais*. Conversation meandered, firing at will. His targets included writer's block—"Mallarmé and his fucking blank page," he said, "he started it all, you never heard of writer's block before that"—as well as the communists; the Muslims; me, *en passant*, with hypocritical apologies; the Americans; his publishers (especially) who refused to bring out a second edition of *The Veil of Bashshar*, his most recent story collection and a total flop commercially; his ex-wife, Katia; the British; the Swiss-Germans . . . Mine? Oh, psychoanalysis, publishers, professors, him, en passant, without apologies . . . It was good, despite the momentary likelihood of fisticuffs. Moreover, it was what had always happened in our friendship, first falling out and each spending days or weeks brooding on the other's flaws; then one of us realizing there was nothing for it—there just weren't better drinking companions anywhere in the twenty-six cantons of the Helvetic Confederation than Guy and Gustave, raved Gax, aggressively—and making the obligatory conciliatory phone call disguised as just one more instalment in the insult sitcom in order to palliate any sign of emotional dependency. He'd called me at the office; I'd responded brusquely. At the restaurant he was the one who was brusque, then, when he thawed, I, going too far, told him about Martine, casually, as if she were a new colleague, or someone I'd met at a cocktail party, implying, indeed, that both were true. He was enthusiastic. I said nothing about her book, however, suspecting that a combination of Nazism and mystics would set him off like a dried-out firecracker.

"A woman, Tavo? A real lady, not a *pute*? Well done, I say." He raised his glass. "Good luck."

"Thanks. But it's early days yet," I said, to counteract the unreasoned and unreasonable bubbling of hope I felt racing through my veins.

For two aging bachelors, dining at the Lyrique was the next best thing to dining at home. We knew the waiters; they knew us. Neither they nor we were in any hurry. Shouts and guffaws and occasional intestinal detonations from our table were all taken in good part by the doddering staff (not one under sixty-five) as well as by the other customers, most of whom we knew—most of whom were, in fact, ex-colleagues, or readers, or once-and-future girlfriends. That night, our appetizers lasted a good hour over the first bottle, before old Alphonse, the head-waiter, an asthmatic from Alsace, wheeled over the second bottle and our *poule des Dombes* and *lapin roti*. It was a convivial place, the old Lyrique, with its gleaming oak tables, its tall gilt-framed mirrors that were like windows into a deep, pure world consisting entirely of one vast café, its long rows of newspapers on rods hanging side by side in a permanent *garde-à-vous*, its Gargantuan portions of *frites* and *moules*. (Now it's part of Internet Inns International, known for whizbang web hookups and complimentary laptops at every table and Gargantuan slices of gooey flavorless cheese-and-tomato pie, laughingly called "pizza." Oh, where are the cafés of yesteryear?)

Gax was undergoing yet more difficulties with his ex, who was threatening to sue him over something or other, and his latest "novel" was proceeding with crab-like slowness; hence the mockery of the great Mallarmé and his no doubt off-the-cuff remark about "the blank page" and the occasional acerbic remarks about my "humble versifying—*very* humble." He reminisced, over our second bottle and a tray of blue cheese—Gex, Bresse, Roquefort—while thanking providence that at our age we still had the stamina for it.

"For what?"

"For all of it, Termi. The reading, the writing, the teaching. The wine, the smoking, the dinners, the long walks by the river in the autumn, the music, the loving, the very waking up in the morning. Life, in a word. It isn't until you've seen the X-rays in the doctor's office that you begin to realize how real the end is and how near it is and how painful it can be and how fucking awful it'll be to lose all this."

He'd had a cancer scare, I remembered. Prostate, or kidney. Anyway, he'd been ordered to stop smoking and drinking, an utter waste of breath on the doctor's part. One might as well

order a politician to stick strictly to the truth, or the bise to stop
blowing.

Still, I preferred not to dwell on the old Final End just yet.

"Speaking of doctors, your LeCluyse is a right horror.
Pederast, he called me. *Pederast.*"

I explained. This occasioned much mirth and led, of course,
into the past. We revived memories of pederasts of our acquaintance, notably a grimy specimen who stalked his prey in one of
the public loos at Cornavin station and a rather absurd teacher
at the World Academy named M. Constantin, whose reputation
as a man-about-town, complete with leather jacket, red MG, and
silver cigarette case, had suffered a fatal blow when he was caught
hanging around the boys' showers once with a Polaroid, from
which emerged —it later emerged—snapshots he later tried to
sell to potential customers on the seedy streets of the Paquis and
Grottes districts. Other memories, seeing these ones enjoying
such a successful revival in the mind-theater, elbowed their way
back onstage, as they will in the minds of former soulmates who
really have so little else to talk about, bar their own troubles and
the multitudinous ways in which the world's going to hell. Of
our trip to London in '69, for instance, a bibulous nightlong
train ride across France then the ferry from Calais on a blustery
March day and the stirring sight of the White Cliffs and Beachy
Head rising through the wind-whipped spume of the Channel;
the orderly Kentish farms and oasthouses and the damply green
fields outside the rain-streaked train window, and in the aisles of
the train an entirely different smell, that of Britain, composed in
equal parts of beer, chips, detergent, and puke.

"Remember that landlady?"

"Ah, God. Mrs. Wicker?"

"Ah, God indeed."

We'd shared that lubricious solitary, a widow with that particularly English blend of obsequiousness and stand-offishness.
At one in the morning on our third night in Earl's Court she'd
scratched at the door of our attic bedchamber and flounced in,
superb in a blue chiffon nightdress that strained to conceal the
proud shelves of her bosom and bum; "oh, so French, you boys

are," she simpered, brandishing three plastic champagne glasses
and a bottle of some Sainsbury's plonk that passed as Vin de
Table. "Swiss, actually," cut no ice, we Swiss having zero identities beyond our borders, certainly not by comparison to our
neighbors and cousins the French (amorous, tetchy, given to aph-
orism), Italians (amorous, petulant, stylish), or Germans (pedantic, toilet-oriented, easily roused, less easily aroused), from whom
we are derived. Even the Dutch have a clearer image abroad
(windmills, gin, rosy cheeks). So: "French, of course, *mais oui.*"
And randy as a pair of Cape baboons. Yet unscrupulous about
sneaking out two nights later without paying in full: a fiver under
an empty glass on the lino'd kitchen table and a note bearing
the scrawled word "Adieu," a quite cinematic and, we'd always
hoped, in Mrs. Wicker's opinion an exquisitely "French" touch.

    Later that night, after Gax had hopped on the No. 3 for his
ride home, after firing off a parting barrage of insults ("dreamer";
"drunkard"; "fasntasist"; "giant wanker"; etc.), and I'd skimmed
off the crest of my drunkenness with a good brisk walk across
Place Neuve and down the Rue de Candolle past the sleeping
university (well, not quite: two lights on in Anthropology) and
so homeward via the Boulevard des Philosophes and puffing
and panting up two flights of stairs (the lift was kaput), I fell
into bed and before diving into sleep I lay there and listened to
my heart stumbling about and thought about Gax's memento
mori: The flesh is weak, and is soon dust. Our memories were
visits to a time and place when the heart was steady, the bowels
regular, the vision crystal-clear, the libido up and running. Now
we were both demi-centenarians, and every day we paid for it.
Of course, I could have taken the American route and joined a
gym, stopped smoking and drinking, and purchased purple or
silver exercise pants; but such buffoonery was not for me. I'd
rather pace myself, take the odd walk, think positive thoughts—
and get married.

    I got around to thinking about Martine again, of course, bed
being an obvious place to do that, but I was reeled in from my
sleepward slide by such impudence on the part of my free-as-
sociating brain: Marriage!? Are you mad? Was there a happier

bachelor in Switzerland?

Perhaps. Solitude had become a carapace; its removal would be painful. But it had become, also, a prison; and its removal would spell freedom.

Then my drowsy thoughts wandered to Stefanie von Rothenberg and her second visitation from down below, and I couldn't help wondering how much of what Martine was passing off as a fictionalized biography was in fact nothing more than a) autobiographical (unlikely, but not impossible) or b) an elaborate tissue of fanciful inventions of her own—the dialogue, of course, had all the flair and fancy of fiction, and she couldn't have possibly known half the things she wrote. I even wondered if Stefanie von Rothenberg had ever existed, or if it had been Martine's little idea of hitting the bestseller lists. If so, she'd failed spectacularly. Yet who would have the nerve to come up with a fresh Hitler squeeze, a new angle on the Führer? And who among us who has lived even a little dares find reality too hard to believe? The mere reality of Hitler himself, engineer of the twelve-year Master Race of sadists, boors, halfwits, and bullies, all men of assistant manager stamp promoted beyond their abilities? Adolf was a marginal, a social castaway, a man marked from birth for failure as absolute as the success a perverse destiny initially awarded him. A man who, I had always believed—and Martine's little book supported this belief, so far—was nothing more, really, than an Austrian petit-bourgeois of inferior intellect thrust into the midst of extraordinary events and times that he had the native instincts to exploit for his own purposes. The combed and pomaded hair, the stiff mannerisms, the fussy little tash, the fulsome and tacky ceremonialism, the idiotic racial and dietary theories taken from half-digested books by crackpots, the long afternoon teas and their lavish helpings of *Torte mit Schlag* and other toothsome *bürgerlich* delicacies: all of it pure undiluted *mitteleuropäischer* kitsch. And Herr Hitler is with us still, behind the desk at many a frontier post; at the wheel of many a city bus in Maubeuge, Bologna, and Aachen; in the assistant manager's office in the offset printing plants and auto parts shops of Seville and Rennes and Glasgow; in the gymnasiums and schoolrooms of Yekaterinburg and Lisbon and Oslo; in the dreary cubicles of educational publishers and chambers of commerce in Hamburg and Livorno and Birmingham. And I speak only of Europe. His like are legion, and they are worldwide, and God grant that another such never walks through a gap in space and time and picks up where nasty little Adi left off.

(But one will.)

I slept well, notwithstanding.

Vienna 1912–1914

Stefanie stayed in bed for two days after the portrait-sitting, drifting in and out of sleep and muddy fever dreams. In between naps she leafed through magazines, the *Neue Freie Presse*, Korvath's *Life of Luther*, and the inspirational memoirs of John of the Cross and Teresa of Ávila; and, when idle, she gazed through her bedroom window at the Stadtpark, now mist-dripping and bare. Once or twice she fancied she saw someone looking up at her, but it was too dark to say for sure. Was it Adolf? Helmuth? The Archangel Michael? Satan himself? There were moments when she felt almost flippant, defiant, devil-may-care (as it were); at other moments the sheer horror of it burst upon her, the horror primarily of having no further doubt, of knowing the Truth that had eluded so many for so long, that both God and devil are real, immanent, and insatiable. With this realization her world, once infinite, once the glorious atelier of art and science, a School of Athens of the mind, became nothing more than a Grand Guignol puppet-show for the cosmic japes of Good and Evil. At the same time, she perversely exulted in the newness of her discovery, the candor of her soul, all ambiguity gone. She, Stefanie von Rothenberg, was either a lunatic or a mystic! There was no other option, no talk of premenstrual hallucinating, brain fever, juvenile fantasizing.

Well! She knew she wasn't a lunatic; ergo, she was a mystic. She had visions, second sight, and the gift. It was the way it was, and the world would simply have to accommodate itself to this fact. She quoted Luther at Wittenberg:

"Ich kann nicht anders."

Truly, she could do no other. It had been thrust upon her. She, too, of course, would have to learn to take seriously what hitherto had been, to her, the domain of muttering peasant girls, or mad monks, or wild-eyed clairvoyants. She was prepared to accept that she had had a vision, no, two visions, of the devil, both, oddly, in the presence of Adolf (but she could hardly blame him, poor half-touched scarecrow of a man), and with the force of character with which she had resolved, against paternal urging, to become a theology student, she resolved to learn what she could from her visions, and people could say what they liked . . .

She drifted past the ceiling as she dozed and dreamed, and the landscape spread out below her was that of Life, not Austria. Her only destination, her only thought, was God, the luminous numinosity at the end of the sky. Far, far below, in the shadows of a crevice cleaving the patchwork fields, torrents rushed and darkness ruled, and from that dark place there surged the spectral figure of the fiend. Why did she see him? Why did she see only him? What did she possess that others did not? Whatever it might be, it hadn't begun with her; there'd been no saints among the von Rothenbergs, but they were regular churchgoers (except Uncle Anton, who had a mistress in Klagenfurt), and some claimed visions. Stefanie's grandmother Anna Maria had steadfastly maintained that St. David lived at the bottom of her garden in Bad Ischl, behind a linden tree. But *Grossmutti* Anna-Maria's temperament, hardworking and down-to-earth, was the very opposite of a high-strung seer's, and Stefanie flattered herself that she was the same. Granted, she was studying theology, and God and the Devil were perforce much on her mind. But the first time she'd had the vision she was still a student at the Linzer Realschule, and she had thought of herself, when she thought of herself at all objectively, as a Catholic humanist, fearful of God, respectful of the Pope and critical of Man; but being fearful of God would no longer be enough. She'd been shanghaied on board His mighty vessel and sent up to the crow's nest and loudly told, "Sing out if you see Satan!"

Finally, she felt as if her knowledge of the world had deepened immeasurably. She felt older, wiser, and chastened, yet proud. Even her reflection in the mirror, while still proffering the smooth-skinned face of a young beauty, nevertheless dwelled in the shadow of a half shadow. Her eyes were sadder, as befits one who had seen what she had seen. Or so she fancied, romantically.

She knew that she knew more, but she knew not how to learn what she knew.

After five days she arose and rejoined the everyday world. Smoking a cigarette with her uncle in the solarium, she described a wide ellipsis around the nature of her problem, while hinting at a matter of great spiritual and/or psychological concern.

"Perhaps Dr. Freud can help," said the Baron. "I was playing cards with him last week. I'd met him once or twice before, you know. Last time he was talking about the new house he's planning to build in Carinthia. Nice chap, if a bit moody. *Ahüüüm*."

"Oh, him. *Himmeldonnerwetter*. The Rat Man man? No, I don't think he's the one I need, Uncle."

In any case, Dr. Freud was far too eminent, and too busy quarreling with his peers and former disciples, to accept new patients; although he did suggest, on hearing from the Baron at their next card game of Stefanie's case, that she might benefit from a close study of transference, as defined by himself: i.e., Read My Book (On Psychoanalysis), which she did, only to return it to the library after twenty pages. Such fruitless casting about! Such dogged gnawing on the obvious! Such mundanity, such indifference to the Poetic! Most of all, such obsession with sex! Now, sex had a place in Stefanie's life, of course, abstract as yet but neither vilified and suspect, as with churchly folk, nor itself worshipped as a deity, as with Dr. Freud; in truth, although she had never practiced it, she fully intended to, at the right moment, with the right man, but in the meantime she saw no need to give it more than its due. Sexuality might not always be with her, but spirituality would.

*

"Spirituality," she said. "What is it, Helmuth?"
"Isn't that partly why we're studying this rubbish, Steffi?"

said Helmuth Meinl. "To find answers to questions like that?"

"No. That's not why I'm doing it. And it's not all rubbish."

They were sitting on a bench on the Schottenring, awaiting a trolley car. It was noon on the twenty-eighth day of June in the year 1914. The weather was wet and mild, with clammy gusts spitting rain and scooping up detritus from the gutters. Helmuth, now engaged to a *débutante* from the Innere Stadt, had taken on the emotional distance of a cousin or guardian.

"I did it," he said, oblivious to Stefanie's non sequitur, "because my family have been in religion for the past four generations. My father knows I'll never be a rabbi, but he hopes I might become at the very least a scholar, with many published books. Of course, they discourage too much study of the Jewish texts here at the University. There was even some fool hawking copies of *The Protocols of the Elders of Zion* last week, I don't know if you noticed. Ach, Steffi, I don't know. Sometimes it's so boring."

"You see, I don't find it boring," said Stefanie. "But of course we Catholics have a different outlook. That was one reason my father opposed me. Catholics aren't expected to know anything about religion, just practice it. Especially women."

"Ah, I know."

"And I was dragged to church too often not to become a little curious about how all this got started, *ja?*"

She said nothing of mysticism. It was her heart's own secret, like a clandestine love affair. Resolute now, she accepted her gift; still, she quaked in her shoes at times when, peripherally, she contemplated its meaning. There would come a time, perhaps, when she would be able to speak of it; but now it would sound bizarre, even outlandish, to inform anyone of the advent of her, Stefanie's, eye on the beyond . . . oddly, Adolf, were she ever to tell him about it, would listen, for once, with keen interest, she was sure: something alien within him would respond to the mystery in her soul, and this was, in the end (she felt), their only, but unbreakable, bond.

But Adolf was gone. She'd heard nothing from him since the day of the portrait, and a visit to the Heim für Männer with a few kroner in hand and a portrait commission from Aunt Liesl had proved fruitless. Neumann and Cohen, the old Jews at the front desk, told her they had no idea where "dat crazy Hiddler guy" had gone.

"He just walked out. Pouf!" said old Neumann. "Dat crazy guy. *Dummes Kerl.* Ha, Cohen?"

"*Ja.*"

When the trolley car came, Stefanie said goodbye to Helmuth and rode home, not to the Palais Ottoheinz, for she was no longer her relatives' ward; at age twenty-four she was on her own, a woman of the world (and beyond, she might add, whimsically), with her parents' blessing and a like benediction from Aunt Liesl and Uncle Ernst, and the use of certain of the latter's connections to secure a three-room flat on the second floor of a "vor-März"-era building on the Mariahilfer Strasse, a building as comfortable, solid, and enduring as the rule of the Habsburgs.

She had an apartment on the third floor. It was high-ceilinged, with tall windows and a large kitchen and French doors opening into the parlor, in which were heavy armchairs and a vast sofa and dark tapestries on the wall. It was a bit like a museum, but it suited her. There she entertained little, and studied much, and read widely in the world of Man and God. She was ready for life, and Life's signposts were clear: In May she would graduate. By August she would herself be employed; she had been offered a teaching position (German, French, a little Latin, less Greek) in a private girls' school in Auerstadt, in the Vienna Woods. It would be a haven for her, a place to write and reflect. She had begun filling a journal with attempts at the metaphysical self-analysis expected in an intellectual's daybook: observations about Man and Woman and their relationship to God, with verbal dexterity in reserve for the next vision, should it ever come (and she prayed—how she prayed!—that it never would) . . . it was to her journal that she turned her attention on that June afternoon in 1914, copying out Hildegard of Bingen's description of her visions:

"The visions which I saw I beheld neither in sleep, nor in dreams, nor in madness, nor with my carnal eyes, nor with the ears of the flesh, nor in hidden places; but wakeful, alert, and with the eyes of the spirit and the inward ears, I perceive them in open view and according to the will of God."

Thus Hildegard, "feather on the breath of God." Stefanie wrote: "In my case, the eyes of the body saw what the eyes of the spirit saw as well. It was real. It smelled, for goodness' sake." She crossed out this last sentence and substituted, pompously, "Have I not, after all, apprehended it with more than eyes and ears?" Frowning, she scored that out, too, and wrote in "And it stank of putrefaction." This got her to reflecting on the fact that mention of the olfactory sense in any of the usual mystical literature was rare, indeed almost nonexistent, with the exception of Blessed Bernadette's scent of roses and St. Teresa's whiff of attar . . . but these were sweet, and good, and were of the Blessed Mother, not sulphurous and metallic and redolent of Hell.

But visions of the fiend were not all that common, either. Stefanie found herself wishing that, as long as her visions were fated to continue, she might at least see the Holy Mother, or an angel, and thus join the ranks of the traditional, the elect, the old guard, the blessed.

She put down her pen, suddenly aware of distant noise, her attention distracted by a growing commotion outside. The even pitch of traffic sounds had been jarred into dissonance. A concentrated shouting rose from the busy street below, the knotted clamor of an accident or other intrusive event. Stefanie went to the window and looked down on the Mariahilfer Strasse. Traffic was moving, but slowly, and a trolley car sat immobile in the middle of the roadway. Some of its passengers were dismounting gingerly, as if dazed, but not, apparently, injured; there was no blood, at least, and everyone was upright. On the pavement small groups were breaking apart and coming together again like plant cells under a magnifying glass, moving here and there with no apparent purpose until, as Stefanie watched, one tight nucleus of a dozen or so rain-coated men made in a body for the neighboring offices of the *Neue Freie Presse*. Shouts rose, faintly. Stefanie opened a window. She heard yells and cries, but none of the laughter that might be expected from crowds celebrating the traditional Viennese feast day of Peter and Paul. Her neighbor,

Frau Schmidt, an aging ex-actress from the Burgtheater of yore, was leaning out her window next door.

"What is it, Fräulein von Rothenberg?"

"I don't know, Frau Schmidt. Perhaps an eminent personage has died." Had Franz Josef applied once again at death's door and finally been admitted? No; the alarums in the street had all the earmarks of something more violent, unexpected, and crowd-creating. There was continued shouting, but no aggression or arguing, therefore no opinions in opposition as there would be after, say, an election, or a sports event. A few men were leaning against the wall of the building opposite, clearly stunned by some great herd-emotion. A unit of mounted policemen was cantering three abreast down the broad avenue with no other apparent purpose than to convey the reassurance of armed authority.

"Franz Ferdinand!" bawled a youth directly below, seeing the inquisitive faces at the windows. He mimed a gun, held it to his head. "Dead!"

"A suicide? Like Rudolf?" screamed Frau Schmidt, leaning so far out of her window that the strong hands of (presumably) Herr Schmidt intervened from behind to grab her around the midriff. "Oh my God! And the Duchess Sophie? Fräulein von Rothenberg, do you know?"

"No, Frau Schmidt, but I will find out."

Impatient at the distraction, but impatient also to learn the truth, Stefanie ran downstairs and crossed the street to the offices of the *Neue Freie Presse*, a short journey that was nevertheless long enough for her to piece together from overheard scraps of conversation the dreadful news that the Archduke and his duchess were dead—murdered—assassinated—somewhere in the Balkans, either Croatia or Montenegro, or was it Herzegovina . . . ?

"What's the latest?" she inquired of a rough-looking man smoking a cigarette outside the newspaper offices. The man shrugged and took a deep pull on his cigarette.

"FF got shot, didn't he?" he said in a Hungarian accent, and pointed to a freshly posted notice on the newspaper's public bulletin board.

"Although we join the entire nation in deepest mourning, as a result of the fatal attack by Serbian nationalists on Their Imperial Highnesses Franz Ferdinand and Sophie in Sarajevo this office will remain open indefinitely for official dispatches ONLY. All other business is suspended. Accredited representatives please contact Herr Direktor Kommerz-Rath Dr. Heiliger for any further information, Telephone (Schönbrunn Exchange) 122–8."

It was a violent re-awakening of the hard world of human reality to which Stefanie, adrift in mysticism and speculation, had given so little thought for so long.

"Please tell me what it means, Fräulein von Rothenberg," begged Frau Schmidt, when Stefanie had returned with the news.

"It means that Charles will be the next Emperor, Frau Schmidt," said Stefanie. "Or maybe we'll get a republic when the old Emperor dies. I really don't know." And of course she knew not what it meant (indeed, beneath her quite genuine shock she was still, foolishly, irritated at having been torn away from her journal, in which she now wrote, "June 28, The Archduke is dead. Sophie, too."), but it carried away beyond the horizon of the irretrievable past a shimmering glimpse of the Archduke and his lady on a fine summer morning in Linz in 1907; and onto the blank wall of the future it cast the ominous shadow of Momentous Change.

But Hildegard wrote of God and His falling stars.

Munich, Odeonsplatz, 1914

In Munich, amid excited crowds on that first August day in 1914, with the sun's rays slanting across the storefronts and in the air the drunken breath of war, Adolf Hitler found himself thinking about—of all things, on a day like that—*her* again. On his way to a rally in the Marienplatz honoring the advent of the long-awaited conflict (quick and easy, over by Christmas, *Gott strafe Frankreich*) he'd passed a photographer's emporium on a side street and the photograph of a young woman—adjoining a black-shrouded portrait of the late Austrian archduke labeled "Our Cousin"—had caught his eye.

"Gott," he exclaimed. "Steffi," using the fond byname he'd never used to her face. His sweet girl from Linz. *Das süsse Linzer Mädl!* It was a near-perfect likeness, or so he thought at first, revising his opinion somewhat as he leaned closer and squinted at the photograph—of a younger girl than Stefanie, he could see that now, blonde, younger and with altogether less character in the face, a photographer's model, or local débutante; still, the emotions the false likeness aroused were dense and entirely unexpected, because stifled for so long. A furious longing filled his heart, a sensation familiar only as yearning for his dear dead mother, or as ardent early morning fantasies of Germanic nationalism. Was he in love? If so, better at a distance, he decided, perversely.

"*Ja, ja.*"

He looked at the black-bordered picture of the dead archduke, for whom he felt no pity (an increasingly alien emotion)—indeed, the anticipation of what was already rumored (mobilizations, ambassadors recalled, Austrian troops shelling Belgrade) tingled in his veins like champagne—yet, nostalgically, he recalled that day when he and Stefanie and the Archducal couple had, in Linz, come together, under the guidance of Fate.

"*Schweinerei.*"

But Franz Ferdinand had been not only a Habsburg but a rumored pacifist, a liberal, someone with decided parliamentarian leanings, a dreamer of French and British dreams, a lover of constitutions and The Vote. Good riddance, then, doubly so. Good riddance to the whole pox-ridden ignorant lot, if the rumors of war were borne out by events . . . and they had to be, he felt it, it was as plain as the sun in the sky, even that fatuous clown the Kaiser had let slip a comment the other day, something about "inevitable corrections in the balance of power." That was clear enough. And now Austria was invading Serbia.

Hitler went on his way with a backward glance at the nameplate next to the shop door: Hoffmann, Photographer, Sessions By Appointment, and promptly he made mental plans for a self-portfolio of photographs, himself captured on many reels, or plates: exaltation, deep thought, provocation, nobility, inspiration, dynamism. And yet, photography was an inferior art, a pale imitation of what could be done with brush and palette; oh, you could count on achieving an effect, all right, usually instantly, no thought required, much like playacting, or the operetta, or ballet, those Viennese distractions, pastimes for the lower classes, inferior arts, all of them, and not surprisingly the pretty exclusive domain of Jews and Moravians and Slavs and other misbegotten groups (this was Adolf trying out his newly minted contempt for entire races rather than individuals, an experiment that made him feel bold, fresh, and reinvigorated, as if a great broom had made a cleansing swoop through the cobwebby obfuscations and parliamentary rationalizations of the mind) . . . speaking of Jews, one was waiting for him now, that rich Steinberger fellow who'd promised him a commission, the synagogue-creeping, carpet-crawling Yid (but his money was as good as anybody else's, never forget that, said Adolf to himself). The Munich Adolf, like the Vienna one, was a hand-to-mouth freelance artist, a purveyor of kitsch on request, a mad but sober bohemian, a slow-simmering ideologue. In Munich, however, there was no Heim für Männer, no Yiddischer Cerberus at the front door. Young Herr Hitler was lodging with a family, the Schroders, in North Schwabing, good German folk, proud and pure and far blonder than Adolf. Thank God (in Whom Adolf believed only as in a kind of celestial aide-de-camp arranging his, Adolf's, future appointments with Destiny) he'd moved out of Vienna, that Babylon of the races, to Germany, land of his heart, land of his blood, land of Hermann's Teutoburg, altar of his destiny . . .

But the Jew and his shekels would have to wait. There was that rally at three o'clock in the Odeonsplatz. Momentous events were occurring, the fate of nations hung in the balance, the upper air was vibrating like a taut violin string under the bow of Fate, mighty armies were gathering, the world was teetering on the brink, nothing would ever be the same again.

For the first time in his life Adolf Hitler exulted in the simple fact of being alive.

Little Adolf's Big War

And then, of course, twenty million died. Cousin Fritzl lost an arm on the Isonzo River and was invalided home to Munich to preside over the birth of twin sons. Lance Lieutenant Helmuth Meinl served gallantly on the Eastern Front and was wounded in Galicia. Aunt Liesl, bored with Uncle Ernst and home life generally, volunteered as a nurse and cared for the wounded in a Red Cross field hospital near Gorizia. In the West, along the Ypres-Passchendaele line, in the Sixteenth Bavarian Infantry Regiment, Corporal Adolf Hitler, company dispatch runner, found himself honored with the Iron Cross Second Class for bravery, in December 1914. He was indeed brave, and comradely, courteous, and fair, with only occasional outbursts of nastiness, but no more, surely, than any other poor tormented put-upon frontline piece of cannon fodder; as his mates said, Adolf's a bit bonkers but that's perfectly all right, under the circumstances; it's the ones who never say anything we *really* distrust. Yes, Jews and Gentiles alike praised Corporal Hitler's soldierly skills and temperance, and they enjoyed his charming watercolor landscapes of the trenches (with, discreetly, themselves in the background, striking soldierly poses). Adolf accepted their praise but kept to himself. Only once, on a windy, wet March evening in early 1915, did he join his comrades on a manly jaunt, on that occasion (arms linked, even) to a snug and steamy brasserie in the Belgian border town of Vélochoux. After three mugs of *vin chaud* containing far more alcohol than he had been led to believe, Adolf allowed himself to be persuaded into a House of Tolerance on the Meuse Canal.

"You're a cute little corporal," said the Belgian girl, no girl: a war widow of twenty-seven dressed in girlish garb, fetchingly Germanic with blonde curls and a dirndl, soon removed. "Do you always wear your cap to bed?"

"Bed?" said Adolf. "Oh, no, no. At the front we sleep in bunks, or on stretchers, if no one's using them."

"You have beautiful eyes."

"Ach, *schweinerei*."

Only the Teutonic spirit of dominance of lesser peoples, and a certain wry Victorian fancy of round thighs framed in garter belts, impelled him onward, and the result was eminently forgettable; indeed, Lison (the whore) had set about forgetting the cute little corporal by the time he departed, bowing, all Austrian airs and graces.

"Yes, yes, good bye. Please leave the door unlatched. Now I need forty more francs for milk and eggs," she muttered. "Eggs I can get, but where I am going to find milk?"

Apart from that incident (unprogenitive, although a near miss in sperm-count terms), and a few political outbursts, Adolf kept to himself for the duration of the war—and how he loved that dear old war! At last, he belonged! How he loved the feeling of being a foot soldier in one of clean, heroic Hermann the Giant German's apocalyptic struggles with Pantagruel the unshaven wine-bibbing Frenchie lout who was congenitally incapable of appreciating true Germanic genius. And Adolf emerged from the carnage that killed, appalled, or maddened so many with a second, finer decoration: the Iron Cross, First Class. (That this entailed no elevation in rank reflected reluctance on his superiors' part attributable to their Austrian corporal's indefinable, sometimes almost spectral, weirdness.) Yes, Adolf Hitler was happy. Surrounded by death, he had truly found a higher calling that sustained him on his daily run from command HQ to the front lines through enemy artillery fire and a parade of horrors that would give nightmares to a lesser man. These horrors would invariably include, amid whiffs of putrescence and sulphur, lice swarming like small knotted torrents over mattresses and shoes alike; the sagging, rat-chewed flesh of corpses; spilled intestines (a hazard to slip on, especially for a dispatch runner like Adolf); shin-deep, piss-scented bilge, freezing cold up to knee-level; friable cairns and knolls of shit eroding seamlessly into mud; the occasional dead outstretched hand signaling nothing, protruding from the mud walls of a trench; the wide-open killing zones through which he had to run, message pinned to his breast, ducking and weaving and zigzagging through the hot breath and zip-zip of bullets and clump-clump of shells landing in the mud and the heavy burp-burp of the lethal French 75s; on spring days a mild sun beaming indifferently through the drifting miasmas and gun smoke; the muddy mess of sloughed-off uniforms, infantry belts, love letters, prophylactics, and other forgotten details of obliterated lives . . . yet to Adolf all this horror was poetry, of a kind. It struck a chord in the dense harmony of his soul; it was the poetry of manhood, of proud Siegfried, of Germany triumphant.

Gustave
Five

"SHE, TOO, OF *course, would have to learn to take seriously what hitherto had been, to her, the domain of muttering peasant girls, or mad monks, or wild-eyed clairvoyants . . .* " Well, maybe she did, that fine Fräulein von Rothenberg, but I couldn't. To me, the most reluctant of mystics—if that was indeed what I was— mysticism still was the domain of muttering peasant girls, and I cursed the luck that had dragged me into its orbit. And, worse: *. . . the sheer horror of it burst upon her, the horror primarily of having no further doubt, of knowing the Truth that had eluded so many for so long, that both God and devil are real, immanent, and insatiable.* Horror? But I thought the girl was a believer. Wasn't it good news, then? Or was it the horror of any certainty displacing life's pleasantly fuzzy doubt? And on the other hand . . . *List, list, oh list!* Papa Hamlet's ghost, roaring on the battlements. Hamlet *fils* and his *There are more things in heaven and on earth, Horatio . . .* that we would really rather not think about, thank you very much. The older I got, the less I wanted to contemplate the possibility that the grinning devils with pitchforks were real, let alone that the moment of their prodding was nearer by the hour. This primordial nonsense, straight out of Calvin's ramblings, flouted Vico: Age of gods, Age of heroes, Age of men? No: Age of ninnies! It appalled my Enlightenment mind. I recalled David Hume's lofty dismissal of visions: "no human testimony can have such force as to prove a miracle, and make it a just foundation for any system of religion," and Diderot's withering putdown of same: "utter rubbish; and please let the cat out when you go." But not even the sages of Edinburgh and Paris could deny that there was a kind of horrid logic in that hint of eternal farce in old-world Christian demonology that would be such a perfect extension of the farce of life . . . yes, an optimist might say it was all of a piece with Leibnizian theodicy, and he and/or she might find hope in the mere fact of God's probable existence. But to me, M. de Voltaire erased that fantasy with a single word: *Pangloss*. And Ockham's razor shaved too close for comfort: If you have to choose from competing theories, he said, choose the simplest because it's most likely to be true. Well, the simplest theory was that I was cuckoo. True? The next simplest, or Theory B, was that I was having hallucinations because of . . . booze? Stress? Sexual deprivation? (I'd see to that one, at least, with Giulia.) Then, of course, there was the less simple, dreaded Theory C: I had actually seen the Archangel. Amusing, no?

(Yes! What terrifies me is God's sense of humor.)

Too, I was getting jumpy, scrutinizing strangers in the street for signs of halos, or wings, and to ascertain that they were firmly rooted, ground-wise. This was taken for ogling, or aggression. I had more than one outraged matron on the street to placate ("but your shoes, *madame*, your shoes, so very elegant, I must purchase a pair for my wife . . . "). And last Monday at the College I was hurrying down the hallway toward Lecture Theater 3 when a cracked voice cried, "On your knees! It's the Archangel Gustave!" I turned and saw the retreating, mirth-shaken backs of two of the younger lecturers, who turned in turn and, giggling like infants, turned away when I turned again. I dismissed them with a rude gesture, but next day (Tuesdays are always dodgy), I was at my desk laboring through a turgid essay on Alpine Poetry of the Proto-Romantic Period when Mme. Brunel, secretary to Dr. Petitpoix, our Director, rang and summoned me to his office. I was loath to be disturbed, but Petitpoix was not to be ignored, so I went, guts roiling. His office was on the top floor, with a view over the St. Gervais church and the Old Town to the Jet d'Eau in the lake shimmying like a swan's wing in the blue beyond, all of which was much more beautiful on that still autumn day than Petitpoix himself. He was in his middle fifties, tall, a meter eighty or more in his knobby stocking feet, white-haired with, like Wagner, sideburns that almost joined under his chin. He was an ardent cross-country skier and cyclist. A Swiss patriot, he had once thrown the *Unspunnenstein* at the ludicrous *völkisch* stone-throwing festival in some Swiss-Primitive forest canton, an event at which grown men turn out in lederhosen and flowery braces and link arms to sing martial songs of an idealized Switzerland that isn't mine. Pictures of the event and of various bicycle races—the Tour de Romandie, the Tour de France—decorated the walls of his office.

He was leaning sideways in his chair, gazing at the ceiling, when the bovine Mme. Brunel showed me in.

"We need to get this place cleaned up, Termi," he said. "I'm certain that's a cobweb up there. What do you think?" He pointed, squinting. I was unconcerned with cobs or webs separately or together.

"What do you want, Petitpoix? I'm busy."

"Well." He looked at me with the expression of an archvillain from twenties films—Svengali, say, heavy on the staring and "faint smile playing over his lips" kind of thing. So I came directly to the point.

"You'll have to drag me up before the Senate if you want to sack me, and I've been here longer than you have."

"Why, I *will* take you to the Senate, Termi," he said, reduced (I was pleased to note) to petulance, "if I get one more report about your public misbehavior. Drunkenness, I suppose—again."

I sat down and demanded an explanation. He gave me a few seconds' worth of the Svengali treatment, then heaved a long, deep sigh, like a man relieved of a heavy burden.

"I'm referring, of course, to the article in *Le Procope Helvète*, which describes a . . . well, I'm sure you've seen it."

"I have not." *Le Procope Helvète* is a gossip rag written by anarcho-Leftists of the permanent-malcontent stripe, the types who wear the same clothes for days on end and drive oxidized 1978 Volkswagen minivans with *Eat the Rich* and *Not in My Name* decals plastered across their cracked windows. "Pure bumwipe, Petitpoix."

"Ha! So you say." He handed the paper to me, tapping the article with a headmasterly index finger. "Read this."

"*Lurid sighting in city centre?*" The article was unsigned, like most articles in that broadsheet of vilification whose existence was a direct result of the Canton's newly lax libel laws, which in turn were a consequence of a slide in values generally . . . The paper had the sneering style typical of book reviewers, hack journalists and undergraduates—and no wonder, as most of it was written by members of one or all of those three groups. I had contributed once or twice (twice) myself, once on Verlaine (pro), another time on *Citizen Kane* (con). This article was probably the incontinent spewing of a discontented ex-student of my own. I read out loud at first, then subsided into silent perusal.

"A fat pompous ugly bellicose toad of a professor and 'man of letters' of fifty-plus is the only one known in Geneva today to claim to be a mystic, to possess that second sight that opens up the heavens for his private delectation. A mystic, truly? A new Thomas of Navarre? Do we in Calvin's city harbor within our borders a future saint of the Roman Catholics? Or a Mahayana Buddhist, floating blissfully above a sacred mandala? Or . . .

"JUST ANOTHER DRUNKARD?" Inserted adjacent to this typographical shout was a photograph of a representative of the grog-blossomed fraternity, a bearded, ragged tramp glaring at the camera, holding high, in the manner of the Statue of Liberty and her torch, a bottle of (I recognized the label) Feldschlösschen beer, while elbow-levering himself up from a recumbent position under a bridge—no doubt the Pont de la Coulouvrenière, traditional kip of the local downs-and-out and, once, the fair-weather home of a young Italian stonemason's apprentice known as "Benny Muscles" to his comrades . . . Reluctantly fascinated, I went on reading. Petitpoix was quietly strumming his fingers on his desk, gazing sky- or cobweb-ward.

"Statistics would argue in favor of the drunkard hypothesis, our city being quite notorious for its many imbibers, less so for its mystics. Certainly our man's love of the bottle is well established: he is a *poivrot*, pure and simple, who sucks on the bottle as an infant sucks on its mother's tit. Or do other drugs cloud his vision? He is, after all, a poet, self-styled, with two banal collections to his credit, or disgrace, confections in a direct and predictable line of descent from Apollinaire's *Alcohols*, yawn yawn, and Baudelaire's *Flowers of Evil*, snore snore. But that he is a poet, and *maudit* for the inferior quality of his verses, there is no doubt. And moreover he is a visionary, for he has seen Michael— and not just Michael Dupont the taxi driver, or Michael Cornet-Rouge the hairdresser on the next corner! No, no, my friends! It is the sacred Archangel of that name whom he claims to have been introduced to, and on the fashionable Corraterie, no less, during rush-hour one banal workday last week!"

This paragraph was separated from its successor by a cartoon depicting a bald, long-fringed and heavily mustached man of bowling-ball roundness clutching a bottle and gazing up at a hovering hippie like figure sporting huge batlike wings. In the background a leering Sino-Japanese tourist was depicted with a camera. I continued, grimly, aloud again:

"Overheard in one of the city's cafés: This well-known man of letters, or just plain *man about town*, or plain old *man*, described in intimate detail within your correspondent's hearing the physiognomy and anatomy of the blond angel who descended in a shimmering cloud of gold dust, like a crowd-pleaser in Zizi Jeanmaire's heyday at the Casino de Paris . . . '"

"Now," said Petitpoix, ignored too long. "What do you have to say, Termi, eh? Angels on the boulevards? It's like one of those Brazilian novels. Of course, we all know here at the college that you've had your problems, and of course we sympathize, but . . . "

I interrupted him. The article wasn't quite over.

"Swiss cinema has fallen on hard times," I read. "Perhaps one of our more enterprising young *cinéastes* should contact the esteemed visionary and propose a docudrama entitled *The Poet and the Angel*. Or maybe they should merely give him the number of Al-Anon, which has several convenient branches around our alcoholic metropolis. The closest to G.T.'s residence is the Rue Haldas branch, telephone number oh two two . . . "

"Ah ho ho," burbled Petitpoix. "Amusing, no?"

"No," said I. It was an outrage. I fumed. The author even

knew where I lived. But it was not a libelous outrage, as my name was never used. Naturally, I wondered about the source. Gax? The treacherous bastard! . . . unless we'd been overheard during dinner. Not impossible; after all, we treated the Lyrique as an extension of our living rooms, and spoke freely there . . . one of the waiters, then? Possibly. I only hoped Martine wouldn't see it, but in her media-saturated milieu reading all the local papers was probably a daily requirement . . .

"Well, Termi?"

"Well, *M. le Directeur*? Under the law, which is all that matters, I wouldn't be able to take action, because it names no one; *par contre*, this also means that you don't have a leg to stand on. Therefore I categorically deny that I am the man described. So put that in your bike clips and pedal it."

I rose and left, my bravado tempered with apprehension. As soon as I arrived home I called Gax. He stammered in a surly and quite unconvincing fashion.

"*Le Proco-cope Helvète*? Why would I have anything to do with that fishwrap?"

"Then somebody eavesdropped on me. It's all in there. Just have a look."

"Calm down, Termi. Don't make more enemies than you can handle."

"Pah."

True, but I wasn't thinking of him; insulting one's boss was a dangerous game, at my age. I wasn't likely to entice further employers, if sacked, and the income from my published writings would barely support a thin titmouse. However, I did have a pension plan and twenty-four years of service, and Calvin College had an age-old system of permanent tenure called "investment," granted to me by Petitpoix's predecessor, that was proof against dismissal in ordinary circumstances. But it could be rescinded in the event of public disgrace, incompetence, incitement to riot, embezzlement, self-exposure, and other malfeasances, and it was my opinion that Petitpoix had been after my hide for a long time anyway, in fact ever since he first set Adidas-shod foot in the place, wearing absurd inner-thigh-revealing blue cycling shorts,

yellow *Equipe Romande* jersey and red bandanna (and I, who
happened to be in the entrance hall, directed him to the service
entrance, taking him for a bicycle messenger) . . . actually, the
precise moment of rupture had been after a public set-to about
some absurd ecological decree he had issued—collect all used
snotrags and deliver en masse to the snotrag bin thrice a week
on pain of death, or something equally ridiculous—and which I
called "shit" several times (yes, it was after a leisurely lunch at the
Lyrique), forever earning his enmity. And I had few allies. There
was Paul Trenet, my *copain* in the Biology department, with
whom I'd gone on a beer-tasting tour of Germany in '94. There
was Mlle. Giroux in Languages, who was one of the few human
beings who'd read, and appreciated, my poetry collections, and
with whom I'd daringly exchanged kisses one midsummer night,
down at the Perle du Lac after a heaping platter of *filets de perche*
and two bottles of Seyssel. But Trenet was nearing retirement, and
had a bad liver, and Mlle. Giroux was rumored to be in Helsinki
marrying a Finn. So if Petitpoix launched an attack, I would be
on my own doughty little Belgium to his mighty Nazi divisions.

As it transpired, I launched the attack on myself, somewhat
like the Arab armies in 1973. It was the Monday after my *contre-
temps* with Petitpoix, when things seemed to have died down; at
least, there had been no more catcalls in the hallways, or obscure
graffiti on the bulletin boards ("Big Angel's Watching You" and
"Fat-arsed Archangel" had been scrubbed off). As usual, my students were sulky, and, good middle-class kids that they were, all
dressed like the impoverished children of cherry-picking illegal immigrants; but there were no overt gestures of derision or
rebellion. I was actually feeling in fine fettle (as one so often
is just before a disaster), having gone for a ten-kilometer walk
the day before across the barren crest of the French Jura range
from the Crêt de la Neige to the Colomby de Gex, just to prove
I could do it: windy and chill under a cirrus-streaked sky of
pale blue with a view across the Genevois basin of the long
finger of Leman tickling Geneva's twat and the sky-high Savoy
and Valais Alps and some of the Bernese Oberland, too, with a
coy peek at Italy from the other side of Mont Blanc's crumpled

bedclothes. I had known this panorama all my life but it never failed to inspire and humble in equal measure. It was here in the eighteenth century that men first looked up at the mountains and said, "How magnificent!" instead of "There dwell demons!" The mountains liberated me from the prison of myself. They took me into the vast anonymity of Nature. They were godly, and I walked with the gods, yet burdened with a mere mortal's knees. It was a splendid jaunt. Oh, my guts cried out from time to time and of course there was the occasional blaring fart and groan and heart-hiccup, but all in all my performance wasn't bad for a man my age and shape. I drove down to Gex afterward, as Mont Blanc started her pink-glowing descent into night, and I followed my foot-feat with a dish of dried beef and fondue at the Bobinette and washed it all down with a crisp Pouilly-Fuissé. During dinner I refused to be drawn out of the pleasant fuzz of my thoughts, despite the intrusive booming of the television, immersing myself instead in the comforting minutiae of school openings, jazz concerts, flooded barnyards, and cars for sale in the Sunday *Dauphiné Libéré*. The drive back, through the darkling plain of the Pays de Gex, amid the twinkling lights of the random farms and thickening suburbs, had been a slow and stately affair, with me paying the utmost attention to the safety of the Citroën and its occupant and the Citroën responding as a well-behaved car should. Bed then at ten, a sober rising, and few smokes and little coffee; so, as I mounted the podium the next day to deliver a lecture on the life and inspired works of Pierre-Alain Deutweiler, Archpoet of Saas-Fee and author of *Paracelsus, a Bombastic Farce*, I was quite alert and relaxed . . . although, by the way, Martine Jeanrenaud had not been answering the phone for some days, which behavior of course I now attributed to the article in *Le Procope Helvète*.

But no other cloud floated in the sky of my life at that moment. Then came the next moment, and enter stage left: Cloud, in the shape of . . . HIM. Yes, the mighty boy-archangel, Michael of the Tanning Salons, scourge of the devil, favorite of bearded Russian anchorites, spitting image of the American actor Jed Ranger. (I hadn't noticed this before, but in the interim had watched a movie starring Ranger (*Pomegranate Juice*, 1999); "hm," I'd self-mused, "he looks like the Archangel Michael. Hic.") This time his lighting was soft and diffuse; yet it seemed to fill the room, like the luminous wash of a lighthouse at night or the aliens' arrival in a sci-fi movie. Slowly, the trembling will-o'-the-wisp fashioned itself into a broad nimbus, rippling like a jellyfish, and drifted across the lecture hall above the oblivious heads of the students. I gaped. This time, I must confess, there was at first a touch of exultation. I recalled the drunken delight on the saint's face in Bellini's *St. Francis in Ecstasy*. I realized, this time round, that it was *unbelievable*, yet I believed it willingly, for there it was. I damned near heard a celestial chorus. I was, fleetingly, one of the elect. I may even have flung my head back and sunk to my knees: St. Gustave the Mystical Tango Dancer! Then doubt—sanity—set in. I heard a distant titter from the human audience, but on the angel's face was the blandly pleasant and quite unmoved expression of a newsreader, or tour guide. In his right hand he displayed his sword, as if offering it for sale; then slowly and soundlessly he sheathed it, smiling all the while. He then calmly folded his wings, exactly as he had done the first time. I was struck by the programmed quality of these gestures. They seemed automatic, as if I were watching a computer-generated image created by someone—or some*thing*—else.

God?

The angelic apparition floated past the back row and paused directly above Kia Dos Santos, bisexual Brazilian anti-nuclear, anti-banking demonstrator and World Music tambourine player and daughter of the Brazilian Ambassador to the UN. Perhaps the faint haze of marijuana smoke around her meticulously tousled head concealed the apparition from her. Or maybe she had a hangover from all that thrumming and drumming the night before. Either way, all she saw was me staring in her direction, misinterpreted this as an invasion of her hard-won private space, and got to her feet ready to do battle with any oppressive representative of white-male sex hierarchy.

"*Tiens*," she shouted, navel exposed, both thumbs hooked into the belt loops of her jeans. "Oy, you, prof! Wotcha lookin' at?"

"Him," I shouted back, pointing. "Don't you see?"

I couldn't believe she didn't. He was looking down at me, with fine Correggian perspective from the feet up; he was higher this time but there was no change in the *posture* of the image relative to the first time I saw it. I was reminded of the *Son et lumière* show at Versailles, where a huge image of Louis XVI floats across the side of the Trianon.

"Man who is born and lives but a day, you are full of doubt and anger," he said in the accent-free Linguaphone voice I remembered.

I found this banal, like a sermon, or a horoscope in the paper.

"You're right, Michael," I said, "Doubt and anger it is. Tell me something, won't you? Just one thing, all right?"

Whether he heard or not I never knew, but the entire class certainly had. I was aware of coarse laughter and a crash, but dimly, as if there were a soundproofed barrier between me and the real, or other, world of the students beyond. What a sight I must have been, to be sure, standing there on the podium, chin thrust forward, waving my hands and bawling into the (to them) empty air . . . !

"The flowery language of men bears foul blooms," said my visitor. "Only remember this: He of whom I warned you walks the earth still. And you and I will meet again upon the brow of the hill that leads to the higher place."

"Oh very well. But that's not what I wanted to ask you. What I want to know is this—where are you going? Wait," for like the Cheshire Cat's his smile faded last, as the noontime sun outside the windows turned to dusk, then back to noon again, and I came to slumped forward, clutching the sides of the podium and feeling as if I'd just emerged from underwater. A semicircle of students was standing around me. Kia Dos Santos approached warily, as to a strange, possibly mad, dog. This possibility instilled in her a strange new respect.

"Excuse me Professor Termi, but are you all right?"

Well, it was hard to say. Not really. Class was dismissed, of course, and I went home, pleading stress—exhaustion—over-work—the usual litany.

Back in my apartment I settled myself in my armchair facing the Salève and watched as the old loaf-mountain turned a mottled violet in the foggy sunset. After a quick Pernod I reached for the phone to call Martine, but, not wanting the renewed disappointment of getting no answer, went to her book instead. Another installment of Stefanie and Adolf would be a welcome distraction from the mad maze of my life, which, until recently, had been as placid and well ordered as my dear country of Switzerland, and was now turning into a bit of a little Lebanon.

Auerstadt 1915

Stefanie's turmoils came from within. She had arrived at woman's estate only half fulfilled. Yes, in some ways she coped admirably with the demands of her burgeoning life. She had graduated near the top of her class, a *Magisterin der Naturwissenschaften* in Theological Studies, and a doctorate had briefly beckoned; but the inverted self-worship of the University, and the incessant incomprehension of men, along with the pressing demands of Life, had decided her against pursuing her studies. Instead, she accepted the teaching position she had been offered at the Girls' Academy in Auerstadt am Wienerwald, a sleepy woodsman's village about twenty kilometers from Vienna. The school was a clean, quiet place with gleaming floor tiles and lace curtains and striped shutters and a flagpole on the roof fluttering the double-headed eagle. It was run by Frau Himmelbeer, a convent-educated spinster of progressive thought. Stefanie had thirteen pupils in her form, a baker's dozen composed of three girls of some promise amidst ten dullards who would never amount to more than mating machines. She coaxed the dullards and tried to fan the bright sparks into flame, with mixed success. Her years of theological studies seemed to have had little value, in the end, except as a sop to her own curiosity, for here she was, teaching languages and savoir-faire to proper young ladies of the middle class. Her life alternated between boredom and worry (like life in general, away from the battlefield); she wondered at times if she belonged in teaching at all, or in Austria, or in this world.

On many evenings, after a meal of war-rationed simplicity, she sat by the lace-curtained parlor window of the small gatehouse she was renting from one of Uncle Ernst's former business associates—another victim-in-the-making, somewhere in Italy—and let her attention drift away from the book on her lap (usually a river-novel of the High Nineteenth or a theological work of an abstruseness that was beginning to seem absurd) and, through the gloaming of the night and the looming shadows of the forest and the unribboning smoke of her cigarette, she felt the oldest yearning in the world, that for a mate, for a nameless shape to define itself from the shadows and emerge as a man suited to her needs, tender, strong, loving . . . in 1915, after all, she was, at the age of twenty-five, nearing, as they would say in some circles, the backdoor of marriageability. She had long since matured into a full-breasted woman of ethereal pallor and dignified bearing. Her eyes, darkened by her visions (or so she fancied), were so deeply bluish-gray as to appear almost black. Her hair fell in long smooth tresses, the way she'd always worn it, braided at the back; in the mornings before school she brushed it vigorously, with the brush held tightly in her long elegant hands ("the hands of a duchess," as one of her elderly admirers back at the University had put it), counting the strokes out loud, one to fifty, with her eyes closed, concentrating. Stefanie was always concentrating, she was driven to distraction by concentration. Yet her pupils reaped the benefits: not a slur, not a yawn, not a mispronounced word escaped Fräulein von Rothenberg's attention. Homework was homework and was handed in on time or else. (Or else the offending girl had to write a punishment line, e.g., "Even if homework is not done perfectly, it must at least BE DONE," one hundred times on the blackboard after class.) The precise elocution of German and French, enemy languages on the front lines, was, in the dozy distance of the Vienna Woods, a crucial alliance, as were poetry recital, and rhetoric, and math, and the catechistic elements of the Catholic religion. Frau Himmelbeer, the school's director, at first distrusted her aristocratic, overeducated but plainspoken Fräulein von Rothenberg, but distrust soon turned to its opposite, and Frau Himmelbeer became for a while (and only for a while) Stefanie's staunchest defender, never more so than when, in the summer of 1915, the gossips of Auerstadt alighted to feast on the lady teacher and her presumed paramour.

Like Adolf, this man was an artist, albeit musical; and, also like Adolf, he had his oddities of mannerism and thought. Even his name was somewhat odd: Arthur. Arthur, whose family name was Lebel, was an orphaned thirty-two-year-old French-descended Jew from Strasbourg in the old French province of Alsace, since 1870 a part of the Prussian Reich. It was as a German citizen and composer, and ward of an Austrian cousin, that he was in Austria, and as an asthmatic that he wasn't at the front lines. He solemnly swore to revive his French citizenship as soon as the war was over, and Paris as a citadel of culture was forever on his lips. As were the names of composers, for he was the Academy's music teacher, and Stefanie happened on him one day, drawn by the sound of a Schubert impromptu played on the faintly out-of-tune piano in the Teachers' Lounge: the music; a dusty sunbeam streaming through the half-shuttered window; Lebel's tousled head, aureoled in sunlight, bent over the keyboard. It was a romantic scene of the previous century, a glimpse of Schubert himself at one of his Schubertiades.

"Herr Schubert?" inquired Stefanie, impelled to a moment's frivolity by this mental association.

"Arthur Lebel," said that worthy, ceasing his performance with a lazy smile. "But yes, thank you. Schubert *à mes heures*." He stood and bowed, with insolence in his posture, uncoiling a taller frame than she had supposed, having only seen him seated, or from a distance. "Fräulein von Rothenberg, I believe?"

He had, of course, noticed the well-fashioned Fräulein von Rothenberg from the first, as she was such a standout in a teaching staff of eight frumps and one artist (himself) in an insignificant Dorf buried in the Vienna Woods, with a flock of uninspiring girls sneezing and napping through Music History, Composition and Art. Arthur Lebel was a man of the world, and as such had little tolerance for provincialism, bigotry, and braying patriots. Fortunately, it seemed that Fräulein von Rothenberg was cursed with none of these flaws; indeed, she combined passion and detachment in an ideal measure. So Arthur and Stefanie became friendly, and more: their interests coincided, their temperaments were superior, and their courses were complimentary, with Arthur's Music of the Revolutions meeting Stefanie's Victor Hugo at the barricades of 1848, and Stefanie's German Romanticism dovetailing neatly with Arthur's Lives of the Great Composers.

"Are you a great composer, too?" asked Stefanie, during one of their morning breaks. (A certain lofty irony was beginning to color their relations.)

"I'd like to be," said Arthur, lighting her cigarette, then his, with a match that then went whizzing into the empty air. "If I were, I'd be Berlioz."

"Not Beethoven?"

"Alas, poor Ludwig. Was there ever an artist so imprisoned by Art? The greatest genius of all, but a martyr from first to last. No, I prefer the hurly-burly of Hector's life, the bold plunge into life's maelstrom. The midnight flights, the mad carriage rides, the love affairs, the lonely dignity of an artist welcoming his muse one starry night, drunk on the terrace of a Montparnasse café."

"My goodness. Well, I admire him, too. Of course, the French are our enemies now, so you have to speak obliquely of their national heroes."

"It is not my style, Fräulein, to speak obliquely of anything," said Arthur, with High Romantic brazenness. "Least of all of my reverence for true art, which is Man's only defense against stupidity and evil—French art especially, let me say, because of its variety and self-confidence. If I speak of Berlioz, it is to laud his name. If I criticize one of your Austrian gods, such as Johann Strauss or Bruckner, or the Habsburg dotard himself, I do so with candor and no thought for the consequences." He completed this verbal flourish with a physical one, flicking his cigarette into the flowerbeds that bordered the school courtyard. He then turned and asked, "Would you like to come on a nature walk with me?"

"*On* a walk as opposed to *for* a walk," mused Stefanie. "You are sounding very Germanic, Herr Lebel. Do you mean a proper nature walk, a ramble through the forest, with the two of us quoting Heine and Schiller like a pair of *wandervögel?*"

"Actually," and here Arthur Lebel looked sheepish, "I'm taking my second form on a field trip to Baden, ostensibly for its Mozart connections."

"Which I thought resided mostly in Constanze's bad behavior."

"Ah, but Constanze has been maligned. The unfaithful wife, the calculating hussy. People are so quick to accept the cliché. In fact, if we know the name Wolfgang Amadeus Mozart today, it is in large measure thanks to his widow's efforts."

"Yes," said Stefanie, "but perhaps she preferred being his widow to being his wife."

"Touché," said Arthur. "You may well be right. Although he is not to be faulted for having had the mind and soul of an artist, infused with greatness and impatience with everyday trivia."

"And with marital fidelity."

"Well, there you venture into a realm I would rather avoid. You, as a student of religion, are no doubt something of a moralist. I prefer to leave moralizing to the theologians, and for the most part ignore their conclusions."

By the time they resumed their classes, they had agreed on the excursion to Baden. In war-deprived Austria, such an excursion, even just down the road to well-known, well-worn Baden bei Wien, was an exciting prospect. For days the girls spoke of little else. Arthur took pleasure in tailoring his classes to the occasion, explaining the intimate connections between the spa town of Baden and not only Mozart but also Schubert, Beethoven, and Johann Strauss, Jr., as well as sundry Habsburg royals, Dr. Freud, and a writer or two (Schnitzler, Zweig); and he never failed to toss in a dollop of scandal for the older girls, usually a reference to Schnitzler's *Reigen,* or the amours of Joseph I, or a reminder why the ladies of Vienna were so attentive to Baden when the Hussars were drilling there. Storms of giggles erupted, eliciting from Arthur a world-weary eyebrow. Why this world-weariness, wondered Stefanie. Was it a pose, as it was with so many of the young Viennese men (many of whom were now posed face down on the battlelines) she had known, the would-be *poètes maudits* and celestial guttersnipes à la Verlaine, Wilde, Baudelaire? Undoubtedly, with an invigorating dash of Verdi. And of course he was an orphan, his parents having died in a brief but comprehensive typhus epidemic. This might account for some of the melancholy and brooding, and the evident indifference to others. And when Arthur played, which he did whenever she asked him to, there was a frown of concentration on his bony face that betokened deeper streams within him than the poseur's trickle, and a genuine anguish lit up his eyes. Asthma could explain only part of it. She kept her distance, observing. It slowly dawned on her that his affectations were a form of self-defense and that Arthur Lebel, at bottom, possessed compassion; and that slow dawning also revealed to her to what degree Adolf had lacked same, and, consequently, why (with the exception of his portrait of her) Adolf's art, and his opinions, missed the point entirely.

She thought of him, now, with bemused contempt that was a vestige of the emotion she had once felt, and in her heart was sorrow for the misguided past, regret for what might have been, and a faint hope for the future.

A Puch motorbus was chartered for the excursion, through the good offices of Frau Himmelbeer's cousin Emil, master mechanic at the Puch works in Steyr. This worthy volunteered to drive, and on a bright day in May, with much roll-calling, last-minute confusion, and rustling of maps, the Auerstadt Girls' Academy expedition set off. They boarded the bus at 7:30 and Cousin Emil stood up at the front of the bus and gave a short speech in a booming monotone.

"We are greatly privileged to be riding in this magnificent Puch bus, made here in Austria," he bellowed. "Which is needed, as are all motorized vehicles, at the front. Yet I feel strongly that Education is a crucial part of the national war effort. Please remember, therefore, that this is an educational excursion, not a picnic. God save our King-Emperor."

Titters and groans. Emil bowed and took his place behind the massive steering wheel. As the bus made its way slowly through the narrow streets of Auerstadt, the brightness of the day seemed an insolent reproach to the massive national bloodletting that was at that moment going on across the dying Austro-Hungarian Empire, from the Dolomites to the marches of Moldavia, but neither Stefanie nor Arthur felt inclined to extend the war's lease by dampening the high spirits of their charges. Music was the tonic of the day. All eighteen girls in the two top forms, many of them amateur players of this or that instrument, had, as Austrians, grown up with the national legacy of great music, and the names Mozart, Beethoven, and Schubert were as familiar to them as the price of radishes to a grocer. Not for them the sordid propinquity of art and vaudeville, the leveling of standards, the false equalization of incompatibles. For those young ladies a waltz was Saturday night entertainment, an operetta a farce, a newspaper a bulletin sheet. (Few of them were at an age to entertain themselves on Saturday night anyway except, surreptitiously, with a Schnitzler story, or a glimpse of fashion in prewar issues of the *Neuer Wiener Illustrierte*.) Great art was supplanting God, thought Stefanie. Or was it complementing Him?

She put the question to Arthur. He was watching the sunlight in the branches of the pines. They were nearing Baden when he replied.

"Great art is God."

Ah, yes, another hat for Him to wear, thought Stefanie, picturing to herself a great Godhead crowned with all the caps and top hats of the world.

*

Baden, shuttered and half deserted as it was, with so many of its agile young porters and messengers and cab drivers serving their King-Emperor on faraway battlefields, nevertheless displayed its attractions—the Kursaal, the Franz-Joseph Park, the Hauptstrasse—like a demure demimondaine . . . like, for instance, Frau Schratt, Franz-Joseph's mistress, whom, incredibly, they glimpsed almost as soon as they tumbled out of the bus. The Empire's most notorious courtesan was taking a stroll in the Englischer Garten, accompanied by a drab companion of the professional companion species. Frau Schratt was carrying a blue parasol and wearing a flowered dress better suited to one half her age. Her nose was held high, her cheeks were rouged, and she carried with her faint airs of an age long gone by. The girls erupted into gales of whispers.

"Actually," said Arthur to Stefanie, sotto voce, "I understand the old monkey hasn't laid hands on her, or on any other woman, in twenty years."

"Old monkey?" Stefanie was, once again, reminded of Adolf. "I take it you are referring to His Imperial Majesty?"

"Ach, don't try my patience with those dusty old titles, Fräulein von Rothenberg." Arthur, flushed, grew quite emotional. "The whole lot are doomed, and you know it, and if nothing else comes of this disgusting war there will be a couple of boons to mankind as a result, and that will be one of them."

"How do you know, Herr Lebel?"

They paused in their discourse to round up errant charges. An ice-cream stand was located, the girls plied with creamy vanilla. A nearby fountain soared and dipped in the breeze, chuckling to itself in its stone bowl. The sun shone unimpeded by even a wisp of cloud. Stefanie, too, shared the ice cream, with a voraciousness that amused Lebel, smoking.

"Such appetites you have," he said.

"So how do you know that whatever replaces our royal house of Habsburg is going to be any better?" reiterated Stefanie, ignoring his implicit psychoanalytical joining of the appetites. "Revolutionaries? Communists or Communards? What, exactly?"

"I don't know," he said. "But there comes a time when any change is better than the status quo. I think that was the real reason for this war, you know. There was never any question of Russia's or France's borders begin threatened by Serbia or Austria's by Serbia or Italy, for God's sake. Our leaders were just bored with peace. Too much peace leads to stagnation. Anyway, apart from the overthrow of the old order, we, that is, France, might get Alsace and Lorraine back. That would be the other benefit of the war."

"Why did you come here, if your loyalty is to the enemy?" inquired Stefanie waspishly. They moved off, shooing the girls away from the ice-cream stand, heading onto the broad, tree-lined and almost empty Grillparzerstrasse, with its majestic statue of Joseph I and view of the Kurpark.

"I see your desire today is to provoke," said Lebel. "Very well. Am I a spy, you ask? No. Surely you don't think your highly efficient Security Police—and even after the Redl affair, the Austrian intelligence services are widely respected as one of the best—would have let me settle down if I had been at all untrustworthy? No. I have relatives here. My cousin is a banker in Graz. I have no quarrel with Austria, Stefanie." (It was the first time he had addressed her thus; the event was significant, but he made it seem casual, which Stefanie admired.) "My quarrel is with Germany, or more specifically Prussia, as the occupier of my homeland for the past half century. Austria? No, no. As a matter of fact, I adore Austria. How could I, a composer, not be a Viennese at heart? As more or less Catholic capitals of art and culture, Paris and Vienna are natural allies."

For lunch the entire group—all eighteen girls, Stefanie and Arthur, and Emil the loyalist—installed themselves on the terrace of the Grand Hotel des Bains (now, because of hostilities, officially renamed Badner Gasthof, a name no one used) and gazed out over the fountain-tinkling gardens and the softly soughing pines of the Rauheneck hill and, in the golden distance, the first outcroppings of what, out Innsbruck way, became the Tirolean Alps. An elderly gentleman served them lunch, apologizing for the sparse menu.

"The war, you must understand. *Schinkenplatte, schinkenplatte*," he said. "That is all I can offer in quantities sufficient to feed a crowd such as this. *Schinkenplatte und spätzle*. And some *marrons glacés*. With lemonade."

"Beer, Uncle," said Arthur. "Beer for me."

"And me," said Stefanie. Arthur raised an eyebrow. In the air hovered possibilities. He was enjoying himself. Man of the world that he was, veteran of a dozen or more seductions, he understood the meaning of all Stefanie's tics and allusions, although their import might be quite obscure to her, inexperienced as she was. It was true: Sensing herself ineluctably drawn into his orbit, she put up token resistance in the guise of barbed remarks, provocative questions, and small acts of defiance such as ordering beer when a lady was expected to abstain, or sip lemonade; but she, too, was enjoying herself, and of course she was quite aware, underneath, of the reasons for the hot flush that invaded her cheeks, and the lingering gaze when she and Arthur conversed, and her urge to hotly challenge what he said, as if passion were so imminent that it must infuse everything. Still, she was grateful for the presence of the girls, as a palliative to emotion, although she—normally such an observant student of humanity—quite failed to notice the narrow, studious gaze of two or three, those inevitable two or three who, out of no future sexual inclination one way or the other, had developed a crush on her, or on Herr Lebel.

An afternoon ride in a landau along the Kaiser-Franz-Ring, a visit to the house where Constanze Mozart had spent so much non-marital time, a stroll through the Kurpark to admire the statue of Beethoven, and a muddy-tasting cup or two of cura-tive waters, and the day was done. Herr Emil, after another short speech thanking the "Herr und Frau" (Arthur and Stefanie exchanged an ironic glance) and the "most excellent young ladies" (no giggles this time, fatigue made sure of that), fired the bus into vibrating life, God-blessed the King-Emperor again, and they were off. The long spring sunlight slanted across the golden fields, cast-ing shadow-claws that lengthened, darkened, jumped ahead and fell behind, in the glades and along the roadside, as they passed through the southern fringe of the Wienerwald. In Stefanie's heart there was a nourishing fullness that she had never really felt before, but by the time they arrived back in Auerstadt she was in a fever, her hands atremble, deeply desirous of a) a cigarette and b) a kiss from Arthur. When Arthur lit her cigarette (after the girls had gone in to perform their ablutions), she smoked it hurriedly; then, without a word being said, he led her by the hand to the Teachers' Lounge and played Schubert's Impromptu in F. In that music dwell love and melancholy, but Stefanie had no time for melancholy, not then.

When she and Arthur Lebel appeared for dinner they were as brickred as if they'd spent the day on an Alpine peak, toasting in the sun. It was at that moment that the first of the gossips swooped down; then another, and another. The older girls knew what had happened. So did Frau Himmelbeer, and her heart turned over in her chest at the thought of the ramifications, the rumors, the scandal.

"Oh, my dear Fräulein von Rothenberg," she said, hands clasped as in prayer, at their next encounter. "How are you, my dear Fräulein?"

Stefanie immediately grasped the import of Frau Himmelbeer's theatrics.

"Fear not, Frau Himmelbeer," she said, with calming gestures. "My upbringing and my character have both taught me the importance of discretion."

"Yes, but. The townsfolk. The school board. The girls' parents . . . "

"Will never know."

"Ah, my dear Fräulein von Rothenberg."

"My dear Frau Himmelbeer!"

And if the truth was that Frau Himmelbeer was envious not of Stefanie but of Arthur, well, Stefanie knew that, too, and her demeanor, while betraying neither encouragement nor approval, conveyed this knowledge with an ideal combination of pity and aloofness, very like that of a medieval saint, while of course exuding from every pore a newly awakened, unsaintly (if very medieval) sexuality. Every night, in the early days, then once or twice a week, she and Arthur awoke each other to varieties of the physical hitherto undreamed-of in Stefanie's philosophy: rudimentary as this was, it seemed to confer a new dimension of being on Stefanie, and as for Arthur, the young roué found himself quite smitten: smitten by her body; by her tumbling hair, and quizzical cobalt-blue eyes; by her humor, and airs of a countess; but smitten especially by whatever it was that was mysterious and deep in her soul, a great unplumbable spirit within her. At certain moments he caught her staring at him as if he were an object on display in a museum, or through him as if he were a sheet of glass. Sometimes her actions were enigmatic, or simply bizarre. For example, one morning during recess they were strolling (hand-in-hand, as was their wont when no one was around) in the woods behind the school. Alongside the path they came across a fledgling bird that had obviously fallen out of its nest; feebly hopping, trailing its wing behind it: pretty clearly cat bait, Arthur said. Not so, said Stefanie, and with slow, gentle movements she picked up the frightened bird, caressed it, and murmured magical somethings to it, all the while fixing Arthur with her eerie, gray-blue eyes; then, to Arthur's astonishment, she opened her hands and the wounded fledgling fluttered gamely upward and alighted on the very branch from which it had fallen.

"Lucky damn bird," said Arthur.

"Oh no," said Stefanie. "Only blessed."

Well bless me, thought Arthur.

*

Stefanie herself had been surprised by the incident, although she said nothing to Arthur. It was as if another person had invaded her, a person of immense power and compassion. This sensation had been accompanied by a calm confidence that dispelled all quotidian worries and petty concerns. Like the tide, it rose and fell, and left behind traces of its passing. One such trace was the glimmer of a vision, a figure of light hidden in the greater light of the sun—in fact, this was precisely the image that came to her in that same forest clearing one morning, and in the breeze there was more than whispering, there were greetings, and exhortations, and instructions on what Stefanie must do, and secrets behind the greater secrets of the wild. She glimpsed a shape, with arms upheld, against a blaze of light, and a loud humming sounded in her ears.

That day she introduced the second form (Great Themes in Literature), skeptics all, to the mystics of the Middle Ages: Teresa, Hildegard, Thomas Aquinas.

"Were these people normal, Frau von Rothenberg?" inquired young Sessi, thirteen.

"By no means, Sessi. They were very different. Which does not mean that they were insane."

"Oh, but surely, Frau, they were quite mad."

"No, my dear. They merely saw and heard things beyond the experience of most people. They understood things most people can barely grasp."

"But that's what crazy people say, isn't it? That they hear voices?"

"Yes. Some crazy people do hear voices. But some people who aren't crazy at all . . . "

"But how can you tell the difference?" another voice piped up.

"Yes, Frau," said a third. "Like that Erik Estlund last month, the one who said he heard the voice of God from farm animals?"

The case in question had provided Vienna with a few days' diversion in the midst of the war: a farm hand arrested on charges of trespass, caught night after night conversing with cows in a neighbor's field and writing down his interpretation of their comments in a notebook. Their ruminating, he claimed, was more than physical. It echoed the music of the spheres. Cows spoke of a sweet resignation to fate that was the secret of the cosmos. Ach, you're a fool, shouted the procurator. Oh yes, said Estlund. A fool who listens to the voices of God all around him while you, Herr Procurator, are a rational man who hears and knows nothing. How dare you, screamed Herr Procurator. Upshot: six months in prison for Estlund and warmth to the cockles for two million war-weary Viennese hearts.

"It's not quite the same thing," said Stefanie, unsure how. "You can't compare a half-witted farmhand to St. Thomas Aquinas."

"But what about St. Bernadette of Lourdes? She was only a simple peasant," said snooty Fräulein Evangelin von Staempferl, twelve.

"No mere peasant," said Stefanie, "could have such glorious visions of the Holy Mother. Sister Bernadette—she's not a saint yet, my dear—was a rare flower in this patch of weeds we call life. I honor her name."

Beloved Bernadette Soubirous and her vision, not of the Virgin, but of Aquero, the holy child—the Immaculate Conception—was, indeed, one of Stefanie's personal favorites of all the mystics: humble, cheerful, witty, yet suffering the most intense agonies from illness, all the while experiencing some of history's most compelling visions of the Virgin.

Meanwhile she had to tame the second form.

"I will tolerate no cynicism in this class," she declared, firmly. "Such cynicism is unearned at your ages. I will insist on respect for the subjects I teach. I demand it for the great ones of the past whose names you are barely fit to utter."

Her words ensnared their attention and an awkward silence was born. So was gossip, inevitably, and here Stefanie ventured into danger, with enough tongues wagging already about Fräulein von R. and the dashing Herr Lebel. Her nature was spontaneous, and keeping secrets was never her strong suit, unless they were others'; her own, in the fullness of time, the world learned of, and so it must be with her visions and the strange new shadow-Stefanie who filled her soul. Anyway, it was rare for her to lose her temper in class. Her touchiness on the subject of mystics and on the need for young ones to respect the great ones of the past, along with a certain otherworldly reputation that she was beginning to acquire: all this gathered momentum like a coal train rushing downhill.

"Frau von Rothenberg is an ex-nun," boldly asserted Evangeline von Staempferl on the playground.

"No, she's not," bleated sad Christina, who adored her Frau von Rothenberg. "She's too young and beautiful."

"That's why she's an EX-nun, silly. Anyway, she's not so young."

"Not so beautiful, either," hissed a Stefanie-hater, one who'd never made the grade. "And if you want to know what I think."

No one did, which guaranteed that sooner or later everyone would; but the Stefanie-hater knew how to bide her time, as do all villains worth their salt. It wasn't for many months, after the girls had moved up a form, and a couple of seasons had come and gone, and Limanova-Lapanow and Caporetto had been fought and won, and Franz Josef was dead, and Stefanie and Arthur were officially engaged to be married ("But after the war," as Arthur explained to lovelorn Frau Himmelbeer, "in Paris"), and the battle of Verdun was nearing its blood-drunk climax, that one day, in a rapid-fire sequence of events, Stefanie:

    1) saw the Holy Mother in the very glade in which she had seen the light and heard the sounds;

    2) conversed, kneeling, with the blue-tinted, hovering, light-ringed Mary (whose German was Austrian, indeed Salzburg-accented), on the subjects of war and sin and expiation of same;

    3) was accosted in mid-vision by her malevolent little enemy, who'd regularly been following her into the forest;

    4) had to defend herself to Frau Himmelbeer, when the truth finally came out.

"What is this young Renate Engelfels tells me, Stefanie? That you converse with the empty air?"

"The little bitch."

"I beg your pardon!"

"I do not converse with the empty air. I was vouchsafed a vision of the Holy Mother, Mary in heaven, for which, having before this seen only the foul fiend, I thank Her deeply. As for that Engelfels creature, I'm going to start by writing a letter to her parents on how not to raise a spy and a snitch."

"Fräulein von Rothenberg, do I hear you correctly?"

And so it went, with Frau Himmelbeer metaphorically placing a judge's cowl on her head and pronouncing sentence on her once-beloved Fräulein von Rothenberg: that Stefanie was guilty of eccentric behavior unacceptable in a serene and close-knit girls' academy; that her unorthodox behavior had already caused concern and shored up the foundations of intra-school gossip; that she was to go from that place to a place of unemployment . . . in brief, she was fired.

"Thank God, Arthur," Stefanie said to him later. "The atmosphere was stifling, anyway."

"But this is terrible. She has no right. We have recourse, Stefanie. We must fight her decision."

"No, they all think I'm mad now. Now they all know. Now you know, for goodness' sake."

"I've known for a while, my dear girl. Or at least suspected. And this will make a tremendously good opera, by the way! I've even sketched out the first act. "

"So our marriage is off."

"*Au contraire, chérie.*"

"No, Arthur, I'm a mystic, don't you understand. A woman of the spirit."

"And so? Can spirit and flesh not be accommodating?"

"Was St. Teresa married? Or Hildegard von Bingen? Or Sister Bernadette Or St. Catherine Labouré?"

"Now you're getting delusions of grandeur. Admittedly, your phenomena are extraordinary and attest to a deep gift, my dear, a blessing or curse from above, or below; but the Stefanie von Rothenberg I know is also a woman of the real world, a woman of flesh and laughter, and I would be sorry to lose her."

Well, be that as it may, said Stefanie. Marriage would have to wait. Unemployed in the middle of the war, she had to cast about for ideas, for support; back in Vienna, she presented Arthur to Uncle Ernst and Aunt Liesl, with mutual esteem and congratulations echoing wide. Then she canvassed the schools. Not hiring, was the response. Arthur returned to Auerstadt and Stefanie scoured Vienna. It was Christmas 1916, a month after the old Emperor's death, and the gloomiest, most sorrowful Christmas in Vienna since the death of Prince Rudolph, but this time a thousand deaths seemed contained in the single royal one. War wounded filled the streets. Ambulances commandeered the roadways. Troop trucks rattled toward the front, blowing melancholy horns. Military trains shunted and groaned ceaselessly through the railyards of the Westbahnhof and Sudbahnhof. A myriad efforts and infinite planning and meticulous organizational skills were required to organize this war, and by thus coordinating the deaths of a quarter million or more, the dying empire was holding off its own death a while longer. But the end was in the air, and two million Viennese sensed it, and many welcomed it, as one might greet with secret relief the death of a long-ailing relative. The historic change was already apparent in the schools of the capital, where plans were underway to rewrite history from a less imperial perspective. The new emperor, Charles, spoke of autonomy, federation, parliamentary democracy, westernization.

Arthur flatly declared him and the empire he ruled doubly doomed.

"Sarajevo was the kiss of death," he said. "Franz Ferdinand their last real hope. The old emperor's death turned the key in the lock. This boy-king has no future except as an exile."

Stefanie lived for a while at home with her aunt and uncle, her marriage plans in abeyance. For many weeks, she hardly gave those plans, or Arthur, a thought. Day and night (mostly at night), the Holy Mother, or an impression of the Holy Mother—a quiet inner surge, like the first drink of champagne—stayed with her as the only companion she cared to have. Arthur, realizing how tenuous is the hold of an intelligent, spiritual woman on her earthly affections, did not interfere. But he spent many a brooding night staring through cigarette smoke at the dark forest outside and wishing for his beloved Stefanie. Haunted by her and, at one remove, haunted by whatever haunted her, he started work on the opera he had cavalierly mentioned to her, the story of a mystic in eighteenth-century France, (until 1789) land of Reason. Once underway, it took on the trappings of *Manon Lescaut*, with elements of *Joan of Arc*, influenced by (as Arthur put it, airily) "Wagnerian chromaticism via Debussyesque use of strings and percussion." *The Mystic* is what he titled it, but he was obliged by force of circumstance temporarily to shelve it, and certainly say nothing to Frau Himmelbeer, or to his students. He spoke of it to Stefanie once, during a weekend visit to the Palais Ottoheinz, but she refused at first to take it seriously.

"The world we know is falling to pieces around our ears," she said. "It's not the right time for operetta, Arthur."

"It's an opera, not an operetta," said Arthur. "And it's precisely the right time. A time of despair and madness: what better time to bring art into the world?"

He was right. Stefanie was, once again, confusing Art and Faith; but the war and humanity's suffering, and God's tolerance thereof, had her wondering if the Jews hadn't had the right idea all along, in not referring to God by name and not trying to humanize Him. The concept of God was too vast, and any attempt to comprehend it (or It) inevitably reduced It (or it) to human terms, thereby negating Its (or His, or Their) omnipotence . . . what was the point, then, of theology? Of her years of hard labor in the precincts of Jerome and Augustine and Martin Luther? Of her determined scaling of the University's male redoubt? Perhaps, precisely, to lead her to this point as a schooled disbeliever in religion's conventions, a self-anointed visionary, a receptacle for the pure balm of the Holy Mother.

And the other, below, the fiend of hell and the *Monchskeller* in Linz and her relatives' anteroom, in this very house . . . ?

"Ach, Arthur, you're right. It's a perfect time for Art. What else do we have?"

In early 1917 Stefanie went home to Salzburg and found part-time employment as governess to the children of a family friend. She was tempted to raise issues of theology and the human condition, but she forbore. Indeed, for a year or so, back home on the Getreidegasse, with the crisp outline of the Salzkammergut visible through the kitchen window on clear days, she lapsed into the normal state of a young woman of her time, saying nothing, not even to her dear mutti, about the visions, or Adolf, or any of the other transformations of her life, except, in passing, Arthur; and Arthur reinforced his own reputation by visiting frequently and bringing Stefanie updates on Frau Himmelbeer and the opera, and Herr und Frau Doktor von Rothenberg, after the initial shock, quite took to the self-deprecating, opinionated young man, who behaved with respect and vociferously admired old Hermann's prowess on the organ in the Benedectine Abbey church—even modestly playing a tune or two (Fauré, Mozart) on it himself.

"Herr Lebel, it is an honor to meet such a true, talented musician."

"Herr von Rothenberg, I can only say I will endeavor to be worthy of such a compliment."

Flourishes; *apfeltorte*; coffee; a snifter of cognac, its origins explained in painful detail out of respect for the Frenchness of their visitor and prospective son-in-law ("*Lieber Gott!*" "Why, this is excellent news!") . . . in this way, through her parents, Arthur re-asserted his masculine significance to Stefanie's life, and they were officially engaged in November 1917, in the wake of the victory at Caporetto, when for a moment the old empire's death throes were allayed. A year later, the war ended, as did the empire—as did Arthur's employment, for reasons more to do with a letter from the director of the Paris Conservatoire than with his students at Auerstadt, or Frau Himmelbeer, although the latter bore him a bitter grudge, seeing in him all of Man's vicious charms and wiles.

"The war's over. I can go home," said Arthur, referring of course to France.

"Splendid," said old Doktor von Rothenberg. "Now I will have an excuse to visit Paris again."

They made arrangements, and Arthur's Parisian uncle Samuel, a former actor and pastry chef from Strasbourg and newly elected Radical member of the National Assembly, found them decent accommodations on the Rue Soufflot, near the Panthéon. They packed, made farewells, acquired letters of recommendation, train tickets and travel permits. Arthur, in the full flush of his Frenchness, was delighted that it would be his last journey as a citizen of Germany, with the lost provinces of Alsace and Lorraine now back under Marianne's protection.

It was their future's time, for nothing was on their minds except what was to be, and what they could make of themselves in their new life; but on the day before they left Austria, the past whistled through the letterbox. Stefanie received a letter from Adolf Hitler, postmarked Munich, forwarded by her relatives in Vienna.

Dearest and Most Esteemed Fräulein von Rothenberg!

It is, I am sure of it, wrong of me to address you in a letter, but for the past two or three days (three, to be precise) you have been much on my mind. The war is over, as you know. We were betrayed, as perhaps you do not realize!! The November criminals who did this must be brought to account. It is now my job to do just that, as well as sound out such supporters as we have left, in the demobilized regiments of the Rhineland and Bavaria. (I am a German citizen now. In the war I earned an Iron Cross, First Class. Good bye, Habsburgs! Good bye, Habsburgland! Good riddance, if I may say so!) It is an exciting enterprise. I hope I am equal to the challenge. Actually, I have high hopes for the future. The world is not as it was. I still paint and draw, but not to earn my bread. I am an agent of the Army now, but soon I hope to be my own master again.

I write because I thought of you. You are a woman I have always admired, Fräulein Stefanie (if you will permit me!), for your intelligence and your elegance. Should you care to journey to Munich to visit, I would be delighted to show you some of the sights. Believe me, Munich is a beautiful city! In some ways, more so than Vienna! At least there are fewer Jews and gypsies and Ruthenian imports. And you can see the mountains.

You may write to me at Regimental Headquarters, Militär-Postfach 16 in Munich (Bayern).

> *Please believe, honored lady, that I remain your devoted servant,*
>
> *Adolf Hitler.*

"The signature looks like cigarette smoke dispersing in the air." Arthur laughed. "Who is this clown anyway, Steffi? 'At least there are fewer Jews.' Lovely, I must say! An anti-Semite of the old school, obviously. How *echt Deutsch!*"

"He's the artist I've told you about. The one who painted that portrait of me in Aunt Liesl's drawing room. Actually, he is Austrian, from Linz. But look at this! Holder of the Iron Cross First Class, if you please. He is no clown, Arthur. I never took his political ideas seriously, but he is a clever man, if a little selfish, like so many artists, eh?"

"Undoubtedly, my dear. You knew him in Linz, of course?"

Purely by happenstance—as a result of insufficient time spent together to explain, to reminisce, to become acquainted—Stefanie's Linz years were a closed book to Arthur, who had, consequently, attributed to them all imaginable qualities of great mystery and romance, although (as Stefanie hastened to point out) she had been a mere girl at the time and had gone home to Salzburg at every possible opportunity.

"So that was where you knew this fellow, eh. Your boyfriend, then?"

Thus forced to define her relationship with Adolf, she found an unexpected word.

"Suitor. Not lover or paramour, no, he was my suitor, if you like, in a very old-fashioned, awkward kind of way. As in, say, a novel by Fontane. But I don't think he's fit for marriage, unless to an entirely meek and submissive kind of girl. As I said, he is self-absorbed, really to a remarkable extent; as Dr. Freud would say, his ego dominates completely. His mother spoiled him, you know."

"Did she now. Listen, perhaps you should drop him a line, hinting that the courtship is over?"

A week later, Stefanie did send Adolf a postcard. On one side was the Eiffel Tower, universal symbol of her new home. *Au verso* she wrote (with the enthusiastic profusion of exclamation marks then common in epistolary German):

Dear Adolf,
Thanks for your letter! I'm glad you're well! I, too, have changed! As you can see, I am living in Paris now. By the way, I'm married! He is a musician, a composer. He loves Wagner, too! His name is Arthur Lebel, so Lebel is my name now, too. You must come to visit us! We live at No. 25 bis, Rue de Soufflot, in the sixth arrondissement. I know you would love Paris.
Affectionately,
Stefanie Lebel, née von Rothenberg.

Paris

From Vienna the Habsburgs had departed like a caravan in the night; henceforth, they would rule only their memories. The ex-Imperial couple, Charles and Zita, were exiles on the Algarve. Stately, stable Vienna, metropolis of ease and affluence and all the world's glitter, majestic capital city girded around by the implicit security of five hundred years of Habsburg history, crossroads of the world and crucible of art and science and *gemütlichkeit*: suddenly, Vienna was nothing. Overnight, with the Emperor's departure, the nation Vienna ruled ceased to be a

sprawling polyglot empire and became a nonentity, an insignificant Alpine republic, a Switzerland with palaces, a domain of
burghers and skiers. Vienna in 1920 was an attic, a repository of
yesteryear's fantasies, from which nine hundred thousand wartime refugees from the former Royal and Imperial hinterland
departed to their new homelands of Czecho-Slovakia, Poland,
and Yugo-Slavia and reduced the city's population by a half million. They thereby freed up living space, most of it substandard;
but the new republican regime was having a painful birth, with
the inflation rate reading like an ailing patient's fever chart and
riots breaking out with boring frequency. A dozen political parties were formed, dissolved, re-formed, banned; then the Social
Democrats took over, and Vienna the Golden became Vienna
the Red, city of welfare committees and workers' communes and
torchlight marches along the Ringstrasse. Bread soared to a hundred thousand new schillings a kilo and the lower-middle-class
dropped "middle" from its name and sank to the lowest of all
classes, the disenfranchised bourgeoisie. Only the *hochbürgerlich*,
and some of the old aristocracy, managed to stay afloat. This
included the Baron and Baroness Ottoheinz, thanks to their
wood pulp holdings and to the continued, indeed, increased,
need of newsprint; the Palais Ottoheinz, however, by joint agreement between the Baron and the new City Council, was now
home to the Municipal Welfare Association for the Indigent and
Dispossessed.

Aunt Liesl wrote to Stefanie in Paris, lamenting the collapse
of everything she revered:

*We are living in a two-bedroom flat on the Praterstrasse, with
most of our belongings still in boxes. Oh, Steffi, I know I shouldn't
say this, but how I miss our old home! How I loved the old Palais!
How I hate what they've done to it! Anarchists and Bolsheviks are
running the city now, or they were this morning. After all, I am
writing this at two o'clock in the afternoon, so perhaps the government has changed hands again! We haven't been well. I have
on-and-off colds, and after the revolution your uncle's sinus problems
grew dramatically worse, proving what I have always maintained,*

that they are psychological symptoms of a deep-rooted pessimism and nervousness in Ernst's character, an inborn Jewishness, if you like. Mind you, there seems little reason to be optimistic these days. Poor Ernst hasn't left his bed in weeks, except at night. Fortunately, we have a fine view of the big wheel and the Prater park for him to look at from his bed. This he does, all the dull day long, until it gets dark, then he puts on his clothes and goes to listen to the music at the Schwarze Katz Keller down the street, hobnobbing with all manner of dispossessed Romanians and Croats and what have you, and he comes home after midnight smelling of cheap cigarettes, perfume and whisky. But enough of him.

As for Fritzl and his family—they have two boys now, did you know? Your second cousins, ja?—they are riding out the upheavals in Munich. Of course, Lotte's family money helps. To tell the truth, I worry that Fritzl may turn into a useless drone. He hasn't held a steady job since the war. Of course, his injury makes it difficult, but I fear he uses it as an excuse all too often. Please check up on them for me, Steffi, if you ever have the opportunity. I know you are very busy in your new life, but it's hard for me to leave your uncle in his present condition—and anyway I haven't been feeling too wunder-schön *myself recently.*

Best regards to your husband.
I kiss you.
Liesl.

Stefanie wept slightly at the thought of dying Austria, her own little ex-empire: poor Vienna, sad Linz, dear Salzburg.

Fortunately, she was in Paris, and Paris was Paris, although even the City of Light, as the capital of the bled-white nation that had given and lost the most during the war, was less than paradise in the immediate postwar years. The city was as stately, bold, begrimed, and audacious as ever, of course, and its skies and gardens were fragrant with the obstinate rebirth of spring, but everywhere also were living reminders of the hell from which humanity had just emerged. The destitute *mutilé de guerre* was a common sight on the métro, in the cafés, on the bridges, accosting passersby with a single accusing eye, or brandishing a rusted stump, or madly reciting the grievances of a ruined life. At the train stations these wretches monopolized the porters' jobs and would spring from nowhere, prosthetics clattering, to open a taxi door, or carry a suitcase. Stefanie regarded them with more horror than compassion, an emotional ratio she tried to reverse, and she reminded herself that other men, the generals and politicians, had been responsible for an entire generation's blight.

"Mother of God help them all," she murmured; and with these words, sacred to her, her mind felt soothed, yet she longed for more, she needed self-abnegation, prayer, penance. Her conscience was her demon, ever spurring her on. For a while she volunteered weekends at a Red Cross soup kitchen in Belleville, a depressed district of northeast Paris composed mostly of African migrants and the indigenous working class, but she felt no deeper compassion stirring at the sight of these human castoffs of great Paris. On the contrary, she, Austrian *grande bourgeoise* that she was, found herself battling revulsion at the sight of human beings with no apparent pride, dignity, or cleanliness, reduced to what amounted to scavenging, and she soon acquired a reputation among the far saintlier women with whom she worked as "The Snotty Boche." Anyway, her command of the French language, good in Vienna, was inadequate here, and her accent lent itself to behind-the-back ridicule. After three months of these weekends, she resigned.

"The quality of my mercy is very strained," she said to Arthur. "I'm just not much good with people, am I?"

"As if that were a crime," replied her husband, his eyes fixed on the short score, on several staves, of *The Mystic*, Act Two.

Food rationing was coming to an end. Certain everyday goods, such as coal and firewood, were still scarce, although following the reconquest of the eastern provinces supplies were slowly becoming available again. In any event, that summer was especially mild and verdant, and in the warm waning evening light Stefanie found a hint of the peace she had always wanted. The Lebel flat was on the top (fourth) floor of a Second Empire building on the east side of the Rue Soufflot, a quiet side street on the Montagne Ste. Geneviève near the Luxembourg

Gardens. Students from the nearby Sorbonne crowded the streets, and from their tiny balcony M. et Mme. Lebel could see the Panthéon to their right; to the left, in the evenings, above the trees of the Luxembourg Gardens, soared the illuminated copper crown of the Eiffel Tower, with— in the mid-1920s, during the tower's unfortunate hiatus as an advertising billboard for Citroën cars—the vertical "CI" of the electric "CITROËN" sign visible, twinkling above the trees. Stefanie gazed at the tower as she took her ease on the little balcony, smoking, drinking coffee, reading, and adding comments, piecemeal, to her journal. Starting in the autumn, she was also correcting the exams and term papers of students at the Académie Werfel, a German cultural institute sponsored by the Universities of Vienna and Munich, "a small enclave of Germanophilia in a wilderness of Boche-haters," averred Arthur, who was a part-time music instructor there. Indeed, the Académie Werfel was a very small enclave, amounting to no more than fifteen in the lower forms and an even dozen in the higher, mostly Alsatians, Swiss, and Catholic Rhinelanders exiled since before the war. Still, the job paid a small stipend, and it filled the dull days, but like most jobs it failed to get the real job done: It gave nothing to the heart and cheated the soul. Stefanie chafed. Others, notably Arthur's uncle Samuel, the ex-actor (whose most memorable role had been the angry chef Joseph in Anouilh's *Les Moustiques*) and member of parliament—and gallant of the old school—had urged her to limit her ambitions to housewifery and dalliance, but that was a notion she instinctively despised, and rejected out of hand with a gesture of contempt.

"Why, then, perhaps Madame Stefanie could join literary discussion groups and get her poems published," said Samuel, cigarette held at arm's length, eyelids drooping in (she thought) infinite condescension.

"Madame Stefanie has no poems," said Stefanie, "and no time for so-called literary discussion groups. I remember such gatherings in Vienna, Monsieur. They consist almost invariably of bookish spinsters with cats, dying for human, preferably male, contact at any cost. I'm not ready for membership in that club yet, thank you very much."

"I should say not," said Uncle Samuel, exploring her with the intrusive eyes of the boulevardier he was.

"Ah yes, *mon oncle*," said Arthur, when Stefanie made a comment. "Well, if you turned the clock back twenty years, half of the middle-class men in Paris would be just like him. He's a living dinosaur of the Belle Époque, Steffi. But he started out as a kosher baker in Strasbourg. Don't take him seriously."

But Uncle Samuel, like Uncle Ernst, turned out to be quite serious in his guise of Jew in masquerade. He confessed (putting on an exaggerated Yiddisher accent) after three digestifs one evening on the balcony that he had been born in Strasbourg as Shmuel Schoen, for which "Samuel Lebel" was a fairly accurate French translation. Yes, he said, before he turned to acting he had been a baker once, as had his father, an immigrant from Poland, before him; indeed he, Samuel, still made the finest *rouleaux d'Alsace* in Paris, when he put his mind to it. His candor made Stefanie think better of him, briefly, but she still distrusted him. She had nothing of the instinctive flirt in her; it was an art she had to learn. In his actor's obtuseness Samuel never noticed. Women were made to respond to him alone. Heavily mustached, tan of visage, and leonine of mane, he avowedly modeled himself on the great Clemenceau. Sometimes, like the Tiger, he spoke with true wit and feeling, but inwardly he saw the world as a charnel house. He treated others with a disdain that at times bordered on cruelty. Once he confessed to Stefanie that, at a dinner party given by the eminent and well-connected Madame Poulenc and attended by Pascal Gide the Royalist agitator, Samuel had slipped a valuable silver spoon into Gide's coat pocket in the vestibule and had then whispered in his hostess's ear, pointing to Gide, "kleptomaniac, I'm afraid."

"How dreadful of you!" said Stefanie when Samuel told her of the incident. "Was he arrested?"

"I neither know nor care. At least he was never seen at Madame Poulenc's salons again."

Yet this lightness and flippancy of manner was his way of warding off despair. Like most men of his generation, and all actors, he flirted as easily as he drew breath, at first putting Stefanie off; but discreet flirtation, she discovered, could be exciting, leading the reluctant traveler to the outskirts of Sex, the forbidden metropolis. Ironically—and, in a way, thanks to Uncle Samuel—Stefanie was becoming more aware, in her early thirties, of the dominion of sex. With Arthur, at first (her first), lovemaking had been unremitting and doubly exciting because of a) love and b) inexperience, spiced up by the paramount need, then, for concealment, but in due course, as happens, the elegiac became routine, the routine found itself taken for granted, and Eros quietly left through the back door. Companionship came to call, then it, too, drifted away: Arthur with his back turned, bent over his opera, uttering monosyllabic replies to the questions she, on the sofa, might ask, with a haunting in her brain . . . not that they couldn't still became flushed and breathless in each other's arms, but they were married, after all, and he was working eight to ten hours a day, and she was caught between the real world and that other world of the Holy Mother and Sister Bernadette, no less real to her but unmentionable to others. Fortunately, as a palliative, there was the great city around her, a living encyclopedia of the human condition, Rabelais and Balzac and Hugo in stone, in which not only sex but avarice and love and gluttony and humor all flourished on a grand scale, as in the world at large; a spectacle to be enjoyed, if one had sufficient entrée to the places where the drama might be observed. Uncle Samuel had such entrée, and he grudgingly shared his contacts with his nephew and niece (mostly the latter); but it was not until a dress rehearsal of *The Mystic* attracted the attention of the exiled Russian pianist and composer Ivan Youzbine that Arthur and Stefanie started moving in more elevated social circles. The great pianist (he had been a student of Rimsky-Korsakov's) wrote a short review of the nascent opera for the emigré newspaper *Novaya Iskra* that was duly translated for *Le Journal de Paris*:

"M. Lebel shows great promise. *The Mystic* develops small motifs, but these are motifs of significance, from which lyrical melody grows, and both motifs and melody conceal subtleties in orchestration and structure and only yield to the greater amplitude of lines and forms. Unfortunately, the story is too silly for words, all about a woman who has visions of the devil and the holy mother and other nonsense, and how she is driven to kill the evil Lord Montacute, who is torturing the local peasants or something or other and how in the end she finds peace by joining an order of nuns and becoming a saint, or some such rubbish. To make matters worse, it takes place in the France of the Enlightenment era, when educated people were sufficiently sensible not, for the most part, to believe in such fantasies. Perhaps M. Lebel needs a new lyricist. Were it not for the music, I would have covered my ears and run screaming out of the concert hall; but the music saved the day."

"Mr. Youzbine's wine soon turns to vinegar," remarked Arthur.

"The man's a maniac," said Stefanie. "Of course, he's Russian."

Although there were undeniably maniacal elements in Youzbine's makeup (but that was all right, because not only was he Russian but he was truly a pianist of Lisztian passion and a composer to rival Rachmaninoff) the acquaintanceship flourished. Youzbine took Arthur under his wing and soon Stefanie saw less of her husband in private than before and far more of his distant profile at high-society functions in vast sitting rooms and chilly salons and Gauloise-redolent nightclubs where Russian exiles and actors and errant artists drank and struck tragicomic poses and pawed one another and her (once exciting Arthur's ire, to the extent of a well-aimed and accurately delivered punch in the nose); it was noisy, raucous, depraved, and exciting, and it demanded immediate concentration, gliding over life's depths, it celebrated only the present, the transient, the moment. Stefanie, erstwhile theology student, found herself surrounded by hedonists, many of them young Americans, mostly actors and writers (genuine or self-styled), exiles in France for the drinking and the high life and the low cost of it all. For them the beautiful Austrian woman with the blonde hair and distant gaze was an oracle, an idol, an exotic, a living souvenir of Mayerling, pure Twentieth-Century Fox.

"Did you ever meet Franz Josef, Madame Lebel?" inquired one night, in his cups, one of the Americans, a handsome

Hollywoodian.

"Once," she said. "On the occasion of my uncle's ennoble-ment. I curtsied higher than he inclined his head, but not by much. Then he got my name wrong."

"Oh, that's quite magical, my dear Madame Lebel," said the young Hollywoodian, marveling in a desultory way at having met a still-young survivor of another, already near-mythical, era. "Do tell me more about decadent old Vienna. The balls. The affairs."

"I went to some balls, of course. The Apprentices', the Butchers'. But I missed the decadence. I was a student. I studied."

"How serious of you. How middle class." The young actor nodded abstractedly, but his gaze welled with interest and con-cern. Stefanie was charmed by his attention and his illustra-tive mannerisms, very much those of an actor, and truth to tell she might have succumbed had she (innocent that she was!) not noticed his glistening gaze settling with greater interest on an adjacent young man of known proclivities. She felt a slight shock, followed by the slow burn of humiliation and the chimes of celestial irony: *Sin, even in thy heart, and see how thou art punished!* Stefanie took her desires home to her marriage bed, to which Arthur, whose name was now a byword in the salons, was more or less a stranger; but during one of his rare overnight visits he and Stefanie embraced as man and wife, and nine months later, in the spring of '23, Ignace (for Arthur's long-dead father, *né* Ignaz) was born, giving greater joy to Stefanie than anything else in her life ever had, with the possible exception of the appa-rition of the Holy Mother, her own mother, and Arthur himself.

Gustave
Six

I WAS LYING on a hospital bed under a spotlight, dressed in a pale green shift open at the back, allowing chill breezes to play over my arse. A doctor and his nurse were concealed behind a screen, like prompters at a play.

"Is there a sensation of a voice?" inquired a voice.

"Yes. Yours."

"Not mine. Like mine?"

"No. A man's."

"Is there a sensation of something seen?"

"Yes; an archangel."

"Pardon. A what?"

"An archangel. You know, an angel of high rank. A field marshal in the army of angels. Or, in Swiss terms, a *colonel de division.*"

Muttering; then the voice coldly resumed its interrogation.

"Is there a sensation of something felt or touched?"

"No."

"How long have hallucinations been present?"

"Hallucinations? You mean visions."

"I mean hallucinations, Mr. Termi. That's why you are here, isn't it?"

"I thought I was here to find out if I'm sick. If I'm not, we might have to conclude that my visions are genuine. And it's *Dr.* Termi, by the way."

More muttering. Then:

"When did these hallucinations or visions first appear, Dr. Termi?"

Aha, I thought. A minor victory.

"Last September 18. And another two days ago."

"Were you falling asleep at the time?"

"No. Very much awake."

"Has there been a recent death or other emotional event?"

"No."

"What medications are being taken?"

"None."

"Is there a sensation of insects crawling upon the skin?"

"Only when they are."

"Is alcohol used regularly?"

"Yes."

"In what quantities?"

"Sufficient."

"Could you be more specific?"

"Approximately a liter of Fendant dry white wine every two days, plus a *cannette* or half liter or so of beer daily, but never before lunch. Whiskey in the evenings before dinner, double, single malt. Red wine on weekends or with strongly seasoned dishes. Occasionally a schnapps or grappa. On feast days a cognac, invariably Napoleon three-star."

Silence, soon broken by more muttering.

"Are illicit or illegal drugs being used?"

"No."

"Are the hallucinations—"

"Or visions," interjected a male voice.

"Or visions . . . related to a traumatic event?"

"My life is stable. I have had no traumas recently."

"Is there agitation?"

"Occasionally."

"Is there confusion?"

"Not often, but sometimes."

"Is there a fever?"

"No."

"Is there a headache?"

"No."

"Is there vomiting or excessive looseness of stool?"

I yawned my way through a loud No. A nurse appeared, severe, sixtyish, holding a clipboard. I sat up. She placed her broad peasant hand on my chest and gently but firmly pushed me down.

"Lie back, please."

I recognized her voice as the interrogator's. Lines of disapproval criss-crossed her brow as she slid me into the gaping maw of the CAT scanner. Inside, lights pulsated, a motor thrummed. I re-emerged, feeling slightly giddy. The nurse took my pulse and blood pressure and after what seemed like a eon or two blood was drawn, urine sampled, eyes probed. Then I was allowed to dress and sit in the waiting room, where well-thumbed copies of *Swiss Highways* and *Helvetic Cyclist* awaited my perusal.

The doctor was a young Indian named Gupta.

"You have a mild case of limited-access porphyria," he said, looking down at his notes through fashonably narrow tinted eyeglasses. "A condition of the blood and urine common to alcoholics."

"Yes, and?"

"And," he spread his hands, "this is causing your, ah, visions."

"But?"

"But nothing. You should stop drinking."

I laughed. He frowned.

"Or at least less whisky."

"And if I do, the visions will go away?"

"Most probably."

"And if I don't?"

"They may continue. Or they may not."

"And the rest of me? Physically?"

"Blood pressure one forty over seventy. Not bad, not too good. Pulse regular. No, otherwise you're all right. I recommend also low-carbohydrate diet. Oh yes, avoid sun exposure. And eat carrots. Like a big bunny, yes? Ha ha ha? And I will write you a prescription for glucose pills you can get filled at the pharmacy downstairs."

A big bunny, indeed. I picked up the pills and went home, where I celebrated with three deciliters of Fendant and a return trip to the cozy yet ghastly world of Stefanie and her Adolf.

Paris to Munich

One day in November 1923 Arthur, holding a well-filleted copy of *Le Gros Parisien*, came onto the balcony, where, in weather that was untypically clement for the time of year, Stefanie was breastfeeding Ignace. She looked up, smiling expectantly, as at an old and cherished but predictable friend.

"Your chum Adolf Hitler," said Arthur. "That's the fellow, isn't it? The one who sent you that puppy dog postcard? Well, he's international news now."

"Oh no." She detached from her breast Ignace, whose face immediately collapsed in on itself, as if inhaled. "Did he assassinate someone?"

"Assassinate? No, no. No one. But I'm not sure it's any better, what he's done. See for yourself."

Ignace emitted three tentative burps, then a full-throated wail.

"All right, I'll read it to you. Silence, you there!" And over the infant's gurgling Arthur read to Stefanie the incomplete first reports ("Melodrama in Munich!") of what history would call the Beer Hall Putsch, starring Stefanie's old comrade and suitor, now, according to the newspaper, a wounded fugitive and a traitor to the German nation.

"There he was, in the center of Munich, marching shoulder to shoulder with General von Ludendorff and a certain Goering, ex-commander of the Richthofen squadron," said Arthur. "After declaring himself the head of the new government and holding three ministers hostage in a beer hall, he took to the streets and caused a riot. Your pal is no longer a nobody, that's clear, but he's pushed his luck a little too far for the Germans, if you ask me. They don't generally go in for this kind of Latin American caper."

"How fortunate he wasn't shot," said Stefanie; but suddenly, as she spoke, the vision-haze passed before her eyes and she saw

Adolf sprawled dead, blue eyes staring blankly in his pale bony face, lank forelock draped across his forehead . . . he was dressed, it seemed, in a gray-and-black uniform, and beyond him was a vast rocky landscape stretching away to the edges of her vision, and the rocks were dappled with blood.

Ignace screamed. Stefanie shook her head clear. Arthur was still reading.

"Shot, you say?"

"Actually, yes. But they don't know where or by whom. He was seen to fall, and when the police started arresting people he was nowhere to be found. 'Police are combing the city,' it says. Sixteen of these so-called National Socialists and three Munich cops dead. My God, Steffi, so your *petit ami* Adolf tried to take over the government of Germany! Give him top grades for effort, eh? But he's had it now, you mark my words."

Arthur went on to read aloud about other world events, notably the opening of King Tutankhamen's tomb and the prophecies that surrounded that event—good material, he said, for an opera; and, having mentioned opera, he fell silent and returned in body and spirit to the nurturing of his own. Stefanie, for her part, saw operatic potential, if only for *opéra bouffe*, in Adolf's escapade, which, she was sure, he had planned as a Wagnerian conquest of the summits. Was he, then, an Alberich or a Wotan? She recalled his last plaintive letter, in which he had sworn to apprehend the "November criminals." She had, of course, heard from her relatives, as well as from her students at the Académie Werfel, about Germany's postwar woes, which were legion. For one thing, the French Army, as if determined to repay the hated Germans by earning the reciprocal hatred of every German, had occupied the Ruhr, and Paris was insisting on the murderous reparations schedule decided at Versailles, a demand that fueled throughout Germany the worst inflation in history and ushered in the brief, horrible era of the four-billion-mark kilo of potatoes and wheelbarrows full of money that wouldn't buy a jam Berliner. Inflation wiped out thousands of families' savings. Even Fritzl, in Munich, with his wife's land holdings in the Allgäu, was hard up, according to a letter Stefanie had received, by coincidence, a couple of days earlier—the first letter, in fact, she had ever received from her indolent cousin, written at Aunt Liesl's urging. She opened it and reread it, skipping over the perfunctory congratulations on the event of Ignace's birth, etc., etc.:

Ja, we're on our uppers, and this damn arm doesn't make things easier, of course, and the twins (Willi and Kurt, you will meet them soon, a real-life Max und Moritz, as Lotte calls them!) are no longer attending Dr. Novotny's School. No, dear cuz, sad to say we are reduced to sending our kids to the Gymnasium, and you can imagine what kind of shape the schools are in these days! Their schedules are, to say the least, irregular. I think the boys went to school yesterday, but that was the first time in about a week, since the last food riots on the Marienplatz at which, by the way, a good friend of ours, Herr Blumberg, was seriously injured and taken to hospital—actually, we're worried, dear Steffi. Thank God Lotte never sold her land in the Allgäu, which she was talking about doing just before the great inflation hit us, if you can believe it! Even so, it seems that everything's falling apart, and nobody knows what's going to happen next, it's crazy and very upsetting for Germans, who love order and peace so much. Everyone's looking for a strong man to take charge and make things better, and there are lots of people who think your friend Hitler is the one, but I'm not so sure, I've heard him speak and there's something unnatural about him, please forgive me for saying so Steffi, I know how close you were to him . . .

Not as close as Fritzl obviously believed, but, she thought, in an odd way (given the little she knew about him, really), as close as anyone had ever managed to get; and yet what was it, really, her relationship with Adolf Hitler? Sexually awakened as she had since become, she recognized it for an unconsummated male-female flirtation on one level, but go any deeper and strange feelings awoke, madness lurked (she remembered the satanic visions, trembling) . . . Driven, then, by a woman's need for correctness and clarity, she accepted Fritzl's invitation to come and stay with him and his family and went, fully intending also to visit Hitler in the fortress to which a court (as she had read in the foreign edition of the *Süddeutscher Zeitung*) had sentenced him to five years' imprisonment.

Accordingly, with little Ignace in tow, in May, 1924, Stefanie went to Munich. Arthur was deeply enmeshed in the final rehearsals of *The Mystic*, with the assistance of the great Youzbine and a handful of budding acolytes, a good number of them female. Uncle Samuel, an ardent motorist, offered to drive Stefanie in a recently purchased Delahaye touring car; but the prospect was too much of an adventure for her.

"I will meet you there, then, dear Stefanie."

"Suit yourself, *mon oncle*."

Stefanie and Ignace took the train from the Gare de l'Est, and as they passed through the ruined heartland of the Great War, she gazed long and hard at the mournful hills of Alsace and Lorraine, source of all the poison of France's wars; and when the train crossed into battered Germany at dusk Heine's sad lines came to mind.

> *Denk ich an Deutschland in der Nacht,*
> *Dann bin ich um den Schlaf gebracht,*
> *Ich kann nicht mehr die Augen schließen,*
> *Und meine heißen Tränen fließen.*

And all through the journey Ignace wailed.

In Munich they stayed with Fritzl, now a heavyset one-armed beer drinker, his placid wife, Lotte, and Willi and Kurt, their two sullen twin boys, in a still-respectable three-room apartment on the Leopoldstrasse. Once Stefanie and Ignace had settled in, she endured many an hour of Germanic griping, not that there wasn't enough to gripe about in Germany in the spring of 1924, except that inflation was slightly better—down to the hundred-thousand level for daily purchases—and Munich's mood was, in consequence, improving, overall; but the griping continued, for there was unease and uncertainty in the air, and stability was a thing of the past. Still, the former Wittelsbach Capital had an immortality all its own, whatever the crisis. The northern face of Stefanie's very own Salzkammergut Alps glistened on the far horizon; the fountains played at Nymphenburg; the birds chirped in the Englischer Garten; trolley cars clanged merrily through the Marienplatz; students roistered in the *Bierstuben* of Schwabing; and the grotesque figures of the Rathaus clock still marked the hour, as they had for centuries, with their jerky clockwork gait. But in conversations at Fritzl's home (and Fritzl himself, beer-flushed, presided over table talk with the bluff dominance of a true German burger) the mood was sour, and dire predictions were made, and the name Hitler came up once or twice, casually, as if in reference to a total stranger, before Fritzl and Lotte remembered, and acknowledged, Stefanie's friendship with the man. This was the first real sign of Adolf's growing fame, and it was somehow even more impressive over Fritzl's dining table than in the newspapers; and when Stefanie thought about it she was still amazed that her dour, melancholy, artist friend from Linz and the Heim fur Männer, with his passionate, semi-articulate and deeply unoriginal view of the world, should have become a household name by instigating a silly political farce in the streets of a foreign city.

"What a crazy life," she thought. Soon after arriving, she had applied to the Interior Ministry for permission to visit Adolf in the fortress-prison of Landsberg am Lech, a small farming town southeast of Munich. After due consultation with the prisoner, who expressed his surprise and consent, the authorities granted permission for a visit ten days from then, provided she came alone and stayed no longer than an hour between the hours of ten a.m. and one p.m.

"This person is a political detainee and as such is forbidden to send or receive missives or messages of any type," cautioned the letter. "Violators will be dealt with in the strongest terms."

"Rubbish," was Fritzl's comment. "Strongest terms my backside. The place is like a holiday resort. There are forty National Socialists staying there, all in near-palatial accommodations, as you'll see."

On the tenth day of her stay Stefanie answered the door to find Uncle Samuel, dressed in a motorist's goggles and overcoat, standing on the step. He gave a sweeping bow.

"Greetings, my dear niece," he said. "I have just arrived from Paris. My car and I are at your disposal."

He was lodging at a Gasthaus nearby, and over the next few days he came to call whenever possible. Fritzl found in him a true arbiter of taste and style, and the two sat for hours in the parlor, discussing motor cars, seaside resorts, cigars, beer, France, Germany—or rather, Samuel lectured and Fritzl listened eagerly, nodding. Entrusting Ignace to Lotte (who, like many mothers of sullen older children, missed the early innocence of baby-care), Stefanie explored the Bavarian Capital, rejoicing in a temporary sense of reprieve from the hauntings of ambition, mysticism, family and politics. She visited the Englischer Garten on the turbulent Isar and admired the quaintly undraped citizens taking the sun. She visited the Pinakothek to see the Dürers: They were spare, haunted, and Teutonic, and they did not disappoint. She stopped in at the Bavarian National Museum, and the Asam Church. It was good to be among German-speakers again. She became aware of a depth of fellow feeling that surprised her; on the other hand, Munich was only one hundred and forty kilometers from Salzburg, and the dialect, the architecture, and the religion were the same, the spirit was Catholic and southern. She felt at home, and more than once, as she strolled hither and yon, she had to shake off the illusion that she was in Salzburg again, that her pappi's house was just at the end of that street, on the corner of that square . . . she also saw the name Hitler, in florid Fraktur script, on posters, in headlines, and most dramatically on a pamphlet thrust into her hands by a hollow-eyed youth on the Odeonsplatz who whispered hoarsely, as she recoiled, "Take it, lady. Germany Jew-free is Germany free!"

On the appointed day, after requesting a ride from Samuel, Stefanie went to visit Adolf in Landsberg Prison.

"Do you want me to give him a message?" she asked Lotte and Fritzl, half jokingly.

"*Ja*. Tell him the anti-Semitism, the antiforeign garbage, the equating of Jews with Bolsheviks," said Fritzl, "it's all stupid nonsense and it won't wash."

"Fritz, you can't be serious," said Lotte. "This is Bavaria. Of course it will wash."

Ignace bawled when his mother left, but was soon placated by helpings of a nut-and-fruit mush prepared from a venerable southern Allgäu recipe.

The Delahaye was oiled and willing, and stood throbbing quietly in the wan autumn sun. Samuel put up the roof and away they went, out the Landsbergerstrasse past the rapid erosion of city into suburbs and suburbs into Bavarian pastureland. The bells in onion-domed churchtowers dinged and cowbells in the fields donged in reply. Horse-drawn carts plodded on their timeless ways. In villages with *fachwerk* farmhouses and cow shit on the roads, small children stood and stared as they passed through. One old man in a coat and tie spat and shook his fist, seeing the French registration.

"*Mon Dieu! Ils nous détestent,*" said Uncle Samuel. "It's a bad situation here, dear Stefanie. And your friend Herr Hitler will undoubtedly have a hand in making it worse."

"Or better."

"No, no. Worse. I've read the man's speeches, my dear. He is of puny intellect and nonexistent morality, being entirely selfish; but he has drive, ambition, and will, and he may yet succeed, although admittedly his present circumstances would seem to argue the contrary."

"Yes, he's in prison for five years. That's long enough for people to forget about him."

"Five years! If he serves more than a year, you can paint me yellow and call me Fu Manchu. Of course, your friend Hitler is merely one among many, and not only on the Right. There are those on the Left who are just as bad, but the Left lacks the crucial ingredient to appeal to a German: nationalism. Oh yes, if you want to appeal to a German, you must do so through his confused sense of inferiority-superiority by telling him how great he is just to be a German. This country is an adolescent among nations, and these days, just like an adolescent, it's sulking after its punishment. Now would be a good time for the rest of us to turn away and leave it alone; but no, on the contrary, we meddle all the more and make matters much, much worse. *Mon Dieu.*"

What is the answer, my dear Stefanie?"

(In the soaring aching sky, above the goiter-shaped church tow-ers, Stefanie glimpsed her answer to everything—or was it merely the question?)

Shortly before ten, the crenellated profile of Landsberg Castle came into view, casting its shadow over the swift-flowing Lech below. The authorities at the Castle were disinclined at first to admit the urbane Frenchman and his coldly poised companion.

"Herr Hitler is at the other end of the prison," said the sal-low *Unteroffizier* at the main gate. "He has very specific visiting hours. He is political, you know."

"We know," said Stefanie. "But we also know that those spe-cific visiting hours are now."

"The gentleman must stay in the guard office. The pass is for the lady only."

"With pleasure," said Uncle Samuel. He whipped a deck of cards out of his coat pocket. "*Spielen sie, Herr Kommandant?*" he inquired. "*Für geld?*" The guard's eyes widened with interest, but he looked nervously around.

"All right, but if someone comes," he said, "I blame you com-pletely, *ja?*"

"A noble impulse," said Samuel. "Truly, we are in Germany now."

Stefanie signed her name and time of arrival in a registry and followed another, lesser guard through a vast echoing domed hall-way encircled with catwalks up an iron staircase to the third floor of the prison. Around a couple of tight bends and a momentary pool of utter darkness was a heavy iron door in front of which a man was waiting, a saturnine individual with a single brow-width eyebrow above feral eyes. He introduced himself, with consummate awkwardness, half bowing and forcing a nervous half smile, as Rudolf Hess, presuming, he rambled on, to have the privilege of addressing Fräulein von Rothenburg . . . ? But hidden ears were listening.

"*Berg*," snapped a familiar, hoarse, querulous voice from inside the chamber. "Rothen*berg*. You may dismiss yourself now, Hess."

And Adolf Hitler appeared, waving a dismissive hand. He inclined his head when he saw Stefanie. Stefanie suppressed a chuckle, for Adolf—heavier than before, and more weathered around the eyes, but instantly recognizable behind his mustache and forelock—sported the clichéd costume of a Bavarian or Tirolean peasant, knee-stockings and lederhosen, with floral patterns on the shoulder straps. She smiled, but he seemed deliberately to be withholding his welcome; instead, he set his jaw firmly and stared into Stefanie's eyes like a policeman seeking to extract a confession.

"Fräulein von Rothenberg," he said, executing a crisp bow. "I am honored. Welcome to Schloss Landsberg."

"Hello, my dear Adolf," she blurted. It was a palpable *faux pas*: Hess, shocked, paused in mid-exit. Hitler uttered one of his barks of laughter.

"*Ja*, look, Hess is shocked," he said. "He's probably never heard anyone call me by my first name. But surely my brother Alois does, eh, Hess? Anyhow, that's all right, the lady and I are old friends. Come back in thirty minutes, Hess, do you hear me?" he said, raising his voice to the softly closing door; then, remembering his manners: "Please. Step into my *Sitzecke*." He motioned to an armchair in a nook next to the window, from which there was a view, partially blocked by an incongruous potted rubber plant, of the winding Lech river between yellowed autumn fields and in the distance, against the serrated silhouette of the Alps, the gleaming lake-mirror of the Floggersee.

Stefanie sat down. With an exaggerated grimace, he sat down on a small wicker chair opposite.

"Shoulder injury," he explained, patting his right shoulder. "My war wound from the Putsch."

Awkwardness intruded. She looked out the window; he sat forward.

"Your parents are well?"

"Well, thank you."

"And your esteemed uncle and aunt, the Baron and Baroness Ottoheinz, they are in good health, I trust?"

"Fair. Thank you." And your mother, she almost asked, then

she remembered that he'd been an orphan for years, and that she wasn't sure whom he might consider family, or whom to inquire after: he was pretty much on his own, only now he had followers like the vulpine Hess, and forty others somewhere within the confines of the fortress . . . Stefanie sat back, affecting ease, and looked around. On the opposite wall, a pair of lithographs caught her eye: sentimental scenes, solid kitsch, one depicting the lamplit interior of a peasant dwelling wherein dwelt ruddy-cheeked Teutons, the other a pastoral landscape complete with dreamy clouds, cloud-reflecting brook, grazing (and no doubt lowing) kine. On the corner of the wall near the door hung a dried wreath looped in sashes, one of which was inscribed "In Eternal Thanks: *Kampfbund Bayern*." Diagonally across from the alcove, on the right, was a neatly made camp bed. Next to the bed was a bedside table atop which were magazines and a book that Stefanie, peering, identified as a biography of Henry Ford. A dresser faced a washbasin at the far end of the room. Judging by the location of various doors, the cell even boasted its own bathroom and built-in wardrobe.

Hitler gazed thoughtfully out the window, chin on hand, as if posing for a portrait, but any dignity in his pose was negated by the naked knees and sandal-shod feet (white-stockinged, grayish in the instep); a slight ridge of hair ran up the side of his thigh, and a blue vein stood out against the pallor of his skin. He seemed stiff, uncomfortable, walled in by artifice. Stefanie momentarily had the feeling she was taking part in some kind of grim amateur theatrical.

"Should I then call you by another name?" she inquired. He turned slowly and considered her with a gaze in which all amicability was held at bay.

"Well, my title in the party is leader," he said. "So that is what they call me: Führer."

"Like a travel guidebook," said Stefanie, perversely determined to jar the old Adolf out of the stern carapace of the new one, who was merely the old one with his defenses permanently up, and his innate prickliness elevated to arrogance. "A human Baedeker, *ja*?"

Mixed emotions invaded his features, and he wrestled briefly with his dignity, but in the end he smiled, uncrossed his legs, and clapped his hands: a small victory. She had broken the ice.

"*Ja, ja,* just like a travel guidebook, ha-ha, but instead of *Herr Reiseführer* Baedeker, I am hoping someday to be *Herr Reichsführer* Hitler!"

"That's quite an ambition! But let us be frank, Adolf, here you are in prison, even if it is a quite comfortable one—this cell, by the way, is probably larger than my apartment in Paris . . . "

"Paris!" he exclaimed, diving for the tangent. "Of course. That's where you live now, *nicht wahr?* Now you must tell me. Are the French entirely corrupt and degenerate? Do they all hate the Germans? How many Jews do you know?"

"Well, you must understand that I have a limited circle of acquaintances, but my husband is a composer, and he of course . . . " But it was fatal to circumlocute. Brief as Hitler's attention span had been in days gone by, it was even briefer now, and during any momentary pause he yielded to the balm of angry perorations on whatever subject hovered vaguely at hand, guided by nothing resembling logic or reason, indeed seething with contradictions and paradox, and driven primarily by his own formidable force of character, the concentrated essence of his awkward charm.

"The French, I suppose you want to know what I think, well, they occupy our territory, they force us to our knees with their reparations, they humiliate us at every turn, so I only feel what any patriotic German feels. Of course, all you need do is examine for a moment the form of government they have in France. Riddled with freemasonry, Jewry and Marxism, bound hand and foot by the Wall Street plutocrats, soft and syphilitic, incapable of firmness or decisiveness at home or abroad . . . "

Was there, then, no lingering scrap of romance, no regret for days gone by, no personal word for her alone? No fond memory of a day in Linz half an era ago, a morning in Vienna . . . ? Was she merely a sounding board, an infinitely replaceable effigy who might as well be one of the guards, or Rudolf Hess, or one of the vacant smiling peasant-faces on the wall? While talking,

Hitler blinked several times in rapid succession, then sustained an unblinking stare for as long as possible, while emphasizing his points with his right index finger alternately prodding his left palm and pointing heavenward; smiles automatically chased frowns, and the carefully combed forelock kept detaching itself and falling across his forehead. This necessitated a nervous gesture of the right hand, eternally to replace the errant lock which would then promptly detach itself and slide downward again . . .

And yet! He smelled of lavender water, or cologne, or something sweetly astringent, lathered on with a heavy hand, and on a man that was on a woman's behalf, and on whose behalf could it be but hers (Stefanie thought, with a faint feeling of triumph)? So, her existence had some small significance to him, after all! The so-called Führer of his own bizarre little fringe! And yet in his eyes she saw nothing but his own eccentricity, his own longing, his own zeal (or was she being too "feminine" about all this? too sentimental?) . . . with a shudder, she remembered her vision of his death, him sprawled on a rocky landscape, and involuntarily she looked down at the meadows outside; but there were no rocks there.

He paused. Stefanie launched a bold question.

"So you are not married, then? Obviously?"

He looked astonished.

"Married? Good heavens, no."

"Yet you are very romantic, Adolf. Deep down."

"Romantic? I hardly know what that means. Hardly, if you mean little precious glittery bijoux like the Russian ballet or clever-clever Jewish ideas or some sugary Straussian scenes from the Vienna Woods or smooching in a horse-drawn sleigh . . . "

"I mean individualism and idealism combined with love of high drama. Goethe and Lotte. Heloise and Abelard. Tristan and Isolde. Do you remember when we met at the opera, in Vienna?" And, she failed to add, when we subsequently met at that dosshouse you were living in?

"Ah, *ja*. The opera. That was where I met your friend Helmuth Meinl."

Stefanie was astonished.

"*Himmeldonnerwetter*, Adolf, how do you remember his name? I had almost forgotten the incident, myself. I'm amazed that you can recall the name of a stranger you met for five minutes what, ten, twelve years ago!"

"I rarely forget a name. Especially a Jewish one." He laughed flatly. "And it's hard to avoid Jewish names in Vienna, isn't it? Meinl, Cohen, Steinberg, Rosenblatt, Kahane . . . "

"Well, of course." The haze passed across her eyes. "In so large a city, you will inevitably encounter people of all origins . . . as in Paris . . . " Kahane was her uncle Ernst's birth name: was Hitler's mention of it mere coincidence? or was he asserting himself in a newly bizarre and malicious way? and did it matter, with this foul mist clouding her eyesight . . . ?

"Ah, Paris, of course," boomed Hitler's voice, hollowly, as from the far end of a tube. "A magnificent cultural capital, I don't doubt. The Opera, the Conservatoire, and so on, but it's still one of the world capitals from which our national humiliation was stage-managed and is still being stage-managed, behind the flimsy facade of the Dawes Plan," *und so weiter*, oh God, thought Stefanie, looking out the window, firmly trying to hold on to the external world-image of mountains, lake, river, the domino-town scattered below; " . . . you must be acquainted with quite a few of them," he was saying, but now the sun, as at Fatima, seemed momentarily to be revolving in the sky as a second sun gradually spun off into the middle distance, somewhere above the Floggersee, a small but piercingly bright light like the Morning Star spreading across the palette of the sky and actually reflected in the lake (did others see this, too?), revealing within itself a shimmering figure haloed in gold, quite the classic Mary vision, almost exactly like those Stefanie had had in the forest at Auerstadt, only bigger, brighter, and speaking in a voice Stefanie had never heard before. " . . . most German banks are run by Jews, that is a well-known fact, and I will not even mention Wall Street, which should be renamed Via Dolorosa, ah ha-ha, ach it's a pity what they've done to America, but America has sold its soul to them, and I consider it my duty to see that the same does not happen to Germany . . . " no, not that voice . . . "I am here to direct you away from evil, my child, for where you go, others will follow . . . " THAT voice . . .

"Look!" cried Stefanie. It was like trying to force herself to wake up during a nightmare. Adolf paused, grasped his knobbly knees, followed her pointing finger.

"Can you see it?" she shouted.

"I direct you away, my child, for it is only with the greatest faith" (broad vowels: the vision was speaking Stefanie's native Salzburg dialect, just as she had before, and as she had spoken to Bernadette in the patois of the Pyrenees), "that I who have appeared to you before do so again in place of the foulness from below: Turn to me and repent!"

"I have, for goodness' sake," cried Stefanie. "What more must I do?" she gasped. "Build a shrine in your honor?"

"A shrine? My dear Fräulein von Rothenberg, are you quite all right? Dear God, what an annoyance." Hitler flapped his hands confusedly. "Do you want a glass of water? *Hess!*"

"Adolf, do you see it?"

"I see nothing, dear lady. Well, I see you, the mountains, the river . . . "

Suddenly, it had passed, and there was no longer a second sun reflected in the quiet Floggersee. Stefanie panted. Her head ached.

"I have visions," she said, quietly, as to a confessor. "Like the medieval mystics. *I see things.*"

As she had once intuitively predicted, this intrigued Adolf almost to the exclusion of his own preoccupations. He at once began to interrogate her, and inquired whether her visions—the actual subject of which appeared not to interest him—had ever manifested themselves in front of a crowd, say in a stadium, or cathedral, or public square? Then, without waiting for an answer, he went on, "You know, this is very interesting, *ja,* highly remarkable in fact. You know that I, too, have had visions. In 1918, when I was lying in a hospital bed at Pasewalk on the Western Front, I had a vision of the future so intense that I felt as if someone had been pressing down on my head, here"— with forefinger and thumb, he made a delicate pincer around his temples"—and believe me, the sight was real, as utterly real as, well, as your vision, just now. I saw the mountaintop, the figure of Germania, the sacrifice of the Jews. Without that vision, I doubt if I should ever have known the way forward. And it makes me think, it reminds me of the events in that Spanish or Portuguese town in which a crowd of, ach, I don't remember, eighty thousand or so were entirely convinced that they had seen miraculous visions in the sky, wasn't it in 1917? *Ja*, Portugal, wasn't it? A town called Fatima. I remember because I was on home leave at the time and read about it in the newspapers: what a propaganda coup for the Church, eh? Incredible, how the human masses are susceptible to delusion! No, no," he said, hastily (he was on his feet now, pacing back and forth, hands clasped behind his back), "of course I am not suggesting that you yourself have been deluded, Fräulein Stefanie," reverting involuntarily to the nomenclature of former times, "unlike the mountebanks who proliferate in Germany these days, the peasant girl Therese, the faith healer von Studenheim . . . *ja, ja*, undoubtedly some people have the ability to see what others cannot, that I can accept." He paused and leaned forward, smiling the cautious smile of one too self-conscious to smile spontaneously. "I am one. Since that time at Pasewalk I have seen wondrous things in the sky and the clouds as well. But these visions are not like your visions. I see the future of this country. I see the sunlit meadows of our future. I see Germany reborn. Percival. The Grail. You see, well, you see . . . "

"I see the Virgin Mary," said Stefanie, clear and composed. "And I thank God for it, for I also have seen her opposite. Twice, actually, both in your company."

"Her opposite?"

"Yes. The devil."

"The devil! And in my company?"

"Yes, long ago. In Linz. And the second time, in Vienna. While you were painting my portrait."

This went down well with the former Catholic altar boy. He goggled, and spluttered a nervous laugh.

"Well, I have never been very good at portraits!"

No, no, he understood! Of course, as he said, he was having his own visions—although it would be blasphemous for you or me to use the name. Let us remember, though, that in 1924 his political career was, to all appearances, finished before it had begun; that he was famous, but only as a provincial laughingstock; that his main support came from half-witted goons like Hess; and that he was in a political backwater of his own making. Let us also remember (well, history will not let us forget it) that he had a native perspicacity amounting to genius; a downright uncanny ability, a paranoiac's ability to probe the weaknesses of others; and a rock-solid (and rough-hewn by life's sharp chisel) belief in himself *über alles*. He was, consequently, the most highly evolved of the genus *homo politicus*, stripped as he was of all morality, impelled solely by ambition, keenly aware of, but unsympathetic to, human frailty; and this political paragon found himself wondering if Stefanie von Rothenberg might not be an asset to his cause. In Stefanie, until now, he had always sensed strength, which jarred with his Waldviertel peasant's view of women as inferior, yielding creatures, beasts of childbirth and burden. Indeed, this perception of Stefanie as iron-willed and self-sufficient had always blocked any open expression of his desire for her (expressed, as was typical of his kind, in the dark, alone and ashamed), but then came her sudden confession, and it revealed two weaknesses to him: hers, as a self-styled mystic; and his party's, as a secular alternative to Christianity in a still-Christian nation. Would it not, he wondered, be a brilliant idea to synthesize? A spectacular move to produce a true believer in both the old religion and the new? On the one hand a genuine mystic, a holy fool, a link to the balladeers of Nuremberg, the Minnesingers, Wolfram von Eschenbach and the mystics of the Middle Ages; on the other a convert to the new church of National Socialism, a statuesque Aryan bearing a bold aristocratic name, with plenty of contacts in the upper classes of Austria and France? And, parenthetically, a contrast to the charlatans plaguing the Fatherland these days: a parallel to himself as antidote to quackery?

Serendipitously—or perhaps not—and unknown to Hitler,

Stefanie wanted to save his soul: she found herself again at that most dangerous stage of womanly infatuation, when explanations proliferate and irrationality is rationalized. Truth to tell, there was a genuine religious impulse at the bottom of her feelings; if she interpreted the Virgin's words at all, it was as an exhortation to convert, to proselytize, to intervene on the brink of atheism, to save a soul, but not, at that stage, her own . . .

It was also true that Stefanie was fascinated by the man Hitler, and she was egotist enough to believe that she could guide him where others could not. So a collaboration was born, based on mostly but not entirely false premises—it must be obvious to the reader by now, after all, that Hitler was the dark thread that ran through Stefanie's life, tracing a course parallel to that other, godly, golden thread of Heaven, and that although Stefanie was a woman of some sense and great intelligence, she was in danger of finding herself in thrall not only to the man but also, and perhaps mostly, to his debased yet evocative romanticism, which in her mind complemented rather than opposed her love of God and her visions. When Hitler spoke, Stefanie (and this was to be the experience of an entire generation of Germans) overlooked his meanderings, threats and contradictory half-truths, paradoxically admiring *him* while ignoring his *words*, just as in Wagner's operas she paid no attention to the leaden intricacies of plotting and dialogue but concentrated, she thought, on the glorious art of the whole. Through Hitler—his name, his person—she glimpsed a future that glamorized the past: the Pöstlingberg out the window of the Monchskeller; the Archduke, and the Danube, and the pealing bells of Linz; she relived that past, which was a place of longing, for it is not only to our generation that the world before the Great War seemed like another era. To its survivors, too, it shone in the receding distance like a dying bonfire. But on the future's horizon flashed turrets of steel. National Socialism was in its youth, it was dynamic and futuristic yet romantic and history-laden; certainly no Wagner-lover could be indifferent to its appeal. Its clarion call was the call of Frederick Barbarossa at Kyffhäuser, the summons to the Teutonic Knights from atop Schloss Nürnberg, the whispering immanence in the pine forests

of the Böhmerwald. It was 1924, and Germany (and their own
Austria, too) had suffered one terrible blow after another. Had
she not the right to hope?

She bade Hitler farewell formally, with a solemnity that
matched his own.

"I hope to see you again soon," he said, searching her face
with his penetrating gaze.

*

"Of course, you're not Jewish," said Samuel on the drive back
to Munich. "If you were, it would help you understand the fellow's craziness and the danger of these Rightist parties. A nation
isn't like a kitchen you can scrub clean, and that's what they all
talk about, 'cleaning up,' the simpletons. In France we have the
Croix de Feu; Italy has Mussolini, England Mosley and Churchill;
in Germany, they have your chum Hitler. *Sacrebleu*, Stefanie, you
should be ashamed of yourself. Think at least of Ignace."

"Samuel," said Stefanie. "I am not a fool. I know what it's
about. I think he can help the nation and I want to help him,
God willing, before it's too late."

"But why, Stefanie? And how?"

"Because I now realize that he understands something about
the Germans. In a way, he too is a mystic."

"Bah! *Quelle foutaise.*"

"You may say so. But you haven't known him for twenty
years, as I have."

"Well, well. And how are you proposing to bring about this
transformation?"

"I will speak. I will travel. And I will try to have him bear
witness to the glory of God at my side."

"God? Oh God. *Bonne chance, ma vieille.*"

As they retraced their drive back to Munich (the same old
man in the same run-down village came to life again to spit at
them and shake his fist and exclaim *Hinaus mit den Welschen
plunder*, chuck out the Froggie garbage), Samuel was for once
neither avuncular nor flirtatious. Stefanie's announcement, upon
leaving Schloss Landsberg, that she was intending to do "a little

work" for Hitler and the National Socialists, had taken him unawares. It seemed a contradiction of all he knew about her, but he reminded himself how many times he had discovered how little he knew about women. Then, in a second, she caught him off guard by taking his side. She agreed, she said, that the National Socialists appealed mainly to the slope-browed, ignorant, provincial bigot, yes; but this was precisely her reason for wanting to influence their leader, who was, she remained convinced, not fated to be a bad man at heart.

"He is an artist, Samuel. Remember, I know him. If he's changed, it's because of politics and the opportunity for power. It's just amazing what politics will do to you, isn't it," she said (as if, thought Samuel, she had made a study of the subject). "Look at Lenin."

Yes, said Samuel to himself, and Lenin too no doubt had been a thoroughgoing bastard before he took over, but an obscure one, like so many; and like him and so many others, Hitler had also been an embittered nonentity, but he was now prowling the backstage of actual power . . .

"And what better time to influence him than now? Anyway, realistically, I don't think he'll get any further than the local level, the Bavarian legislature perhaps. After all, the economy's improving, isn't it? And the world's at peace!"

Brave words, in 1924.

Gustave
Seven

AFTER AN UNSETTLED night of sweats and many trips to the bathroom—but no more visits from on high, thank (so to speak) God—I did what any man in my situation would do: I went to see my *mamma*. I had no classes to teach that day and no urge to do anything else. Mamma was now a hale eighty-one. She lived in Confignon, in a new house with a view from one window of the Salève and from another of the city that twinkled at night like ships' lights on the sea.

I drove out in a pelting rain. She answered the door. We kissed.

"*Ciao, Mamma.*"

"*Ciao, Tavo.*"

In the living room Ferruccio, her old pug, waddled over to inspect me, barked hoarsely, then returned panting, with many a dubious backward glance, to the comfortable concavity of his hassock. Mamma handed me an espresso and a grappa. I bolted the latter and sipped the former and sat back in the damask-patterned wingchair I remembered from the old apartment, from the days of my youth when I was small and slim enough to sit reading in it on the cushion of my tucked-under legs. Across from me now were, side by side in metal frames on the bookcase, Mamma's two men, cranky Papa glaring through his shades from a sun chair on the balcony of the chalet, and me at age twenty-five or so, obnoxiously kitted out in some kind of Scottish university scarf and blazer, with the Camus-like touch of a cigarette dangling from my lower lip and Edinburgh Castle behind. Who did I think I was? Or rather, who did I think I would be? Not a damned mystic, that was certain. I averted my eyes from that arrogant innocent and stared at the Salève.

Our conversation meandered around Mamma's gout, my indigestion, her reading (all Italian authors now—Sciascia, Levi, Bassani), my writing (nil). She delicately avoided mentioning my job and inquired instead after my car.

"Running well, *Mamma*. But a little uncertain in third. I'm going to change out the water pump next week." She nodded enthusiastically, as if keen on water pumps. She wasn't, but it was diplomacy, not senility, that caused her to inquire; thank God, her mind was still sharp. When I finally nudged the conversation around to problems at work, after another long lull in a conversational byway devoted to last night's TV movie on TSR6 (*Unterkampf*, with Bettina Faustus) she interjected,

"But you have some personal problem, don't you, *caro*? What is it? *Che c'è? Una donna? Sei malato?*"

I took a deep breath.

"No, I'm not sick—well, not really. I have a mild case of something or other. Not that I can tell, most days . . . and yes, *Mamma*, I *have* met a woman. But that's not it."

"Tavo!" she exclaimed. I sat up. "That's not it? You meet a woman after fifty-three years and it's not important? You're making no sense. Oh, dear. I hope she doesn't turn out like that Françoise of yours. *Dai, dai.* Tell your mamma what's going on."

So I did. Sitting straight-backed in her chair, she listened with appropriate gravity, sipping her coffee, ignoring my cigarette smoke, spasmodic throat clearings, spurts of nervous flippancy and digressive tendencies, to all of which she had long been accustomed. When I was done she asked,

"Have you spoken to a priest?"

"Oh come on, *Mamma*, when was the last time I or anybody in this family went to see a priest?"

"Oh come on yourself, when was the last time a Termi or a Caldecotto went about having visions of the Archangel Michael?"

I admitted to having consulted a doctor and a psychiatrist,

and told her in detail of the LeCluyse debacle.

"OK, so you got that far then you ran away because you thought he insinuated you were *finnochio*? Tavo, Tavo." She heaved a deep, very Italian sigh that despaired of sense in this universe of fools. "You know the psychiatrists think sex is at the root of everything. They are narrow-minded, like the communists your papa loved blindly, or the bad priests who want to make us all feel guilty about life. But a *decent* priest like Padre Sanzio who baptized you, and I say this as a non-believer for more than fifty years . . . "

"Ever since I was born, as a matter of fact."

"*Ma si*, you know that. After you were born, even though we had you baptized I never believed. In a God who gives me one child in His image, then tears apart my insides so I can never have more children? Then gives other women who don't use contraceptives dozens of children in Africa, only to kill them all off? *Basta cosi*. But I respect the best of religion. I believe it answers a need. Didn't St. Augustine say that God has placed a longing in our hearts? And the heart of a fifty-three year-old unmarried man is full of longing, *carissimo*, and I don't care how many poems and books you publish. And a decent Italian priest like Padre Benedetto can understand these things. He's half retired now, I think, but they still keep him on at St. Martin's, over in Onex, you know, that ugly modern church on the left as you go toward town . . . ? He can listen to stories of visions and spirituality without laughing at you, and he can even offer you a glass of Chianti." Ah, *mamma mia*. "And speaking of all that, who is this woman you mentioned?"

I got out of answering that question by inventing an appointment—well, almost got out of it. As I was leaving she put her hand on my shoulder and said,

"Call me, Tavo. Come for dinner some day. And bring the lady."

To appease my conscience, as soon as I got home I made an appointment to see the old priest.

"Termi? Who? Ah, Tadzio's boy?" said Father Benedetto, who'd picked up the phone with the alacrity of a man with time on his hands. "Ah yes. To see me? But of course. Time? I have nothing but. Who needs me? Everyone is an atheist now. Or a Muslim."

Father Benedetto Sanzio was a Ligurian priest from Savona who would no doubt have been our family confessor if any of us had ever had an inkling of standard Catholic belief. He'd always been welcome in our house, though, even when Papa was alive; no other priest would have been permitted to baptize me, certainly. For one thing, he liked cars and used to drive a red Alfa Giulietta that he always dutifully had serviced at my father's garage. For another, he was a people's priest; he'd been in Nicaragua, and Honduras, and had led strikes against Agnelli back in Italy, and this drove up his stock with the commies. For a third, as I recalled, he was a jolly sort, a bit Friar Tuck-ish with hints of Pope John XXIII. In fact, he looked a bit like Mamma's pug Ferruccio, I thought on meeting him later that day for the first time in a decade or so, with the pug's image fresh in my addled mind and no afterimage of Father Benedetto at all after all those years. He even looked slightly Chinese, as do many old Latins. He exuded a cozy pong of cigarettes and armpits casually scrubbed. He extended a warm, plump hand and we shook, gravely. Like him, his office was small and dark and smelled of Caporal smoke. It occupied the toe end of the L-shaped parish hall of St. Martin Catholic Center in Onex, that vapid suburb best half seen in pouring rain, as I saw it that afternoon through the Citroën's wildly flailing windscreen wipers. Somewhere across the highway was the actual church, a circular '60s-modern effort with a stubby open spire. It could as easily have been a post office or the headquarters of a shoe factory in Zambia. Still, Father Sanzio had managed to endow his office with the appearance and exiguity of a traditional priest's sacristy. It gave off a faint air of ancient sanctity. Jesus smiled down at me from one wall and writhed on the cross on another. The pale faces of saints gazed upward, hands clasped. In an evocation of the ancient darkness inside many an Italian church, the shutters were half closed against the dull daylight, and my mind supplied me with memory's scents: incense, mustiness, floor polish . . .

"A real *professore*, eh?" said the priest. "I used to call you *professore* out of irony, in the Italian way, but now you really are one. *Dio* it's strange to meet like this. How many years? Didn't I see you about twenty years ago, at someone's wedding? Do you speak Italian?"

Twenty; and yes; and yes. The wedding was my cousin Alfredo's, now as then a boring civil servant in one of the UN agencies.

"And how can I help you, *professore*?"

Well! Strange was the reason that had brought me here, I averred, casting jumpy glances at the squirming figure on the crucifix above the yellow-paned window that reminded me of the institutional windows in Frédy Girardet's sublime restaurant in Crissier. Through the gap in the shutters I saw a car park and cars, including a red Alfa . . .

"Yours?" I welcomed the diversion from my purpose.

He turned, swinging his entire upper body around like a machine-gun turret. He was dressed in standard left-wing priestly casual: a black polo shirt buttoned up to the neck, a dark gray jacket, nondescript trousers, an ensemble of blacks and grays. Then, paradoxically, like the unexpected flashes of gold in Matthias Grünewald's gloomy triptych, or Calvin's hideous beast-visions of Alfas and Citroën-Maseratis past and present . . .

But it wasn't his.

"No, no," he said. "I gave up driving. I had a bad accident two years ago. It's a pity. As a good Italian I enjoyed driving. Pardon me." He could barely contain himself, taking a pack of Murattis out of a desk drawer. "Smoke?" I accepted. He coughed loosely, contentedly, as we exchanged lights and inhaled. "I was driving to Valence, in the Rhône Valley, where there is a retreat run by the Church for depressed priests, alcoholic priests, sex maniacs . . . you name it. Quite a zoo, eh? The church opened it after the scandals of the nineties. I was looking forward to it, *professore*. I hoped to spend a month or so down there, as my duties here are light—I am the curate *in solidum* of St. Martin's, but they rarely call on me . . . anyway, I never made it, because just outside Vienne this drunken *testa di cazzo* took a turn too

fast and hit me broadside, *wam*! Like that," slapping the back
of one hand against the palm of the other, "and making me a
very depressed priest, I can assure you. I was in traction at the
hospital down there for three weeks and, as they say, 'my life was
despaired of.' So now I take the bus, taxis, trains, even sometimes," he grinned, "I walk."

It didn't take long after that for him to take a walk over to
his cabinet and extract a bottle of —as Mamma had predicted—
chianti; not the best by any means, drinkable table plonk I'd
seen for ten francs on the shelves of the co-op, but it was the
middle of a rainy afternoon and the somewhere the sun was over
somebody's yardarm and there was a warm and fuzzy Italianness
in the air which never fails to make me sentimental and prone
to Chianti-tippling (of course, Barolo, Nebbiolo, Valpolicella,
Montepulciano, Dolcetto, Brachetto, or Moscato will do at a
pinch). Father Benedetto motioned me towards a pair of well-
worn leather armchairs in the corner of the office. We sat and
sipped.

"Well," he said.

I shrugged.

"It's hard to know how to begin. I feel like a *pazzo*."

"Ah. Never mind that. I've heard it all."

"Well, Father, I don't know if you've heard this. I don't
believe. I haven't gone to church, except to admire the art, in
forty years. But I've started to have religious visions."

"Visions!" His face lit up and he hunched eagerly forward.
"*Bene*! *Bene*! I haven't talked to anyone who had visions since,
well . . . since the seventies, back in Italy, a retired doctor who
saw St. Peter hovering over his dining table upside down as he
was during his crucifixion, a detail the doctor, a lifelong atheist,
couldn't have known . . . but come, *professore*. Tell me."

So I did, without mentioning the porphyria. He was, after
all, a doctor of the soul, not a physic.

Then, that night, musing over what he'd said, I took up
Martine's book with renewed interest, for when I'd brought it
up (having told him everything else), the old priest said, "Sister
Stefanie von Rothenberg? *La tedesca*? *Si, si*. I met her once."

The Thirties

A month after Stefanie's visit, Adolf Hitler was released from Landsberg Castle. He had served nine months of his five-year prison term. Back in Paris, Stefanie first heard about it at the Académie Werfel, then, along with official notification of the event on Party stationary she received an official Party membership card and a signed photograph of Hitler. Arthur snatched it up and peered long and hard at it.

"What's going on here, Steffi?"

"Arthur, I told you everything."

"I don't think so."

He left, and only returned a week later. Soon he left for good. He had long had his suspicions, he said, and Hitler's picture was the limit. He sent for his belongings, and in January 1926 Arthur and Stefanie separated, an Anglo-French contralto named Nancy Poirel being the proximate cause. No church divorce was possible, of course, and an annulment was unlikely; not that secular Jewish Arthur cared. But Stefanie endured a brief season in hell, then she shrugged her shoulders: so Arthur was gone. He'd really been gone for a long time. The modest success of his operas—especially, with the tired irony of these things, *The Mystic*—had transformed him into a socialite and womanizer, abetted in both by Ivan Youzbine and Youzbine's entourage of Russian libertines. Sadly, the amorous flame of the Vienna Woods and the Auerstadt School had flickered out long ago, since when Stefanie's true rivals had proliferated beyond counting: the operas; the girl-friends; her holy visions; Adolf Hitler; but perhaps most of all, her past and Arthur's future.

Her only condition was that she keep their son, and Arthur, who had never taken to fatherhood, assented. Papers were drawn up and approved by a civil court, but Stefanie dreaded the idea of a fatherless son, so Samuel—no longer "uncle," just "Samuel," even "Sami"—moved into the neighboring flat on the Rue Soufflot, initially on the basis of guardianship and as a token masculine presence. In the spring of '26, having done well on the

Bourse, he purchased both apartments and had a door installed in the adjoining wall, enabling him to come and go as he pleased. It was a fine Parisian arrangement, and in due course Stefanie realized that a cynical lover two decades her senior suited her far better than marriage to a man her age; the transient quality of such a loose arrangement, acknowledged from the start, matched her temperament and the world's unruliness.

Her parents regretted Arthur's removal from the family scene.

"I was happy that you married, Steffi," said her mother over hissing phone lines. "Now you're living apart from your husband. That's very modern, I know. But in Salzburg we still prefer marriage. Look at your father and me. Thirty-four years."

Shortly after their thirty-fifth anniversary, in July 1927, her father, depressed by the failure of Stefanie's marriage and other malfeasances of life, died of a cancer of the pancreas. Stefanie returned to Salzburg for the funeral. She wept, for she had dearly loved her Pappi. She embraced her poor mutti, and left little Ignace with her. Then, shortly afterward, she visited Munich, and spoke to a gathering of NaSos.

Hess was there, and introduced her as a worthy friend.

"*Ja, kameraden,*" he bayed, "this lady has been one of us at heart for many years. Let it not be said that our party excludes this man because of his low origins or that woman because she is upper-class! I, Rudolf Wilhelm Hess, and Fräulein Stefanie von Rothenburg, are living proof of that!"

The meeting hall, a converted Lutheran church in the suburb of Haidhausen, was packed, and full of working-class odors: sweat, cheap cigarettes, beer, and schnapps. A poster hung at the far end of the hall, exhorting the faithful to march. On one of the walls was a portrait of Hitler against roiling Romantic storm clouds. The German that was spoken was coarse, guttural, Bavarian: Adolf's German. These were *his* Germans, too, mostly men, small folk left behind by progress and democracy and the twentieth century. These were the Germans of the Wars of Religion, or the Middle Ages, rustics adrift in the city, restless barbarians, anomalies in the modern age, ignorant, brutish, and embittered. Yet they, too, had families to feed; they, too, needed to belong to a great crusade.

"Hello, comrades. I speak to you as a sister," said Stefanie. Her voice was strong and clear, as if she were in front of a class. "Like you, I want the redemption of the German lands. I sincerely believe we have been mistreated. I live in Paris"—catcalls, boos, hisses—"and I have many French friends"—more booing, cries of "*Welschen raus!*"—"but I firmly believe that they must give us a chance. But we, too, must hold firm on principles of civilization and Christianity. I have come to you from the Greater German marches of Catholic Austria. Heed the call! We are yet a Christian land. Pay attention to She who loves you, for She is truly the voice of us all."

She went on in like vein, rambling yet infectiously spontaneous, for another ten minutes or so, and toward the end she settled into a conversational style, trading one question for another, and the subject of Jews arose.

"It is absurd," said Stefanie. "We are a Christian nation."

"That's why we have to get rid of them," bawled a proud anti-Semite from the intellectual precincts of rural Bavaria. "Keep Germany pure and Christian!"

"*Ja,*" chorused some of his peers. "Throw them out!"

"But they are Germans, too," said Stefanie, but her moment was over. Hess unctuously escorted her off the stage.

"We would like to thank, um, Fräulein Rothenburg," he shouted hoarsely, outshouted by the Jew-haters.

"Where is Hitler?" inquired Stefanie, out of breath and ruffled.

"He is negotiating the purchase of land," said Hess. "Near Berchtesgaden."

Farcical as it was, Stefanie's first public appearance before the NaSo faithful, and the vileness of their hatred, and the unplumbable depths of their provincialism, disturbed her. She realized that to these people "German" was not a mere expression of nationality, but a term of sanctity, of racial purity, that resolutely excluded whole swaths of Germans, notably Jews. After all, if Jews were German, what was the virtue of being German?

She fretted and prayed, and was about to return to Paris

when, while having breakfast in the Café Heck, she read an article in the *Münchener Post* about the increasing fame of a local mystic called Therese Neumann, who had recently begun to show signs of the stigmata.

"This reporter," said the article, "embarked on his investigation in a spirit of the most devout skepticism. However, confronted with the reality of the young woman's personality, as well as the undeniable fact of her stigmata, he had a change of heart. Whether she is a saint is not for us to say, but there can be no doubt that she is one of the elect. In these perilous times for our country, we must listen to what she has to say if we are to survive."

Therese Neumann lived in a convent in Konnersreuth, north of Munich. Stefanie visited her the day after reading the article. A nun ushered her into a dimly lit bedroom. Therese's stigmata were not in evidence, but the girl's goodness emanated from her person like the Ávilan scent of rose petals that also filled the small bedroom where she lay (and which Stefanie traced to a vase of the moldering flowers in a small nook near the door). Therese's face was wan but not wasted, and she regarded Stefanie with shining eyes and clear recognition, as of a fellow sufferer.

"You have too much of the world with you," she whispered. "Without it you would know better what you must do."

"I, too, have visions," murmured Stefanie. "I see both good and evil things."

"And you consort with those of this world, which contains both good and evil," said the peasant girl. "Take heed of this warning: you will be chosen to perform a great deed of cleansing. And remember: Your only friend is the Mother of God."

With the words of the strange bright-eyed girl in her ears, Stefanie returned to Paris and the iron demands of life.

The teaching was going well, despite shortages, and the weather was mild, but a series of minor but annoying health problems (gastritis, tinnitus), troubled Stefanie's sleep, and life's everydayness closed her mystical eye. Still, every Sunday she visited the shrine on the Rue du Bac where St. Catherine Labouré, a twenty-four-year-old novice, had had her first vision on the night of July 18, 1830, being politely escorted into the convent chapel by an usher-like figure surrounded in shimmering haloes of gold whom she later took to be the Archangel Michael himself.

[Gustavus Interruptus

Well, well. Speak of the . . . no, better not say that. See, I'm turning superstitious. Anyway, my Michael is less shimmering than quietly gleaming, but still recognizably the same chap, so add another name to the distinguished company of Archangel spotters: St. Catherine Labouré! Actually, I remember visiting that church once, after a boozy lunch at the Drouand with an editor who turned out to be a devout Old Catholic and fell to his knees at the saint's grave, then, quite drunk, slowly arranged himself into a recumbent position and slept it off for the next four hours or so, oblivious to the steady stream of pilgrims, most of them hunchbacked Spanish grandmothers . . . honestly, this is becoming more and more absurd . . .]

A blaze of light above the altar resolved itself into the figure of Mother Mary, who descended the steps and sat, rather casually, in the spiritual director's chair and told Catherine, in fluent Parisian-accented French, that she had a mission for her. Bad times were to come, but she promised help and grace for those who prayed to the Miraculous Medal.

"Times are evil in France and in the world," she said, "but do not fear; you will have the grace to do what is necessary."

(So she spoke in Stefanie's dreams, but in the dialect of Stefanie's native Salzkammergut.)

At the shrine Stefanie prayed like any good Catholic, and like any good Catholic she heard and saw nothing in reply. She thought of the words of Therese Neumann and wondered uneasily (with a slight upsurge of hope, as of yearning for a normal life) if her visions were over, if she had offended the Holy Mother in some way.

"Forgive me, Mother Mary, but what do you expect? I'm no peasant girl. I'm no stigmatic. I'm a university graduate. I think, I argue, I dispute, and I cloud my faith with argument and reason."

There was no reply that day (a Sunday), but somewhere outside a bell started pealing joyously.

Vienna Again

In early March 1932, Uncle Ernst telephoned, grumbling all the while.

"Your aunt is going from bad to worse, ach *ja*, Steffi, it's a terrible sight," he declared, in the overly loud tones of the hard of hearing. "But of course she might rally if you came to visit and of course I would be delighted to see you again, dear Steffi, and by all means bring your little boy Konrad. What? *Ja, ja*, or Ignaz."

Samuel bid Stefanie and Ignace a formal farewell.

"*Au revoir, mes petits*," he said. "Save a place for me at the Vienna Opera."

"*Adieu*, Papa Samuel," said Ignace. He stood tall and proud, and already resembled a miniature Arthur, even at age eight, right down to the confident manners and the worldliness he absorbed from the Paris air.

Stefanie briefly kissed Samuel; then the whistle blew and the scenery shifted from the echoing quais of the Gare de l'Est to the gray suburbs and the sad green countryside under weeping gray skies.

The familiar scent of roast chestnuts and tea leaves filled the air. A band at the Westbahnhof was playing *Cagliostro in Vienna*. Uncle Ernst was waiting for them on the platform.

"We hired a nurse, two nurses, a *therapiste*," he said. "Ach, the expense! It's enough to drive a man mad! Never mind, we do what we must, not so? So! How is Paris? Things here in Austria are a little worse now, with Dollfuss and his fascists . . . hello, this must be Konrad."

"Ignace Lebel. *Enchanté, mon oncle*."

"We're in Austria now, boy. Speak German."

"*Guten tag, Onkel Ernst*."

"That's better. Good boy. How would you like to ride on the great big Prater wheel, Konrad?"

"Ignace, sir."

"Bah! Ignaz, then."

The Ottoheinzes were living in an apartment on the Wiedner Gürtel, next door to the Hotel Kongress, where Fritzl and Lotte were staying with the boys. Friztl was beer-bulkier and more brooding than ever, but spoke hopefully of acquiring a prosthetic arm. Lotte as always hovered in the background, part of the landscape, except when she ventured an opinion, which usually detonated like a small grenade.

"Steffi, how is that French uncle of yours?" inquired Fritzl. "Now there's a man of the world."

"Sami is quite well, although he has certain dubious financial holdings."

"More to the point, how's that Hitler friend of yours?" said Lotte. "Are you still on the NaSo after-dinner speaking circuit, Stefanie?"

"No. I have serious misgivings about the National Socialists."

"Well, God be thanked. If only Germany were as wise."

"Ach," said Fritzl. "Germans are morons. Only Austrians are civilized. And maybe the French."

Aunt Liesl was gaunt, glitter-eyed, cancer-ravaged. From her bedroom window she had a view, as she proudly showed Stefanie, of the Ostfriedhof, the main cemetery in the east of the city. In the distance towered the Prater wheel.

"All I can think of when I see it is the Buddhist wheel of life," she said. "The mandala. Ironic, isn't it, that I should be dying when for the first time ever I think of such a thing, such a serene symbol, so reassuring it might have been when things were better. Who knows, if I had been a Buddhist, with such symbols, I might never have fallen ill. It's the worry, Steffi, listen to me now. Worry is the killer. Let worry eat your soul and before you know it cancer will be eating your flesh. *Ja*, ironic." She pointed to the cemetery. "But when I'm gone, all you'll have to do is pop me in the box and carry me across the street," she said. "Isn't that considerate of me? Ach! How healthy and voluptuous you are. If only you could spare some for me."

She huddled into herself, as she did a great deal. The slightest draft was an arctic gale: She shivered almost constantly. The

nurses gave her spoonfuls of hot soup, and warned the visitors
against tiring her. She drifted in and out of a drugged doze.
Soon she would be dead, thought Stefanie as she publicly hid
behind the standard bromides of reassurance ("oh, you'll be up
and about," "I say, you're really looking quite well," "now you
just rest and you'll be better in no time," etc.); but she knew,
and Liesl knew, and in the others' guarded gazes there was the
same foreknowledge of death. Stefanie caressed her aunt's sleeping face, overwhelmed by the monstrous banality of extinction,
the seeming pointlessness of persisting with life, of dragging
oneself from A to B closer and closer to death year after year
until the spark goes out and only bones remain, detached from
the soul, the learning, the wit, the memories and the desires of
the soft fleshly creature that had housed them for six decades,
seven, eight . . . Aunt Liesl's sleeping dying face had the noble
but abandoned look of a ruined church. *Why sleep*, wondered
Stefanie, *when sleep is no longer restorative?* Aunt Liesl was Death,
she was the uninhabited realm to which, a week later, her soul
finally fled.

As she had predicted, her journey across the street took no
time at all, and Stefanie offered up a prayer to accompany her
on her other, invisible journey. Liesl's tombstone looked out over
the city where she had spent all of her sixty-seven years: to the
west the Belvedere, to the northeast the Kahlenberg's woods and
wine gardens, southwestwards the Prater's great wheel of life and
death. Twenty or so mourners attended. Fritzl sobbed loudly and
theatrically, buttressed by Lotte on one side and Ernst on the
other. Ernst's eyes were dry but his mouth was set in a thin line of
resignation. Fritzl's boys, unmoved, nudged each other, glancing
surreptitiously at Ignace, who stood apart, next to his mother, as
she gazed aloft at Heaven, where Liesl now was, and at the fluffy
pink Baroque clouds floating away eastward, toward the open
marches of Burgenland and the galloping Hungarian steppe.

In the days following the funeral, Fritzl staved off collapse
only by dint of deep consumption of Wiener Weissbier. Soon
he and his family went back to Munich. Ernst and Stefanie were
not sorry to see them go.

Uncle Ernst was depressed but oddly fit. He sniffed less, and stood taller and lean, as if, perversely, his wife's vitality, when she was well, had sapped his own, but now that she was dead he had shed the extraneous and recovered his health. And in truth, although the Baron Ottoheinz might some day be quite gaga, it was good to see him in tolerable health, and he was firmly in command as he and Ignace planned their excursions. Stefanie was happy to leave her son in the old man's care. She herself walked the streets of her beloved but now-mournful hometown, uncertain if she should stay. Vienna, like the rest of Europe, was bracing itself. The Dollfuss fascists who were running Austria had clearly, Uncle Ernst said, taken against Jews, foreigners, "and the like" (as he put it). Indeed, twice he had had problems from former customers and once from an ex-business partner (the one who had rented Stefanie her lodgekeeper's room in Auerstadt): anti-Semitic comments made loudly, within earshot, blandly feigned ignorance of same when confronted . . .

"If they just had the courage of their convictions, however unsavory, it would be preferable," said Ernst. "Swine! Jewish-born that I am, I'm still a Christian Austrian knight of the realm, so far above them in status it's laughable. Miserable wretches. No class, no education. All they know is what they hate. Like the communists. And these people are all cowards, too, you know. But I greatly fear they will soon be in charge everywhere."

And once again Stefanie found the name Hitler to be the refrain in the chorus of political complaint. The Viennese were keenly aware that the NaSo leader was an Austrian, an ex-Viennese, a onetime urban castaway on their streets, and that he was making news again in Germany, first, after the Geli Raubal suicide hit the newsstands, as the bereaved lover of Geli, his dead half niece, then, more respectably, as the Coming Man of Destiny. In 1930 his National Socialist party swept the popular vote in the parliamentary elections, overtaking the Reds; for many, he was the knight, the visionary, the Guide. Stefanie listened as others talked of him, remembering her gaunt portraitist and awkward suitor. Hermann of Teutoburg, Siegfried, Frederick the Great: Every German mythological cliché was embodied in

the man. Most spoke of him in favorable tones, even one or two
Jews, Helmuth Meinl for one, who met Stefanie at Landtmann's
with his wife, Grätel, a smiling porcelain doll of Frisian origin.
The Meinls were prosperous, even in those lean times. They had
three children, Helmuth said. All were in the charge of their
nanny; one was about to go to boarding school in England.
Helmuth had done rather well as a stockbroker and dealer in real
estate futures, and from those blandly comfortable heights (Benz
phaeton, villa in the suburbs, winters in Davos), he recalled with
an easy laugh his once burning notion of becoming a religious
scholar and the shabby life of aching ambitions he had left so
far behind.

"*Ja*, well, that was a long time ago, Stefanie," he said. "Then I
suddenly discovered I had a wife and family to feed! And believe
me I had no intention of sacrificing comfort to scholarship. The
dusty garret, the frayed sleeves, eh? The nervous ailments, the
disrespect from everyone. So I went into business. I also converted to Christianity, you know. *Ja*, I'm no longer a Jew. *Adieu,
vie de* shtetl!"

"He had to," said Grätel. "If we were to get married. They're
like that where I come from. And now he's a churchgoing
Lutheran, *nicht wahr, schatz?*"

Steel beneath the porcelain. Helmuth chuckled as his
wife leaned over and pinched his cheek in a proprietary and,
Stefanie thought, patronizing fashion: Poor Helmuth! But there
he was, the happy victim. And he looked well, still bony and
loose-limbed but distinctively silver around the temples, with
Habsburgian whiskers shaved an inch short of the jaw. The three
of them drank a couple of *Kapuziners* and enjoyed a slice of
guglhupf and talked of the world and its ways. When talk turned
to politics, Helmuth dismissed the stark anti-Semitism of the
Nazis, as the NaSos were coming to be called, and that of their
Austrian cohorts as mere posturing long familiar to Germans
and Austrians, Austrians especially, going back to the days of
Mayor Karl Lueger.

"They'll change when they get power, just like Lueger. He
talked, but he never hurt anybody. This Hitler will be the same.

You'll see."

"I hope you're right," said Stefanie. "I think it's possible, from what I know of him, which is considerable. Actually, you met him once, Helmuth. Do you remember?"

Helmuth put on a good show of squeezing the memory from his wrinkled brow and twenty years.

"At the opera, yes, of course. The little man in the suit. That was before the war, wasn't it? 1913 or so?"

"1912."

"My goodness," said Grätel. She held her coffee cup halfway to her lips. "You know *Hitler*, Fräulein von Rothenberg?"

"Oh *ja*," said Stefanie, savoring the moment. "Old friends."

Of course, Stefanie had not seen him since her visit to Landsberg in 1924; he had not written, nor had he summoned her to address any more party meetings after her brief disastrous appearance in Munich, since when her misgivings vis-à-vis Nazism had only deepened. In any case, spiritual anguish kept her away from political life. In politics even at the best of times there was a meretriciousness and moral grubbiness that repelled her. In Nazism, it was clear, malice was coming to dominate moderation. The socialist wing was weakening. Adolf was beginning to trumpet the nationalist call to the hordes.

"Our fatherland, free and pure," he roared at a rally in Augsburg in April 1932, "our old Germany, rid of Jewry and the Church, cleansed of Freemasons, gypsies, socially unproductive elements, and Bolshevism. Out with the foreigner! Out with the masonic Jew Bolshevik! Our old Germany, proud and pure, born again under our flag."

Surely it was mere politicking, Stefanie thought. "Rid of Jewry *and the church*"! It was horrible, what he was saying. She considered writing him, then decided against. He probably would not answer a letter from her, he was becoming too prominent. He'd hardly remember her; anyway, what was she hoping for? He was on his way into another, greater arena, where *her* opinions wouldn't matter. No conversion there. He'd always been his own man, an artist first and foremost, and he was now a kind of a master artist, a manipulator of destinies, a performer on a vast stage; but an artist, still, and beyond her grasp, or God's. On the day after the Augsburg rally, however, Hitler issued a public statement of regret, addressed to the Archbishop of Munich "and all my fellow Catholics of pure German origin" (no apology for promising to rid Germany of Jews, accordingly); and a few days later, in the ironic way of life's happenings, quite unsolicited, he got in touch with Stefanie. Ernst was standing in the hallway one morning when she returned from fruitless job hunting. He bustled, and there was a light in his old eyes.

"Steffi," he said. "My goodness. You had a telephone call from Munich. This number." He handed over a scrap of notepaper. "From Herr Hitler's office in the Brown House. I believe I actually spoke to him. Such a strong accent he has, *ja?*"

"Are you sure?"

Stefanie dialed the number and navigated the powerful currents of secretaries, receptionists, and other haughty underlings before she heard his voice announcing his name in a hoarse mumble. She imagined a large office with blinds drawn and a solitary desk in one corner. He sounded half asleep.

"Hitler."

"Hallo, Herr Hitler! Here is Stefanie von Rothenberg."

He *had* been half asleep—he rarely rose before eleven, and it was barely that now—but his mood lifted when he heard the voice of she who was, in his mellower dreams, sister, mother, and lover to him. Her spirits sank when she remembered the long road behind, the steep climb ahead. Thus did they seem fated ever to play counterpoint to each other's moods. But that moment, in April 1932, was one of Adolf Hitler's rare moments of vulnerability, and one of the last he ever allowed himself to expose to an outsider; at that moment, at the crossroads of his life, with a sordid affair behind him in the most sordid way possible, and the limitless fearful future ahead, he needed to confide, to unburden himself, to be reassured. (And the Communists seemed to be taking away votes from the Nazis again, especially in Red Berlin and its suburbs.) Normally he would have turned to his half niece Geli, or Geli's mother, his sister Angela; but young (but by no means innocent, oh no, coarsened by men

long before he'd met her) Geli had killed herself for love of him
(so *he* said), and his native arrogance ruled out an apology to her
mother, who would come around soon enough, anyway: People
needed him, but he needed only The People. And yet, just this
once, in the stark loneliness of days and nights spent in fitful
sleep and brooding, in the chill hallways of Party Headquarters,
in the little universe of his mind; *this once*, he needed a companion, a confidant, a caresser, a woman to make him laugh and
remind him of his greatness.

He chose Stefanie. She understood. She had always loved
him, he was sure. She would be at his side when others made
excuses. She was the seer, the confidante, the one who saw
God or what (or whom-) ever it was she saw; like him, she was
accountable to no one for what made her different. He'd been
disappointed, of course, by her (to all accounts) foolish speech
in Munich, and Hess had recommended against asking her to
any more party functions, saying (in his humorless way) that she
was too sincere, too ladylike, too Christian, apologizing for the
Jews, for God's sake. Well, needless to say Adolf had agreed they
couldn't have that, but all that had happened seven years ago, she
was a lady after all, things had changed, she was older now, and
entirely (as far as he could ascertain) respectable, except for that
left-wing Frenchman she was living with; somewhat permanently
at loose ends, though, as if unappreciated by the world for talents
none shared—and how he could understand that!

Had she heard his news? He was, he said, at somewhat low
ebb personally.

"Your niece?"

"Half. Yes. And they accuse me of murdering her."

"That's politics, Adolf. You need to have a thick hide."

"She calls him Adolf!" whispered Ernst to Ignace as the two
of them huddled behind the door and eavesdropped indiscreetly,
Ernst struggling in vain to mute the sinus clearings that afflicted
him at moments of excitement. "*Hûûûûm!*"

Her husband (Hitler said, disingenuously) in Paris had given
him this number, her uncle and aunt's . . . *not* her husband?

"Well, well. Who, then?"

"A friend."

He offered no comment. She was still naive enough to think the omission might be from discretion. In fact, it was from indifference. But he feigned concern well enough when she said—in response to a banal question about Vienna—that the Baroness Ottoheinz was dead. Her aunt and uncle, he exclaimed. He remembered them: fine people, *ja*? Ah, so the Baroness was dead? So sorry. Nevertheless. He wanted to call, to talk. To invite her to visit him.

"An invitation?" she repeated. "To Munich?"

No. Not far from her dear old home town of Salzburg! *Ja*, he had, he explained, recently purchased a fine property on the Obersalzberg, near the resort town of Berchtesgaden, some thirty kilometers from Salzburg, on top of the world, clean vistas, no crowds . . . didn't she read the papers? Not even the Austrian rags? Well, anyway, he was having some guests—the Hesses, the Goerings, the von Ribbentrops—over for a weekend to inaugurate the new house, the Haus Wachenfeld, and its annex, the Kuhlstein house—oh, that was what he'd, somewhat fancifully, named the teahouse on the Kuhl rock . . . would she like to . . . ? She would have her own room, with a splendid view of the Obersalzberg—and, by the way, she was the only one he had telephoned personally!

"Just like in the old days, *ja*?" he said, attempting a laugh. Stefanie laughed dutifully, not catching the reference until she remembered his hoarse stammering voice over her Aunt Marie's telephone line in Linz, those many years ago. She was, once again, surprised by his ability to recall the seemingly insignificant, but she understood that recognizing the difference between what others saw as insignificant and what was *truly* so was the gift of the master strategist; and her scrawny artist from Linz was showing signs of being just that, wasn't he? She wondered why he'd called, although she sensed his loneliness and that avid desire she'd felt in him before, a desire for closeness, praise, companionship. Reluctantly, she felt grateful. Now might be the moment, she thought, to influence him: like him, she felt the other's weakness. Perhaps he wasn't lost to God, after all.

"How do I get there?" she inquired.

"Ach, for you it's easy. Just go to Salzburg and turn left!"

Arrangements were made, tickets and brochures mailed, a map enclosed. Many of the brochures bore the sign of the swastika, sign of the times, wheel of life, wheel of death-to-come; but Germany was still under the creaking yoke of the Weimar Republic, Hitler still a politician-in-waiting.

Stefanie made preparations. She gave thought to her appearance, a rare event. At forty-two she was full of figure, the von Rothenbergs being a stocky breed, but she was scarcely fuller than she had been ten years earlier, and by no means fat. Her introspective, melancholic character deprived her, much of the time, of an appetite, or any settled routine. Occasionally she drank a little too much, usually white wine, frequently Riesling. In the evenings, like so many of her kind, she smoked. Digestive problems plagued her from time to time, the consequence of a temperament unsuited to normality. But overall she was fit and looked less than her age.

"How do I look, Uncle Ernst?"

Old Ernst was proud. He was proud of Ignace, too, who was accompanying his mother as far as Salzburg, where he would spend a day or two with his grandmother. At the Westbahnhof Ernst and Ignace shook hands, and Ernst watched the train pull out. Through the puffs of steam he saw the blue sky above Vienna, and in that sea-sky the swallows swooped and sailed like fragile vessels tossed by the wind.

Gustave
Eight

AT AROUND SIX o'clock on Saturday night I sat at my usual table in the Lyrique, awaiting Martine's arrival within the half hour. Yes, she'd finally responded to my five or six recorded messages ("Allo, Martine, this is Gustave, give me a call at 337-7797"; "Allo, Martine, this is Gustave, give me a call at 337-7797;" "Allo, Martine," etc.); no, she hadn't been avoiding me. Swearing she'd never look at a Pakistani again as long as she lived, her mother had returned abruptly from Karachi after walking out on Omar or Abdul after the umpteenth beating and/or attempt at group sodomy. The first thing she did, said Martine, was change into jeans and T-shirt, drink two cold Cardinals, and smoke a Gitane. That night they both went to a singles bar in Carouge and sixty-two-year-old Maman snuggled up to a half dozen guys and refused to leave until Martine threatened to clock her on the noggin with an umbrella if she didn't get into a taxi.

"So things are a bit topsy-turvy at the moment," said Martine. "Poor *Maman*, she needs me around. It's not over yet. They've relations here, her husband's lot. Geneva's full of Pakistanis, as you know. So we have to be careful. But I'll get a bit of relief Saturday. She's going away for a few days. I can meet you then."

Hence, Saturday night at the Lyrique. It would make a change for me to dine with a lady instead of with Gax, and it would benefit those old gossips of waiters to see me with one for a change. Meanwhile, over a Lismore single malt (one of the lesser-known but better Speyside whiskies) and a Caporal, I paged through Father Benedetto Sanzio's surprisingly (or perhaps not) un-dog-eared copy of the *Concise Catholic Almanac.*

"Read through this," he'd said at the conclusion of our interview. "You are traveling in a strange land, so it would benefit you to learn the dialect of the natives, as it were."

"So, do you think I'm *pazzo*, Father?"

"Oh, undoubtedly. The question is, to what degree."

"And Sister Stefanie?"

"Oh, yes. Nutty as a fruitcake. But most people who make a difference one way or another—most *interesting* people—are, to a certain extent. You know," he rose and escorted me the short distance to the door, "it's most instructive that you are reading this book as a result of your experiences. It calls to mind what the great psychologist Jung said about synchronicity. One thing happens here, another, unrelated thing happens over there, and suddenly a third thing happens as a result of these seemingly unconnected events and there is an unexpected confluence in someone's life . . . eh?"

"Indeed. I am familiar with the works of Jung, Father."

"So. Here is a synchronous series of incidents. First you have the vision, then you find the book, then you meet the author. *Addio, professore.* We will talk again soon and then I will tell you of my meeting with the Sister Stefanie you are reading about. But I don't want to spoil your reading, ah? *Ciao.*"

I took my leave of Father Benedetto with warmth in my heart. I liked the old priest's matter-of-factness, his Italian skepticism, his deep seriousness concerning my visions. Many had had them, he said, including half the population of his native town in Liguria; only the priests never seemed to. Of course, these days it was attributed to bad diet, or stupidity, or sex, or something such as a physical ailment of the blood (or urine); but, he assured me, "you are by no means alone." Well, yes, I mused later in the Lyrique as I flipped through the pages of the almanac, but in whose company was I? John Calvin's? Fools and cretins? (And wasn't *cretin* just another word for *Christian*?) Or inspired otherworlders like Stefanie von Rothenberg? Or just Porphyriacs Anonymous?

The old pope smiled shyly at me from the frontispiece of the *Concise Catholic Almanac*, assuring me in easy prose that I had in my hands the genuine, Vatican-approved summation of all facts relating to the history of Holy Mother Church and Her progenitor the Christ and His family and all the massed angels and saints and *their* families and friends. Eagerly, I turned to the entry for my old mate the Archangel: an entire section. There were colorplates of him floating about in blue and gold and wielding the blade in various fields of conflict; and of course the Castel Sant'Angelo gig was depicted, himself sheathing his sword and silhouetted against a stormy sky with Pope Gregory gazing up at him, slack-jawed. (I wondered if Michael spoke demotic Greek, or the Latin of the barracks, to rough-and-ready Gregorius.)

> *St. Michael* [said *The Concise Catholic*] *is one of the principal angels; his name was the war-cry of the good angels in the battle fought in heaven against the enemy and his followers. Four times his name is recorded in Scripture.*

I was flattered to be visited by so distinguished a personage.

> *In Daniel 12, the Angel speaking of the end of the world and the Antichrist says: "At that time shall Michael rise up, the great prince, who standeth for the children of thy people."*

Children of thy people: sounds Jewish to me. Not that I have anything against, etc., of course not; what am I, a Nazi? But where is the relevance of this phenomenon to a Swiss-Italian agnostic of part-Scottish descent?

> *In the Catholic Epistle of St. Jude: "When Michael the Archangel, disputing with the devil, contended about the body of Moses," etc. St. Jude alludes to an ancient Jewish tradition of a dispute between Michael and Satan over the body of Moses, an account of which is also found in the apocryphal book on the assumption of Moses (Origen, "De principiis", III, 2, 2). St. Michael concealed the tomb of Moses; Satan,*

*however, by disclosing it, tried to seduce the Jewish people
into hero-worship. St. Michael also guards the body of Eve,
according to the "Revelation of Moses."*

And our man went toe-to-toe with Old Nick himself. No
wonder the face he'd pulled for me was so chilling: *it was from
the life.* Warning or entertainment, as the gods besport themselves with men? Perhaps both. And in a sense, didn't it mean
that, like Stefanie, I'd seen the Evil One too (although she had
two to contend with, didn't she) . . . ?

*Apocalypse 12:7, "And there was a great battle in heaven,
Michael and his angels fought with the dragon." St. John
speaks of the great conflict at the end of time, which reflects
also the battle in heaven at the beginning of time. According
to the Fathers there is often question of St. Michael in
Scripture where his name is not mentioned.*

Well now, here was the action sequence, no doubt about it.
Certainly, I was impressed by his credentials.

*They say he was the cherub who stood at the gate of par-
adise, "to keep the way of the tree of life" (Genesis 3:24),
the angel through whom God published the Decalogue to
his chosen people, the angel who stood in the way against
Balaam (Numbers 22:22 ff.), the angel who routed the army
of Sennacherib (IV Kings 19:35).*

Feeling faintly faint, I accepted a freshening of my Lismore
at the gently trembling hands of old Alphonse.
"How are you this evening, *Monsieur le professeur*?"
"Well. I'm meeting a lady, Alphonse."
"Why?"
"Because she's *sympathique*. I like her."
"Ha!" He directed an age-moistened gaze at me and shook
his head—or maybe it was Parkinson's. "At your age, I'd learned
to control myself," he remarked, and shuffled away. But surely

he was married and had six or more children? I wondered, wondering then if that mightn't be precisely the point . . . ah, well. So then, back to the Archangel. He was, as I discovered, just about everywhere at all times, and Everyman to all men (even atheists?):

VENERATION

It would have been natural to St. Michael, the champion of the Jewish people [Well, where were you at Auschwitz, then, *mon brave*, I wondered . . .] *to be the champion also of Christians, giving victory in war to his clients. The early Christians, however, gave to St. Michael the care of their sick. Tradition relates that St. Michael in the earliest ages caused a medicinal spring to spout at Chairotopa near Colossae (Greece), where all the sick who bathed there, invoking the Blessed Trinity and St. Michael, were cured. The pagans directed a stream against the sanctuary of St. Michael to destroy it, but the archangel split the rock by lightning to give a new bed to the stream, and sanctified forever the waters which came from the gorge. The Greeks claim that this apparition took place about the middle of the first century and celebrate a feast in commemoration of it on November 12* (Analecta Bolland., *VIII, 285–328*).

Blah blah blah. I skipped ahead.

At Constantinople likewise, St. Michael was the great heavenly physician. His principal sanctuary, the Michaelion, was at Sosthenion, some fifty miles south of Constantinople; there the archangel is said to have appeared to the Emperor Constantine. The sick slept in this church at night to wait for a manifestation of St. Michael; his feast was kept there June 9. Another famous church was within the walls of the city, at the thermal baths of the Emperor Arcadius; there the feast of the archangel was celebrated November 8.

I reflected that it had been November 8 when I saw him for the second time. It was an annoying fact, because it should have been a mere coincidence but didn't feel like one. Worse, it should have been insignificant but wasn't. Of course, I could say the same about my induction into the Pantheon of the Mystics generally. And the Greek apparition date, November 12, was the coming Friday. Beware! I thought again of Marley's ghost.

> *The Christians of Egypt placed their life-giving river, the Nile, under the protection of St. Michael; they adopted the Greek feast and kept it November 12; on the twelfth of every month they celebrate a special commemoration of the archangel, but June 12, when the river commences to rise, they keep as a holiday of obligation the feast of St. Michael "for the rising of the Nile."*
>
> *At Rome also the part of heavenly physician was given to St. Michael. According to an (apocryphal?) legend of the tenth century he appeared over the Moles Hadriani (Castel di S. Angelo) in 550, during the procession which St. Gregory held against the pestilence, putting an end to the plague.*
>
> *Well known is the apparition of St. Michael (a. 494 or 530–40), as related in the Roman Breviary, 8 May, at his renowned sanctuary on Monte Gargano, where his original glory as patron in war was restored to him. To his intercession the Lombards attributed their victory over the Neapolitans, 8 May, 663. In commemoration of this victory the church of Sipontum instituted a special feast in honour of the archangel, on 8 May, which has spread over the entire Latin Church and is now called (since the time of Pius V) "Apparitio S. Michaelis," although it originally did not commemorate the apparition, but the victory.*

I underlined November 12, May 8, and June 12 with a light pencil, intending to later write them in my agenda and reminding myself to be especially wary on those dates.

In Germany, after its evangelization, St. Michael replaced for
the Christians the pagan god Wotan, to whom many moun-
tains were sacred, hence the numerous mountain chapels of
St. Michael all over Germany . . .

This surprised me. Michael was really Wotan (*"Loge, hör!"*)?
The archangel Odin!? The Saint of Walhalla . . . ? Then the honor
was double!

Sensing a presence—no, let me put it this way . . .

A shadow fell across the table. I looked up.

"Well!" I exclaimed. Martine Jeanrenaud was standing there.
Her mouth ripe with a restrained smile, she was looking awfully
attractive, her eyes blue and bright behind her owlish eyeglasses,
and red-cheeked from the boreal bise that swirls across the empty
spaces of our city in the colder months. Her maroon overcoat
went perfectly with her disheveled auburn hair . . . now, I don't
usually notice these things, being a firm believer in the old adage
"if you like the clothes outside, you don't like the woman inside,"
but she had a fine sartorial touch, and her clothes were graduated
just so, in varying shades of red: dark, then darker. It accorded
perfectly with her satiny skin, her auburn hair. A promising sign,
I thought. It implied a sense of order, a respect for the aesthetic
basis of civilization, for the necessity of keeping chaos at bay.

Or perhaps I was reading too much into too little, as was
my wont.

"Hello, Professor," she said.

"Mademoiselle Jeanrenaud!"

I looked at her with something of that mild discomfort mixed
with incredulity one feels on seeing in the flesh the object of one's
recent dreams—as if she might suspect my guilty secret (or share
it). Of course, through another fogged-over lens I was also, with
intimations of awe, seeing the author of *Adoration*, fictionalizing
biographer of Fräulein von Rothenberg, in whom I could not but
help detect elements of her creator—in such paragraphs as *Her*
introspective, melancholic character deprived her, much of the time,
of an appetite, or any settled routine. Occasionally she drank a little
too much, usually white wine, frequently Riesling. In the evenings,

like so many of her kind, she smoked. Digestive problems plagued her from time to time, the consequence of a temperament unsuited to normality. But overall she was fit and looked less than her age.

Overall, she was fit and looked less than her age. I ordered Riesling; we smoked. Was hers a temperament unsuited to normality, I inquired? Fortunately, she didn't reply with the standard modernist trope "Whatever *normality* means"; instead, she studied the menu and answered me, her eyes scanning the *plats régionaux*:

"You *have* been reading my book, haven't you, Professor?"

"Please. Call me Gustave."

She looked up.

"Yes, yes. Of course I will, my dear Gustave." (My dear!) "I just like the word *professor*. And you do so look like one." She was flirting; had she, then, wasted some time in idle thoughts of . . . *me*? Delightedly, I prepared to respond in kind, then I saw that she saw what I was reading, and thought, no doubt, that the cat was out of the bag . . . well, it was all her fault, in a way, wasn't it? I no longer thought it would be fatal to advertise my visions. I'd made up my mind that if this relationship had any future it would be on the basis of candor. I could hardly conceal or deny my visions of the Archangel. So it was time, I reckoned, to make a clean breast of things. Yes, I'd had visions, and that was that. If she couldn't take it, she couldn't take me, *et voilà tout*. But I didn't really feel so cavalier about it; I was rather counting on anyone who'd written a copious book about the life of Stefanie von Rothenberg having a bit of a soft spot for visionaries.

Alphonse interposed himself to serve the Riesling and to write down our respective orders: *poulet de Bresse* for her, *magret de canard* for me—with a side dish of carrots. It was blustery outside, warm inside. I was seated at my favorite table in my favorite café in my favorite city with . . . well, my favorite woman. Things could be worse. For the moment I put aside thoughts of mysticism and visionaries and we chatted of this and that. My classes? Well, well. The usual, you know. The halt leading the blind. Her job? Stressful, as always. Deadlines, deadlines. There was talk of sending her to Rome to cover the Christmas blessing by the pope. Ah, Rome! Yes, a fine city. She would take the train, she thought; she wasn't keen on flying. Had I heard? A plane from Russia had made an emergency landing at Cointrin that very morning: Thank goodness no one was injured! Russian planes, eh? And the traffic had been awful on the highway from the airport. Of course, there had also been a demonstration in front of the UN, something about banks in East Africa, tying up traffic even more. And the weather! Colder by the day; sometimes, it seemed, by the hour. Ah, yes: well, it would soon be winter. Cigarette? Oh no thanks I'm smoking too much again, I really must, etc.

Truly, the contentment was extreme. My cup ran over. I toasted the moment. The moment reached its climax. Martine, with idle curiosity, picked up the *Almanac*. I heaved a deep private sigh. Confession was at hand.

"*The Concise Catholic*! Are you religious?"

"No. I mean, not really. Although an old priest of my acquaintance made a good case for staying in the Church, which he calls the one thing that prevents a man from the degrading servitude of being a child of his own time."

"Ha ha! Very good. I did a documentary once on rebel priests, mostly in Latin America. I enjoyed the trip, but frankly I wasn't impressed with the priests. A bunch of self-promoters and womanizers. Anyway, I think I'm very much a child of my time, for good and bad. Are you thinking of converting, then?"

"No, no. No need for that, even if I were. I was baptized into the Catholic Church, and of course I wouldn't consider any other. Good Italian, you see."

"Of course. And I, Genevese of good Protestant mountain stock, am Reformed Church on both sides. My two uncles are both pastors: one in Neuchatel, the other in Delémont. My father, the mountain-climber, was a committed materialist, and as for my mother . . . but, speaking of her!" She put aside the book, animated by other thoughts. "You remember I told you about her dreadful marriage and her return from Pakistan and all that? Yes? Well, the other night after I spoke to you I received an anonymous phone call—or rather, she did, but she handed the phone to me right away and told me to say she wasn't there."

"Who made this anonymous call?" I inquired foolishly, then, hastily: "I mean, a man? A woman? A . . . ?"

"It sounded like a very young man or a boy, with a high-pitched voice and a strong Middle Eastern accent. First he asked to speak to Madame Suleiman, that's my mother's married name. I said, of course, she's not here. I didn't offer to take a message, because there was something in his voice, you know. And sure enough, right away he became extraordinarily abusive."

She frowned at the memory. Alphonse swooped down with dinner. After tucking in for a while (she ate heartily, unaffectedly), we resumed.

"Now, tell me. In what way did this crackpot abuse you over the telephone?"

"He yelled at me. 'You'"—she put on a mock-Arabic accent and wagged a forefinger—"'you are another whore like her! If we need to we will come and kill both of you! Tell her she belongs in her husband's home in Pakistan and if she does not come back we will come for her!' Then he screamed, 'Allah yew haw lala Allah hew ha la de dah willy willy willy lalah,' or some such gibberish, and rang off. *Charmant, n'est-ce pas?*"

Well, naturally, I became quite agitated.

"This is serious. Did you call the police?"

She waved an elegant, dismissive hand. Police? Of course not. Police meant upheaval, lights flashing, muddy boots, neighbors peering out of their doors, the long nose of inquiry sniffing everywhere. No, no police.

"Well, really, Martine. I mean. When a woman is threatened by a screeching lunatic over the phone, it's no small matter. You must call the police. Immediately, please."

"There's no need to lecture me, professor! It's not that I'm not taking it seriously, you know. Mother's going to Paris for a few days to stay with Laure, my sister."

"But . . . does this mean you'll be alone in your apartment?"

She popped the last morsel of her *poulet de Bresse* into her mouth and, smilingly, chewed.

"Well, that depends where else I might find accommodation,"

she said, and the winsome glance she shot me could have only one meaning.

"Might I suggest a humble scholar's garret on the picturesque Boulevard des Philosophes, with the city's best collection of Italian opera records and an unparalleled view of the Chemistry Faculty over the rooftops?" I blurted, with bold verbosity.

"Hmmm. It sounds irresistible."

I was flooded with a hot and cold fever of anticipation as delicious as dinner, but it was followed immediately by near panic as I made a mental inventory of my flat (I was, after all, a bachelor of lifelong standing, unaccustomed to ladies, or indeed anyone, visiting): the singlet draped over the radiator; the stack of half-read books on the coffee table; the pajamas hanging on the kitchen door, the ashtray in the study piled high (well, there was no need to go into the study); the bed maladroitly made (but made, at least, after a fashion) . . . I excused myself and cooled down amid the tiles and plashing of the gents', where I took my glucose pill and gazed at myself in the mirror, marveling at the chance that had led this far, and mentally damned myself to hell if I failed to take full advantage of it.

And yet I had still not told her the tale of Gustave and the Archangel. Perhaps it wasn't quite the moment.

Alphonse bowed as we left. I reciprocated, with irony. Martine and I walked briskly down the nearly deserted Boulevard du Théâtre. The bise roamed the streets, bullying pedestrians into corners, alongside walls, or inside. Dead leaves and scraps of discarded newspapers and wrappers rose, flapped, and fell, with the slow spasmodic movements of deep-sea creatures. Ragged cloud-shards striated the black moonlit sky from which howled the cold pure wind. My heart swelled with a strange exhilaration I hadn't felt since youth. I felt like Berlioz, or Casanova, or Garibaldi at Naples, or one of those travelers in meditative poses from Caspar Friedrich's wondrous wanderworld. It was October, season of ghosts and memories of the hopes of Octobers long gone. At the corner of Place Neuve we stopped and shivered theatrically and looked across the square at the beckoning trees in the Parc des Bastions, their swaying come-hither sporadically illuminated by the bluish light of the streetlamps. In their shadows phantoms lurked. I told the tale of one: The Lamenting Widow, never seen, sometimes heard, plaintively sobbing, whispering words unspoken since the seventeenth century, mourning her husband killed by halberd-toting Savoyards.

"Have you ever heard her?"

"Once I thought so. And I was quite sober. It was after midnight, one New Year's. But it could have been the wind."

"And you were sober? At New Year's? Pull the other one, professor."

Martine slid a warm gloved hand under my arm. We headed south across the vast emptiness of the Place Neuve. General Dufour and his mount continued their time-frozen prance atop their pedestal. The mansions on the centuries-old escarpment of the Rue des Granges haughtily drew up their skirts and turned their gray backs on us. A tram slid smoothly by on its gleaming rails. Several cars raced by in single file, like ducks seeking shelter. There was a shout from party-bound students near the Music Conservatory. Shadows flickered under the Doric portico of the Rath Museum. A man paced back and forth in front of the Grand Théâtre, glancing at his wristwatch. The wind lifted my sparse hair into a feeble crown. Martine's grip tightened. When we came to a crosswalk and waited for a clanging tram to pass, I turned and took her full female warmth in my arms and kissed her with all the ardor in my bottled-up soul. Our eyeglasses collided, with a plastic crunch.

"*Merde*," I said. She laughed softly and took her glasses off and we resumed. A young man's craziness surged through my veins. Suddenly it seemed a dreadfully long way back to my apartment, but the cold windy square was no place for ardor . . . and I discreetly draw a curtain over what followed.

Suffice it to say that, as the poet has it, that night we were not divided.

Berchtesgaden 1932

The road to Haus Wachenfeld led into the clouds. It looked like the summit of the world. Hess turned, with a sour expression on his face.

"Are you all right, *Frau*?"

"*Sehr gut, Herr Hess*. Lead on."

Hess resented being the packhorse, that was obvious, but Stefanie felt no pity for him. He was a saturnine, sullen man, entirely devoted to his leader in an unhealthy, village-idiot kind of way. Halfway up he paused to catch his breath. All around them the mists swirled, lifting here and there to reveal rock, a patch of dark green meadow, a peak as sharp as a stalagmite. The chilly air smelled of pine, and in the distance cowbells clinked.

Stefanie was surprised to learn that the fading beauty waiting for them at the top of the path was Frau Hess. She would have found it hard to imagine how a Frau Hess could compete with the prime object of Hess's desire, namely, his Führer.

"Frau Lebel?"

"*Ja*. Also Fräulein von Rothenberg."

"A fine German name," said Hess, no doubt implying contrast to the French-sounding married name.

"It's Austrian, in fact," said Stefanie. "From just over there," and she pointed east, toward the Salzburg highway along which that morning she had traveled in a Mercedes saloon that had been waiting for her at Salzburg station. The driver, a cheerful red-faced man named Kohler, had willingly dropped Ignace off at the Getreidegasse ("Birthplace of our own dear Mozart, *nicht wahr*?"), where the boy's grandmother was waiting. Startled, the elder Frau von Rothenberg saw the automobile and her daughter next to the driver, and in that moment she fully savored the alienation of parent from child that comes about by mere virtue of the years passing: *Can that woman of the world be my own little schatz?* A few minutes later, as they were speeding through Salzburg's sparse suburbs toward the Bavarian border, Stefanie caught the echo of her mother's sentiment, as it were, on the wind; and she shivered, as if that wind were a wintry one.

She shivered again on the Obersalzberg.

"My goodness! It's cold," she said to Herr und Frau Hess. "I've been away for too long. Vienna feels like the Riviera compared to this." Frau Hess smiled wanly, uninterested in Vienna, the Riviera, Stefanie, or indeed anything at all, except possibly her husband, who deposited Stefanie's bag and unceremoniously, but with evident relief, hailed an acquaintance in the parking lot and took himself off, mumbling an apology. Stefanie looked around. A bus labored up the narrow mountain road, its engine echoing off the walls. Two or three uniformed figures were standing at the foot of a broad stone staircase that led up to the main compound: the SA, Ernst Röhm's Brownshirts. Stefanie felt their eyes on her, even at that distance.

"The Führer is expecting you?" inquired Frau Hess in the desultory manner of one seeking confirmation of a weather forecast.

"Well, I hope he is," said Stefanie. "He invited me here." She felt unaccountably superior to this woman, perhaps for her all-too-evident subservience to a man who was himself little more, as Stefanie had noted, than a cipher.

Frau Hess nodded and smiled nervously, then bustled off after her husband, glancing over her shoulder. Somewhat annoyed, Stefanie followed her gaze. The SA had scared away Frau Hess, it seemed. At least, one of its members had, the one approaching with a desultory swagger. He was young, beefy, and blond: the new ideal.

"Allow me, *meine Frau*," he said, snatching up Stefanie's bag disdainfully. "This way, please."

A funicular railway ran up the side of the mountain atop which sprawled the Haus Wachenfeld compound, renamed (according to a construction billboard) *The Berghof.* The composite main chalet was still a work-in-progress. Scaffolding encased one end, and bulldozers and cement mixers stood about amid patches of mud and marl. Construction workers, not strapping Aryans but swarthy foreigners—Croats or Slovaks—were getting off the bus. Somewhere, dogs barked. A security patrol strode by, giving Stefanie the once-over. The SA man motioned for her to precede him into the funicular. He stepped inside and pulled a lever. A bell clanged and the doors shut with a hydraulic sigh. Stefanie and the young thug were the only passengers. As the car jolted and shuddered slowly up the mountainside, she became uncomfortably aware that her companion was scrutinizing her. As if to admire the view on the other side of the car, she turned suddenly and caught his gaze, cold and lubricious, like that of a Saturday night teenager with too much to drink; and like such a teenager he was leaning against the wall, arms folded, feet crossed, the very incarnation of the untamed juvenile.

"Do you live here, *junge*?" she asked.

Languidly, he transferred his gaze upward until their eyes met; it was the slow insolence of a stupid man endowed with authority. Stefanie stiffened in annoyance. Was she not, after all, to be treated with respect, even as their Führer's guest?

"Nah," he said. "I'm from Mannheim. They sent me up here to help with the security."

"You know that I'm a guest of Herr Hitler," blurted Stefanie. She was certain that she was betraying her nervousness, but it hardly mattered: She was furious. Impudent young lout!

"Ah *ja*, but we're all his guests here, *Frau*." It sounded as if the boy were talking of God: the unnamed *His*.

The cable car jerked to a halt. "Here we are. Watch your step."

Stefanie had to endure the boy's company all the way up another, more manorial, flight of stairs. When they got to the entrance of the Berghof itself, he deposited her bag with a curt nod.

"You will be assigned your quarters shortly," he said, and went off to join a small group of other Brownshirts standing around talking in undertones, heads bowed, their demeanour modest, quite un-Brownshirtlike. Stefanie was surprised at such discreet behavior on the part of men she had read about in the press as being permanent brawlers and troublemakers. Then, noticing an equally subdued group of regular army officers standing a little way off, she followed with her eye the strands that led to the heart of the invisible, yet almost palpable, power-web from which this daunting influence emanated. Standing just inside the doorway, wearing a gun belt, black shirt, swastika armband, and jackboots, was the Spider-King himself, their Führer, Stefanie's one-time portrait painter, would-be ruler of the universe. Hitler had developed a martial way of standing, a militant pose she assumed was in some way associated with manliness and leadership, the right hand tucked into his waistband, the left on his hip, one foot jauntily in front of the other. Next to him, mimicking this pose, was a portly man with slicked-back hair and an expression of wilful joviality made sinister by his piercing blue eyes, wearing a Brownshirt uniform heavy with medals and shoulder straps and tapering into knee-high boots polished to a high gloss: This was Goering, the air ace, commander of the SA. Stefanie remembered him from photographs and newspaper articles. A romance—him landing a Fokker biplane on the lawn of his wife's estate—followed by a tragic death, his wife's—some debilitating disease—came to mind with the sugary pang of cinematic emotion. So this was Goering. He was an important man, and looked it, and what's more, judging by his stance, he knew it, too.

Various other bystanders, in uniform and out, milled about, talking in undertones. The whole scene was so staged that Stefanie looked around half expecting to see a photographer or film crew but seeing only the reverential upturned faces of soldiers and Brownshirts. Hitler and Goering continued chatting, Goering doing all the laughing, Hitler with the rabbit-toothed grin on his face Stefanie remembered so well from Linz and Vienna, the grin he grinned when he was well into an anecdote, or caustic castigation of his enemies. She stared, briefly lost in her memories of the bizarre and mysterious journey that had brought the man from where she'd first known him to this literal and figurative pinnacle of his existence. She felt a faint half swooning go through her, and hoped it heralded no visions. She wanted crystal clear concentration, she wanted to talk, to instruct, to influence . . . *She*, influence *him*! The moment the thought crossed her mind a smothered laugh followed. Just as incredible as Adolf's ascent, she thought, berating herself, was her exaggerated sense of her own importance, her grandiose notions of mission and God. Still, you couldn't expect her to totally disregard the importance of her visions—not so much the visions themselves *but the mere fact of her having had them at all* (although this line was perhaps a little too Jungian for her

liking); still, precious few had ever had visions unaided by artificial stimulants, least of all members of the blasé bourgeoisie,
so if she was a little vain because of it, well, the *progenitor* (or
progeni*trix*) of those visions would soon settle that (but not, she
hoped, for good), she had no doubt . . .

"Fräulein von Rothenberg?"

The Summons had come. A valet took her carryall and led
the way up the stairs. Hitler looked down at her from the top
step, hands clasped in front of his crotch (she suddenly, briefly,
remembered the Vienna Opera, 1912, Adolf meeting Helmuth,
the same gesture . . .). She curtsied, awkwardly, with a hint of
deference, but by this time he was beaming broadly and extending his hands in welcome.

"My dearest Fräulein von Rothenberg. Welcome, welcome.
Welcome to Haus Wachenfeld. Or should I say, the Berghof on
Obersalzberg."

He bowed over her hand and clicked his heels, creating an
audible impression among the murmuring onlookers; a flash-
bulb did, in fact, go off, and Goering lost no time in following
his leader (amazing *how much* The Leader he already seemed to
be, mere provincial politician that he still was) and muttered
nonsensical expressions of greeting, taking her hand in both of
his, presenting her with a brief view of his pomaded head on
which each hair was visibly distinct from its fellows, all combed
ruthlessly back.

"Ever so delighted to make your acquaintance, Fräulein von
Rothenberg, the Führer speaks very highly of you."

"That's enough, Goering, you'll embarrass the poor woman!"

Hitler's easy high spirits were new to Stefanie. They came,
no doubt, with the position, the stature, the adulation, the
long-fought-for acknowledgment of his importance. "This way,
dear lady." He hurried with stiff jackbooted steps up another
short flight of stairs and stood aside for her to enter. As she
did so, slightly dazed, she imagined she heard from somewhere
the exquisite rising note of the horn in the Prelude to Act I
of *Parsifal*, the sublime music of an apotheosis, as if her own
bodily assumption were at hand, the Life Eternal, Nazi cherubim

frolicking in the castle-clouds of Heaven, a clear beam of light shining down upon the earth from the domain of the gods in which *he* now dwelled . . . operatically, he took her hand, and, bowing again, led her through the ornately Bavarian vestibule with its stags' antlers and rustic motifs, past a tall window through which she caught a glimpse of mist flitting through valleys of near-Amazonian green, across a vast seafloor of Tirolean tiles, up two more carpeted steps and into the main foyer at the opposite end of which stood two oaken double doors. Hitler gently let go of her hand, opened the doors, and stood aside like a conjuror eager to display an effect. Beyond the doors was a sitting room as vast as the promenade deck of an ocean liner, with red leather armchairs interspersed with coffee tables, newspaper racks, and canapé trays. Gilded paintings (Stefanie recognized Bismarck and Frederick the Great enframed on either side of a Titian nude) hung on the pale larchwood walls, and a bust of Wagner stood out prominently on a side table, but the dominant feature of the room—indeed, of the whole house—was the gigantic picture window which took up the best part of the north wall from the floor to the ceiling, that ceiling being very nearly as high as the house itself. Half of Bavaria and the entire Salzkammergut lay at their feet. Hundreds of meters below, sprinkled like dice on a tablecloth, were the huddled houses of Berchtesgaden, and a giant's-leap away, across the mist-shrouded valley, soared the peaks of the Chiemgauer; farther south, the summits of the Wetterstein and the Karwendel range lofted into misty oblivion. All of these mountains she, as a Salzburger, recognized, and she named them, pointing. Hitler followed her pointing finger with slight interest.

"*Ja?* H'm! I never knew these names," he said. "I only knew the Zugspitze from geography class back in Leonding. We had a dreadful teacher, a Jew named Stein. And, speaking of the Zugspitze, you know it's the highest peak in Germany, of course, but do you know exactly how high it is, my dear Fräulein von Rothenberg?"

She did, but forbore.

"Two thousand nine hundred and sixty two meters," he said,

beaming, as if he'd built every meter himself. "*Ja.*"

She knew not what to say. He was still smiling, hands behind his back, looking out the window. It was the moment, if there was to be one, to mention God, charity, Christian forgiveness, the greatness of a Christian Germany. Stefanie desperately cast about for a cue: Easter? The mountains, domains of the gods? The Führer, like Moses, on a mountaintop? The vanity of human wishes? She cleared her throat and turned towards him with the bright expression of an ingénue.

"It's . . ."

But it was too late. He turned away. They were joined by the entourage, and the rest of the morning progressed snail-slowly amid suffocating pomp and bourgeois convention carried to an absurd degree. In a room adjoining the ship's-promenade sitting room were two great dining tables, one round, like King Arthur's, the other long and rectangular, like a picnic table. Promptly at twelve, Hitler and his guests proceeded to take luncheon in the lustiest Viennese tradition, with rich helpings of gravied noodles, braised cabbage, *guglhupfen, gateaux à la crème, Linzertorten mit schlagobers*, and assorted *petits fours*. The lords of the party sat on either side of their master at the round table; the assorted uniformed guests and their spouses sat at the picnic table. Stefanie was positioned among the elect, next to a Herr und Frau Rosenberg (Jewish? she wondered, doubtfully), diagonally across from Hitler. Conversation was generally low-key, with a great deal of personal reminiscing from their host along the lines of My Years in Vienna; My Enemies, Jews One and All ("The Jews are definitely a race," he thundered, "but they are not human," eliciting uncertain titters): The New Art; My Talents as an Artist; German Women; Cars; Dogs; etc. Occasional thunderclaps of laughter erupted from Goering. Two liveried valets were on hand to serve, supervised by a worn-looking woman in her early forties with a face that hinted to Stefanie of familiarity, although she'd never seen the woman before—then, at a quick rabbit-grin, Stefanie caught the resemblance and realized the woman was Adolf's sister Angela, mother of the recently deceased Geli. Adolf treated his sister in an offhand fashion that was fully as Austrian as the pastries. Most of the guests—Stefanie; Goering; the Hesses; the Rosenbergs; Herr von Ribbentrop, a former salesman of *Sekt* wine, "I'm convinced our German wines are quite as good as French champagne"—drank, in huge quantities, coffee and tea; but Adolf, she noticed, drank first milk, then elderberry juice, and ate a *guglhupf* and three large helpings of *Linzer torte* with dollops of *Schlag*. After tea, the guests rose and mingled, genially dismissed by Hitler, who stayed seated, probing his teeth with a toothpick, and conferred with Hess and Herr Rosenberg, whose job was apparently to convey news of this or that political development: The party was doing unexpectedly well in the by-elections in Oberöstwanger *gau* in Thuringia, but the Reds were ahead in Berlin-Kreuzberg; the Duce had just received the French Prime Minister, M. Herriot, in the *Quirinale* in Rome; a donation of ten thousand Reichsmarks had been received in the Party coffers from a certain Herr Krapf, a Bremerhaven industrialist (this enlivened Hitler more than all the other news together: "Give him honorary membership and a signed copy of the book—oh, and a guaranteed place at my table in Berlin, but make sure he understands the rules"); a lady in Schleswig-Holstein had bequeathed the National Socialist Party her estate, including a vineyard and three Horch touring cars ("Horch! A fine German automobile, if not quite as prestigious as Mercedes-Benz; but what would I do with a winery? Ribbentrop! This is your problem!"); the city council of Lörrach in Baden-Württemberg were inviting Herr Hitler to address them, on the occasion of the city's six hundredth anniversary; Hitler's rival for the Presidency, Feldmarschall von Hindenburg, had a cold but was going ahead with an appearance in Hamburg; *und so weiter . . .*

"You know, I remember him when he hadn't two gröschen for a sandwich. I believe you do, too." The words were Goering's. He had materialized from the ether to stand beside Stefanie. As abruptly as he had spoken, he produced a gunmetal cigarette case. "I believe you smoke, Frau von Rothenberg?"

"Well, yes, actually. But I have my own, thanks . . . "

"Allow me to insist. But not in here. He's a wonderful host

in most things, but he can't stand people smoking around him, especially women. Yes, I know, it's very old-fashioned, but I daresay your father was like that, too. I know mine was. No, we have to go out there, discreetly, if we want to smoke. *Discrètement, Madame*," he added, with a smile, proud of his French and the implied knowledge of her link to that culture. He pointed to the terrace that extended the length of the house; again, Stefanie was put in mind of an ocean liner sailing through the clouds . . . she followed Goering's confident bulk through a silently sliding glass door onto the terrace and took the cigarette he was insistently proffering. A man in a black overcoat looked sharply around when they stepped onto the terrace but walked away in response to a curt nod from Goering, who then produced a brass cigarette lighter and lit their cigarettes, inhaling extravagantly.

"Ah, my first today," he said. "Trying to cut back, you know. I was up to forty a day, and Turkish, if you please. I'm down to about ten now, and I aim to keep it at that. Brrr! Are you warm enough?"

Stefanie folded her arms and shifted her weight from one foot to the other.

"It's quite bracing," she said, not entirely sure what she was doing alone on a windy terrace with the gross yet charming ex-commander of the Richthofen Squadron and, if rumor had it right, somewhat self-indulgent fancier of women and *gourmandise* . . .

"Beautiful, isn't it?" The comment was strictly *pro forma*; with a painfully obvious lack of interest, he waved a desultory hand at the mountains, the tattered clouds, the green meadows.

"Oh, it is," she said. "It is. Of course, I've known these mountains since childhood, you know."

"Of course. You're a Salzburger. But your home is now in Paris, *ja*?" His face, folded into smiles, suddenly unfolded like an awning, and he gave Stefanie a stern, sharp stare that made her look nervously away; then, annoyed at herself, she forced herself to return his gaze, which was now clouded over with thought.

"I'm sure you are aware, Fräulein von Rothenberg, that the party is building its influence here and abroad. We intend to be ready to assume power when the moment comes, as it will very soon, perhaps later this year . . . and it is of capital importance to us to have friends—collaborators—compatriots—sympathizers, call them what you will" ("Spies," thought Stefanie, "might be apt") "in strategic places. Like for instance, London. Moscow. Or Paris." Goering blinked through the smoke. "And of course you live in Paris, don't you?

"Most of the time, yes."

"And I understand your, shall we say, gentleman friend is a member of the Radical Party?"

"I beg your pardon?"

Of course, of course, he cooed, soothingly. Yes, they knew all about Sami—or should he say *Schmuel Schoen*? Mind you, he didn't give a damn one way or the other, and as for Jews, quite frankly (and this was between him and her and the fencepost) he could take 'em or leave 'em, his feelings were quite neutral on the subject, not like some people's . . . anyway, his fiancée, an actress, had plenty of Jewish friends who were always coming around to the house . . . yes, Stefanie's cooperation would be very helpful, and moreover it would be an investment, he explained, smoothly deploying the argument to confront her predictable, if muted, indignation (she was shocked by the sudden intrusiveness, the unexpected laying bare of her private life, like dirty fingerprints on fresh linen). An investment in the future, he added. The National Socialist Party was coming to power sooner rather than later, that was certain, she had to see that. When they did, they would remember who had helped them, and those who *had* would reap huge benefits, and not merely financial (although there was that). The world was changing, Fräulein. The new world would be Germany's, and Germany would be theirs.

"And after Germany . . . ?"

"Ach, one war in a generation is enough! No, no, our people are peaceful enough. We only want the best for the Fatherland. We want the respect of our neighbors, especially France. But we need partners, collaborators, representatives. Agents of influence, I believe the Bolsheviks call them. Also, we can afford—because of recent generous endowments—to pay quite handsomely. I understand you are," the creases returned, heralding a smile that, Stefanie saw, was quite automatic, "currently unemployed? And your son, is he well?"

"My goodness, Herr Goering, what you are saying is quite simply that you know everything about me, is that it?"

"Hardly *everything*. I have no idea, for example, what your amorous or cultural tastes are—except that you have, on occasion, attended the opera performances of Wagner. However, I do know that you claim to have seen visions of the Virgin Mary, or is it Jesus Christ? And now that I have met you, I am satisfied that you are not the raving lunatic I half suspected you might be. Others, however, might think you were, if they learned of your visions *outside the frame*, so to say. You know what people are like. I can imagine that sort of thing not going down at all well with employers, colleagues, publishers, and so on, don't you agree? Sad but true, eh?" How suavely Herr Goering made his threats! With what panache, style, and dash, and the kindliest sense of fellow feeling! He drew deeply on his diminishing cigarette and looked down at Stefanie with an almost benign expression. "Please remember that you have in the past offered your services to us, and that the Führer has a very high opinion of you—and let me add that this is not the case with very many people, especially women. You are an old acquaintance from the Führer's past, and you earned a place of honor when you visited him in his prison cell at Landsberg. You are, so to say, one of us, and we are the future of Germany, of Europe. Your spirituality has a place with us. We are keen on reviving some of the old ways—combining this and that, you know, all of Germany's spiritual traditions! Having a visionary such as yourself to run the program might be just the thing. After all, this is a moment unlike any in history, Frau von Rothenberg."

"You forget one thing, Herr Goering. I am an Austrian and your party is German."

"Ha! Austrian, German? Is there a difference?" He strolled over to the balustrade and placed one jackbooted foot on the bottom rail. Looking down, he sent his cigarette end spiraling wildly into oblivion. "There's one for the goats," he said, chuckling, then swung around, arms folded, and gave Stefanie the frankest of open stares. "When you go to Munich, does it seem foreign? Augsburg, Bayreuth, my own hometown of Nürnberg? When I am in Salzburg, Graz, Linz, Vienna, I am in my own country, actually far more so than when I am in Rostock, or Danzig, or even Berlin. Blood is blood, Fräulein von Rothenberg. Austria and Germany are one, will be one, mark my words, one forever. This Dollfuss, the Austrian Republic . . . " he snapped his fingers, crisply, with a bloody insouciance that would have quite chilled Stefanie had she not already been chilled to the bone by the high mountain air and the man's sinister charm. She shivered. He tut-tutted solicitously and rubbed his hands; like Hitler, he noticed everything, especially weakness. Again, the smile.

"Yes, even I am beginning to feel it, and I have more natural defenses than you!"

They returned to the turgid warmth of the chalet. The briefing session was over. Goering, heartily hailed, hailed heartily back and disappeared toward the front door. Stefanie, as in a daze, accepted more tea, but more urgently wanted a drink. She looked around for someone to whisper this to, but there were no friends among the invited. Only Hitler, standing next to the picture windows, was looking her way, smiling, and he would scarcely be sympathetic to her need for a bracer. He beckoned to her. Simultaneously, Hess and another man, both of whom had been standing at Hitler's side, sidled away like scolded dogs.

"What do you think of my house?" inquired their Führer as she approached.

"It's magnificent," she said.

"Ah, you remember the man I once was," he said, clasping his hands behind his back. "More than anyone else, except for my own family, of course. Do you realize what a unique position that places you in, my dear Stefanie?"

"*Ja*, well, I suppose . . . " *My dear Stefanie*? Not since Linz, and not even then . . . ! As for her, she avoided all modes of address, not knowing whether a simple "mein Herr" would suffice, but she was most reluctant to call him "Führer," as his toadies did, and "Adolf," in the circumstances, much less "Adi," seemed quite unsuitable, and there was something suffocatingly bland and officious about "mein Herr" or "Herr Hitler." Formality's demands would have to be met with no more than the distinction between *du* and *sie*.

"You know," she said, "Herr Goering said something similar to me, just now."

"Did he," said Hitler, not seeming terribly interested in what Goering had said. "That Goering, *ja*? Listen to me now, Fräulein Stefanie. Come," and he led the way over to a pair of heavy armchairs. He sat, so she followed suit, but made sure not to sprawl as a man would into the chair's plushness; instead, she perched, à la secretary or adoring mistress, on the edge of the seat, and gazed at him as he, without compunction, sank manfully and luxuriantly into the chair's depths. Such an odd mixture, she thought; such a sybarite at heart, but such a jittery, fastidious, nervous man on the surface, so supernaturally aware of the thoughts and desires of others, like a quivering antenna'ed insect . . . They were, she noticed, being left alone. No valets or maidservants were near. Only Hess, at the far end of the great chamber, hovered, but out of earshot.

"I am not married, nor do I intend to be," announced Hitler, his eyes fixed on the Chiemgauer range through the window. "I recall your asking me that when you came to see me at Landsberg—I never told you how important that visit was to me, did I, no, of course, not . . . well, it cemented our friendship. It was a bright light in the darkness of my years in the wilderness, which are, by the way, finally coming to an end, believe me. I know it, I feel it." He clenched his fists close to his breast, then slowly relaxed. "And if I've not been in touch, well, you understand. For one thing, you were married to that Frenchman!" His gaze drifted downward and alighted on her. "No longer except in the eyes of the law, *nicht wahr*? But there you are, living with this other Frenchman," he waved a deprecatory hand, "in Paris, possibly in a leaky garret, like some Mimi and Rodolfo couple, *nein*? Ach, it's fine for students and romantic painters and poets. But not for Fräulein Stefanie von Rothenberg of Salzburg! Her country needs her. *I* need her." Now the appeal was followed by the probing stare, the election-poster Hitler touting for votes, the Corporal versus the Field-Marshall.

"But I tried, I failed, it was a disaster. They shouted me down."

"The meeting in Haidhausen, *ja*? You're right, it was a disaster, and not because of you. I blamed others for that." He glared at the distant Hess. "But I'm not talking about that. You're a spiritualist, a visionary, in your own way a leader like me, but not a politician, or a people's tribune like Rienzi. Of course, I should have realized that. But to come to the point. I would be very pleased if you would accept my offer of companionship."

"I'm sorry?"

"Ah, I thought I was being sufficiently clear without having to be specific."

A certain mincing coyness in the drift of the conversation, an awkwardness Stefanie recognized as old-fashioned Austrian petit-bourgeois code for "Please let's get it over with as quickly as possible" (she was Austrian, she'd read her Schnitzler), pointed unavoidably to . . .

"You mean?"

She sank abruptly into the chair, aghast. The leader of the National Socialist German Workers' Party and putative future President of the Republic leaned forward to get a clear view of her from around the wings of the armchair, peering at her anxiously and pressing his fingertips together.

"Of course, I am speaking in terms of a semi-permanent arrangement, with your freedom of movement largely intact. And by the way this is quite separate from whatever Goering may have been talking about. Whatever that was, you must discuss with him, *ja*?"

Once or twice before she had trembled in Adolf Hitler's proximity, but not from desire, or not desire alone, but more from of a combination of the desire she'd perhaps once felt, many years ago, and her own struggle against the natural yielding of the weaker to the stronger—and the visions had followed such moments, *not visions of the Virgin*, she reminded herself, *but of the devil himself*, and both times in Adolf Hitler's company; easy to dismiss then, in the parlor of her aunt's and uncle's house, or in that Monchskeller in Linz (for why would the devil appear to nonentities?), but now that Adolf was on the mountaintop, the Guide and Leader, the next great shepherd of the Teutonic flock . . .

Or perhaps not. A provincial he was and a provincial he would remain. And how far did provincials get, in a world of silk-hatted globetrotters?

(Sallow, slick-haired, fidgety, odd-scented, with the staring eyes of an insomniac, and the ravenous dog-hunger beneath it all.)

But what better means could she find to influence the man, who was now on the brink of eternally placing himself beyond her or anyone's influence . . . ?

"I am honored," blurted Stefanie, dishonored.

"And I," he barked with laughter, "am honored that you are honored! Many women would have been insulted. My goodness, I was nervous, I can tell you!"

"But I cannot let you know yet."

"Why not? You've seen the house, you know me. Ach, woman's eternal shilly-shallying. A man's not like that. A man, he decides, he makes up his mind, so!" He clapped his hands, once. Stefanie recalled the male ditherers she had known—her father, her uncle, her husband, her cousin—and recognized Adolf Hitler's definition of manhood as something pure and artificial, the manhood aspired to by the man unsure of his own, the power complex of the sexually indigent (of course, there had been Geli). Perhaps his need of her fell into the same category. She was known, she was easy. It was a comfortable flirtation for him. And why not? Had they not strolled the streets of Linz together arm-in-arm, a quarter century past? Was he not the same awkward, impassioned artist she'd half loved then? Was she not the same insecure, eternally questing, half-mad daughter of God?

Boldly, she said:

"I must remind you that my faith comes first."

He waved a hand.

"*Ja, ja*, faith, faith. I had it too, once. Please don't forget that I was an altar boy at Lambach Monastery. *Ja*, and what I wanted most was to be a priest. Did you know that?"

"Yes, you . . . "

"And I admired the abbot, a fine man, he had the right combination of knowledge and power, ah, you should have seen the way he ruled those monks, you know I think it was the first time I had ever seen authority dispensed in so effective a fashion, it predisposed me to good opinions of the Church," and so he continued, picking up stray thoughts along the way as a broom picks up dust, weaving the half-baked thoughts of *Mein Kampf* into the cast-off nighttime ravings of Gobineau, Liebenfels and Nietzsche; in short, the purpose of their conversation was soon lost in a flood of speculation, contempt, reminiscence, and criticism. Stefanie, still perching on the edge of her chair, watched fascinated as, quite oblivious to her, he lectured the empty air, his eyes, blinking rapidly, fixed on a point directly in front of him, his hands shaping arguments, counter-arguments, the pillars of the Church, the two sides of the debates, his own inevitable victory, bells, hats, cats, and the devil himself . . .

(Who was standing on the terrace outside, watching them with eyes the size of dinner plates and the *rictus sardonicus* of a dead man, but they saw him not, for they had eyes only for themselves.)

Andante

And so Stefanie von Rothenberg became, for a brief time, Adolf Hitler's mistress, in the wake of Geli, and in between, as it were, Mimi and Eva. He was distant but considerate, at least in the early days. Materially, she lacked for nothing. She could at last afford to send money home, to her mutti thirty kilometers away and to her baby boy Ignace back in Vienna. In the autumn, she told him, she hoped to enroll him at the Académie Werfel in Paris. To Sami she sent only regrets. He replied coldly, citing Pascal's wager.

Sexually, Adolf Hitler was hasty, unimaginative, and—as in so many things—entirely a petit-bourgeois Austrian, with that class's penchant for enemas, heavy underwear, and darkness. He indulged in some rather odd foreplay, involving much staring, heavy breathing, and sudden movements, but Stefanie lived through the entire experience as in a trance. She felt the weight of penance, made heavier by the tiny thrill of being *his* woman, her Adi, not the Führer of the National Socialists: Her Linz and Braunau artist, her awkward suitor, bohemian paramour. Hitler reciprocated at first, gruffly, clumsily, then slowly returned to the utter inwardness that was his normal state. He slept in his own room on the first floor; she, above the garage, adjacent to the room occasionally used by Johann Kohler, the number-two chauffeur, a genial duffer she chose mostly to ignore. Kohler seemed not to notice, and continued to greet her heartily, and with some deference, as she fulfilled the demands of her routine. They were few. She arose in the morning and breakfasted, then read, wrote, and drifted through the great ocean-liner rooms attended by the reticent Angela or one of her assistants. On the terrace when Hitler wasn't around she stole a smoke. In the afternoons she took the bus down to Berchtesgaden, or went walking through the woods. In the evenings she dined, and occasionally joined the others in watching one of the inane American films Hitler prized, and read, and prayed, but her prayers went unheard: She knew it, she could feel the hostile silence from Heaven. Guiltily, she redoubled her efforts to speak to Hitler of her faith, but he was hardly ever at home, and Hess relished keeping her at arm's length.

"*Nein*, Frau von Rothenburg," he would say hoarsely, knitting his single brow-width eyebrow, "not today, not tomorrow, and probably not for the rest of the week. Go for a walk, read a good book. May I recommend *Mein Kampf?*"

Through the presidential election of 1932, lost by Hitler but not by much, and into the autumn campaign during which, it seemed, the Nazis' support plunged, Stefanie stayed at the Berghof, invisible to the public ("no one must see you, no, no, they must think I live for Germany and Germany alone"), tormented by her adoration of God on one hand and the magnetism of her truculent human demigod on the other.

One rare morning, of perfect blueness above—rare, too, in his presence at the breakfast table (orange juice, fried bread)—emboldened by her menses and a sleepless night, she seized the initiative.

"What you are doing is irreligious," she said. "What you are preaching is sacrilege. What you are planning is horrible."

Like any irritated husband, he put down his paper (*Völkischer Beobachter*) and peered at her quizzically.

"What are you talking about?"

"I have heard you calling for the removal of the Jews. And the others. It is un-Christian. It offends God. And me," she added.

"Un-Christian?" He barked with laughter, then became frowningly solemn, as if mulling it over. "Are you serious?"

"I have had visions, Adi." (The mode of address question had been settled, in private; in public she called him nothing, with respect denoted only via the *Sie*.) "Bad visions. Visions of you. Of terrible things."

"Visions, bah. Who knows what causes them. Feminine problems, no doubt. After all, why is it always women who have these visions? You never hear of some, of some *guy* in a field talking to Jesus Christ . . . "

"There were many men who had visions. John of the Cross, the English poet Blake . . . "

"Ach, now you talk of English poets. Please. I have things on my mind of such weight that you cannot conceive of them. Listen to me, *liebchen*. I follow my life with the precision and security of a sleepwalker. It's all mapped out. So go and have your visions, but leave me out of them, all right?"

In September Sami came from Paris on his way to Munich to meet with Social Democrats. They had tea in Berchtesgaden.

"What can one say?" he exclaimed. "You are the most extraordinary woman, Stefanie. Casually you depart our home to attend your aunt's funeral, and, next thing I know, you are living with Adolf Hitler in the Goddamned Bavarian Alps. And you complain that he doesn't take you seriously! To me!"

"I never know where my life is going, Sami," she said. "But I have faith in my heart, I follow its lead. I heed my heart. That is one thing you must understand."

"Follow the lead, you're not a dog, for goodness' sake." Sami

looked and acted entirely out of place. All around him stout and
rubicund Bavarians crunched on their apple torte and *spätzle*.
Sami's Jewishness stood on the table, it danced the hagana, it
davened, it pleaded to be recognized. But his Frenchness was its
equal, even its superior. Stefanie heard no "*Jude*," but did hear
a muttered "*welsch*," and warned Sami with a glance; but he
ignored her, and raised his voice slightly.

"These Germans," he said, "what will they do next? re-crucify
Christ?" Glared at, he glared back, and quelled the onlookers,
mustache bristling; he, after all, had faced down hecklers in the
Assemblée Nationale, including Herriot and Fauche, and once
had humbled great Poincaré himself. Cavalierly, he summoned
a schnapps, and with it a cigar. The ladies at the next table arose
and stalked out, muttering sentiments that were clearly anti-
French and anti-cigar, and probably anti-male as well. Stefanie
watched them go, dreamily, unfocused, enjoying a moment's
respite from the madness of her life.

Sami chimed in.

"This is lunacy, Steffi, as you must know. Lunacy! Come
home with me. If only for Ignace. Your Hitler is mad. He wants
to get rid of Jews and foreigners, well you've heard him, is that
his pillow talk, too?" With these words Sami made as if to spit.

"You don't know him, Sami. He is like a force of nature. He
will lead this country into a new age, I am convinced of it. He
stands poised between all the good he might do and the evil he
is tempted by."

"Good. Fine." Sami made dismissive gestures. "Let him lead
his fucking country. Let them follow him like the Pied Piper.
This is not your business. This is not even your country, *pour
l'amour de Dieu!*"

And yet Berchtesgaden and the virgin-white Alps were beautiful that autumn day, with just a shiver in the shadowy valleys
of the winter that was coming; the sky hummed with blueness,
a Dornier flew overhead, birds squabbled, and the snowcapped
peaks of the neighboring mountains shone blindingly white.
Limpidly, a church bell chimed down the valley, and the buses
taking the construction crews snarled and growled back and

forth, never stopping in the village.

Swastika flags had blossomed like zinnias, vying for space in the window boxes and in the flowerpots on the quaint wooden balconies.

They walked. Sami shivered.

"Fucking Nazis," he said. "I'm not a praying man, Stefanie, but I'm figuratively on my knees right now before you or God, whichever one does me the courtesy of listening. Please come home."

She was moved. Sami returned to Munich by train from Salzburg, and thence to Paris. Stefanie stayed on at the Berghof, dressing in doll's costume or (and this was her penance) dirndls for her master's pleasure on the rare occasions when he was home, and for her own amusement reading, kite-flying, hiking. Once, not long after Sami had returned to France—leaving in his wake assorted regrets, longings, and nostalgic thoughts—she was on the balcony having a smoke and Hitler, unannounced except by the panting of his Alsatian dog Blondi, joined her. He was wearing a double-breasted suit with a small swastika button in the lapel. He looked like the assistant manager of a packing plant, but the light that burned in his eyes was the light of a crusader, and there was more than an assistant manager's soul reflected in the restless mobility of his face.

"Things are going well. Sometimes it feels as if God Himself were dictating my program to me," he said, with typical grandiloquence. He never said hello, or offered an inquiry after her health; usually he said nothing, or launched directly into a soliloquy. His only social abilities were concealed behind the formalities of the heel-clickings and hand-kissings of bourgeois practice. As in the past, intimacy was a foreign language to him; his mother tongue was bombast. Yet in certain circumstances, as Stefanie had discovered, he could be charm itself. For example, she had never seen an adult who so plainly enjoyed the company of children, with whom he could safely inhabit a sympathetic dream-realm. Ignace, on his two visits, had enticed Hitler to play cowboys and Indians behind the sofas of the grand sitting room for an hour or more each time, and had, since then, spoken fondly of his Onkel "Wolf." Hitler was contradiction; Hitler was mad.

"I am sane. Everyone else is mad. I am the last hope for Germany, and Germany knows it. Wait and see, you just wait and see. The election results are mixed, *ja*. We have the Reds to contend with, especially in Berlin, but there will be ways. Blondi! *Los!*" He tossed a bone. The dog frolicked, well trained. "*Ja*, they all feel it. There is a tremendous desire, a hunger, among the German people. Only I can appease them and take them to the heights of which they dream. Only I can mobilize their hatred for the alien, the Bolshevik, the traitor. The November criminals. The Jew." He gazed at the Jew-free heights spread out before him: already he was the political god, the uncrowned king, the self-anointed savior of a nation. Stefanie stood aside, hoping he wouldn't smell the tobacco smoke on her breath, not wishing to displease her lord and master. The impulse disgusted her, and she saw herself anew, and saw him for the new man he was. Gone forever was the hesitant, awkward Adolf of long ago, Stefanie's Adolf, the earnest artist of Linz and Vienna, the sidling, sideways suitor. Gone, too, was any chance of her influencing him beyond what was on the menu at dinner. Gone, finally, was her own life. Looking down on the tumbling summits of the Bavarian Alps, she felt as if a fever had broken and found herself thinking of the cafés, the side streets, and the trees in the Luxembourg, of Paris, where her life might have continued unimpeded, had it not been for him, his mad magnetism, her own mad impulse. Paris: the Seine, sanity, Ignace, the Académie. Paris: lurching Citroëns, Sami's robust rage. Paris: France, not Germany, not Hitler, not the Nazis. The thought was a momentary relief until it brought in its train, like a clunking goods wagon, the bulky image of Hermann Goering. The jovial air ace had been noticeably less of a presence at the Berghof recently, and word had it that between his fiancee and his recent election to a high position in the Reichstag, he had important business in Berlin. Stefanie hoped his new responsibilities might cause him to forget their conversation, and in any case she decided—on the spur of the moment, on which spur she made all her life-altering decisions—to confront Hitler with talk of departure.

"I want to go back to Paris," she said, on that fifteenth day of December, 1932.

"Go," he said, shrugging. "Go."

She challenged him with a glare.

"Will you miss me?"

Blondi cantered up, gazed at her master, raced after the bone, tongue lolling. Hitler turned slowly and looked at Stefanie.

"Miss you?"

"*Ja*. Miss me."

"I hardly know what you mean, Fräulein von Rothenberg. Your company has given me pleasure enough, but as you know, I don't use such sentimental expressions. I seek in every way to harden myself, to be better prepared for the struggles of life. Hate unites men; love divides."

"*Ja*." Stefanie smiled. "But if Blondi went away, you would miss her, *nein*?"

"Of course. Blondi is my dog."

"And I am—your bitch?"

His face darkened. He frowned. Expressions of great intensity chased each other across his face. Stefanie had never seen a face so mobile, so expressive of the turmoil within.

"I don't understand your anger," he said. "Aren't you happy here?"

She chronicled the desolation: her humiliation; his bedroom games; the intellectual emptiness; the swarming sycophants; the endless talk, politics, politics, politics . . .

"Politics? But of course. Of course! All is politics. Your life, my life, all. Germany awaits us. The last election was not so good, admittedly. But we will assume power. Germany will be transformed. No more thirty-seven political parties. No more of the doddering Jew-financed cowards of Weimar. No more bending the knee to the French. No more decadent art. The world will learn where the repository of true civilization is. I will teach the world. As for the rest of your complaints, they are meaningless. Sex? It's of no consequence. And when you speak of intellectual emptiness, I can only laugh! When was your most recent contribution to our intellectual life?"

The dog returned, the bone was thrown. He had his back to her. She hated him at that moment with a dry, visceral hatred. She thought how much she would love to be with him in an even higher place, the Kuhlstein rock behind the house for example, or the mountain opposite; and, once there, rush at him and push him over the side and rid the world of him forever. She thought crazily that she should do it, that it would be the best thing for her and for the world; and that it would meet with the instant approval of She who watched over her. She briefly remembered the vision she'd had, of him sprawled lifeless . . . was it a premonition? But she did nothing. She suddenly felt weak in the knees, and wanted to go.

Behind his back, after he had thrown the bone, his hands sought each other and clasped in a nervous union. Sadly, she remembered the swishing of his silver-topped cane along the Danube on a July afternoon in 1907.

"Thanks, Adi, for making things so clear."

Leaving the Führer to survey the landscape he coveted for his own, she took the lift down and set about readying her things. Angela offered to help but Stefanie curtly said no, then ran after the woman and held her around the shoulders for a silent moment of understanding. Angela stood stiff, then relaxed and patted Stefanie's shoulder.

"Thank you, Fräulein von Rothenberg."

As Stefanie was locking her suitcase and glancing one last time around her dimly lit room with its dark furniture and heavy drapes adorned with scenes from the *Nibelungenlied*, Johann Kohler appeared in the doorway, twirling a key attached to a swastika-shaped keychain.

"Going my way?"

"I will take the village bus, thanks."

"His orders. I'm to drive you to Salzburg. Please say yes. I haven't been out of the house all day, and it's lovely weather for a drive."

Stefanie saw no reason not to accede to his request, which was, after all, an "order." They departed the house, Kohler with her bags underarm and overshoulder, through the great promenade deck and the baronial entrance hall with its view of plunging valleys far below.

"Not a bad place for a vacation, but as for living, I'll take an apartment in the city any day, thank you very much," said Johann.

Stefanie's last sight of Haus Wachenfeld was of Frau und Herr Hess standing at the top of the stairs. Hess's arms were folded, and he was nodding slightly, as if in confirmation of long-held suspicions. He raised a hand in languid salute. Frau Hess was standing so close to her husband that their shadow fell as one along the wall that bordered the stairs. Stefanie got into the Mercedes roadster without another backward glance.

"Yes, it's a cheerful little place, isn't it?" said Kohler, firing the twelve cylinders of the Benz into life. "Frankly, I've been in stockades that were more fun. At least you could smoke there. Oh, you're well out of it, *meine Frau*. Believe me. Cigarette?"

There was certainly something symbolic in that cigarette, which she accepted; and with the blue smoke wisping out of the car window went, for a short time, images of the past, worries about the future, and all manner of apprehension and fears.

Gustave
Nine

As a man newly confirmed in his love, and one who had every right to believe himself loved in turn, I hardly minded when I received word in my office from Mme. Brunel, M. Petitpoix's secretary, that the not so great man had me on his schedule for an unscheduled (by me) 9:00 meeting on the morning of that Monday following the most memorable week of my recent life. Nor did I especially object, when I arrived in the director's office, to see a strange bullet-headed man in thick glasses and a business suit sitting on the sofa. But when Petitpoix—who was, uncharacteristically, himself wearing a suit, albeit one that looked as if it had come direct from the Flea Market on Plainpalais—introduced his guest as Dr. Martin Dürrenmatt, consultant psychoanalyst, and made it clear that the good doctor's subject at Calvin College would be *me*, I became somewhat tetchy.

"Psychoanalyze?"

"At the college's expense, of course. What I am proposing, Termi," intoned Petitpoix, making a chapel of his fingers and gazing upward, at cobwebs or beyond, "is that you take the three or so weeks remaining in the Christmas term as a paid leave of absence during which we will all of us together try to come to terms with your ah. Condition." He made it sound as if I were expecting a baby. "And reach a mutually agreeable conclusion."

"Meaning, Petitpoix," I suggested, "you want to find out if I'm bonkers or not before you chuck me out, just in case I decide to take you to court."

"No, no, no, my dear professor," interjected Dr. Dürrenmatt in a voice both high-pitched and hoarse. "No one's suggesting anything more drastic than a short medical break and a series of casual conversations with me. Everyone is well acquainted with the widely varied forms that overwork and stress can take. Why, once, after a particularly trying course of teaching at the Zürich Poly, I went around the house saying nothing but '*FIGUGEGL*' for three days! My wife was threatening to call the police by the time I snapped out of it."

"'FIGUGEGL,' eh? Charming, I'm sure. What does it mean?"

"'*Fondue isch guät und git e guäti luunä.*' Zürich dialect for 'fondue is good and puts you in a good mood.' Well, to be quite frank," and here he lapsed into a series of powerful wheezes I interpreted as his version of laughter, "my wife thought I was headed straight for the *Burgerhölzli.*" He smiled blandly. "The loony bin."

How Swiss-German, I thought. How banal. Despite several spells in the army surrounded by Swiss-Totos, as we Genevese call our Swiss-German compatriots, I had never had the slightest interest in learning to speak their fractured patois. High German, *aber jawohl!* The language of Mann, Luther, Goethe, and Kant? *Natürlich!* But *schwyzertütschi?* The dialect of goatherds and barmaids and Zürich busdrivers? *Nay, merci!* as they said in Bern . . .

"So: Nothing formal at all," said the excessively amiable Dr. Dürrenmatt. "We can meet at a café, if you want."

"And if I say no?"

Petitpoix lowered his gaze from the ceiling and tried to level it at me in a menacing fashion, but his eyes flickered, and I realized, with a small feeling of satisfaction, that I made him more nervous than he made me.

"If you say no, of course, we will have to discuss alternatives. But I strongly urge you to agree, for all our sakes."

"How conciliatory of you, Petitpoix. I thought the gossip column in *Le Procope Helvète* was the last straw for you. Now you're giving me another chance?"

He shrugged and said nothing. He didn't need to. For all his lust to give me the sack, he'd come up against reality. This

psychoanalytical caper was only the first act in the entirely predictable drama of easing an employee around the various obsta-
cles our benevolent confederation has placed in the way of an
employer eager to give said employee the heave. But it would
be a long and tortuous process, and I had cards to play, too; in
fact, in Switzerland the government bureaucrats are, theoreti-
cally, entirely on the employee's side, unless gross misconduct or
malfeasance of spectacular dimensions can be established, and
I quote from memory: "assassination planned or actual; regular
embezzlement from the company finances; clandestine filming
of management procedures and/or washrooms; daubing graffiti;
using coarse language in public places"; etc. And I was guilty of
nothing worse than claiming to have seen the Archangel Michael.
In the Age of the Videohead, when the young are raised with,
if not by, rapid-fire, ever-changing, unreal computer images, it
hardly seemed like much of a transgression. (Yet I still hadn't told
Martine, even or especially after the other night when we'd had
so much, and so little, to discuss . . . I still reeled, incidentally,
sitting there in Petitpoix's office, with Dr. Dürrenmatt perching
on the edge of the sofa, as if ready to spring if I made a move—
yes, I still reeled, and in my stomach flowered the thrill of knowing that I loved and was loved . . .)

"Yes, of course, Dr. Dürrenmatt," I said, breezily. "By the way,
I went to a doctor who told me I have a touch of limited-access
porphyria that might be the cause, but that then again might
not be."

He frowned.

"Porphyria? But this is a disease of old people, Asiatics, peasants . . . "

"Quite. So I'd be delighted to have a chat. Which café do
you frequent?"

Petitpoix emitted an audible gasp of pleasure. Dürrenmatt
beamed, etching a surprising network of deep Amazon-delta
wrinkles across his broad *schwyzerdütsch* features.

"Actually, my favorite's the Temple," he said. "In Carouge."

"Good place," I averred. "Good wine list."

Bathing in bonhomie, we agreed to meet there in three days'

time. Petitpoix was so delighted he rose and came round his desk to shake my hand before escorting me out his office door, a dry run for the much-anticipated day when he would escort me out of the building for the last time . . . but the more I thought about it, the less that prospect worried me. I had a solid twenty-four years' service and a reasonable pension plan and a good case for early retirement; I had my books, my poetry, my music, my mamma, my car . . . my woman . . .

. . . my Archangel . . .

So I was only too pleased, that chill, still, gray November day, to abide by the Senate's injunction and take a leave of absence. I stopped at the Café des Philosophes across from my flat and had a coffee and a *boule de Bâle* and a small bowl of steamed carrots in garlic butter and enjoyed the snug warmth and quiet chitchat of the place, where occasionally that old Homer of modern Geneva letters, Marco Baldas, holds court for a worshipful clique of student admirers through a fug of Gauloise smoke and exhalations of threadbare philosophy and cheap *eau de vie*.

Casually, I filleted the papers: *La Tribune, Le Temps, Le Dauphiné*, the latest *Le Procope* . . . and yes, there it was, on page three.

"Follow-up," mewed the rag, "to last week's epic spectacular 'The Professor and the Archangel.' (We received more hits on our Internet site as a result of this article than for anything else we've published since Rabid Taki's outing of the gay Iranian ayatollah in the March 17 issue.) Said mystical prof, now certifiable, waved arms and legs jointly in an access of dementia and bayed like a keeshond in heat and claimed once again to be in the presence of the Archangel Michael, whom by the way no one else could see, before collapsing in front of some twenty students in a lecture theater at one of our venerable local educational institutions which is, even as we speak, exploring ways of putting the old lunatic out to pasture. (Unless this was a ploy on his part to enliven one of his notoriously puerile and insanely boring Alpine Literature classes.) Any openings for part-time Buddhas in the local Chinese eateries would be greatly appreciated. More anon." The article was, like the last one, unsigned. I read on, but the next item was tedious droning about the rights of squatters in the St. Jean district. Fuming, I smoked. There was an irritating familiarity about the style of these Procope pieces, not just the usual sneering of the professional malcontent, but an extra *soupçon* of disdain, that reminded me of the style of a certain writer of my acquaintance . . . although to be fair to him it was a style much prized by modern critics (especially the ones on the way out), who, no doubt as a result of May '68, urban terrorism, the downfall of the family, and Andy Warhol, see their job as one not of elevation but of mockery. And yet! "Max Menninger," Gax had once written in one of his more amiable pieces, "produces big, brown words in the same way that a prize hog produces big, brown shits." Gax was the guru of a whole generation of so-called critics whose ultimate goal has nothing to do with inspiring a love of literature (ha!) but is, rather, to steer their own revolting little persons into as many television studies and beds as possible. "Notoriously puerile and insanely boring": hm. I could almost hear those words hanging in the air. Yes, it sounded like an inside job, these being the kinds of word pairings best uttered in the lofty drawl of unearned juvenile irony. There was a mole in my class. And there was an accomplice outside, and his initials, I greatly feared, might well be G. G.

I crossed the street to my apartment building, narrowly avoiding death from the speeding front end of a Fiat, and climbed the stairs with scarcely a wheeze. In my flat dust floated quietly about and the refrigerator hummed tunelessly to itself. There were no messages on the phone machine, not that I ever got any. Martine was in Interlaken for a "quickie shoot," as they called it, of the opening of the Edelweiss Supreme, a new Chinese-owned but *echt-Schweizerische* resort hotel complete with a hundred waltzing Heidis and strutting alpenhornists. She would be away for another two days. (And when she came home it would be home to her professor. Already I envisaged crisper window curtains, polished parquet floors, a solid queen-sized captain's bed to replace the sway-backed old backbreaker I'd been snoring on for these fifteen years and more.)

I weighed the merits of returning to my half-hearted new

poem (how dated already, those celibate fulminations!) but instead read my e-mail on my sluggish secondhand Bell computer. Amid the exhortations for larger dick size and eternal youth: One anonymous misspelled group posting ribbed me for my visions and alluded to the Procope piece.

"Arch Poseur and His Angels, in *Le Procope* . . . or Are they Demons of Drink?"

The address was Swiss, the pen name Schtroumpf. I contemplated a reply but deleted the message and napped, then made tea and returned to the adventures of S. and A., albeit somewhat reluctantly after the deeply nauseating images of sex with the Führer (Good God, Martine! What were you thinking?), to the unusual life of Frau Lebel, *née* von Rothenberg. (Why didn't she just get an annulment from the wretch and have done with it?)

The Long March Continues

In 1932 Sami had made ill-advised investments in a Bayonne bond-corporation that declared bankruptcy one year later, precipitating financial crisis, the collapse of the government, the disgrace of the Radicals, the supposed suicide of the financier A. Stavisky, and financial disaster for Sami himself. Stung by accusations from right-wing deputies, he resigned his seat in the Assemblée. Rioters pelted his Delahaye with bricks as he drove away from the Palais-Bourbon. François de la Rocque, the Fascist leader, derided him, calling him "Herr Goldenstein." Leaflets bearing the star of David and caricatures of Semitic noses fluttered in his wake.

"Your friends," muttered Sami to Stefanie. "The damned fascists. Everywhere. They say the whole business was our fault. And who killed Stavisky?"

"He killed himself."

"Don't be so sure."

Gaston Doumergue, ex-president, stepped in and spread the balm of his blandness over the roiling political seas. The Third Republic got shakily to its feet, preserved to collapse with finality another day. Sami watched from the sidelines, unshaven,

beset by indigestion and headaches, usually garbed in his dressing gown until late morning, smoking Gauloises and drinking
five-to-eight petits Ricards a day and seated, in clement weather,
on the balcony. On rainy days he dressed and went downstairs
to the Café Gueuze and harangued the barman, a Communist,
on the contemptible corruption of France's Right and Left alike.
Also, Sami those days was an inattentive, even indifferent lover
(and who could blame him?), and every letter or newspaper from
Germany inspired a small diatribe of incomprehension.

"My God, he's the damned Chancellor of the Reich now, isn't
he. Well, why aren't you by his side? Now's the time. Off you
go. Go on, away with you to Berchtesgaden. Who's romping in
his bed now?"

In fact, most letters Stefanie received from Germany came
from Fritzl's wife, Lotte. Although he had had a prosthetic arm
fitted, Fritz was sinking seriously into beer and despair. He had
found a job as assistant shift manager at the Bavarian Motor
Works, quite a comedown for him but a job was a job, it was a
question of self-respect as much as anything else. Of course, there
were all kinds of new restrictions now, with the new government,
and Fritz had run into a bit of trouble because of his Jewish background, which in his usual blockheaded fashion he continued
to deny. This only made matters worse, of course. There were
all kinds of nosy people in uniforms at work these days, and
one or two had even stopped by the house when Lotte was out
and chatted with the boys, tried to find things out behind their
parents' backs . . . it was contemptible. Fritz hadn't lost his job
yet, but she, Lotte, felt that it was only a matter of time. And by
the way, speaking of the new government . . . They had heard
rumors about Cousin Stefanie, but being well-bred did not want
to come right out and ask. Still, there was a great deal of nosing
around, of delicate sniffing at the edges. Was she back in Paris
for good? Did she plan any trips to Germany? Say, to (ahem)
the Alps, near Salzburg?

The combination of deference and indignation in these letters was unique in Stefanie's experience. Finally she sat down
and wrote a reply.

Dear Fritz and Lotte,
How are you? How are the boys? I am well. Ignace has started
his second term at the Académie Werfel, so I can say he is
getting the best of French and German culture.
How kind of you to inquire about me. Yes, I have returned
permanently to Paris. My sojourn in Germany was an
extraordinary interlude in my life. I do not regret it; quite
the contrary. It made clear several things. One, that politics
has no place in my life. Two, that faith in God transcends
all else. Three, that I do not tolerate heights well. Four, that
Adolf Hitler is a great man, but that greatness does not mean
goodness.
Meanwhile, I make a living at my son's school. 'Will you be
my teacher?' he asked me, the day before he started school.
'Only in the upper forms,' I replied. That gives us seven or
eight years!
Although my flat is small, I am sure I could arrange to accom-
modate you if you decide to visit me here in Paris. God bless.
Stay in touch.
Kisses from your loving cousin!
Steffi.

Lotte soon replied. Fritzl, it seemed, had finally been taken
in for questioning by the police after arriving at work drunk
and, in an about-face, loudly proclaiming his Jewish heritage
while insulting his colleagues as "stupid Swabian swine." Lotte
said he'd been knocked about quite a bit, and threatened with
imrpisonment. It was lucky, she said, that it had been the police
and not the Gestapo. However, young Willi and Kurt had again
been interrogated, this time after school at a local *Konditorei*
by the father of one of their schoolmates, a Herr Liebnitz, "a
sallow man who affects a leather trenchcoat," who was either
in the state security police or worked as an informant for that
grim agency. He had bought Willi and Kurt strawberry tarts and
chocolate milk and, after bland commentary on childish things
such as electric trains and carousels, had proceeded to question

them closely on the customs and beliefs of their parents, notably their father; was he a Jew? An observant Jew? Did he have Jewish friends? Did he attend a synagogue? Which one? Herr Liebnitz had promised the boys greater inducements than strawberry tarts, going as far as mentioning uniforms and air guns and rides in the country if they agreed to cooperate by writing him, Herr Liebnitz, weekly "letters" reporting their father's comments, conduct, and movements, especially if they agreed to join the new youth organization called Hitler-Jugend; he would even make efforts to ensure that (in view of Lotte's impeccable Aryanness) their polluted ancestry was overlooked, or reclassified, as was being done in so many areas, some too high to name . . .

Fully as disturbing as the invidious anti-Jewishness and gross interference in privacy was the revelation that both boys had cooperated in the persecution of their own father. It had only been Lotte's discovery of one of Willi's "letters" to Herr Liebnitz that had brought the whole matter to light.

I found the man's address and went to see him, to accost him, to accuse him, to present him with the tokens of his evil. He was at home (he lives in a respectable suburban villa in Au). He himself has two children, girls, as sweet as can be. I was embarrassed with them standing around—I saw no sign of a wife—but obviously he has them trained. He was nauseating, Steffi. This is the kind of man who will thrive under your Hitler. Utterly without morals. Only concerned for his own welfare. I thrust the note under his nose. 'How dare you turn my children into spies?' I said. He feigned ignorance! 'I do not consort with young boys,' he said. 'Are you accusing me of perversion?' All this in front of his daughters, too. I was so sickened I merely stood and stared at him, torn between fury and fear, real fear, because this man is the type of the new man, he has no compunction about destroying lives, he does it as nonchalantly as you or I might squash a bug . . .

The upshot was twofold emigration, the boys being sent to stay with their Grandpa Ernst in Vienna, and Fritzl and

Lotte coming to stay in the already-cozy apartment on the Rue Soufflot. In spite of the cramped quarters Fritzl's arrival had a noticeably cheering effect on Sami's spirits. The two men had found each other congenial during Sami's brief visit to Munich ten years earlier, and although Fritzl was stouter, more florid and louder than ever, and Sami more melancholy and embittered, their friendship matured, via shouts of "You Old Jew" and "You Fat Boche" and several weeping evenings of wine and beer downstairs at the Gueuze. Sami was disgusted by Fritzl's troubles and the sinister tale of Herr Liebnitz, but in a perverse way the whole affair gave him the satisfaction of having been absolutely right about a regime whose advent he, Sami, had long predicted, and he couldn't resist saying so to the former mistress of that regime's progenitor.

"It sounds like the new way in Germany is pretty much the old way of, oh I don't know . . . Vlad Dracul? Eh, Steffi?"

Eventually, after lengthy discussions with Sami and some of his friends in various government ministries, Fritzl and Lotte decided to settle permanently in France. Through contacts in the government Sami got Fritzl residence papers and found him a job as a security guard at the Dewoitine airplane works, despite his two obvious handicaps: the prosthetic arm and his fractured French.

"One real arm is enough," said Sami. "As long as you can salute. As for your French, if you can say '*bonjour*,' '*oui*,' '*non*,' and '*vos papiers*' you're all right."

Sami himself at last, reluctantly, returned to work in early '36, first as a file distribution manager at the Ministry of Agriculture, then as a full-fledged Huissier in the Foreign Ministry on the Quai d'Orsay. Both positions necessitated regular hours and a daily shave. He quite missed his sodden, self-pitying days, but welcomed the chance to wear a clean shirt again.

"There," he said. "I have arrived. Look at me. Another indentured drone in an office, cultivating his hemorrhoids."

Eventually, after lengthy correspondence and shouted telephone conversations had satisfied their parents that the Herr Liebnitz episode was not necessarily a harbinger of the future,

Willi and Kurt arrived from Vienna and moved with their parents into a small semi-detached house in the working-class suburb of Montrouge. In the spring of '36 the boys began attending the Académie Werfel with Ignace, who was wary of them, although they seemed to be the soul of friendliness, eager to learn French, getting high grades on their lessons, joining in other students' soccer games, canoeing on the Seine on Sundays. It was far from an ideal situation, but things had been worse. Fritzl was alive, at least, and drinking less; and Stefanie was satisfied that the family was safe and reasonably content, for the moment.

Her own state of mind was restless and dour, and she awoke every day with a knot in the pit of her stomach, as if in dread of some nameless event. In the early mornings, as the street sweepers swept and the lorries rattled and groaned, she walked the streets of the Latin Quarter. Cafés in which men sat smoking and reading papers over the early morning *verre de blanc* were opening for the day's business. *Clochards*, many of them war veterans, gathered on the steps of St. Sulpice and passed around a bottle. On the boulevards, taxis puttered by, shopkeepers raised their shutters, bookcases were wheeled onto the freshly hosed-down pavement, and everywhere there were smells of roasting coffee, gasoline fumes, and Caporal smoke mingling in the air. On sunny mornings Stefanie would end her morning walk with a stroll around the pond in the Luxembourg Gardens, the so French order and design of which so contradicted the disorder and illogic of everyday life; but the French happily live with the illusion of order. Abstraction rules in a country where theorizing has the weight and illusion of reality, a country where theories have even found themselves translated *into* reality, as in the Luxembourg Gardens, or Versailles, or even the Maginot Line . . . unlike the Germans, who were less cerebral and (like everyone else) resented the French for their cultural confidence and sheer ability to live well under any circumstances. Stefanie brooded much about Germany. A strange addiction bound her to that nation, and her own connection with Hitler, and Fritzl's recent experiences, only bound her tighter. Germany overshadowed the world. The Germans were entering a new Age of Empire that future generations would look back on with amazement and wonder. All Europe would be under their sway. Stefanie's former lover and teenage swain would, like Louis XIV, stamp the age with his name; like Bismarck, he would move boundaries as it suited him; like Charlemagne he would fundamentally change the world he found.

In part of her mind she was a prisoner of Berchtesgaden, subjugated to the power of he who was now a colossus on the stage of the world.

Classes at the academy generally kept her focused on the day-to-day, and Ignace, in the upper forms, was turning into a stalwart young man and outstanding student; but in the evenings and on weekends Stefanie wrote, dwelling inwardly on thoughts she found as incredible as the events that had given rise to them. In the background was the muttering of the great city and, usually, the sound of RTF on the radio. Sami was seldom at home. He played bridge at Fritzl's, or visited "friends" Stefanie suspected of being unattached and female. Her sojourn with Hitler had opened up a chasm between them that would be forever unbridgeable, she feared; under the courteous commonplaces they were indifferent, cold, mutually finding fault. More: she wondered if he hated her.

As for her, she was ashamed, but too proud to admit it.

Blum

But in 1936 Sami and Stefanie came together again, reunited in body and spirit by (as Stefanie said) "of all things," politics: the New Dawn of the socialist-communist alliance and its victory in the May elections and the renewed, if short-lived, hope it inspired, not only among the Reds, many of whom were suspicious of these "boudoir radicals," but also in the ranks of the moderate Left-leaning and the antifascists, among whom Stefanie counted herself. Sami was ecstatic beyond all reason, certainly beyond the straited skepticism that was his usual response to world events.

"At last!" he roared in the Gueuze, the evening the news of

the new government was announced. "*Vive la République! Vive la France! Vive la gauche!* A republic we can live for! Drinks all round! Pastis, please!"

A month later Léon Blum was named Prime Minister. He was an old friend of Sami's. They had been fellow book reviewers for *Le Matin* and (sporadically, on Sami's part) fellow travelers in the Socialist Party Blum had done so much to revive after the murder of the great Jaurès on the eve of the '14–'18 war. Yes, they'd been friends then and were friends now, said Sami, although he conceded to the lesser intellect and the greater disposition to debauchery at the time ("Léon was always at his books, always") but professed equality when it came to literary essays and the like, Blum having stumbled in his judgment, reckoned Sami, at around the time of Proust's first rejection by Gallimard's reader, young André Gide, while he, Sami, had snared the absinthe-bibbing Apollinaire for an interview in *Ces vents qui soufflent*, an interview that was still talked about, in certain (admittedy narrow) circles . . .

"Pah, that's all past."

In any event, the "Blum coup," as the Rightists called it, sent a chill through the ranks of the establishment, which despised all republics, of course, as being of suspect Judeo-Leftist origin (like Blum himself, incarnation of their darkest fears) and preferred the more solemn, hewn-of-granite, racially pure idea of The Nation, with its square pillars, solemn visages, and worship of technology. But for a moment it seemed as if the Right was in retreat. Blum's government started a second revolution.

"Oh, it'll have them shitting their pants, the monarchist bastards," said Sami, gleefully. "Long live Léon!"

"Better Hitler than Blum!" retorted the Right; but in most households, and across all of industrial France, not least (reported Willi and Kurt with the air of savvy correspondents at the front) in the depressed backways and nineteenth-century alleys of industrial Montrouge and adjoining Billancourt. Indeed, a desperate relief was in the air, as if the country had broken a bad fever. Stefanie read the papers with greater pleasure than usual, and even her sullen charges at the Académie

Werfel reacted to the news. Then the strikes began, first at the Breguet works in Le Havre, then across the industrial North. Workers long accustomed to being utterly ignored were now being grudgingly given a voice, and long-pent-up anger spilled over into industrial action, although most of the strikes were so good-natured that the workers more often sang *Auprès de ma blonde* than *The Internationale* (except for the Cusinberche fiasco in Clichy, in which an Arab immigrant was shot dead). Finally, settlements were reached; and joy of joys, the workers' demands were met, paid vacations and a 40-hour workweek were suddenly on the agenda—as well as nationalization of the Bank of France and, rumor had it, votes for women . . .

"*Vive Blum*," said Stefanie. "*Vive Léon*." As if in penance for her past sins, she desperately wanted France's first Jewish leader to succeed. At school she conducted civics classes crisply and unsentimentally, but with a decided bias.

"Blum must prevail," she said one morning.

"But M. Blum, he is a Jew," observed one Manfred Dieselmann, son of the Austrian attaché.

"Yes!" exclaimed others, responding, like dogs to the odor of a cat, to the ambient anti-Semitism of their households and nations.

"Yes," said Stefanie. "But he is a Frenchman first. And we should give credit to his country for upholding the spirit of the Enlightenment."

"*Vive la France*," mumbled the kids.

"But he is still Jewish," muttered Dieselmann, obstinately. "And a Bolshevik."

On a drowsy day in September Sami rushed into Stefanie's classroom, waving his hands briskly at the students.

"Class dismissed," he shouted. "Run along, all of you." Beaming, he seized her by the arm. "Come," he said. She gaped. "To meet Léon," he said. And without further word he had propelled her before him to the street, to a taxi, then across town to the Restaurant Drouand, a large public dining room with high ceilings like a salon, incongruously located on the third floor of an office building behind the Opéra. It was a food- and coffee-redolent room in which floated a dim haze of cigarette smoke barely penetrable by the light of sun or lamp, a room abuzz with the clamor of hearty lunchtime voices, the din of commerce, the newspapers, politics, a room that was the forum and clearing-house for anything alive and kicking and making money in central Paris: art buying, car and horse-trading, haggling, smuggling, prostitution (discreet, of course), commodity trading: all co-existed at the Drouand, cheek-by-jowl with the confits and foie gras and *pichets de rouge* on its *tables d'hôte*.

The Prime Minister of France, officially known as the President of the Council of Ministers, was seated with a young man with a round face made owlish by round spectacles. This was the new Education Minister, Jean Lussac, as Stefanie knew from *Le Matin* of that very morning. They were at a long table covered with notepads and briefing papers, in the corner directly opposite the entrance; a strategic placement, Stefanie thought, and said so to Sami, who ignored her, intent as he was on capturing the Prime Minister's every glance. He strode across the room, hand upheld in salutation.

"*Mon vieux*, or should I say *Monsieur le Président*? Dear old Léon, anyway, arrived at last."

"But where, *mon ami*? On a precipice, I fear. It feels like 1914 all over again, doesn't it? And I am no Clemenceau, I fear. I don't even look like him, as you do. I am an armchair revolutionary leading a revolution in pearl gray gloves, as Daudet said, eh? But how are you, *mon cher*? Would you like a job in my cabinet? No, I should say: Would you like *my* job? Ha ha. You know, this is the first time in about three months I have been able to schedule a lunch meeting. So many things, my dear Samuel. What an age. But we are here to lunch, not to talk politics. And this is Madame . . . ?"

"This is Stefanie von Rothenberg," Sami added to the tail end of many more effusive greetings exchanged with Lussac, whom he had known in the Assemblée as one of his firmer supporters. Stefanie inclined her head.

"*Monsieur le Président*," she said, suddenly painfully aware of her sex, her dubious situation, her accent . . . but with gallant nonchalance Blum rose to his feet. He was tall, slightly stooped, dressed in an elegant charcoal gray suit, his black hair neatly combed over and a heavy mustache half concealing a weary smile. His gaze, behind a pair of thick, round spectacles, was cautious and steady, like a conscientious bank manager's.

"*Enchanté*, Madame!"

Blum settled into his seat and he and Sami conferred, and Jean Lussac uncoiled himself silently and snapped his fingers for a chair—and got one within seconds—and joined in the conference in gruff undertones that was punctuated with great snorts of derision and explosive clouds of blue Caporal smoke. Blum and Lussac at first regarded Stefanie with a combination of indifference and wariness, which she attributed to her sex and her Germanic name; but when the conversation began to cart-wheel uncontrollably out of control—"Ethiopia"; "Mussolini"; "Herriot"; "the nationalizations"; "Daladier"; the "Comité France-Allemagne"; and yes, inevitably, "Hitler"—and she was beginning to feel as out of place as a rose in a mire, Léon Blum leaned forward, signaling silence to his companions by so doing, and smiled, proposing lunchtime delicacies. Stefanie decided on a salad, Sami on a cassoulet and liter of rouge; but Blum proved to have the tastes of an epicure, and recited the menu with expertise.

"*Caille farci aux raisins verts*," he said. "It's my choice. For once in our lives, Sami, let's overdo it."

"Ha! Once in our lives? Speak for yourself. You don't mean a drink, do you? Léon the dry?"

Blum smiled with his eyes, not his lips, although his heavy mustache did seem to twitch at its extremities.

"Not entirely dry, my dear Sami. A good *ballon de rouge* with dinner, generally nothing more. One needs to be alert, these days, if one is to be a truly subtle Talmudist." All present knew he was quoting the Jew-baiting Xavier Vallat in the Assemblée: "We welcome the subtle Talmudist," he had said, upon Blum's ascension. "Exercise, eh? But I leave all that to Jean here, with his holiday colonies and fresh-air Fridays."

"Fridays now," said Lussac, with a half smile. "But every day soon enough, when we get the legislation written. It's not only the fascists who respect physical fitness, you know."

"Ah, so you are an abstainer as well, Jean?" inquired Sami, with a shade of disdain.

"Not at all. Even the contrary. I am from the Loire, where we are raised on the world's best wine."

"Pah! Best? Compared to Burgundy?"

"Oh, but absolutely. Our Bourgueil; our Vouvray . . . "

"An excellent idea," boomed Sami. "One of each, and a Burgundy for purposes of comparison. Waiter!"

"I knew this would happen if I let you order the wine," said Blum, with mock sorrow. "Now my Minister of Education and my future personal private secretary will get into a drinking contest and possibly fisticuffs and the government will be disgraced and go the way of the 101 other governments of the Third Republic."

"Personal private secretary?" echoed Sami. Blum, eyes twinkling, repeated himself, and elaborated: a job for a man of vision, a radical like himself, a man of the Left; but also a confidant, a friend, one worthy of trust. "And I know none better. What say you?"

"I am honored, *Monsieur le Président*. And let me also say: It's a wise decision, *mon ami*. My loyalty will be second to none."

"It's true," blurted Stefanie. "He will be your best." She was pleased for Sami, but more than slightly resentful of the masculine clubbiness that quite firmly kept her at arm's length. The University came to mind: Herr Professor Schnitzel; the jibes; "does your father have a telephone number we can call?" . . .

Blum gave her a nod in acknowledgement.

"*Messieurs?*" The wine steward, deferential, menu bearing, loomed. Sami ordered.

"Good thing I've made a second career out of ordering wine. Not that I ever overdo it, please understand. As for yourself, speaking of overdoing it, I think you already have, *Monsieur le Président*," said Sami, smiling. "With your 40-hour week and paid holidays and collective bargaining *et j'en passe*."

"*Our* 40-hour week, *mon cher*," said Blum. "*Our* 40-hour

week, *our* paid holidays. *Our* collective bargaining. All that is now the property and right of every Frenchman. And woman. This is my pledge. And if I commit errors it will be because of being *not enough* of a leader, not because of being *too much* of one." A propos of women's rights, he courteously turned his attention to Stefanie. Was she, he wondered, German; and if so, acquainted with the works of Goethe? No, she replied; and yes.

"Ah, but you must know Goethe, then," he said, in one breath. Sami leaned forward, eager to interject, like a teenage boy with a hot secret.

"Léon wrote a book about Goethe once," he said. "Brilliant." Blum raised a dismissive hand.

"Brilliant it may have been, but with all the copies unsold I could build a bridge from here to Narbonne. Still, Goethe was, and remains, my great passion. His Faust! His Werther! How sad that the murderous trivialities of a bully boy like Hitler should insult such genius," the Prime Minister said. "Hitler represents the very opposite of culture. But it is necessary for all of us to examine our consciences in the face of such a catastrophe. Especially we French, who have been so, ah," he waved a hand in the air while searching for the word (but kept his steady gaze on Stefanie all the while), "*vengeful* in our demands, post-Versailles. It's crazy, my friends. Crazy."

Sami looked significantly at Stefanie and raised his eyebrows, as in query. She, catching his look, shook her head. No, she would not parade her acquaintanceship with the bullyboy of whom Blum spoke, not for lunchtime entertainment, not for anything (she who had studied men so closely was fairly certain the Prime Minister spoke with earnest spontaneity and not out of any calculation to draw her out on the subject of his nemesis across the Rhine). Would she do it for France? wondered Sami, and then wondered what, exactly, were his lady's feelings for his country; after all, an Austrian, a fellow countrywoman of Hitler's, an ex-mistress . . . he shook his head to dispel this last, this smoke pot that would forever befoul their lives together.

Meanwhile, Blum was talking.

"Actually, I spent some time in Weimar," he said, seeming

to be under the impression that Stefanie was, after all, German. "The town of Goethe's Lotte, of course. I had a rewarding time. I learned some German, at least! *Ein bisschen, ja?* Of course, I knew some Yiddish from my youth." He considered her, gauging her reaction, as a presumptive German, to his bold Jewishness. She smiled pleasantly. He went on: "The people were most welcoming, despite my, shall I say, double burden of nationality and religion? Yes, I must admit I was never confronted there as I have been here in my own country—in a physical sense that is." Both Sami and Stefanie knew he was referring to the previous year's Camelots du Roi incident, when he was pulled from his car and brutally beaten by the extravagantly named Fascist thugs.

"Filthy swine," said Jean Lussac, who had otherwise been smoking slowly and meditatively and jotting items on a notepad.

"Well, we got rid of them, Jean," said Blum. "We legislated them out of existence. Poof! Like that." He snapped his fingers. A waiter hurried over. "No, no, monsieur, thank you very much," said Blum, with elaborate courtesy, seeking to not embarrass the man. "Merely a gesture of emphasis, you know."

"*Monsieur le Président.*" The man retreated at a half bow. A small encounter, thought Stefanie, but deeply illustrative of character. Already she saw the very opposite of Hitler in this Blum, the two countervailing forces on the continent. *Der alte Jude, das ist der mann*, as Bismarck had said of Disraeli. Would Hitler ever say the same of Blum? How ironic, she thought, if the two of them should turn out to be the great force of Europe and its opponent, Blum's Jewishness only adding spice to the irony (a man who had been bar miztvahed, who had attended a shul, who observed the Jahrzeit, all of this grist to the fascists' mill); how could Hitler ignore him? Premier of France, legislative leader of the other great European power, Mussolini notwithstanding . . . ?

But there was a conciliatory softness about Blum and the opposite in Hitler.

"No, Léon. They'll be back, calling themselves political parties," said Lussac. "It's all coming from across the Rhine, these days, anyway, *n'est-ce pas?* Everything bad and obnoxious. The Right is flexing its muscles. We're the last hope." His fist landed softly on a pile of papers. His spectacles flashed blindly in a random sunbeam from the windows. "Maybe for all Europe."

They had lunch, an expansive old-fashioned bourgeois spread with three courses and a bottle per course, followed by the cheese, the brandy, the coffee, the cigarettes, and one cigar (Sami's). Spain came up, and the Rhineland, and the prospect of an alliance with Russia against Germany—Blum's pet project in foreign policy—and again and again the name "Hitler." Stefanie resisted the temptation to say "But I knew him when he was just a," whatever he was, "little shabby painter," and what he'd become, "and I was his mistress for a month," which was a nice way of saying it . . . in any case, she noticed Jean Lussac staring at her.

"What do you think, Madame?"

Flustered, she retreated into the reserve proper to a well-brought-up Austrian girl.

"Oh, I don't have any thoughts on the subject, Monsieur Lussac," she said. "It's all politics." A bark of laughter came from Sami.

"I can hardly credit that, Madame," said Lussac. He was a man who understood seriousness, Stefanie thought. Distress had already found a home in his eyes. "But I respect it."

After the lunch, and the hasty departure of the Prime Minister and his aide amid the salaams and jeers of the crowd outside, Stefanie and Sami took the Métro home and strolled up the Rue Soufflot to the Panthéon in the gray evening light.

"I'm very pleased M. Blum made you that offer, you know," said Stefanie, feeling somehow the need to remind Sami that he mattered, that she cared. "You'll be wonderful."

"Oh, I don't know," he said. Head bowed, frowning, lines of weariness on his face, Sami looked very Jewish, like an aging rabbi from the Auhofstrasse in Vienna. "As long as it lasts, my dear Stefanie. As long as it lasts."

As long as anything lasts, she thought, but said nothing as they stood outside the sepulcher of Voltaire and Rousseau, aliens both, in a way, yet French by adoption, by sympathy, by culture, a culture that had lasted, one way or another, for a thousand years . . .

"God I hope there isn't a war," said Stefanie, who had just felt the first shiver of one.

"Oh there will be," murmured Sami. "There will be. The question is, when? Tomorrow or the day after?"

Brüder Hermann

Walking along the Rue Vaugirard to the Prime Minister's residence one night early in March 1938, on the eve of a crucial debate in the Senate on Blum's plan to reopen the border with Spain ("Steady on, Léon," said Sami, and reported to Stefanie that his old friend, out of power in '37 but now Prime Minister again, had only replied, "Time's running out, *mon cher*; I have business to take care of before the Right kicks me out for good"), on the Rue de Medicis at the corner near the gates of the Luxembourg gardens Sami crossed paths with a group of ex-Croix de Feu agitators on their way to the Palais des Sports for an anti-Blum rally organized by the Camelots du Roi and Action Française and their allied entities. One of the mob, Didier Buecher, a former fellow pastry chef from Strasbourg, recognized Sami and stepped into his path as officiously as a policeman, broadcasting alcohol fumes and belligerence.

"Oy, Shmuel Schoen, Rabbi Blum's poodle," he said. "How many businesses has the Old Yid confiscated today, Monsieur 'Lebel'?"

"Well, well, Buecher," said Sami. "All grown up but still smelling like dogshit on a hot summer's day, God that stink brings back memories."

"Watch it, jewboy."

Circling like jackals, the others started alternating chants of "Better Hitler than Blum," with "Down with Yids," "Blum Blum Ka-Boum," and other witticisms. Sami, as untrained in the fine art of self-control as he was in the arts of self-defense, rushed at Buecher and the pair of them exchanged wild flailing body blows, neither inflicting any real damage on the other until Buecher's comrades heroically piled on top of the despised Jew and gave him, as he later said, "the Gentile baptism of a lifetime."

Summoned by a phone call from Jean Lussac from the bedside of the influenza-afflicted Ignace, whom she had left in the
care of his uncle Fritzl ("give my regards to Sami, now"), Stefanie
spent the taxi journey to the Salpêtrière hospital cursing the vio-
lence and bitterness of the age and calling upon . . . not God,
of course, but the adjunct and comforting holiness of Mary, to
manifest herself, for once, in response to humanity's need for
understanding, if not peace . . . or at least to show the way. Or
at least to show herself to Stefanie, again, and reassure her all
was not lost; but no manifestations occurred in the taxi, which
was, mused Stefanie, probably just as well, in her current state of
mind, with a perky Marseillais driver who insisted on telling her
how tasty the shrimp were at this time of year down in Marseilles
and how he was planning to take advantage of the new two-week
paid vacation—"and all thanks to that Monsieur Bloom, there
are plenty of people who'd shoot him just because but I, I salute
him, he's a man of courage, Madame"—to take out his old fishing boat at Stes. Maries de la Mer and make some real money, as
he said, catching shrimp to sell to the rich foreign visitors farther
along the coast at Juan-les-Pins and Cannes . . .

Stefanie got out of the taxi on the Boulevard de l'Hôpital at
one of the side entrances of the Salpêtrière, that immense campus
of prison-like buildings, between the Gare d'Austerlitz and the
Jardin des Plantes, which turned its back on the world, like a
convent. In one of the hospital's long, gray, dimly lit corridors a
reporter from *Paris-Soir* wearing a hat with his press card tucked
into the rim lunged at Stefanie, camera and notepad at the ready;
but Jean Lussac, looking as gangsterish as the reporter and his ilk
always described him, in his pinstriped suit and Borsalino hat,
was there to intervene.

"Not now, Monsieur from the press. *Allez.*"

"Are you M. Lebel's wife, madame?" insisted the reporter.

"We've said enough to the press," said Lussac. "Take yourself
off now, and give my regards to the readers of *Paris-Soir.*"

"Thank you, Monsieur Lussac," said Stefanie when the
reporter had gone.

"It's the least I could do." Lussac removed his hat. He looked unshaven and underslept, and smelled of cigarettes. "Léon sends his best wishes, of course, but he's in the fight of his life at the Senate tonight, so he couldn't leave. But I know he misses not having your . . . Monsieur Lebel at his side."

A sister told them they could go into the Emergency Ward.

"But be quiet," she whispered. "Poor Monsieur Lebel! Truly, these people will do anything. Happily, he looks much worse than he is. Just be sure not to excite him, overly."

Stefanie wondered, irrelevantly, if the sister knew Sami was Jewish. Lussac immediately expressed the same thought, somewhat cynically, with the harshness of the age in his voice.

"Would she be as concerned, do you think, if she knew she had a *youpin* on her hands?"

"She is a 'good sister,' Monsieur Lussac, and one hopes she has good Christian feelings."

"*Peut-être, Madame*," said Lussac, with a twisted smile, "*Peut-être.*"

In fact, Sami was fairly alert, or as alert as he could be under the circumstances. A glucose drip was attached to his left arm. His lips were swollen and chapped, like those of a burn victim. His left eye was a welter of purple turning black, his right cheek a maze of broken veins overlaid with blackish bruises. Stefanie took hold of his unbandaged hand, but let go when he winced.

"Hello, Steffi. Lussac, is that you? What the devil are you doing here? Get on with you, man, Léon needs you more than I do. God, I wish I weren't stuck here."

"You are right, my friend, but I only wanted to come as a gesture of solidarity, to express my disgust at these fascist mobs. We've all suffered at their hands, and I fear it's only beginning. But you're right: I must go, and I will," said Lussac.

"Yes, Léon's had it," said Sami. "They'll lose the vote tonight, there's no doubt. God, I've had it with this country," he mumbled. "They kicked the shit out of me, you know," he said with some effort to Stefanie. "Buecher, an old right-winger from Strasbourg. Of all people. A pastry chef, for God's sake. A good one, too, more's the pity. Oh, Stefanie, I've had it. *It's* had it. The whole country. The whole continent. Between the Buechers and

the Doriots and your friend across the Rhine, Corporal fucking
Parsifal. So I've had it, well and truly. As soon as I get out of this
bed I'm off. How does it go?" He licked his dry, swollen lips.
Stefanie couldn't understand a word, then she realized why: Sami
was speaking, in Hebrew, the age-old vow of the exiled Jew.

"*L'shana ha'ba'ah b'Yerushalayim.*"

"Next year in Jerusalem?"

"Good, Steffi. Good. Well, not next year, no thanks. How
about next week? Care to join me? How about you, Lussac? After
all, you're half Jewish, and a half equals two full parts to those
guys, I can tell you."

"Oh God," said Stefanie. Sami, adrift in self-absorption,
gazed up through his good eye at the glass globes of the ceiling
lamps.

"Yes," he said. "They've the upper hand, all right. It's really
too late for the rest of us, so all I can say is, Time to go, because
we're all fucked right up the . . . "

Partly to stem the coarseness in which Sami always indulged in
his moments of Weltschmerz, Stefanie blurted, "But Sami, Léon
—I mean M. Blum—needs you. I need you. *Ignace* needs you."

Sami turned and looked at her. His good eye blinked nervously, repeatedly. His bad one stirred under its swollen lid.

"You aren't listening, Steffi. Nobody needs me," he said. "You
haven't needed me for ages. Ignace has you and you're all he
needs. And who cares? You're not Jewish. And with your connections . . . " He snapped his fingers. "Anyway, we all know
Léon's had it, too, and with him go," he coughed, "any chances
of democracy in this Godforsaken . . . " His tirade dissolved
into coughs. Lussac leaned forward and gently touched him on
the shoulder.

"None of that is true, *mon ami*," he said. "Of course you
feel this way now. I understand absolutely. In fact, I remember
Léon saying the same kinds of things after the Camelot incident. Only he wanted to emigrate to America, where, I believe,
he has cousins. But he stayed, and look! What a difference he
has made already to the lives of the workers of this country.
Anyway, if he is out of office soon—and you may be right—he

needs your support more than ever. You're a *combattant*, Sami. And you know your way around parliament. Believe me, our hour is coming, *mon vieux*." His eyes for a moment were fanatically intense. He looked like a mad fakir. "Believe me, Sami." He glanced at his watch. "I must go. So, what shall I tell Léon, then? That you are moving to Palestine? Or that his old comrade stays and fights on?"

Sami groaned.

"Ah, my God, Lussac, once you get a bone between your teeth . . . "

"Good. We'll talk later, when you have recovered. *Au revoir, Madame*." Jean Lussac popped his hat on his head, nodded and was gone, nimbly sidestepping on his way out two sisters pushing a cart full of bandages. One looked after him and said something to her colleague, who nodded; then both glanced at Stefanie.

"*Ah du Gott der Gott*," muttered Sami, closing his eyes. Suffering for his Jewishness seemed to bring out his Jewishness to a degree Stefanie had never witnessed: this talk of next year in Jerusalem, the degree of Jewish blood possessed by Jean Lussac, the remark that she "wasn't Jewish" . . . absurdly, she felt slighted, even insulted. Excluded. Because the political sympathy that had united them again was now on the verge of disappearing, along with so much else. And despite everything, to be perfectly honest (well, perhaps to be less naïve, for a change), she had never *really* seen people as Jews or Gentiles or Moslems or whatever they happened to be, not even her own Jewish relatives, or her own half-Jewish son; not really, not any more than so-and-so was a postman, or a driver, or a schoolteacher, and so on, and so what? But with a downward spiraling of dying hope she realized that in the brave new world of Adolf and his kind these identities were all that mattered. And the flip side of this coin of the day was the way Jews like Sami, long indifferent or even hostile to the idea of being Jewish, suddenly reawakened to their identity and set their sights on Palestine or America—two places, incidentally, that held no appeal for Stefanie (well, New York perhaps, and the towering California forests) . . . but realistically, just in case Sami was serious: She was a European. For better or for worse.

Sami turned his ravaged face to her and opened his good eye wide.

"Hello, Steffi. Still here? Give me a cigarette, will you."

"Oh, Sami. I forgot to bring any."

"Ah, never mind. You run along home now. I expect my nephew, your ex, will be coming by, if he can spare the time from his latest concert at Pleyel. He'll have smokes with him. You don't want to run into dear Arthur, do you?"

"Ach Sami, I don't mind."

But after this outburst of lucidity—Arthur, Arthur's concert, the smokes—Sami was overtaken by weariness and mumbling and was half asleep when Stefanie, in great agitation of spirit, left the room, hoping, despite herself, that Arthur wouldn't suddenly appear. The sister who had shown her in was standing outside the door to the ward, arms folded, a gatekeeping gesture that conveyed a change in her demeanor and vindicated Lussac's skepticism—or perhaps Stefanie was overly aware of such things now.

"*Bonne soirée, ma soeur,*" she said.

"*Bon soir,*" said the sister, ostentatiously omitting "madame." Stefanie felt a sudden flare-up of fury: How dare that condescending bitch . . . !? Who was she to . . . ? *If only she knew . . .* !!

Knew what? Vanity of vanities. Stefanie von Rothenberg, visionary? Lover of powerful men? The Joan of Arc—the Teresa of Ávila—the Saint Catherine Labouré of her age? No; it was an anxious mother, an ineffective teacher, a despairing exile, and a failed wife who passed by the glaring sister and through the corridors stretching off into an infinity of grayness and globe lamps, until she finally found herself at the main doors of the Salpêtrière and caught the No. 57 bus from the Boulevard de l'Hôpital back to the Panthéon.

The streetlights were dark. Another temporary blackout, explained the bus driver when Stefanie got off.

"It happens all the time nowadays, as you know. But what do you expect, Madame? The lunatics are running the asylum."

On the Rue Soufflot, lights from gas lamps and candles glimmered inside the cafés. It was a mild evening for early March in Paris, except for the occasional chilly gust of wind, and the tables outside were full. No one seemed to mind the blackout; in any case, thought Stefanie, the bus driver was right: the electricity went off a couple of times a week these days, so everyone was used to it, although whether Léon and his "lunatics" were to blame was doubtful. More likely the electrical workers' unions. They were all communists who hated Blum as much as the fascists did. The real lunatics, in other words.

Cigarettes glowed red in the semi-darkness outside the Gueuze. Glowing, too, was the polished finish of a sleek black car parked outside the café with its running lights on. Stefanie noticed the diplomatic license plate: CD 75. Coming closer, she recognized the car as a Mercedes, with the long hood and three-pointed star. A stocky man in a chauffeur's uniform sat at the wheel, reading the *Völkischer Beobachter*. He looked up and leaned across to roll down the window when Stefanie paused alongside. A cheery, jowly, Bavarian face. It was Johann Kohler, the number-two driver from Berchtesgaden.

"Frau von Rothenberg?"

"*Ja.* Herr Kohler? *Grüßgott!*" She switched to German. "*Himmel!* What are you doing here? Is this your car?" she asked, aimlessly.

He grinned.

"Nah, bless you. It's the Embassy's. I'm still the same old car jockey, been one for years but all I get out of it is a five-year-old Peugeot. Listen, I hope you don't mind me coming round like this, I got your address from the embassy. I mean, I don't want to impose, but if you have a sec, there's one or two things I wanted . . . "

"Of course. I just have to go upstairs for a minute."

He pointed to the Gueuze. "Soon as I stash this barge somewhere less conspicuous, I'll meet you in that café."

After checking on Ignace, who was in his bed asleep and snoring lightly, with his Uncle Fritz also asleep and snoring loudly in an adjoining armchair, his prosthetic arm held firmly across a sprawled-open copy of *Le Parisien* shouting "Blum Goes Down Again" on the front-page, Stefanie touched herself up in the hall mirror and went downstairs. She found Kohler sitting at a table with a Kronenbourg in front of him. He seemed paler than before, almost washed-out; then she realized the café lights had come on again.

"Prost," he said, raising the glass. "Who'd have thought the Frenchies would make the best beer around?"

After assuring anxious M. Juliot, the café proprietor and ardent Communist, of the good prognosis for recovery that awaited Sami, who had, after all, been one of his best customers over the years, Stefanie had a *ballon de blanc* and a pair of quenelles, then another pair as her appetite awoke. Her curiosity followed suit.

"Well, Herr Kohler! It's so good to see you here! *Ja*! You're looking well, too."

"And you too, Frau von Rothenberg, if I may say. Maybe Paris agrees with both of us, eh?"

There was the hint of a lubricious, or tipsy, glow in his eyes, and she remembered him as the kind of fellow whose happy-go-lucky deviltry would be quite appealing in the grim surroundings of Berchtesgaden but less so in the real world outside. In any event, their ages—he was, if anything, ten years her senior—and the situation rendered any further thoughts along those lines quite absurd, and he at least had the sense to see this. The glow died, enabling Stefanie to get down to business.

"Now, Herr Kohler. Your news . . . ?"

"*Ja*. Well, I lost my job at the Obersalzberg when you know who moved up to Berlin most of the time and left the day-to-day running of things to Frau Angela, that bitch. She hated me from the word go. So before things got worse, I mean you never know what can happen in Germany these days, on a whim I packed up and brought the family out here. I always wanted to see Paris. Now I've been here a couple years, chauffeuring for Count von Welczeck, the Reich ambassador. My dad was his cousin's chauffeur, you see, and my auntie was the cook at their estate in Baden . . . well, anyway, strings were pulled, as they say, and here I am. It's a living, and I get to live in Paris. Not actually in the city, I'm out in Passy, rue Gros, across from the gasworks. But it's a nice house, with a garden and a garage for the Peugeot . . . "

ROGER BOYLAN

She let him ramble on for a few minutes. He was clearly a man (on his second beer already) in need of an audience, the kind whose wife had heard it all too many times; but suddenly he interrupted himself and leaned forward, eyes darting melodramatically from side to side.

"Anyway, Frau von Rothenberg, what I wanted to say was this . . . you know I get to hear a fair amount at the Embassy. So. Well, I recently had the honor of driving . . . well you'll never guess who." He drained his beer. A pair of motorcycles and a bus rumbled past outside, causing the metal ashtrays on the café tables to vibrate and drowning out Kohler's words.

"He's well shall I say not slim. Drugs, they say. Riding accident or something. But it can't be all drugs, you should see him eat. We went to Fouquet's. Count von Welczeck suggested Maxim's, but the Minister-president—or shall I say *Reichsjägermeister*? He has so many titles now. Well, he insisted. Fouquet's is where the film stars go, he said, and he especially wanted to meet what's her name, Arletty. Sure enough she was introduced, and you could tell by the look in his eye . . . well. Anyway, he . . . "

Kohler ordered another Kronenbourg in stiffly Teutonic French. Stefanie had another *ballon de blanc* and kept the man company for want of anything better to do. He resumed his meandering account of the very important person he had been assigned to chauffeur around the city. It slowly dawned on Stefanie, who until that point had been too uninterested or too tired to inquire, that he was talking about Hermann Goering, who, she knew from the papers, was now the Reich Minister of something or other (the Luftwaffe?) as well as being the Prime Minister of Prussia and half a dozen other things, including "a real art-lover" according to Kohler, who added, finally getting to the point,

"Well, what I wanted to tell you was that I overheard him speaking your name. Do you know him?"

"We've met," she murmured, knowing full well that Kohler knew when, and where.

"Of course. Up there? *Ja*. As I thought. So anyway one evening last week, just before he went back to Berlin, I heard him say 'Does anyone know a Frau Stefanie von Rothenberg, a charming Austrian lady who lives here in Paris? I told her ages ago to come and see me any time,' but then he went into another room and that was it. But it was enough, it got me to thinking about you and how you'd been. So. Tell me. Have you received any messages from Bruder Hermann?"

She had not, of course, until now, and told Kohler so; but the reminder of her encounter with Goering at Berchtesgaden ("it is of capital importance to us to have friends—collaborators—compatriots—sympathizers, call them what you will") chilled her, as did so many recollections of her year in that place that was in retrospect more and more like a fairy-tale rewritten by a lunatic . . . with a jolt, she realized that Kohler was looking at her now with an entirely different kind of ardor, that of political impatience..

"Well, let me tell you, *gnädige Frau*, he didn't need to actually spell it out to me. We all know you're connected. Word has it you're best friends with this Jewish prime minister they've got here, this Blum. Oy oy! There can't be too many like you, best friends with both Hitler and Blum, eh? Hey, here's an idea, why don't we invite them both to a cocktail party? Think they'd hit it off? Ha ha ha. Anyhow I'd say that makes you a pretty ah. Valuable commodity, Frau von Rothenberg."

"Oh I don't think so. You know, I've had no contact with Germany or Austria in a while," Stefanie replied, stiffly. With Kohler, as with all unsubtle people, she had no idea how to put things plainly without being rude. He was clearly a boorish type, and probably a devoted Nazi. "My life is here now."

"Well . . . " He grinned. "Yes and no, eh? *You're* here, but as for Austria, now. You still have a relative or two in Vienna, I believe. Not to mention your dear old home town. *Salzburg, mein liebchen.*" His grin disappeared as he suddenly leaned across the table and rapped the marble surface with an urgent knuckle. "Listen to me. Here's a tip from me to you, lady. Those relatives of yours. Call them tonight. Get 'em out of dear sweet little Austria. Especially that old Jewish gentleman in Vienna. Your Baron Kahane. Or . . . " He made the sensationalist's beloved gesture denoting violent death, the flat of the hand across the throat, and sat back with grin restored. Fear trickled coldly down Stefanie's spine.

"God," she said. "You mean *Anschluss*, don't you? They used to talk about it all the time, but I haven't heard much recently. Anyway, it was the Left who wanted it in the old days, not the Right."

"Well, Left or Right big things are in store for little Austria, believe you me. Don't ask me how I know, but I know." He tapped one side of his nose. "You can take it to the bank."

"I don't doubt it, Herr Kohler. How much time do I . . . how long would you say . . . ?"

"What's today? The seventh? About a week. Probably less."

He finished his beer and sat back again, his pudgy frame jolting with after-belches.

"So! Maybe you should let Bruder Hermann know you're still around, willing and able, ha ha. He's not a bad fellow, the Reichsminister. He'll repay you. Eh?"

So this *was* the message from Goering. It was more subtle than she'd have expected, delivered this way; but on second thought she remembered being struck by the man's intelligence, if not by his goodwill. He was offering help on the one hand; on the other, making a threat. But she'd ignore the latter. She had no choice if her family were in danger. She'd simply do as advised.

Kohler accurately read her glance at her watch.

"*Ja*, they might be still up. Unless she's like my old mother. She's in bed by seven, especially in winter."

"But," she began, then fell silent. It was none of his business, and anyway the boring old sex hunger was stealing back across his now-flushed features. She could have written his next line for him.

"So you live here alone, do you, Frau von Rothenberg, here in Paris?"

"Actually, no. Come, Herr Kohler, do you mean you don't know that?"

She got up, having had enough of everything on offer: him, wine, the café. He sprang to his feet and assisted her with the chair. She took out her purse, but he frowned and wagged a finger.

"Allow me."

She allowed him, or rather the German Embassy, to pay the bill, although M. Juliot briefly and feebly suggested it might be on the house, given the sad circumstances of "M. Lebel's injuries"—"ah yes," said Kohler, who claimed to know so little about her living arrangements, in his Germanic French, "the gallant Jewish *monsieur*, he is recovering, I trust?"—but Stefanie was tired and the thought of her mother and uncle and Austria itself was pressing upon her like a bad dream. Kohler tipped, as she expected, with vulgar excess, and walked her outside. A cool breeze had sprung up and was amusing itself by propelling a newspaper across the street in fits and starts. Stefanie extended her hand.

"*Tschüss* then, and thank you."

"*Ja. Tschüss.*" Kohler looked serious, and stiffened slightly as he spoke. "Remember that I'm available, if you need anything from, or via, the Embassy," he said. "I know I'm only a lousy chauffeur, but you'd be surprised where I get to go, and what I get to hear. I keep my lines of communication open, you know." He took a step back and clicked his heels. "*Gnädige Frau.*"

"*Vielen dank*, Herr Kohler."

And she meant it. She murmured an after-thought prayer of thanks as she rode the creaking lift upward. It was a double blessing, if true; and the fact that Kohler was undoubtedly on two payrolls, as both Embassy driver and low-level intelligence agent, i.e. a hired snoop (and the corollary fact that Goering himself was probably behind the evening's message), in no way detracted from the importance to Stefanie of the service he'd rendered.

Indeed, she returned to the apartment with an odd, smug feeling of vindication. Kohler's warning—"big things in store for little Austria"—had only confirmed her deepest feeling: that her artist-madman wouldn't stop. Onward, devil, onward! She remembered him pouting in a Linz tearoom and wanting the world.

Was he any different now?

Gustave
Ten

"HE LOOKED UNSHAVEN and underslept, and smelled of cigarettes"? "There was the hint of a lubricious, or tipsy, glow in his eyes"? "His pudgy frame jolting with after-belches"? Well, of course: Martine was a *writer* and writers feast on the idiosyncrasies of others (never mind Derrida's employment of concepts *sous rapture*) and I was the very embodiment of Idiosyncrasy, from my receding hairline via my burping voice to my increasingly carrot-incarnadined visage down to my spatula-shaped toes. Good God, what a hoot I must be to her! Had she mentally been taking notes the whole time she and I . . . ? Undoubtedly. How, then, could I contemplate marriage? The woman was a novelist; there it was. For a brief horrid moment I saw myself as I imagined a novelist might—not Gax, or Baldas, or any of those fellows, but a *lady* novelist. Martine, to be exact. Women were notoriously more observant than men to start with. They had to be, they were the hunted. A woman novelist is therefore a forensic scientist with a pen (or word processor). Sweat stood out on my brow; I put the book down.

In any case, to a literal-minded academic a little slow on the uptake, the tale was meandering down byways only a novelist could have taken. What had started out as a quasi-biography of Stefanie von Rothenberg was now in full fictive flood. The plot was thickening like chilled fondue, what with Kohler popping up again and the streets of Paris aswarm with intrigue and the heavy breathing of all those Hitlers and Goerings in the background.

I always preferred breezy wordplays in the Sebald or Banville (or Kafka) style, those rambling yet fluent efforts (Joyce was another) that avoid like the plague all attempts at plot structure and end up where they started, usually squarely on the author's navel. Give me atmospherics, I say, and damn the whodunits! Still, my gal's book was an easy enough read, and the atmosphere rang true. And the lunch with Léon Blum—now *that* was a nice touch, in fact—although I'd never met Léon, dead two years before I was born—I knew the Restaurant Drouand, I'd dined there often during my regular visits to Paris (which any educated Genevese considers his *real* capital city, and which must, of all cities, take the palm, and bow its head to none bar Rome). Oh, Mlle. Jeanrenaud had the atmosphere all right, the smokiness, still thank God a characteristic of hostelries in the City of Light; the loud hum of lunchtime voices; the intrigue . . . this was all very well, but truth to tell, despite the glowing memories of the other night (or because of them, unbesmirched by further experience) I was feeling a little shy of seeing Martine herself again, and shyer yet of proposing any long-term arrangement for us. The gulf between our ages, backgrounds, social positions, and mentalities seemed to gape wider than Hades. I was a shambolic woolly mammoth of a man; she was a graceful, elegant sylph of a woman. The other night suddenly seemed like a dreadful mistake, a formula for humiliation. Especially when I saw her again in her telereporter guise, after tuning in for my midmorning news digest on the television. Yes, there was the woman who'd recently joined me in my bed, pert and pretty, not wearing glasses, dressed in three shades of auburn with her hair contributing a fourth, pointing at a legion of dirndl-clad Heidis assembled on a hillside behind her. Alpenhorns droned; bells tinkled. A choir burst into dreadful song.

"The hotel's Chinese owners are taking Swiss-German lessons," said my girlfriend, smiling at me and a hundred thousand others. "But they confess they find it very difficult. The manager of the hotel has suggested it might be a better idea if the staff learned Chinese. Stay tuned. Martine Jeanrenaud at the Grand-Hotel Wong-Edelweiss Supremo in Interlaken. Back to you, Geneva."

And she was gone, replaced by a bland studio visage of no consequence that I extinguished with a flick of the remote, fighting back a sudden urge to telephone Martine, a sudden need for reassurance, a black panic that I was wrong, it was all a dream, that I'd destroyed my last chance at love, I'd been obnoxious and drunk as usual, she'd only tolerated my gross caresses because she was afraid I was a psycho. No, she'd never come again, celibacy and bachelorhood were my natural habitat and it was too late to change.

Enough, I self-chided. Best to let the pot simmer, not boil over. So I went out and walked across town to the Naville bookstore across from the bus station on the Rue Lévrier. There I ran into Paul Trenet, my chum on the Biology faculty, buying a copy of Max Menninger's latest Charlus Prize-winning blockbuster *The Fatal Squeeze*. On the cover was a blonde model's face pouting fellatial lips against a macho backdrop of a sinister male in half shadow and St. Tropez-style blue sea, speedboats, beach, and palms.

"Utter rubbish."

"Yes, but so what?" said Trenet, peevishly. "I just want a distraction from my everyday life, Termi, without necessarily reducing my liver to pâté. Surely you can understand that."

"Of course. Much easier to reduce your brain to pâté."

But Trenet was an old mate, and I forgave him much. We repaired to a small out-of-the-way tearoom in the quiet courtyard of the old building on the Place Grenus that had once housed the nineteenth-century Hôtel de Russie, which had itself once housed the nineteenth-century Russian expatriate rake Fyodor Dostoevsky, who spent his entire sojourn in Geneva sitting at his hotel window growling, at least when he wasn't crossing the lake for a self-hating fling at the roulette tables of Évian-les-Bains. An unsmiling Iberian-looking woman with a handsome mustache (probably Portuguese, from the lesbian *fado* bar down the street) served me orangeade and a side dish of sliced carrots, Trenet a hot chocolate and cinnamon *escargot*. As she retreated, we indulged in simultaneous coughing fits. *What old men we are become!* I inwardly wailed as the vibrations diminished, the

oysters ejected. Once he'd coughed himself out Trenet attended
to his chocolate with the rapid, puckered sips of a humming-
bird, although he otherwise resembled a stoat, being skinny
and nervous, with bulging eyes. Strands from a once-abundant
chevelure lay limply across his parchment-pale pate. He had the
sort of ridiculous dignity that I prize in men. He was married
to an admirably tolerant Lausannoise named Odette who let
him depart on brewery tours and wine-country jaunts without
demur and was rumored to even put up with his frequenting of
a certain *dame des Paquis* I'd once seen him with late at night at
the Palais Mascotte, through a fog of smoke and the sounds of
badly played Dixieland jazz. Odette and Paul had two kids, now
grown and absurdly respectable: one a teacher, the other a doctor.
To all appearances a happy family; but I'd often wondered what
Odette got up to in her free time . . .

Trenet was given to finger-wagging lectures of his friends and
proceeded to indulge himself.

"Now look here, Termi, you really can't let yourself be pushed
about. Well, first of all you're quite safe, quite safe. Rest assured
it's only Petitpoix doing a power number on you to see if you
can stand up to the pressure. But just in case you should find a
decent lawyer who won't take you round the block to the cleaners
and leave you high and dry with an ice pick in your nose and
cotton swabs in your ears, as you might say. I know one: Maître
Levine of Eaux-Vives. He stepped in when they tried to ease me
out a couple of years ago, do you remember that . . . ?"

I did. Trenet had signed a contract with a textbook publisher
to edit a biology book and the college had swooped down like a
wolf on the fold, claiming conflict of interest.

"So they couldn't fire me and they can't fire you, Termi. You
have investment tenure. You're as safe in your job as the Pope
is in his. It's that simple. God bless Switzerland. We're not like
America, where they hire and fire on alternate days of the week.
Yes, you just ask Maître Levine. I mean, you're an authority
in your field, a published poet, a respected professor, and God
knows what else . . . No, you have to be the one who takes the
final step out the front door."

"Well, now that you mention it, yes. I've been thinking I'd do exactly that."

"Excellent. I mean, just because you've been having these visions . . . "

"Aha!" I said. "How did you know about that?"

"But my dear fellow, it's all over the college. You can't swoon in ecstasy during class and not expect it to get around."

I felt the prickles of acute self-consciousness dance over me from top to toe.

"*Merde.* They must think I'm an idiot."

"Not at all. I have a cousin, Lise Chaudet, who for a while saw St. Edith Stein every Sunday night in the dining room of her house out in Versoix and *she* went on to become a Federal Councillor in Bern and Ambassador to Israel . . . of course, she lives alone, too . . . but anyway, listen, you've been in that job for how long? Twenty years? You're a known quantity. Brusque, yes; your own man, well, as much as one can be and keep a job; pretty much a loony, yes, I can attest to that; but an idiot? Not at all, my dear chap. Now." He finished his *chocolat chaud* with a slurp, pushed his cup aside, and leaned forward, arms folded, eyes unblinking, momentarily resembling a gargoyle more than a stoat—the winged one on the southeast corner of the south tower of Notre-Dame, to be specific. You know, the one with the huge beak and bulging Trenet-like eyes.

"I'll give Maître Levine a call and ask him to get in touch with you, if you like. He specializes in wrongful termination cases."

And of course, out of friendship I let him ramble on, not filling him in on the porphyria diagnosis, which would only provoke a litany of blood-and-urine specialists.

I hadn't the slightest intention of speaking to. But a certain intensity of spirit had always been typical of Trenet, entirely well motivated, mind you. He had others' interests at heart; although like so many idealists he could be a pain in the arse with his nagging. We'd always been like a mismatched pair of animals—he the stoat, as previously noted, I some kind of puffing walrus. We met in our early days at the college, and amazingly had sustained a friendship, based on our deep and abiding skepticism toward life and people in authority, and our mutual love of good food and drink, ever since. We had little enough else in common. We never talked about art. He was a biologist, he'd not know a work of art if it flung itself around his neck. As for biology, although I was of course an example of it, however lamentable, it bored me stiff. Oh, he enjoyed a spot of Mozart, a touch of Debussy, and a dash of jazz; and he'd labored his way through Apollinaire and (God help us) Blake; and I could stand to read Darwin, and Joliot-Curie, and a few of the more mass-market scientists like Hoyle and Andersen and von Ranke. But mostly we enjoyed the rising heat and loosened tongue of too much beer consumed over a plate of oysters or a wiener-schnitzel. So he traveled to countries known for beer and I'd gone with him on three such journeys: one to Germany and Norway, one to Belgium, and one to Sweden. He'd always been the one to arrange things and make plans. Back in the '80s, deep in my bachelor years when the only women I knew were my mother, a colleague or two, and those whose company I paid for, he was my boon companion. He enjoyed the theatrical touch. He'd phoned me one morning during the Easter break in '87 and told me to meet him at Cornavin station in half an hour, and I did, having nothing better to do, and no responsibilities to anyone but myself; and so our German tour began, progressing from the rim of the ex-Reich at Rosenheim and making our way up the map via Munich and various capacious beer halls associated with a certain lovelorn mini-mustachioed fanatic to Hof in Saxony at the then-formidable Iron Curtain that separated us, but not for long, from the Stalinist slumber of Dresden and Leipzig and Magdeburg, where I received an acute sense of the undead, Nazi past—for the dictatorships had only, really, swapped slogans, Brotherhood instead of Fatherland, Capitalism instead of Jewry. Admittedly, the communists eased up on the anti-Semitism, but not by much, and anyway the Nazis had done their best to make anti-Semitism redundant by killing most of the Jews. Breweries there were still, however, in abundance, although administered by the dead hand of the DDR state. We tasted *hopfenperle*, *dunkelbier*, *hefeweizen* of full-bodied, preindustrial strength. The hangovers were considerable. Then it was on to Berlin East and West (although it was only in the West that the other side was conceded to exist; in the East they had street maps that showed everything beyond Checkpoint Charlie as one huge gray blob, the wonderful stage-management of totalitarian fantasy) and more fun times in seedy Kreuzberg strip joints and Ku'damm bars and so onward, via rattling, tobacco-scented and Stasi-staffed East German railways to the windy pebbled coast at Travemünde on the Baltic and over the Zone to vibrant, no-nonsense Hamburg and lovely, placid Friesland and its red-brick churches and thatched-roof farmhouses amid wheat fields under the big blue Nordic sky. We'd shared all that, and Norway and Belgium too.

So I let him prattle on, for old times' sake. But then he stopped and looked me full in the eyes.

"Tell me, Termi," he said. "What does this archangel of yours look like?"

"Why, the Archangel Michael, of course."

"Of course. And what does the Archangel Michael look like on a good day?"

"The statue on top of the Castel Sant'Angelo."

"Ah. Big chap, as I recall. And do you really believe you see him?"

"I do. And not only do I see him, I hear him. Sounds potty, doesn't it?"

He shook his head.

"Not so much. Remember my cousin Lise. And had you ever seen him before?"

"Not that I can recall."

"Do you remember that night in Bremen?"

I remembered several nights in Bremen, but only vaguely. There'd been the Hansens Brau night, the St. Pauli Girl night, and the Holstenbrau night. And a woman named Ursula who kept asking me if she could touch me. (I let her, in the end.)

"Yes. Well, the less said about Ursula the better. No, I'm thinking of when you and I were standing on the docks around one a.m., waiting for the night ferry for Oslo. You went to get some cigarettes, I think, and when you came back you had a dazed look in your eyes . . . "

Then I remembered. The lost cry of the gulls, the damp air, the smell-sonata of diesel and seawater and harbor muck, the slick cobblestones gleaming in the streetlights, the snarling Mercedes taxis, the muted farting of foghorns, the Turkish currywurst vendors . . . I went back the way we'd come, down Am Wall to the steamy, seamy quayside bars full of jersey-clad whores and their exuberant clientele from all the coasts of the North Sea, the Baltic, and beyond. (*Ah, truly, the spirit of Brueghel still rules in the old harbors of Northern Europe, the wild spirit of pagan fun so far from the tut-tutting of nanny states and health zealots and the hundred and one rules of conduct in today's hypochondriacal world! Dans le por-r-r-r-t d'Amsterdam . . . !*) I was tempted to stay and buy a round for a couple of jolly tarts in the Kneipe Zur Hafen, but funds were diminishing and we had Helsinki and the North yet to conquer; so after I'd bought a packet of HB filters I headed back to the ferry dock via a shortcut down a wet alleyway off the Am Wall, puffing away contentedly, pissed out of my gourd, having a great time until my way was blocked by what appeared at first to be a lorry with its bright headlamps on, then a helicopter fully lit and slowly ascending, then a large human figure surrounded by a bluish light and rising slowly and mechanically from the ground. My first thought was: Fuck. Aliens. Just my luck. (Of course, those were hot times for the little green men, with new sci-fi films coming out every other month.) Then I noticed the halo.

"God, Trenet. You're right. *It was him.* But he didn't say anything to me then."

"Maybe he did but you were just too pissed. Or maybe it was in Bremen dialect and you didn't understand."

"No, I'm sure of it, he said nothing. As if it were the first try, you know? To see if he looked right. Although of course there was that other time . . . " I remembered the cemetery in Edinburgh, the chill spookiness of the unraveling mist . . . no porphyria then, surely? "Maybe not. Anyway, it took me a minute or two to catch on. First of course I thought it was an alien, then I reckoned it was a hoax, or a pantomime, an escapee from one of those raucous North German festivals, you know, the kind of mad uproar that can erupt in Germany during the autumn and winter. (They say the Brazilians go wild during carnival, well my God they haven't seen the Germans when they get going.) But now I can clearly remember my feeling of awe at being slowly and painstakingly scrutinized by a mighty intelligence *that was taking notes*, studying me as a scientist studies a specimen. Afterward I had a good puke and took off, of course already busy working out the explanation in my head: too much beer and mussels, the effect of shellfish on the brain, never mix your drinks, etc."

"Yes, when you came back I think I said you looked as if you'd seen a ghost. Not very original but to the point."

We sat in silence for a minute or so. The Portuguese lesbian contemptuously tossed us our bill. On the way out Trenet tapped me on the elbow.

"The odd thing is, Termi: I believe you. I know you're as rational a man as I am, and I don't think you have the DTs or hashish flashbacks or anything like that. Personally, I've seen ghosts all my life. Did you know? Our house in Charmilles is teeming with the buggers, including, Odette insists, a nineteenth-century postman forever trying to deliver a registered letter to long-gone residents. And I say this as a materialist and atheist and worshipper of the ground Darwin and Pasteur walked on. Never told you all that, did I? No, well; I thought this might be a good time. Remember Sir Arthur Conan Doyle."

"Ah yes, the fairies."

"No, not just the fairies. The most rational mind of his generation."

"It's kind of you to humor me, Trenet. But honestly. You think I'm crazy, don't you?"

"Oh, I'm not just humoring you. If I thought you were really bonkers—dangerously so, as you might say—I would make my opinion known. No, Termi, what I'm doing is expressing a certain degree of fellow feeling."

We paused at the corner of the Rue du Mont Blanc and its

hurtling traffic. I was on the point of telling him about Martine, but for reasons that felt more like superstition than common sense I didn't; or maybe I was becoming a little less certain myself, or self-conscious. Or maybe I just wanted Time to take care of things one way or another.

He was heading home to Charmilles, I the other way. We shook hands.

"Now, the next time the angel comes, take a picture of him, there's a good chap, all right?"

"Of course. I'll carry a video cam at all times."

At home I picked up the phone to call her but put it down again and picked up her book instead. It was easier that way.

A Summons

Since the glories of the Anschluss and the peripheral distraction of Kristallnacht ("Jews get out! That's all we've been saying. How much clearer can we be? Tickets? Road signs? Engraved invitations?"), the Führer, Adolf Hitler, vegetarian, philosopher ("all Jews are subhuman"; "the United States will sink under its miscegenation"; "it still astonishes me that so few in my younger years recognized in the shape of my profile the sign of my future genius"; "Strauss was a Jew, of course—no, not that Strauss, the other one"), animal lover, and Time magazine's Man of the Year, continued his inexorable progress toward becoming the world's most monstrous artist. Food and drink, never very important to him, appealed less and less, except for Sachertorte and sweet tea, and the occasional sweet sherry. Cars he enjoyed, usually Mercedes-Benzes, but only if someone else was driving, usually Erich Kempka. Sex? Now and then, briefly, à sa façon. There was his funny little *Tschapperl*, a pallid creature called Eva Braun from Hoffmann's picture studio in Munich who willingly submitted to the underwear game where others had not, but she smelled sometimes of cigarettes, and that spoiled the game's mostly olfactory fun. He liked her, in his way, but he certainly didn't admire or respect her. So his favorite pastime, his own earthly Valhalla, his portal of joy, had nothing of the pleasures of the table or the bedroom about it, nor did it derive from his former incarnation as an artist, except perhaps vicariously. This great pleasure was, quite simply, the private, nocturnal perusal of maps, which he ogled in the avid, secretive way of an adolescent perusing pornography. Maps, and the Map Room, were a true relaxation in the midst of the magnificent but somewhat cold expanse of the monumental new *Reichskanzlei* ("*ja*, what a fine railroad station!" had been Goering's first, muttered comment in response to Hitler's enthusiastic, almost boyish "See, Goering? Isn't it fine?") Hitler's pet architect Albert Speer—identified behind his back as "*Groß Arschküßer Des Führers*" by those who should know one—had had the foresight or the instinct to set aside, on the mezzanine behind the gigantic lobby, an anteroom that was, by contrast with the stylized monumentalism of the rest of the place, almost relaxing, if not quite *gemütlich*, what with the network of exposed heating pipes that had yet to be covered over, either with a dropped-panel ceiling, or the carved, kitschy, neo-hunting lodge beams that adorned certain of the other rooms; Speer was inclining to the latter, with his Führer's approval . . . The room was called the "Map Room," logically, for upon its floor-to-ceiling shelves were stacked approximately a hundred gazetteers, twenty atlases, and two hundred maps; ordinance survey, military, navigational, and touristic, maps new and old, mostly of Europe East and West. There were a few of Asia, a matched pair of Latin America, a half dozen of the United States, none of Canada, Australia and/or Antarctica, for who cared about those places? The Japanese? (Strange, copper-colored people, a bit like Red Indians; not really quite Aryan but possessed of a certain savage dignity; undefeated for a thousand years, after all! Still, it was good you didn't have to deal with them every day.) But there were many maps (twenty-two to be exact) of the Führer's favorite, his own native and—thanks to him since a year ago last March—nonexistent land: Austria. Specifically Linz, his not-quite-birthplace, of which more maps than ever before were now being printed by the Reich publishing house. Fine maps, too. But the old ones were the best. The most powerful artist in the world enthusiastically sandpapered dry palms together when first he set eyes on the Map Room with its soft lighting, its Turkmen carpet with swastika motif, its potted plants (native, of course), its Arno Breker painting of nearly naked blondies against a tedious backdrop of theatrical clouds breaking apart to reveal the rising Aryan sun, and its mahogany map shelves with brass railings. In his office upstairs that was bigger than all the churches in Braunau combined, in the midst of leading the nation that would soon lead the world, the former landscape painter often found himself anticipating with a premonitory *frisson* of delight a late night alone with imaginary landscapes evoked by the rustling maps in his hands: maps of Linz, soon-to-be capital of a New Europe, *Weltstadt* Linz (or another name: Führerburg? Hitleropolis?), a German Budapest that would not commit Vienna's error of turning its back to the Danube, along which a mighty *autobahn* would run. Great factories in Linz would turn out the world's best machines. He saw a statue of himself in place of the pigeonshit-covered Holy Trinity Pillar on the Hauptplatz. And the Gau Haus, with his crypt down a wide somber flight of stairs. The Bruckner monument (how did it go, the Fourth Symphony? Da-da-da-da-da-*DAAA*? Or *Da*?). The Anschluss monument, Austria unchained. Art galleries for the works of Weichsler and Breker. A grand stadium, named after . . . well, *him*. Yes, he was rebuilding the world, but he would start with dear old Linz. It was a solitary passion. Only Speer was welcome to drop by, but Adolf suspected his young acolyte didn't give a toss about Linz.

So at night, when the real business of running the German Reich straight to hell was over for the day, and the Chancellery's three hundred minor and middle bureaucrats had rocked and swayed their way homeward aboard sundry buses and unreliable cars and rattling U-bahns; after the jackbooted and clean-uniformed sycophants of this or that security service had gone about their dirty business; after his personal secretaries, Fräulein Ulla Jungemann and Frau Christa Schröder and Fräulein Sieglinde (*aber ja!*) Rappersweiler had been granted permission to join the diminishing homeward trickle at eight p.m. or so (but they didn't get in until just before noon, because HE was never there

before then) . . . then the world was his. Of course, he intended
to make that literally true, in due course; but for now the nighttime world of a boy's fantasies would suffice.

It was 1939. He was a god. He would, shortly, be the god of
war, he whose spirits are hurricane, his servants flames of fire!
He who goes on the wings of the wind! He whose laugh is the
mockery of Hell, whose love is a murderous lightning flash!

He who was once the laughingstock of the Heim für Männer!

The ex-laughingstock's profile, with its sloping Waldviertel-
peasant forehead, prominent Mitteleuropäischer hooter and
weak village-idiot chin, all straightened-up and rendered stern
and determined like the prow of a dreadnought, had become the
silhouette of Germany on her postage stamps and party posters.
He, Adolf the painter, Adolf the dosshouse dweller, Adolf the
hapless suitor, Adolf the mamma's boy, Adolf the street corner
bawler: HE had become the mysterious deity whose mighty granite visage he had long imagined glaring from behind the clouds
upon the so imperfect world, upon the poor artist's foot-aching
inward-wailing pilgrimages around cold, aloof Vienna. And now
glory was his. Vienna was his. There was justice in the world,
if you made your own. The world was yielding to him, to his
magnetism, his power, his aesthetic and military genius. Roehm
was long gone, the Rhineland was wrested from the Frenchies,
the ridiculous toy Czechoslovak pseudo-nation quite properly
dismantled, the Sudetens brought back into the fold, nasal con-
stipated old Chamberlain—who, as he'd told Mussolini, liked
to take weekends in the country where he, Hitler, preferred
to take countries in the weekend: Oh! Ha ha that was a good
one, *Führer*, said the Duce, slapping his thigh with a glove—
Chamberlain, with his perpetual *ahem*! *ahem*! and look of a
disheveled sheep, sent away with a flea in his ear and a boot in his
baggy striped trousers, and (best of all) Austria—Adolf's native
land—Austria of bitter memory and the decadent Habsburgs—
Austria of his humiliation—of pullulating Judaism—of a thousand lonely nights in Leonding and Vienna—*Austria* had been
brought under control, tamed, muzzled, made docile, renamed
Ostmark, made German. In his own, admittedly fine, words

(one crawler had described his speech in Linz as "a sure sign that Germany has a new Pericles"): *When I first set out from this town I felt in the depth of my soul that it was my vocation and my mission, given to me by destiny, that I should bring my home country back to the great German Reich. I have believed in this mission, and I have fulfilled it.* Dixit!

And Vienna! Vienna was his now, as she deserved to be. Not that he wanted her, the old whore. The fabulous anteroom of Empire, as Metternich had it? No, no more now than a far-flung suburb of Budapest, as von Schirach had more felicitously put it. Yes, more than anything else in the magnificent, squalid, stirring, ludicrous, and tragic story of Hitler's life, he had savored that moment in the cold night air on the balcony of the Hotel Imperial, saluting the bestial adulation of the Viennese who had formerly and so often rejected him and all his works. There he savored his revenge, his triumph, his victory, there on the very Ringstrasse where he had once had (or maybe not—but it made for good reading in *Mein Kampf*, or so Hess had assured him) his life-changing revelation about the, well, excessive Jewishness of the Jews, specifically one malodorous old rabbi direct from the shtetl in greasy ringlets and beard who'd elbowed young Adolf rudely aside in the streetcar line, spilling his roasted chestnuts and spitting out through crooked yellow teeth some Yiddischer imprecation about "*dummes hanswurst*"—indeed, that precise streetcar stop was visible from the Imperial's balcony, *nicht wahr?*—where the Fates, the Norns, the blondie-godlings of Teutonworld, had placed him, their anointed one, to receive the balm of Vienna's abasement, soon to be followed by Europe's, then the world's . . .

And, with the help of all those fine Aryan citizens who wrote to him daily in their thousands to denounce this Jew, that gypsy, those suspected half-breeds ("Dear Führer! It has come to my attention that the Jew Feldstein downstairs is having carnal relations with an Aryan woman named Schultz across the street, no doubt against her will!" "Dear Führer! I have reason to suspect my supervisor of being a half Jew!"), he would erase from the world all race defilers, rapists, sexual degenerates, and habitual criminals, especially those with hydrocephalus, cross-eyed deformed whole- and half Jews, and a whole series of racially inferior types even he had never come across (Wends, Rhaeto-Romans, Moldavians, etc.)!! It would be a world conceived by him, painted by Arno Breker, scored by Richard Strauss!!!

Well, no. Forget Strausses, Richard *and* Johann. Wagner, now and always. (Except for *Die Fledermaus*, of course. Ah, the opening waltz . . .) Hitler heard in his mind, as he often did, the opening chords of *Parsifal*, Act One. Or the overture to *Rienzi*. Actually, on *that* night, the second night of the Anschluss, he had attended a performance of *Tristan* at the Vienna Opera for the first time since 1912. Not that he'd ever been that enamored of *Tristan* with its (as he said so often at table) Frenchified sentiments, swooning love carry-on and dying with a kiss and all that *quatsch*; but he had to admit the music itself was wonderful, stirring, magisterial. Almost as good as the peerless *Rienzi*. And how right, how just, to attend the same opera in the same opera house, with memories still vivid of spending that entire winter's day in 1912 at the Heim für Männer before the opera, assiduously brushing off those old hand-me-down trousers, only to be escorted by some pederast of a gypsy baron or snooty Hungarian-Jewish usher to the paupers' gallery, the standing-room-only section of the theater; then, after finally getting to his seat, meeting that friend of *that friend* of his . . . that Helmuth Meinl fellow, Jewish of course but he was one of those you had to watch, he didn't really look like one, of course that was nearly thirty years ago and he might look like one now, and if he was still in Vienna well too bad for him . . . and as for her?

On this night Adolf Hitler, Führer of the Greater German Reich, holder of the Iron Cross First Class, with an excellent background in cheap lithographs and postcard design, raised his head from his maps, some of which were of Poland and would soon prove useful on the road to world conquest, when things would be set right, November '18 avenged, the many slights of Vienna buried for good . . . The slights of an artist, a painter . . . no, not quite *all*. Gazing at the Breker portrait, he remembered the portrait he'd painted of Stefanie. *Lieber Gott*. A portrait, the only one he'd done. The reason the desiccated Jews at the Vienna Academy had turned him down had been because, allegedly, he couldn't paint people; well, they'd never seen his portrait of Stefanie, it proved he could. But to make it public would be to destroy another myth while revealing too much about certain aspects of the past, so none could be permitted to see it, to speculate on its origins, to discover its Jewish connections, the *normality* of his infatuation with that girl . . . ! *Christus*, there were so many tracks to cover, even now. But anything could be done if he willed it.

So, with the godlike decisiveness that had brought him so far, he picked up the telephone, pressed the Security button, listened to the despairing parp of the dial tone. Finally young Corporal Burger on the *Sicherheitsdienst* switchboard responded, breathlessly, with an almost audible clicking of the heels, having just realized Whose line was ringing . . .

"Heil Hitler," said he to his caller, who was exempt from this formula.

"*Ja, ja.* Listen, *knabe*, I want you to connect me to Vienna. To Gauleiter Seyss-Inquart's office." The man stayed up late, he knew that. Telephonic clicks ensued, but suddenly, on second thoughts, Adi remembered how thoroughly he disliked Seyss-Inquart, his man on the Ringstrasse; oh, a good administrator and all that, but a man with the soul of a bookkeeper and a voice like broken glass and no taste in music at all . . . "No, no, forget that," as more confused clicks emanated from the earpiece, "just make sure Seyss-Inquart gets this message. Now, there's a Baron Kahane somewhere there," said ex-Corporal Hitler, Commander-in-Chief of the Armed Forces of the Reich, in the hoarse undertone he used on the telephone, to the nearly comatose Corporal Burger, a mere staff corporal, for goodness' sake, and only filling in for Oberst Hahne, who was with his mistress. "*Ja.* K-A-H-A-N-E . . . He's a Jew, of course, but that's beside the point. Listen, boy, there are two possibilities. One, they've already gone to his house; two, they haven't. If they haven't, tell them to make sure they get hold of a painting there. It's a portrait of a woman, signed. Seyss-Inquart will know the details.

Bring it here, to the Reichskanzlei. No," his voice rose slightly, "not the old Jew. His luck ran out. It's the painting, *blödmann*."

He replaced the receiver, breathing heavily at the boy's stupidity and at the thought of the portrait that from across the gulf of the years seemed to stare at him with a baleful gaze that spelled disaster . . . and he knew not why, when everything was falling into place otherwise. Well. Never mind. They would find it, bring it back. They'd found the others, the drawings of Geli, the Cranach forgeries. That portrait would be his to do with as he wished: burn, hide, even paint over, or cover with architectural plans he'd work on with Speer.

In a somewhat inevitable mental next step even for an utterly self-absorbed egomaniac like Adolf Hitler, he then thought of the portrait's subject, Stefanie von Rothenberg, and he thought of her with all the limited tenderness of which he was capable. She had so nearly been entirely his own, ex-sweetheart and ex-mistress and the only woman he had ever loved to the admittedly very narrow degree that he was capable of love of anyone not himself—which meant that she'd pleased him at times, and had shown more of an understanding of his mission than most women, and he'd liked her at times, too, and even desired her, once or twice, certainly in Linz, where she was unattainable, and occasionally up at the Berghof, where she'd been less alluring by becoming attainable; but then she was gone, like so many passing ships on the limitless ocean of Adolf's grand and lonely life. He couldn't recall exactly how, or why, but he remembered *where*: Paris.

Next to him was an empty teacup that had contained sweetened chamomile. In it were sugar crystals, dissolving into a small residual tea-puddle. He stared at it fixedly, wishing for more but reluctant to summon Kannenberg, the valet. Next to the teacup was the internal Chancellery telephone; next to that, the external phone, with lines to Hess, Ribbentrop, Goering, Himmler, and Heydrich. A third phone linked to Bormann, directly. The Führer cracked his knuckles, staring at the trio of telephones with a butterfly leap of anticipation in his stomach and a dreamy sense of perfection in all: his war, his life, his mission. All except (he almost laughed; he was becoming mawkish) the right kind of woman to impress, behind the scenes (the Volk couldn't know about women, they had to keep on desiring him, their solitary swain, their head *wandervogel*, their god; or the spell would break). Not silly Eva, who was only good at skiing and dancing and the underwear game. No, a woman who was Aryan and a lady and knew her place, one who was educated and discreet and who could understand the sacredness of his crusade, a kind of cross between a mother superior and a secretary but with a handsome appearance and a "von" in her name. Ach, that "von" was still important, even in the New Germany! And of course Stefanie had had it all. And he'd had her. And he could find her if he wanted. If she was still alive. Paris was a place much like Vienna, no doubt. Decadent to the hilt, a city not bad to look at, but rotten to the core. Artists, writers. Arno Breker, for one. He'd studied there . . . Adolf mused dreamily about garrets, stage-lit rooftops, accordions . . . Yes, he'd take Arno with him, when he went. He wasn't there yet, but he would be, *lieber Gott,* this he knew with as much certainty as he knew his own name. The French, hold out? The generals were dead wrong there, as they were on so many things. France's time was past. Look: they'd even had a Jewish prime minister, that pathetic Blum. Paris quite soon, then. What would she think? He'd have to find out if she was still alive. Of course she was, why shouldn't she be? She wasn't Jewish, or Slavic. He picked up the phone connected to the Security Police. A quacking voice answered, soon hushed into reverence.

"The address of Frau or Madame Stefanie von Rothenberg in Paris. *Ja.* No, RothenBERG. Immediately."

"Right away, *mein Führer.*"

Then he rode the reverie, with a slight dreamy smile few ever saw. Would she remember their clandestine rendezvous, that day in Linz, thirty two years and a century or two ago? Surrounded by hussars and Hungarians and Habsburgs? *Ach, ja.* And now. He could make things easy for her, now. True, she had Jewish relations. Too bad for them, unless she insisted, as they'd done for that old fraud Freud, and Dr. Bloch. Because he could, if he wanted. He could do anything . . .

The external phone's jangle slashed the velvet silence of the Map Room. Expecting Seyss-Inquart with a question about the Vienna portrait, or Heydrich of the Security Police with Stefanie's address or the latest news on the secret maneuvers in Silesia that would unlock the gates of war (a dodge that had occasioned as much smug mirth and palm-rubbing in the inner circle as a small boy's conker game), Hitler greedily snatched up the receiver. But if it was Heydrich the man was drunk or insubordinate, and he was too much of a sycophant to be either; and Seyss-Inquart didn't drink, and was, if anything, a bigger *arschkriecher* than Heydrich.

Besides, there was something in the sound at the other end of the line that was familiar and very disturbing.

"*Ja-a-a-a?*" warily inquired the Führer of the Greater German Reich.

Over the line came a phlegmy baritone laugh interspersed with a breathy whisper redolent of the most devastating sexuality and foulness and somehow also evocative of unpleasant places like overflowing public toilets and the damp and moldy corners of ruined houses and under stairwells and stained nighttime beds and dank groves and the trenches of the War.

"Hey ho, oh you, my Faustus," said the voice. "Oh son of mine. My brother. My lover. Oh my gift to me, I sing your song but not as well as you sing mine." And the voice—the *sound*, rather, less a voice than a rough wind from untold waste-lands—emitted a long low gasp followed by a laugh to chill the blood, then the laughs grew shorter and shorter like a locomotive accelerating until an unnaturally high pitch was attained and the sound, all sounds in one, soared away like a distant rocket hastening to the heart of destruction—and vanished. Then came the hissing of a dead line and the mundane drone of a dial tone and the blood thundering in his ears.

Hitler jiggled the cradle until the operator, Oberst Hahne, who was back from his tryst, replied.

"*Ja, mein Führer.*"

"Tell me who made that call."

"What call, *mein Führer?*"

"The one that just came into my office. Find out where it came from."

He put down the phone. The odd thing was, it wasn't the first time he had heard this sound. The last time had been, as a matter of fact, Vienna in March 1938, after the triumph, after the balcony speech, alone in the bathroom of his suite at the Imperial following much bowing and heel-clicking and hand-shaking and fending-off of lickspittles. Then, too, there had been a sudden presence, but a visual one, a kind of murky mist in the shaving mirror. And a smell, like matches being struck. He had ordered investigations, of course, but the hotel staff found nothing, and anyway he knew in his heart that the matter was beyond investigation, beyond the Gestapo, beyond even human agency, nonsensical as that seemed.

The phone rang. It was Hahne.

"I'm very sorry, *mein Führer*, but we have no register of a Frau von Rothenburg in Paris."

"That's because it's Rothen*berg* . . . oh, never mind. And the call?"

"We have no records of any calls coming into your office since just after six p.m. when Gauleiter Mutschmann called from Dresden and the train company called from Hannover about your personal carriage at 8 . . . "

"Good," muttered Adolf. "Good. So. *Ja.*" He hung up. "Anyway, I knew that. *Gott*," he muttered, suddenly aware of the inappropriateness of his usual repertory of curses—*Gott, Christus, Heilige Mutter*, and the rest . . . yes, it was as if, having risen so high, he, who had never in the conventional sense believed in God, the Trinity, etc., had encountered a spirit born of *their* belief, a spirit of the upper air at variance with low-er-dwelling Mankind, believed in but unseen by the boring ones with jobs in offices who go to the shops and raise children . . . it was a daemon, a great rival, jealous of his power. After all, was he not a god? And did a god not need an opponent? Wotan—Alberich? Rienzi—Orsini? Winnetou—Old Shatterhand?

One thing he knew: He would never speak of it—him—the

creature—his nemesis. No, for speaking of it would make it all the more real, and would lead it closer to him. And if he still had a shred of belief in a God Who was not him, he'd pray to that God to never hear the voice again.

Then Adolf Hitler, Führer of the Greater German Reich, lowers his head as in, but not in, prayer, and . . . what is this? Can it be a tear welling up in his stern and steely eyes and falling on the map in front of him and trickling like the meandering Danube into the heart of Linz?

No, of course not: It is a drop of condensation from the ceiling-mounted pipes for the still-new heating system.

But:

"I've defeated them all," he said. "I'll defeat you, too." And he made a fist of his right hand, as on the poster on which he appeared as Siegfried, holding a spear, with in the distance all the crenelated towers and high mountains of the future, perfect, Jew-free, sun-kissed New Germany.

The Last Golden Days

Paris basked in the sunshine of the lilac-scented days of May, 1940. The war was on the blue horizon, still safely distant, as all wars should be, and the city was calm, apart from the odd air-raid siren that everyone ignored. Seen from the roof of Stefanie's apartment building traffic, interspersed with military vehicles, was light on the Boulevard St. Michel, and a purplish haze veiled the outskirts around Aubervilliers and St. Denis, beyond which, somewhere, the old adversaries clashed again, as they had done so disastrously in 1870 and 1914, and times before that beyond the counting; but this time it wouldn't be like the last time, or times before. There'd be no Sedan disaster or Marne miracle, not with modern technology and the superb skills of the biggest and best armed force in the world, equipped with the finest materiel, led by seasoned commanders such as the venerable Gamelin, and with the nation safe behind the formidable Maginot Line as far as the impenetrable Ardennes.

First reports had the French and their British allies holding the line everywhere, repulsing the Germans, throwing bridges across strategic waterways, building a bulwark of steel across the Low Countries. The French First and Seventh Armies, crème de la crème of France's fighting forces, had advanced into Belgium ahead of units of General Gort's British Expeditionary Force to thwart the untested (except in Poland—poor Poles) Wehrmacht Panzers and the droning phalanxes of (tested) Luftwaffe Heinkel and Stuka bombers. There'd be no cavalry charges this time, no "over the top, boys." No, *this* time they were going on the "dynamic defensive" while mobilizing their heavy industries, the pride of Europe, to fight a total war. France's generals planned to take the offensive at their leisure, some two to three months after the start of "active" hostilities—according to the papers, which were, for once, unanimous, from the *Petit Parisien* to *Le Matin*. All agreed that this one would be over in a jiffy, possibly by Christmas (now, when and where had suffering humanity heard that before?). "Oh we'll be hanging out our laundry on the Siegfried Line," sang Ray Ventura at the Casino de Paris, against swirling stage sets painted by languid Jean Cocteau, whose lover Jean Marais, who looked simply divine in uniform, darling, was playing football on the Maginot Line. Marc Chagall and Pablo Picasso were busy bringing to life on canvas the dreams of shtetls and demiurges past and to come; and the all-seeing unseeing Irish magus Joyce, just down the street from Stefanie, rocked back and forth in his lonely ecstasy, uncomprehended by all. The limousines still drew up to Maxim's and disgorged their elegant charges. Fouquet's, where Louis Jouvet held court at his corner table, was fully booked, its legendary waiters overworked; Longchamps was a sea of elegant hats and silk ties; at the Ritz, the titled guests came and went. At the Salle Pleyel, Arthur Lebel conducted his first piano concerto from the piano and intro-duced a blind composer from Spain, Joaquin Rodrigo, to lead the first Paris performance of his sparkling new *Concierto de Aranjuez*. Paris, as Chevalier was wont to insist (especially later), would always be Paris.

So the papers brayed their bargain-basement patriotism and sham confidence and blandly reassured everybody it would all be over in the blink of an eye.

"Idiots," fumed Stefanie. "How can they say that? Look at Czechoslovakia. Look at Austria. What about Poland? *They* don't exist any more. How long do they give us?" ("Us" for her, after two decades, was France.) Indeed, in less than three years her ex-lover the onetime watercolorist had gobbled up half of Central Europe, forged alliances with three great powers and declared war on two others, and in so doing had become more, much more, than the bony-kneed, concave-chested *bürgerlich* Austrian dauber she so vividly remembered in a mental picture album of many portraits: him in his ludicrous leather shorts in Landsberg prison; him in his *loden* suit at the Berghof, complete with Tirolean hat and plume; him ranting at the microphones; him in the dark, absurdly . . . and the name of this absurd person now bannered the very sky, he was the most famous man in history, yes, more famous than Beethoven, or Goethe, or Genghis Khan, or (in our day) Stalin, or Roosevelt, or the new prime minister, Churchill (whom Sami dubbed "the aristopig"); in fact, in fame Adolf Hitler, ex-illustrator of gemütlich postcards, graduate *summa cum laude* of Leonding High School and the Heim fur Männer, was second only to Him Whose Name he was unfit to speak—He Whose Message he despised . . . and yet Stefanie still prayed for him. Not by name; she hid her prayers for him inside her broader prayers for all humanity, where only God could find them. But her thoughts turned constantly to her former suitor and how she and, more importantly, the grace of Mother Mary, through her, might have changed him, had she cared enough to try. Such thinking was arrogance, she knew that; the man's destiny was set, and had been from the first. On that distant day in Linz, his destiny pointed to where he led the world today. And the memory of her days with him loomed in her mind like a memory of terrible sin.

Bereft for long years of the vision-haze, she spoke her confessions to a dour Auvergnat priest at the shrine of St. Catherine Labouré on the Rue du Bac, the one church in Paris in which she felt she belonged, more than in majestic Notre-Dame or the whited sepulchre of Sacré-Coeur or the exquisite

Sainte-Chapelle—or even the nearby Saint-Étienne-du-Mont, tomb of Ste. Genevieve, patron of Paris. St. Catherine Labouré was the site of the eponymous saint's famous encounters with the Virgin whom Stefanie had not encountered in so long . . . IF she had ever really done so, memory being the filter of the imagined past (encountered? *Seen*, rather, if not *glimpsed*) . . . but then no one claimed to be on such excellent terms with the Virgin as to see her every day. Not even Catherine Labouré. Stefanie met an old nun who had known the cheerful Saint Catherine at the derelict's hostel where she had worked for forty years. "Catherine was the incarnation, dear lady, of complete spiritual peace," said the nun. "Even after having lived through revolutions, civil war, poverty, disease, and the good Lord only knows what else, she radiated contentment of the spirit."

And there's the difference between her and me, thought Stefanie . . . well, one of the innumerable differences, the others being motherhood, teaching, the modern world, the war, the family . . . especially the family. Ever since the Anschluss and Johann Kohler's timely warning had permitted Stefanie to alert her mother, at least, to come to Paris, "only for a few days, *Mutti*," it had now been two years that mother and daughter had been sharing quarters. The old lady, seventy-four when she arrived, at first saw no real reason to stay away from Salzburg, but then she heard about the Germans' thuggish assault on Salzburg's much-loved anti-Nazi Archbishop, Sigismund Waitz, and the near destruction of the Residenz palace and its occupation by an SS unit.

"At that moment," she said, "I knew bad things were on the way, so I went to the bank for a cup of tea with Herr Muller, the accounts manager, and we succeeded in transferring whatever remains of your old trust fund to a bank in Geneva."

"My God, *Mutti*, that was bold of you."

"Yes," said her mother. "But now it's safe. I was beginning to understand what was going on, you see, and how hard it would be to reverse it. Because then those SS brutes sacked Klosterneuberg monastery and it dawned on me how bad things were and that my escape that seemed so ridiculous, like a bad novel, was actually quite well timed, and I thank you for it, *Gans*, and you can thank your German friend, even if he is Austrian . . . but the house on the Getriedegasse? We've had it for a hundred years, Steffi. And once this nonsense is over I'm going back, and so are you, and young Ignaz will have a home there."

Shaken as she was by the loss of her home, at first the old lady took against the French, as did everyone, for what she anticipated to be their arrogance, self-satisfaction, and smug superiority. Then she met actual French people, such as Sami and Léon Blum and her own grandson Ignace, and found them to be much like Austrians, depending on class, only more approachable. But she still railed at Stefanie for abandoning her homeland; yet only once did she mention the word "Führer," and then in sarcasm.

"I sincerely hope," one windy day when her arthritis was crippling, "*their* Führer isn't still *yours*, too. And if he is why he lets you knock around in a flat the size of a breadbox."

Stefanie forgave her that; there were moments, too, of comfort and ease between them, although there was barely enough room in the Rue Soufflot flat for Mutti, along with Stefanie, Ignace, and Sami, if mother and daughter doubled up and Sami slept on the sofa next to the balcony in the parlor—which he was only too happy to do. As he said, "looking out over the rooftops of Paris makes me feel young." He, too, was showing his age, even if he was spryer by far than Mutti. But at the outset of hostilities in '39 even he permitted himself an outburst of optimism, fueled by a drink or two—a Ricard at the Gueuze when he could obtain it, as the Government had measured its seriousness in waging this war by outlawing alcohol on Sundays. So it was wine at home, or at Fritz's house in Montrouge, until war was declared and overnight, before anyone could intervene, Fritz and Lotte and the boys, as enemy aliens, were sent to an internment camp at a place called Gurs, near the Pyrenees. The last Stefanie had heard, they were trying to get to Spain, and Sami was pulling whatever threadbare strings he could to make it possible. He had, he said, a couple of debts to call in from a former consular official in Madrid . . . "the old cuckold. Olé!"

Sami and Stefanie were allies now, both chastened by the

onrushing of war. Sami, for all his professed cynicism, had hardly recovered from the abrupt drama of his friend Blum's rise and fall, and his beating at the hands of Didier Buecher and his fascist mob had hurt his soul more than his body. He was distantly courteous when sober, elaborately so when drunk, and he and Stefanie were rarely if ever intimate, by inclination, logistics and temperament; yet in all circumstances he was quite sincerely concerned with Stefanie's welfare and that of her mother and son, and as devoted to them as the most uxorious of husbands, the most loyal of sons, the most loving of fathers.

And on Sunday, the thirteenth of May 1940, the scent of lilacs and iris and distant smoke floated on the warm spring air. Sami, Ignace, Stefanie and Stefanie's mother were in Stefanie's flat on the Rue Soufflot celebrating Sami's sixty-third birthday with a plate of rouleaux d'Alsace baked by the honoree himself.

"Hmm," was his verdict. "Crusty, not chewy enough. My skills have atrophied. I fancy I'll go back into baking for a while and learn to do something useful with my life, at long last."

The war, his birthday, the coming collapse: a call to arms to a tired ex-warrior. Retired from politics since Blum's last exit from the Prime Minister's office, Sami had backslid with gusto, taking on all his old bohemian habits, lambasting politics and politicians, and trying once again to play the part of dashing boulevardier; but the times were wrong for such a pose, and he knew it. Ever since the murder of the German Embassy attaché vom Rath by the Jewish boy Herschel Grynszpan (a *crime passionel* that Johann Kohler, one night at the Café Flore, had warned Stefanie about, based on his—smirk, smirk—observation of the boy's regular comings and goings at the side door of the Embassy, and his appearance one morning tousled and disheveled at vom Rath's side, and fierce gossip from the Embassy staff) and the raging Kristallnacht pogrom that had ensued in Germany, Sami had had only the grimmest forebodings. And when Stefanie's mother had arrived from Salzburg with the news that the Baron Ottoheinz had "disappeared" from his home in Vienna, Sami was, unhappily, vindicated.

"Disappeared?"

Ja, for Uncle Ernst it was too late, or so said Mutti.

"I talked to him once, just after it happened, the so-called Anschluss that made us into what they call Ostmark. Poor man, he told me things were terrible. Life changed overnight. One day life was all right, more or less, but the next day he was in hell. They'd been to his flat and ransacked it and carried out all the furniture and the artworks and left him with just the clothes he was standing up in. Then they started passing their horrid laws. Jews could go shopping only at certain times and only in certain shops where they had signs outside saying *Nür fur Juden*. You know your uncle, Stefanie, you know how he hates to be called *Jude*. But you wouldn't believe what else he had to put up with. Him, the Baron Ottoheinz! He was forbidden to take a taxi or sit in a tram or go into a laundry or a dry cleaner's, or to make a call from a public telephone or visit a coffeehouse or cinema . . . your uncle Ernst, not allowed to go to a coffeehouse! Or attend a concert or a play or even go into the parks and gardens, just imagine him without the opera to go to; and he told me he'd heard they were soon going to forbid all Jews to walk on the pavement on the side of the road next to the parks."

"God in Heaven."

Of course, she'd read the papers, she knew what was happening. But to have it all fall onto the frail shoulders of Uncle Ernst . . .

"So he went and stood for hours every day for three days in the Jewish post office, trying to get an emigration permit—yes, in all Vienna they have only one post office the Jews are allowed to use—by the way, he mentioned your friend Helmuth Meinl, it seems he and his family wasted no time in finding a friendlier place to do business in Lisbon, Portugal! But as I was saying. When Ernst finally got to talk to somebody they told him he was in the wrong place and had to go to another office. That was the last I heard from him. He was very upset and didn't sound well. He had a lady in to look after him but he was afraid she would leave because she was 'Aryan' and not allowed to associate with Jews. 'Aryan!' What nonsense! Aryans? It's the Indians who are Aryan, isn't it? Or the Persians? So I tried to telephone just before I left, but they said his line was disconnected," she said, shaking her head. "And a very nasty man told me to mind my own business and called me an old Jewess. In a Swabian accent."

"So now what's left?" inquired Sami, rhetorically. "Palestine, America, or more Ricard, thank you very much?"

"Well, they got Dr. Freud out in time. Then he died, of course. But he was with his family. In London. He was a friend of Ernst's, you know," Mutti said, absently.

It was agony for Stefanie to think of the humiliations visited upon her dapper, self-confident, oh-so-Viennese Uncle Ernst. (But even then, she briefly entertained the thought that Adolf Hitler had been lied to, or was too wrapped up in his fantasies to care.) She wondered if she might call Kohler, who might know how she might get a message through. She tried, but the man she spoke to was quite as rude as Mutti's Swabian had been to her; and now there was no German Embassy to call. Telephone contact with Germany itself was erratic and downright dangerous. So in desperation she wrote a letter to the Führer and Reichskanzler at the Obersalzberg ("... *can the life of Dr. Freud be worth so much more to you than the life of my beloved uncle, who never harmed you; on the contrary, don't you remember, he once gave you a painting commission when you were near starvation?* ... ") and dropped it in the post box on the corner of Boulevard St. Michel; but had she known how suspicious were the French Post Office's employees of letters addressed to Germany, never mind one addressed to Hitler himself, she would never have bothered. Her letter, with its bold address, was intercepted, sorted, and sent to the Quai d'Orsay for analysis, but events intervened before some third-rate intelligence hound could either send it on or trace it to its source, so it was put aside and forgotten for months that grew into years . . .

"With the world the way it is, no one knows what's going to happen next," Sami said. "Just remember, Stefanie, that this lad of yours is a Jew, as far as your ex-compatriots are concerned, never mind if he used to play cowboys and Indians with dear old Onkel Wolf. And if things go bad, what happened to your *real* uncle will happen to him and all of us *youpins*. Best to go on that little jaunt to Aunt Julie in Switzerland."

"So who's Aunt Julie, then?" inquired Ignace. "And Switzerland? Pah. It's too boring."

"You're absolutely right, young man. It *is* boring. But boredom is precisely what we should all be in search of. Indeed, I would elevate the accomplishment of universal boredom to be the prime indication of a society's degree of civilization, these days."

"So she's *Aunt* Julie, is she?"

Stefanie saw a twinkle, rare these days, in Sami's eye.

"Yes." He stroked his mustache. "Well. Not really. A nickname, you know. She's an old friend. Julie Rabochon, she used to be. She was on the stage. Started out in humble routines at the Moulin Rouge and Folies Bergère but moved up to serious roles at places like the Théâtre de l'Atelier and even a couple of times at the Comédie. I worked with her in some piece by Anouilh. Léon would be able to tell you which one . . . was it *Le voyageur sans bagage*? Perhaps. I forget. Trivial, although rather entertaining, as I recall, and my part was a fairly solid one, not that I ever went in for modern drama. Give me the classics in everything! But yes, she runs a theater in Geneva now, moved to Switzerland after her father, like me, lost damn near all he had in that Stavisky swindle back in '34 and shot himself in their flat on the Avenue des Ternes."

Stefanie felt herself stifling an absurd and quite pointless surge of old-fashioned jealousy . . . pointless because, after all, Samuel Lebel had never been faithful to any woman except to her, briefly—as he candidly confessed—and then she had to go and cuckold him with *Hitler*, "so after that I lost all faith in everything except what's safely dead and gone." As indeed he had, and faith not only in Man and Woman but in God, at Whom he scoffed. Sami's only counterpart to Stefanie's spiritual quest was his sporadic belief in some kind of enlightened socialism, of which Léon Blum was such a perfect representative: honest, cultured, civilized, and devoted to a better life for all. But all such enterprises turn into dogma sooner or later, and Blum's socialists were now no more than another squabbling flock of parliamentary chickens, uncertain whether to back Blum or Daladier or Reynaud or to vote themselves out of existence and join Thorez's now-banned Communists in the dark.

The somber mood was sustained over the next fortnight, with wildly contradictory reports coming from the Low Countries— Eben-Emael fortress captured, not captured, captured again; Brussels bombed, then not; the French surging ahead, then falling back (this was accurate) . . . then more welcome news came that Lotte and the boys had crossed the Pyrenees, thanks to Sami's friend in the Madrid consular office, and were now in still-smouldering Barcelona, recent headquarters of the world's freelance anarchists and Stalinists, and now quiet, under the amiable jackboot of Generalissimo Francisco Franco. Unfortunately Fritz was still at Gurs, and likely to be moved elsewhere, as an alien Jew and a German/Austrian one at that. Worse yet, by the month's end the myth of Fortress France was finally crumbling, along with the Army. The best troops were stuck in Belgium. The lines north of Amiens had split like a rotten log, letting the German torrent through. The joint expeditionary force was bleeding a slow death at Dunkerque, and all the householders and farmers and respectable citizens of northern France were fleeing to the still-peaceful south. From her balcony window, on the twenty-seventh of May, Stefanie could see, heading south on the Boulevard St. Michel, a procession of tumbrels slow but not stately—ragged, rather, and episodic, like a children's game—upon which tottered stacks of kitchen utensils, family treasures, and sundry bric-a-brac, drawn by wheezing cars and trucks and morose but phlegmatic horses; automobiles sagging under the weight of sofas and bedsteads; more bicycles, some with entire family groups perched upon them and upon one another like acrobats; ancient coal-lorries seconded to civilian duty and carrying Grandma's rocking chair and Grandpa's armchair, and people on foot pulling children's wagons with children and pets and aged relatives on board. At first the police tried to maintain order, shepherding the refugees away from the intersections, handing out violations, and dealing in various other forms of bureaucratic harassment; but gradually the gendarmes, too, yielded to the near-palpable sense of fatalism that hung heavier and heavier like a storm cloud over Paris and all of France, and the sad parade shuffled on. It was a scene of utter disintegration and unholy disorder quite alien to the Cartesian constraints of the French mind. Stefanie knew, then, that France was doomed.

On the morning of May 28 the news came over the radio that King Leopold had sued for terms.

"That's it. Belgium's gone belly up," growled Sami over his morning aperitif in the Gueuze which, as a Belgian bar run by a Belgian communist, would close down that afternoon in protest and sympathy. "The rosbifs are back home, thanks to the aristopig, that Churchill. He was responsible for the Dardanelles disaster in the war, did you know that? Oh, he's a fine one to pick to lead the English nation now. Straight to hell is where they'll go. And it'll all be over for us before you can say *ramoneur*. Our government's disintegrating as we speak. Reynaud's finished, and Daladier and Pétain will throw the gates wide open for friend Adolf. No, comrades, we're buggered. It's time to get out. Now."

"But our air force?" exclaimed the suddenly patriotic M. Juliot, the Belgian communist. "Our tanks?"

Sami shrugged.

"In mothballs or destroyed. Either way, there's nothing to stop the Boches anymore. We have no spirit. What's our moral purpose? Where's our national morale? We have none. Go into the street. You can feel it. Everything's stunned, paralyzed. We've lost. Bye-bye, France. And good riddance, if this is the best you can do."

Back upstairs he met with little protest from Stefanie. She agreed to send Ignace to Geneva, and she tried to insist that Mutti go, too; but the old lady, having uprooted herself once, was adamant on staying.

"No. It's too much. You have these stupid Germans getting you into a panic. It's unbecoming. No Germans will harm me. I am Friederika Amelie von Rothenberg of Salzburg and Mittelheim, and now of Paris. I stay."

So Sami got in touch via telegram with "Aunt" Julie Rabochon, now Julie Schwab, wife of a Swiss elementary-school teacher. With the blowsy generosity he so fondly recalled from days of yore, she at once invited the entire family to move in with her, Sami included; she had, she said, a huge old farmhouse in the Genevese countryside and only herself and her husband to occupy it. As for Ignace, he at first refused, then sulkily consented, with reservations, but where would he play soccer? What about Felicienne, his girlfriend? Did the Swiss have radio? Rugby? Airplanes? Was there a Métro?

"Oh, all right."

Ignace pouted and grimaced and by the time Sami and Stefanie were ready to take him to the train station, his mood had shifted with the weather-vane abruptness of his age, and he was quite looking forward to it all. Just before he left he telephoned his father, who was, surprisingly, at home, not dallying with some actress or soprano, or rehearsing a new piece. Stefanie spoke to Arthur for the first time in two years.

"Well, not exactly," said Arthur. "More like a year and a bit, isn't it? You know I've been busy, my dear, what with concerts and rehearsals. My new concerto's being performed in Rome next month and they're even talking about Washington in the autumn . . . no, listen, I *have* been checking up on the boy often enough. After all, he is my son too."

"Yes, Arthur. He is. And you have not."

Awkwardness intruded.

"So you're sending him to Switzerland?"

"Yes. Your uncle's idea. And you should go too."

"Switzerland? Me? Why, for goodness' sake?"

"Arthur." Stefanie found herself, suddenly, trembling with rage. "This may come as a surprise to you. But you aren't above it all, you know. The universe doesn't revolve around you and your music. Arthur, you're Jewish."

"Yes, yes, but this is France, not your friend Adolf's Aryan fantasy land. Liberty, equality, fraternity and all that. I'm French, my dear. Wasn't that the first thing I ever said to you?"

"No," said Stefanie, who remembered as clearly as if it had been that very morning. "You introduced yourself as Schubert. 'Schubert *à mes heures.*'"

"There you are," he said. His voice was harsher, hoarser, no doubt the result of a million Gauloises a day and a way of life in general incompatible with good health: cognac, actresses, late nights in belowstairs clubs. "It was *in* French, anyway."

Oh, Arthur, thought Stefanie. Oh, God.

"Say good bye to your father," she said to Ignace, and handed him the receiver.

Ignace's train left from the Gare de Lyon. The north-south Métro lines were packed, so they walked down the Boul' Mich' and across the Île de la Cité to the Place du Châtelet to catch the No. 1 Neuilly–Vincennes train eastbound. The flood of refugees down the Boul' Mich' appeared to have dwindled, but it had merely been diverted to the outer boulevards to permit greater freedom of movement in the central city to military and police. Indeed, on the avenues of the inner *arrondissements* there seemed to be little traffic other than taxis commandeered by the government, lorries loaded high with ministerial documents and filing cabinets, nervous gendarmes on bicycles, and army trucks and ambulances containing stained and weary soldiers from the ever-approaching front lines. The few people left on the streets were standing in small groups, brandishing newspapers *(the Petit Parisien*: "The Day of Reckoning Is At Hand! Pray to Ste. Geneviève!"). The words "*le Maréchal*" were invoked in measured, reverential tones, like the name of God, Whose grand old Gothic house of Notre-Dame was filling with worshippers as Stefanie, Sami, and Ignace walked by. The Cathedral's great bell, Marie-Thérèse, tolled as she had tolled so often in the centuries before for plague and famine and worse, for the catastrophes of Man's making, war and siege and massacre; *dong . . . dong . . . dong* she rang, into the sweet breezes of May and out over the paralyzed city and across the golden wheat fields of the Île-de-France toward the approaching darkness from the east. It was a funeral service for the nation.

Sami spat.

"*Fumier*," he said. "They're praying for a miracle. Poor fools."

The Gare de Lyon was seething. On the quais for the south-bound trains were groups of foreigners eager to get out, Parisian families dispatching children to relatives in the supposed safety of the provinces, lesser stars of stage and screen heading to the balmier climes of the Côte d'Azur ("Look!" said Ignace erroneously; "there's Jean-Louis Barrault!"), and insurance salesmen and estate agents spotting the main chance in the midst of chaos ("we'll take over your house and garden while you're away, get you a good price, Boches or no Boches"). Loudspeakers crackled incessantly and incomprehensibly. Whistles blew; locomotives heaved mighty sighs. Porters were being tested to the limits of their strength. Ignace hoisted his modest valise onto his back and trotted happily toward the train, as if headed to Arcachon for a fortnight at the beach. Stefanie, hurrying to keep up, admired her son's carelessness, his unthinking health, the fluency of his muscles, and she saw him—with the pride none but a mother can know—as an affirmation of life, hers and his; as her legacy to the world, a vigorous young man with all the setbacks and sadness of life before him but with much joy ahead, too, and love, and creation—even if it was only in the sound of an airplane engine, or a racing car . . . with God's grace, and the Holy Mother's.

"*Revoir, Maman*," he said, muffled by Stefanie's devouring embrace. He was leaving her for the first time, really, except for a cycling trip in the Vendée two years earlier. But that had been only for five days, and this would be for God knew how long. Sami shook hands formally, with a slight inclination of the head, like an ambassador presenting credentials. Impatient, the boy elbowed his way onto the train through the leave-taking couples and bawling children and officious conductors and reappeared, waving, at the window of a compartment in the middle of the carriage, directly above the waybill on the side of the carriage that read PARIS (Gare de Lyon)-Sens-Auxerre-Beaune-Mâcon-Bourg-Bellegarde-GENEVE (Cornavin).

"I want to go, too," said Stefanie through her tears.

"You should," said Sami. "You must."

She agreed.

But then she changed her mind and insisted on staying in Paris. The Académie Werfel, catering as it did mostly to the

children of German and, formerly, Austrian Embassy person-
nel, had lost half of its enrollment when war was declared, and
the inculcation of Germanic language and culture had suddenly become a low priority in the jittery new wartime France,
although there were voices murmuring in the tones of appease-
ment that would soon become so familiar: "Might be a good
idea to learn their language . . . " So the school remained open,
and someone was needed to oversee the few remaining staff and
students. This task had fallen to Stefanie.

"If you want to stay, stay," said Sami, with a shrug. "At least
you and your mother aren't Jewish, and Ignace should soon be
safe. And you have your certain, shall we say, connections? But
as for me, I'm heading off. Any day now."

"Where? Aunt Julie's?"

"Perhaps eventually, *ma chère*. In the meantime, well . . . " He
winked. "I can't tell you that. I hardly know myself."

But she was certain he did know. On the morning of the
thirtieth she awoke to find his sofa-bed neatly made and most
of his clothes missing from the wardrobe. The mingled scent of
his cologne and the Gauloises he smoked was dwindling in the
air, and a note lay on the writing desk.

"Doddering dotard or not, I'm off to give your friend Adolf
a boot up the arse. *À bientôt.*"

In a hasty postscript he had written:

"War or no war, I still love you, poor fool, poor fool that I
am."

Stefanie wept for them both, for them all.

Glory—and Its Opposite

June 28, 1940, eight a.m., under a cloudless sky, the temperature
a pleasant twenty-two degrees C, winds freshening in the east.

Jean-Xavier Durand, fifty-two, was head porter at the Hotel
Gray de Rastignac on the Avenue de Maine. He was a native
of Dole in the Jura and a communist *de pure souche*, the son
of communists, 1906 graduate of the Lycée Louis Pasteur in
Besançon, father of one, grandfather of three, husband of Amélie

Dudevant of Annecy in Haute-Savoie, part-owner with her of the Dudevant bakery on Annecy's Rue Rousseau.

On June 28 Jean-Xavier stood atop the staircase at the entrance of the distinguished old Second Empire hotel, on the job even with no job to be on. He looked down the splendid avenue of swank shops and fashion houses that was deserted at eight in the morning of a weekday, except for a row of parked and empty RATP buses; a peculiar-looking German military vehicle with a rigid swastika flag on its right front wing, driven by at high speed by a uniformed German soldier; a Citroën Traction driven slowly past by a man in a broad-brimmed hat, next to whom sat an identical man who gazed thoughtfully at Jean-Xavier *en passant*; and a coal delivery wagon drawn by a sprightly horse whose master coaxed him past the entrance of the hotel in a gentle monotone, as if they were on a country road in the windswept marshes of Charente rather than in the stilled heart of the metropolis. Over on the Champs-Élysées there was no traffic to speak of, but the night before the Germans had been parading up and down, celebrating their victory. The brass and drums and woodwinds of their marching bands had been audible all night, depending on the direction of the wind, but with the four o'clock curfew still in force not many natives could go and see their damned parades, not that anyone wanted to. Anyway, they didn't care what the French thought. The French were defeated, finished, humiliated, in a word: *kaput*. And some would say, Quite right, too. Jean-Xavier, for one. He would say that, and had, being known for his bolshie tendencies. *Vive la Révolution!*

He was wearing his head porter's uniform and smoking his last Caporal, and he was more worried about where he would buy his cigarettes than about the country's fate. France was corrupt, eaten away, everyone knew that, hadn't old Blum been saying it for years? And Blum was no saint, no genius, no, he was just a silly old Jew who read too many books, but he was right about a few things. The collapse came as no surprise to any true socialist with half a brain. It was historically inevitable, like the worldwide proletarian uprising that would be led by the Soviet

Union. Meanwhile, there were the Boches, and say what you would about them, efficiency was what they were made of, so maybe things would start working a little better for a while, until the Soviet Union triumphed over the capitalists. Efficiency was certainly at a premium at the Hotel Gray de Rastignac, which, like every other business establishment in Paris, was in something of an uproar. In the lobby, the few remaining guests were forming different queues depending on nationality and ability to bribe the manager, M. Blond, who was insisting the hotel be shut down for the duration. But the owners, the Paoli brothers from Nice, visions of crisp Reichsmarks dancing before their eyes, were demanding it be kept open. The staff came down on both sides at once. None of it mattered, because everyone knew the ultimate decision belonged to the Boches, who had already taken over the Crillon and the Meurice and the Ritz. And as for him, Jean-Xavier, head porter? *Bof*, he'd wait until things died down in Paris and then he'd make his way down south to Annecy, in the unoccupied Free Zone, and help his wife out with the bakery for a while. The sooner the better, because trips down south weren't as easy as they'd been. Jean-Xavier's stints at the hotel were for six months on, six months off, and he hadn't seen Amélie in four months; and he didn't like the sound of the fellow she'd just taken on to help grind the flour . . . a "baker" from Alsace, *hein*? A runaway Paris banker or loan shark, or he, Jean-Xavier, was a singing Jewish rabbi from Poland . . .

Jean-Xavier's wandering thoughts were immediately diverted into the channel of the here and now when the eerie quiet of the Avenue de Maine was softly interrupted by the appearance of a shiny Mercedes landau followed by another, identical Mercedes, then a Wehrmacht staff car, then a soldier riding a motorcycle with sidecar, in which sat another soldier, machine gun at the ready. The motorcade came to a slow halt, exuding Importance. Jean-Xavier tossed aside his cigarette and tugged nervously at his lapels. A man in the lead car, wearing a German military cap with a long visor and a gray leather overcoat, stood up and looked around.

"*Pardon!*" The driver of the second Mercedes was beckoning.

"You, monsieur. Here, please."

Ensuring with a glance over his shoulder that no other monsieur was intended, Jean-Xavier buttoned up his vest, patted down his hair, and obeyed the beckoning finger, not daring as he hurried down the steps to look at the standing man in the gray overcoat in the first car because he didn't need to look, he already knew who it was, it was unmistakable, the mustache, the hat, the way he just stood there, one hand on the windscreen, the other on his hip, surveying the horizon . . .

"I am hoping this way is the right road for the Trocadéro, monsieur," said the driver in a pleasant German accent that reminded Jean-Xavier of his Swiss neighbors back in the Haute-Savoie. "We have a very urgent schedule."

"Yes, yes," said Jean-Xavier. "This is the right way. Continue on this street down to the Place de l'Alma. Then straight on and you will see the Eiffel Tower, across the river of course. The Palais Chaillot is at the Trocadéro, on this side. There is a fine view from . . . "

"Thank you, monsieur." The driver drew a wrinkled fifty Reichsmark banknote out of his breastpocket, unfolded it, and handed it to Jean-Xavier as the convoy moved away and Jean-Xavier the head porter at the Hotel Gray de Rastignac caught the eye of Adolf Hitler the conqueror of France, and without a second thought, as if governed by instinct, both men saluted each other.

"*Bien oui, vous savez*, I couldn't help myself, it just happened, like I was a marionette having its strings pulled," Jean-Xavier excitedly explained later in the staff kitchens to his intimates, from whom he purloined cigarettes, and to whom he displayed the fifty-mark note as evidence of his adventure. "I mean, you can say what you like, oh I know I know I know, you don't need to tell me, *ben oui* he's crazy, he's the enemy of the working man, he wants to conquer the world and kill everybody and all that, *mais oui*, and of course there he is lording it over us, waltzing through our country he's just kicked the shit out of, but I can tell you, and don't laugh, he had such an air, such an authority, you know, just standing there in the front of his car like, I don't know, like a captain of the winning football team, an admiral on his destroyer, standing in that beautiful polished gleaming Mercedes Benz . . . and then what do you imagine, he returned my salute, no, no, I'm serious, I gave him a salute, perfectly normal, as you do in the army, you know, like that, just out of respect, and I swear to you he returned it, like that, I mean the *sacré* Führer *des Boches, nom de Dieu,* saluting Jean-Xavier Durand, *petit français moyen de rien du tout.*" He grinned. "And you know? If I'd had a gun, I could have shot him there and then!"

Hitler had less to say about the encounter.

"I told you Avenue de Maine was the correct route, Kempka. I have memorized the city."

Erich Kempka silently concurred, concerned primarily with keeping his job as personal driver to the Führer and head of the Reich Chancellery motor pool, a responsible position that had its perks such as this totally unexpected side trip to Paris: out of bed at four in the morning, onto a plane, off the plane at Le Bourget and into one of the two Chancellery cars already waiting for them . . . and now, after they'd already spent an hour at the Opéra, *he* wanted to see the Eiffel Tower, then Voltaire's and Napoleon's tombs. And Kempka, who had only been to Paris once before, in '29, for the car races at Montlhéry, had no more of an idea of the French Capital's layout than he did of the moon's. But they soon arrived at the Trocadéro. Speer, Breker, Heischler, and the others got out and went first, then *he* stepped down from his perch next to Kempka in the main car and followed the others slowly, hands clasped behind his back, looking up at the sky as if expecting it to look different from the sky in Germany, then he looked behind and to the left and to the right, while Hoffmann clicked away with his Leica. It was a fine day on which to admire the glories of the disgraced metropolis. He admired the Palais de Chaillot, and kept his counsel, as he did so well, when Speer jokingly said that the German and Soviet pavilions had been face to face at the '37 World Fair.

"Of course, they didn't know then, and neither did we, that we would actually be standing side by side some day!"

For the time being, he mused, and turned his mind to the grand panorama of conquest that lay at his feet like an architect's model: the Seine, river of kings, interspersed with unkingly barges on which he could see laundry, dogs, children; that soaring masterpiece of radio-tower art with the German name Eiffel, topped by the New German flag, *his* flag, the *Hakenkreuz*; behind the tower, the rectilinear expanse of the Champs de Mars, where Louis XIII and XIV and Napoleon had drilled and marched and trained the troops that had once dominated poor fractured Germany and most of the world . . . It was the greatest city on earth, and the capital of the greatest power in Europe, and both were under his boot, his to do with as he pleased. It wasn't a reward that came in everyone's life, to have one day all France as a plaything.

Two days earlier, in the historic Compiègne forest, a solemn act by the Führer and Supreme Commander of the Defense Forces wiped out the iniquity of 1918. The French delegation received the armistice terms from the Chief of the High Command, and the armistice was signed at 6:50 p.m. on June 22. At 1:35 p.m. on June 25, the German and Italian defense forces ended hostilities against France. The greatest victory of German forces, culminating the greatest campaign of all times, had been concluded within six weeks.

He took a deep, pure, hero's breath and restrained himself from breaking into loud laughter, or dancing a *ländler*, or suddenly bursting into coarse oaths. People were watching, from a distance, ordinary people, passersby, the French. He saw them pointing but decided against acknowledging them: *always maintain the godlike stance!* Hoffmann fussed about, getting poses, camera angles, adjusting his lenses, and so on. Speer hovered nearby, then wandered down to the Trocadéro with his camera, then back again and stood to one side talking to Breker, who was quite visibly excited, and who, as an ex-resident of Montmartre in the twenties, was the only one who really knew his way around. During the party's years of struggle, the years of hiding in dirty alleys and sliding on snowdrifts to hand out pamphlets and stepping into puddles and trying to make oneself heard above the wind and the rain and the jeers to handfuls

of embittered and usually drunk Freikorps vets and bribing the
police and taunting the Communists and shivering or sweating
in unheated or uncooled halls and going underground during the
ban . . . during all that time, Breker was playing accordions and
fucking Parisian girls and learning his craft under the thousand
chimney pots of Montmartre, La Bohème, Paree.

He envied him, truth to tell.

"I've seen enough here. Now we go to the Panthéon."

Discussions of boulevards, back streets, the quickest routes
along the Seine, etc., were cut short by the imperious command:

"Go. *Ruck zuck.*"

Then:

"But first I have a stop to make. Kempka, drive to No. 25
Rue Soufflot."

Across the river and left along the Quai d'Orsay and right
turn along the Boulevard Saint Germain past the Assemblée
Nationale and the empty government offices of the France that
was, whose government had decamped first to Tours, then to
Bordeaux, and was now scattered to all points of the compass
but fast converging on a spa town called Vichy; and right again
near the venerable Sorbonne (which name he pronounced with
the greatest respect) and the lead car, his car, drew to a halt on
the Rue Soufflot, just up from the Luxembourg gardens, just
down from the Panthéon, and across from a café with the odd
name Gueuze. Hurried negotiations resulted in Breker being
designated to accompany him.

But just as the two men were preparing to cross the street, an
old man in a beret and blue veteran's overcoat leaning on his cane
on the street corner—evidently quite drunk—started shouting.

"*Mais merde, c'est pas vrai! Venez voir! C'est pas vrai! J'y crois
pas! Venez donc voir! C'est lui!*"

Breker, who spoke good French, was sent over with more
Reichsbank notes to ease compliance, but the old man backed
away and pointed and kept shouting, like an irate toddler.
His voice resounded up and down the street, which was, like
most of Paris that day, almost entirely deserted; but here and
there a window opened stealthily. Then the old man, ignoring

Breker's increasingly impatient entreaties, stood to attention and launched into a quavering and hoarse but powerful rendition of his own version of the Marseillaise, adapted to present circumstances.

> *Aux enfants de la patrie-ie-ie-yeuh,*
> *Le jour de . . . HONTE . . . est arrive-é-é-é!*
> *Avec nous c'est la tyrannie-ie-ie-yeuh,*
> *Son étendard sanglant est levé-é-é-é!*

The commotion in the street awoke Stefanie. She was at home with a damp cloth pressed against her throbbing temple—the vision-haze had come and left a migraine but no vision. Looking out the window, what she saw appeared at first to be a raid of the kind they had been warned to expect ever since the collapse: three or four German vehicles, a number of military-looking Germans standing about, an old man waving his cane in the air and bawling continuously what sounded like a speech; then she realized it was the now-banned Marseillaise.

> *Entendez-vous dans les campagnes*
> *Mugir ces féroces soldats ?*
> *Ils viennent jusque dans vos bras*
> *Égorger vos fils, vos compagnes.*
> *Aux armes, citoyens!*

A shout was followed by explosive coughing and more shouts, then the slam of a car door. Stefanie braced herself for worse: gunshots, screams, explosions . . . but she heard nothing except the sound of the cars speeding away. She stepped onto the balcony and looked down. The old man was waving his stick at the cars which, accompanied by a motorcycle outrider, drove up the street as far as the Panthéon, where their passengers emerged and fanned out around a central figure in a coat and cap who got out and started strolling towards the entrance.

Mutti came out of the kitchen with tea.

"*Was ist los, buzi?*"

"*Mutti.* Oh my God." Suddenly Stefanie understood. "It's him."

Mutti, too, understood, as soon as she had joined her daughter at the window and as soon as she saw the convoy parked in front of the Panthéon, at the end of the street.

"Him," she said. "Hitler? Our new Kaiser? The *schleimer* from Braunau? Bring him to me, I'll stick this teapot up his . . . "

But Stefanie, wild-eyed, possessed by God only knew what illusion (the illusion, perhaps, that she could yet make a difference), her migraine forgotten, her hair in disarray, flung herself out of the apartment and down the unlit stairwell into the street. Out of breath, she slowed her pace, as Reason once again resumed its throne and reminded her of the stark verities of war, occupation, general dissolution, murder, and the fact that the figure ascending the steps into the Panthéon at the end of the street was no longer a part of her past but a part of everyone's, and architect of everyone's present and future. He was now remote, fearsome, and detached from humanity, on an Olympus of his own making; and there was no room for mercy or forgiveness in his soul. Truly, what could she do? Fling herself at his feet? Burst into tears? Plead for Uncle Ernst's life by interposing herself between the conqueror and the tomb of Voltaire?

Seduce him again?

Too late, *Gans*, she said to herself. Too late. He was no longer hers, if he had ever been; but he was now the world's, entirely, and God pity the world.

She turned and wearily climbed the stairs to her apartment; wearily, but feeling less alone.

The Nighttime World

"Well, they dragged him out in the end, of course, but first Blum got his own back, according to this. He started in with the armistice, then the October 4 law against the Jews, saying how these so-called laws and treaties were flagrantly illegal. They shouted at him but he shouted back, so they threw him out and now it looks like they'll close down the trial altogether."

"Good old Léon."

"*Nein. Poor* old Léon. They'll probably be sending him to one of Germany's famous and attractive holiday camps to be *umgesiedelt*, resettled, as they say—in lovely Dachau, maybe? Or scenic Ravensbrück?"

"Oh God."

The first speaker was Fritz Ottoheinz; the second, his cousin Stefanie. Fritzl was reading from a letter from his wife, Lotte. Stefanie, listening, felt herself slowly being drawn toward the abyss. The signs of civilization's end were everywhere in the daily life of Occupied Paris. Stefanie and Frau von Rothenberg had a small allocation of coupons for basics like clothing and food— Stefanie the A permit, good for 1200 calories a day, issued to citizens between the ages of twenty-one and seventy not employed in vital industries, Mutti the V permit, for "*vieillards*," the old, who rated 1800 calories per diem, if they were lucky—but Mutti, recalling days of deprivation in the first war, ingeniously made clothes out of dyed curtains or blankets. Shoes with wooden soles were now in the shopwindows. Still, at least there were ways of bypassing the clothes shortage, with that combination of cunning, artful dodging and imagination known by the French as "*le système D*"; but food rationing was harder to avoid by early '42. The ration for an adult with the A card was 250 grams of bread a day, 200 grams of sugar a month, 300 grams a month of a dreadful ersatz coffee made of chicory, and 350 grams of meat (including bones) a week, in all cases less than a quarter the prewar average. Cuts of beef had virtually disappeared, although brains, livers and kidneys spilled out across the tiles of many a *boucherie*, creating the illusion of abundance. Pork and chicken supplies were erratic, but anything could be had for bribes, frequently sexual favors. Propositioned by the local butcher, a florid Norman with whom she'd done business for ten years, Stefanie withered him with the acid insult "*Monsieur, je vous ai pris pour un gentilhomme, mais je vois que vous n'êtes qu'un satyre!*" and refused to set foot again in his shop. She or Mutti took the Métro one stop to an Alsatian butcher in the Châtelet who was sympathetic to the plight of German-speaking non-Germans. As for bread, the cornerstone of the French table, Stefanie had to queue for an hour or more for a hard, black ersatz *baguette* made of Brazil nuts and, so it was rumored, sawdust. Taxes had been imposed on things deemed luxuries like pets, sheet metal, firewood, and wax matches. Cars had disappeared, except some converted to run on gas or coal and those belonging to the German administration and its French fellow travelers. Rickshaw-like *vélotaxis* had taken the place of taxis on the street soon after the fall, and now making their appearance in the city were bizarre coal-powered cars with prominent smoke-belching smokestacks, capable of moving only at a snail's pace, malodorously and with great commotion.

There were myriad other indications, too, of society's downward course. Trains moved through the night eastward from the Paris suburbs, carrying human cargo. Jews, newly required to wear the yellow star (Fritz refused), were restricted to one shopping hour a day and denied access to all the professions. The war was now worldwide—finally, said Fritz, who was confident the Yankees would win. But there was a long way to go yet. In the last few days, posters had appeared around the city. They depicted the star of David against a violently black background between the German and French slogans "*Wenn Du Dieses Zeichen Siehst . . .*" and "*Quand Tu Vois Cet Enseigne . . .*" and at the bottom was the telephone number of the Gestapo headquarters on the Avenue Henri-Martin.

In that miserable cold, wet and windy early March of Year III of France's ineradicable shame Fritz and Stefanie made up a household consisting of themselves and Frau von Rothenberg. Sami was away, none knew where; but that was to be expected in these times. Rumors, and a message routed via Ignace and the Red Cross in Geneva, placed him somewhere in the southeastern so-called Free Zone where Vichy's writ ran, in the Haute-Savoie or Ain departments. Resistance activity was on the upswing down there, and Stefanie was positive Sami was involved, aging and occasionally infirm that he was; what else had he to live for, after all, but his love of a France that had probably never been and his contempt for everything that was? Ignace, happily, was established as a Swiss resident, thanks to "Tante" Julie Schwab. The boy was in his first year in the Applied Mechanics department at the University of Geneva, and had a Swiss girlfriend.

[Gustavus Interruptus—*I feel I must say that these Geneva connections are proof the world is becoming smaller. For one thing, down the street from my mamma in her placid suburb of Confignon lives a retired old professor named Lebel whose wife is an occasional shopping companion of hers. For another, the name Julie Schwab has long been emblazoned across the top of the theatrical posters of the Comédie, and the lady even has a street named after her somewhere, I believe, in the Petit-Saconnex district. Well-deserved, judging by this.*]

Overall, circumstances had, so far, spared them all. Even Arthur was safe, having at the last minute sailed for America with a Russian couple named Nabokov to whom Arthur had lent a thousand francs for passage, the husband being a lepidopterist and minor novelist and apparently quite respectable. Arthur was now in New York playing the piano at a hotel while awaiting repayment by the imperious but impecunious Russians. Yes, things could be worse, so far, by far; but in those days "so far" was a perilously fragile safeguard against the future. Fritz, as a one-armed, red-faced, peppery "German" had been turned down by the "*Groupement de travailleurs étrangers*" because of his handicap, with or without his prosthetic arm, which in any case was beginning to creak and show signs of age. With no apparent Jewish antecedents or relations (to his shame, he had hotly denied having any when asked, "just to get out of that hellhole") he had been released from Gurs after the *feldgrau* avalanche of 1940 and the appointment of the military dotard Pétain as make-believe Head of State in his opéra bouffe capital, Vichy. Lotte and the boys were still in Spain, but Fritz was caught and turned back at the border by Pétain's newly vigilant gendarmes and threatened with imprisonment in the camp at Le Vernet next to which, those in the know had it, Dachau was a holiday resort. But thanks to the general confusion of the times and a gendarme heeding nature's call, Fritz had strolled out of police headquarters in Perpignan and, posing as a demobbed Alsatian serviceman, had headed in the opposite direction from the southward flow of refugees, into the occupied zone and Paris via back roads, river barges, farm carts, and the occasional spine-jarring bike ride.

"I was the only one going in the wrong direction," he said, "so nobody paid any attention." He had finally attained the sanctuary of cousin Stefanie's flat on the Rue Soufflot three weeks after leaving Gurs. His and Lotte's house in Vanves had been boarded up by the same mysterious powers who'd removed his name and night watchman's job from the Dewoitine payroll. He survived, ironically, on a half pension from the German administrators of the Ottoheinz estate in Vienna. Yes, in the midst of war and chaos, the payment of 450 Reichsmarks to a one-armed half Jew in France arrived with clockwork or Teutonic precision in the third week of every month, forwarded by the Vanves post office and containing a receipt entitled *Empfangsschein* stamped by the Gau Groß Wien, with at the bottom of the page the signature of Austria's Nazi Governor *du jour*. The latest payment had arrived simultaneously with the letter from Lotte, making that day a rare bright one in the drabness of Germanized France.

Fritzl brandished the letter, which had been smuggled from Spain via the Pyrenees "pipeline."

"It's a miracle, getting this," he said. "And it doesn't have their greasy fingerprints all over it."

Lotte's news was brief, apart from the clandestine updates on the Blum trial that she heard on Spanish radio and from the BBC (and that no collaborationist newspaper would print); she had a job in a German toy shop in Barcelona. The boys, Kurt and Willi, were in the German school and paid for their lessons by giving German lessons to eager Spaniards, most of whom were pro-Nazi and still expected Germany to win. Fritzl chafed at the thought of his wife's probable Spanish suitors, "all mustaches and liquid eyes and guitars and that Latin palaver."

"I'd worry more about the Germans," muttered Stefanie.

And, with the apparent inevitability of the new world order Kurt and Willi were eager to get involved—on different sides, lamented Lotte.

"Kurt's all for the Allies," she said in her letter, "because of

Betty Grable and Hollywood movies, mostly; but Willi's turning into a little Nazi. His Francoist friends around here don't
help any."

"*Willi, ach, du Lauser,*" lamented Fritzl. "A little Nazi, my
own little man?"

"Oh, he doesn't know what that means. If he tried to be a
real Nazi, they'd send him off to the camps. He's a quarter-Jew,
after all."

"A quarter Jew, a quarterhorse, a quarter kilo . . . God, what
a world. Léon Blum is right," said Fritz. "We've succumbed to
our worst nature. But *he's* had it now, too. You know what's happening, even to French Jews. I mean, you think we have it bad
with our ration cards . . . "

"Oh I know. Mother of God."

Blum, Vichy's prisoner, had lambasted Vichy from the dock,
and had spoken with such sarcasm and eloquence as to embarrass Pétain's goons and Hitler's henchmen, not to mention the
slavish Vichy press like *Je suis partout*, whose headlines screeched
"Silence! The Rabbi Speaks" and "Blum: Once a Liar . . . "

"*I*, a defeatist?" roared Blum—"with," as Lotte, no philo-Sem-
ite, put it, "the dignity of an old-fashioned German headmaster"—"*I*, a fifth columnist? *I*, a traitor? When those who purport
to sit in judgment upon me wear the blood-soaked uniforms of
their oppressors? When my critics serve at the bidding of a foreign government that has trampled our fair green France into
the mud and filth of slavery and humiliation?"

Then cowardice, the spirit of the age, silenced him and muzzled the once-garrulous yellow tabloids. Blum was deported to
Germany. For it was 1942, the age of compromise and collaboration, and Hypocrisy was the crowning virtue; and the rain
in that March of 1942 was steady and cold and never-ending.

And Sami was gone.

In his place came Johann Kohler, now in the SS, with a
proposal.

Kohler's Proposal

"*Ja*, in the SS, me, Johann Kohler the car jockey from Salzburg? A pretty big surprise, eh?"

"*Himmeldonnerwetter*," was Stefanie's only comment.

"*Ja*, I can I tell you, I was surprised, too, I mean I never went in for all that military stuff, so you know actually it was the idea of one of the higher-ups, well, just between you and me and the lamppost working for Brüder Hermann can really pay off when he's on one of his binges. I knew a guy who got a brand-new Horch drophead out of him! But listen, I'm only an *SS-Schütze*, just a lowly private, so practically anybody can give me orders. You too, Frau von Rothenberg. Go ahead, try! And don't worry, I'm not going to shoot anybody, ah ha ha, I'm still just a humble chauffeur at heart."

He came to call, bowing formally. Fritz stayed with an invalid Polish friend from his former workplace, and all traces of his residence were hurriedly swept away, or locked into drawers. Stefanie introduced Kohler to Mutti, whose presence in Paris was, after all, a direct result of his warning, that pre-Anschluss night in 1938. But Mutti, only recently recovered from a bedridden bout of "life fatigue," looked him up and down and grumbled, "bah, I'd have been better off if I'd stayed in Salzburg. Turn your back for a minute and there they are again, these *wapplers* in their stupid uniforms, marching all over the place like toy soldiers, one-two one-two *links links*."

"Ah ha ha. Well, *Mutter*, we can arrange it, if you like, for you to return to Salzburg," said Kohler.

"And can you arrange for Salzburg to be returned to Austria, and Austria to Austrians?"

"Oh, I never talk politics, *Mutti*! One of my few principles."

Well, he'd finally found his true place in life, thought Stefanie. His ruddy jowls and now-graying hair were set off by the black and silver of the SS uniform, and his bluff way would win over or dominate many a duller dullard; and he was the kind of second-rate sensualist who'd take full advantage of his position, and was already trying to.

So now he, she said with false enthusiasm (by way of deflection), had ended up among the elite of the new Germany! Congratulations!

"*Europe*, my dear Frau von Rothenberg. Not only Germany. Europe. We have Frenchmen, Belgians, Italians, Ukrainians, even a couple of Englishmen, or maybe Irish. I tell you, it's a real League of Nations, the SS."

Their first meeting place was once again the Gueuze, but it sold no more Belgian beer and Provencal pastis since M. Juliot had splashed *A Bas les Boches* across the shutter and fled into the country to join the embryonic Communist resistance. Fewer dishes were served, and the wine and beer were mediocre. There was no pastry, and what passed for coffee had seen better days under the roots of oak trees; but a German, especially one wearing the SS uniform, was guaranteed access to hidden delights, such as *cassoulet* and *confit d'oie* and *caneton farci*, as Kohler was boyishly eager to prove. Stefanie had doubts about sitting in public with an SS man ("are you crazy, *Gans*?" said Mutti; "they'll shoot you"), but the Gueuze was hardly "public," being run by and for the German military and its local acolytes. Sitting there, watching the occasional leg-powered *vélotaxi* or coal-fired bus or German military vehicle lumber past, Stefanie felt like the sole survivor of a unique disaster, surrounded by ghosts: the ghost of Sami, haranguing Juliot at the bar; the ghost of Arthur at the piano; the ghosts of Blum, and Jean Lussac, and the once-hopeful band of '36, now scattered, or under arrest, or dead . . . and here was another kind of ghost of her past, a man in the uniform of the SS, making eyes at her (more boldly this time than the last) . . . at *her*, a fifty-one year-old matronly hausfrau and part-time mystic and ex-schoolteacher!—and, what was more, he was offering her a job.

"You deserve more than this," he said, not making entirely clear the subject of his "this" but implying the circumstances that confined her in a small apartment with an aged mother. Unfortunately, he was right; she did need work. Fritz's monthly pension check and Mutti's dwindling savings weren't enough for the three of them, and the Académie Werfel, along with all other German-affiliated institutes, had been merged into

the new Haus der Deutschen Kultur at the Hotel de Sagan
on the Rue St. Dominique, near the Eiffel Tower. There, it
was hoped that Frenchmen would painlessly be transformed
into good little Nazis—"German Culture" of course being a
euphemism for *Eindeutschung*, Germanization, or Nazi indoc-
trination . . . and indeed, Kohler's idea was for her to run a class
on "Germanism."

"I mean, as an Austrian, you know something about regional
differences. It's going to be important, in the new Europe, for
everyone to grasp the subtleties of our German language and
cultural habits. Things to do, things to say, how to pronounce
this and that. Things to avoid, words with double meanings.
You know. Like a class in etiquette. *And* you're a lady, and a *von*
into the bargain. An adornment to any institute, if I may say so."

"Most kind, but . . . " She stopped herself from blurting out
that she didn't want to work for the Reich in any way, shape, or
form. She needed the job; that was that. But it was hardly the
time for haughty dismissals. She reminded herself that for all
his apparent geniality Kohler was, after all, one of *them*; and so
often, she had found, surface geniality and bluff good humor are
masks for quite the opposite. His face was heavy now, teased into
a semblance of handsomeness by hair oil and eau de cologne,
vanities he'd never displayed in the past, not having been able to
afford them . . . and the attentive ways he had, now, were those
of a man with some little power over others, especially women—
and was this not the reason nine out of ten men sought power
in the first place? His gaze was less uncertain than it had been,
and his deference was gone. He spoke with greater authority. He
flirted, but his flirting had an automatic quality to it, like the
heel-clicking and hand-kissing that were part of his *kleinbürger-
lich* Austrian background . . . like Hitler, she thought. Still, he
held himself sufficiently in check for Stefanie to be able to agree
to work at the Institute without feeling like a whore. Education
was education, and she would never abandon her love of the
German language; and who better to teach it?

"I only hope I won't have to wear a uniform," she said. He
laughed.

"Oh, on the contrary, my dear Frau von Rothenberg, I hope you do. Isn't that one of the best parts of this war, getting to wear a uniform? And getting to get out of one, at crucial moments?"

She ignored his lewdness.

"Well, I won't teach anything called German*ism*," she said. "But I'll teach *German*, if you want me to."

"Done."

"Are you mad, girl?" raged Fritz, when he heard the news. "Why not just sign up with the League of Nazi Whores? Or the Girlies' SS?"

"It's German I'll be teaching, Fritzl. Not Nazism."

"German, Nazi, it's the same now. I tell you, Steffi. I tell you."

With beer all but unavailable, Fritz had taken to quaffing the cheap Algerian wine that had become the mainstay of lower-middle-class Parisian households, and his face, and his torrents of anger, were redder and fuller than ever. He smoked heavily, mostly reconstituted discards, or the cheap Francisque cigarettes with the image of Pétain on the packet. He felt useless. He missed work. He missed Austria; he missed the old world from before this rise of the cretin class: he missed his parents; he missed Lotte and his two boys; and in his cups he swore he'd join them, one way or another. The apartment was full of lamentations and Viennese waltzes from scratched gramophone records.

Then one day he, and about half of his meager wardrobe, disappeared into the wide world.

"*Viva España!*" read his note on the kitchen table. "I'll send the same message from Spain. See you after the war."

Truthfully, his departure was a relief, given the exigencies of the apartment and the circumstances of occupied Paris. But Stefanie, worried already about so much, worried too about her poor cousin, imagining dark horrors visited by the ruling sadists of the day upon the stubborn harmless fool, with his pathetic single arm and childlike outbursts. But after three weeks she and Mutti were relieved when a crumpled postcard arrived, postmarked Barcelona and bearing the words "Viva España!" Only much later did the details of Fritz's ordeal emerge: how, sober and alone with only twenty occupation francs, a handful of Reichsmarks, and his last rent check in his pocket, he had "borrowed" a bicycle from a gendarmerie near the Porte d'Italie and ridden into Burgundy down nighttime back roads; how he crossed into the Free Zone with a group of schoolchildren near Châlons, then forded a rain-swollen stream in the foothills of the Jura and, after drying out in the loft of an abandoned métairie, had then taken local trains south as far as Perpignan, changing at every junction, zigzagging across the country, never sleeping more than an hour at a time; how he had then walked through bracken and wasteland and broken-down farms to Collioure, near the Spanish border; how, hidden in a haycart bringing eggs and milk from poor France to even-poorer Catalonia, he'd successfully made the crossing from Cerbère to Port-Bou, and how desultory and anticlimactic was his reunion in Barcelona with distant Lotte, now deeply in love with Señor Andres Garcia y Moreno of the Guardia Civil, and the two bemused boys, who'd nearly forgotten they had a papa, let alone an irascible, portly, red-faced one with one arm and a taste for booze . . .

But this all came out later. Now, with Fritz gone, Stefanie felt at liberty to proceed with her teaching plan. She introduced herself to Frau Hilda Epting, the director of the pompously named Haus der Deutschen Kultur, in the former Hotel de Sagan, once the Polish Embassy. Frau Epting, the wife of a senior attaché at the German Embassy, greeted her with a hearty "Heil Hitler!" then expressed some surprise at a recommendation from this SS-Private Kohler, whose name she did not recognize.

"In any event, we would certainly not act on the suggestion of an SS, of whatever rank, never mind a mere *Sturmann*."

However, as she was in need of a good teacher, and as she had in front of her someone with experience who was clearly, in appearance and bearing as well as speech, an ideal candidate, she overlooked the SS stigma—to which she was sensitive out of old-fashioned snobbery rather than distaste for SS methods, Stefanie sensed. But Frau Epting, a native of the Breisgau, spoke German beautifully, and at least there was a bust of Goethe on a bookcase in her office, frowning across the room at the mandatory Führer portrait (War Lord: uniform, sword, stormy skies). So they shook hands and shared mutual recognition of Germanness beyond the grubby everyday, beyond the Third Reich.

Stefanie's students were an unprepossessing and cynical lot of French bureaucrats, bootlickers and go-alongs, who needed the language in their office careers. Two of them were members of the *Bureau des Renseignements*, i.e., Gestapo *à la française*. It was a matter of indifference to them if German was the language of Goethe and Schiller, as long as it was the language of getting ahead and filling out this form, that application, those deportation orders.

"Madame, in a couple of years we'll be learning English for the same reason we're learning German now and we all know it," said one of the cynics, a squint-eyed young man named Yves Chatillon. "If we survive, that is. Meanwhile, I need to keep my black-market contacts happy. Let me know if you need a telephone number or two when the larder's bare."

Classes were twice a day, three days a week, and Stefanie welcomed payment in ration coupons, with promotion to a T ration card, as one deemed to be part of a vital industry: Propaganda and Influence. Having a T card (1800 calories a day) made the food queues easier to bear, and at least she wasn't being paid in Reichsmarks—a slight salve to her conscience for having taken a collaborator's job. Yet what choice had she? And in spite of the Führer portraits in Frau Epting's office (the Teutonic Knight one had been added, with the armor and the battle standard) and the entrance hall (that was the early one with the leather trenchcoat and the wistful look of a dog eyeing a distant bone) and the abundance of Wehrmacht and SS uniforms milling about on the stairs, it became, almost, a job like any other. But Sturmann Kohler soon came visiting, much to the visible displeasure of Frau Epting, and as the days went by, his visits required less and less of a formal excuse. He waited for Stefanie after classes like a teenage swain, and eventually hinted that he hoped two things of her: one, that she should report to him anything "unusual" ("or intriguing") about her students, such as useful phone numbers and clandestine contacts, and to do so punctually twice a week, telephone number given (not his); and two, one Friday in May, that she should have lunch at his SS-supplied apartment on the Avenue de Neuilly. She refused; he insisted, less smilingly; she consented—to the second, while promising to mull over the first. He agreed.

A mere Sturmann, was he? Not likely, or he was a liar. Or a double liar. That was hardly surprising. What was surprising was that Stefanie found herself less put out by his attentions than she should have been. Indeed, at moments (in her exhausted nighttime bed, listening to Mutti's snore-rhythms broken by sudden gasps of geriatric astonishment) there was a definite perverse titillation to the idea, SS uniform and all. Sex was sex, and the man wasn't *totally* repulsive, and it had been some time . . . and she had been in Paris long enough to acquire some of the pragmatic Parisian spirit that treats sex outside of courtship as a bodily function no more romantic than any other . . . and, to be honest, Sami's detachment from her, and sex, had wounded her pride. She was a full-figured women, in her middle years, yes, but still in good trim as the war, at least, did not allow for excess at the table. Yes, she was still desirable, and she knew it, and so did numerous men on the street and in the Métro who glanced slyly, or looked boldly; and at least Kohler had the good taste to know it, too.

On the other hand, the man was a shameless crawler, and a Nazi, and a member of the SS, and almost certainly a great liar, so she resolved at least to get what she could out of the connection for her family's sake, if nothing else.

Kohler's Nightcap

That Saturday Stefanie took the Métro, more crowded in those carless days than before the war, and walked from the Étoile stop. The click-click of her wooden heels on the pavement echoed down the deserted avenue, as abrupt a contrast with the heaving press of the crowds on the Métro as a sudden cool breeze on a muggy day. The dream-like emptiness of the city still seemed unnatural and surreal. She would never be accustomed to a quiet, dreamy Paris. Three years earlier, the cars, buses, and lorries on the Avenue Foch would have formed two blaring, snarling, horn-blowing opposing rivers of metal, but now the street was as nearly devoid of any signs of the modern age as an eighteenth-century print. In the long intervals of quiet between the snarling and hiccoughing of a coal-fired bus or the rumbling passages of the Métro beneath the pavement, she could hear the birds chirping on the trees, and passing cyclists exchanged brief greetings but fell silent at the sight of three Wehrmacht soldiers in a *Kübelwagen* who slowed down when they saw Stefanie, seeming to mistake Woman Smoking In Street for Prostitute Ready For A Romp. But they drove off when she turned and walked purposefully away, the determined Parisienne who could still intimidate fresh-faced oafs from the asparagus farms and pigsties of Thuringia and Lower Saxony.

The apartment was on the fifth floor of a handsome Belle Époque building on the Avenue de Neuilly. She took the groaning lift and Kohler greeted her at the door, glass in hand. He appeared especially keen to assure her that they wouldn't be disturbed by his "roommates," a pair of SS officers, fine fellows who, he said, had been sent on a hush-hush top secret reconnaissance mission to the so-called Free Zone . . . They sat in the living room. It was cavernous and gloomy and, apart from copies of *Kladderadatsch* and *Signal* on one chair and *Der Stürmer* on another, it bore no traces of the current residents. The previous tenant's tastes, on the other hand, were still evident. A dagger and an ivory-handled sword were displayed on the coffee table, the bust of an African princess with pointed breasts towered upon the sideboard, and a jungle painting by Henri Rousseau or a convincing imitator hung on one wall, facing a tapestry of Arabesque pattern on the other. The armchairs and sofa were covered in green leather, and there was another Oriental carpet on the floor.

"Whose place is this? Or was?" inquired Stefanie.

Kohler shrugged.

"Some antique dealer. Jewish, of course. He got out, so I heard. To Montevideo, wherever that is. Drink?"

Kohler, changing the subject, proceeded to make much of Stefanie's "statuesque" appearance and ruddy good health and even mentioned her Aryanness.

"Seen in profile, you have a most admirably Germanic facial structure. I've studied the subject, you know. Have you ever read Hurzlheimer's *Semitic and Aryan Physiognomies*? I highly recommend it. Indeed I would say you would make a good Brunnhilde."

This caused her to snort in derision, any more vocal expression of contempt probably being ill-advised; it was a tightrope performance, this game, and she was uncertain at every step, with no safety net below.

Luncheon was *poularde de Bresse* and *pommes vapeur*, courtesy of a discreet figure in a white steward's uniform who kept his head averted as he came and went and seemed, as the evening progressed, to fall into an oddly stooped pose until he was almost sidling in and out of the room. Once or twice Stefanie caught a fleeting scent in the man's wake, a smell, whether symptomatic of poor digestion or charred cooking, of which Stefanie was eager to be rid, and of which, fortunately, the roast Bresse chicken, at least, proved not to be the source. In fact, the roast bird was tender, crunchy, tangy, and sweet. It was the best meal Stefanie had had since the war began. The wine was a Pomerol '26, and also beyond reproach. But the circumstances reduced the experience to an endurance test. By the second course Kohler had had four glasses and was flushed and full of himself and well into the realm of boasting.

"You know, I may be a mere *SS-Schütze* but you wouldn't believe what this organization can get done when it tries. For instance, take me, even I can get you permits to go pretty much anywhere, as long as you're not Jewish, of course . . . you won't turn Jewish on me, will you? Mind you, you've certainly been hanging around 'em enough, haven't you? Your husband, your boyfriend, your son, your cousin . . . ah ha ha. Just joking, Stefanie. Do you mind if I call you Stefanie? Good, good. And do please call me Johann. Or Hans, yes, Hans, that's better. I'm quite an informal chap, you know. Even though I'm just a

Schütze and you're a 'von,' ah ha ha."

They had coffee, or mostly cognac in Kohler's case.

"So, by the way, Hans, how hard is it to get to the Free Zone?"

"Oh, not hard at all if you pull the right strings. For example," he leaned back expansively, "take your son in Switzerland. Well, it's been a pretty long time since you saw him, eh?"

She had never mentioned Ignace to Kohler, but he had the unsettling and childish habit of showing off by tossing out hints that he knew everything about her—about Arthur, for example, "his career as a pianist is finished here, he should get out, go to America, the Jews' paradise—oh that's right, he did, didn't he?" and Sami "your Jewish boyfriend, the old dandy, Blum's bosom buddy, well, you can kiss his circumcised dick bye-bye pretty soon, begging your pardon"—and she never knew whether he expected her to appear impressed, or intimidated, or simply awestruck. This psychological toying reminded her of the school playground as well as of Goering: the man's shrewdness, his icy gaze, that amoral intelligence . . . less so with Kohler, whose intelligence might best be described as above that of a beast, below that of a man, as she had read in some old Gothic horror tale—and that seemed to sum up the Nazis' offhand cruelty, actually; their jocular inhumanity, their schoolboy coarseness, their crude *bierstube* mannerisms that masked undiluted evil, every nasty little horror carried out with the unthinking efficiency of Stuttgart bookkeepers . . . and she thought of that shadowy tavern in Linz, all those years ago.

In the event, she nodded non-commitally, encouraging him.

"Well, as it so happens I know a bloke in the SD office here who makes pretty regular runs from our embassy here in Paris to our embassy in Bern to—to be perfectly frank, but mum's the word you understand—to meet people from the other side in neutral surroundings, do some horse-trading with Tommy Atkins and Yankee Jack, you know. *Any*way, my friend has been known," said Kohler with irritating coyness, "to travel with a lady posing as his wife as a means of, shall we say, diverting suspicion. How much less suspicious a married couple looks than a man on his own, *nicht wahr* . . . ?"

By the time the servant brought them their dessert *flan flambé*, Stefanie had decided the price for the privilege of posing as the man's wife was too high, but Kohler was on his fourth cognac and inclined to insist.

"Oh, come, come, it's a trip to Switzerland on a silver platter I'm offering you, all you have to do is keep the man company on the train, maybe give him a wifely peck on the cheek now and again, and once you get to Bern you're free to go on to Geneva and see your boy, no questions asked and no one's keeping score."

"Well, I have to admit it's tempting."

"So you'll consider it. Good. And as for the rest of the afternoon?" he inquired, rising to his feet to refill his cognac and busying himself with a gramophone in the far corner, from which there soon emanated a series of rapid clicks and scratches and a husky female voice purring Norbert Schultze's "Lili Marleen."

> *Vor der Kaserne*
> *Vor dem großen Tor*
> *Stand eine Laterne*
> *Und steht sie noch davor*
> *So woll'n wir uns da wieder seh'n*
> *Bei der Laterne wollen wir steh'n*
> *Wie einst Lili Marleen . . .*

The lights in the sitting room, already dim, like Lilli Marleen's streetlight, got dimmer when Kohler drew the draperies in an attempt to enhance the romance of the atmosphere. He lit a cigarette and offered one to Stefanie. She accepted, more to postpone the inevitability of his advances and to combat the revived burned-cooking or plugged-sewer scent than because she actually wanted to smoke. Her heart was pounding. She really didn't want to smoke or stay or have another drink. She wanted simply and urgently to be back in her tiny flat, away from this man, away from this world, this war, oh mother Mary . . . but not even granting her the time to smoke a cigarette he was upon her, first ogling wildly with eyes adrift in a purplish-red face, then pawing and grunting, heavily alcohol- and tobacco-scented, kissing her mouth, nose, and cheekbones, forcing his hand under her thighs, and as he plucked her unfinished cigarette from her hand, the better to grope upwards, downwards, and sideways, from the corner of one eye as she struggled for purchase on anything that wasn't him she saw someone—the servant?—come in and sit in an armchair beyond, as if prepared to relax and enjoy the show; and beneath the effluvium of Kohler's cognac/cigarette/eau de cologne/sweat she smelled, strongly, the sharp scent of burning, and she remembered—and she knew.

But Kohler, iconic *dummes mann* of the modern antiheroic age, knew nothing. He knew not God, nor even Satan; unknowingly he did the latter's bidding, believing it to be the former's, or just the rules of the game. Like a child or an animal he knew only his needs. Now his trousers were loose, his belt askew, his face darkening, and, fiddling incompetently with her buttons and his belt, he was trying to force Stefanie back against the cushions. The look in his face was that of a hungry animal: hunger, nothing more or less, impelled him. All personality was gone. It was frightening in an abstract sense but ludicrous in the specific. Stefanie felt a volcanic laugh rising inside her; but as Kohler persisted in his maladroit attempt to rape her, the visitor, too, tittered drily, and killed her mirth.

"All these years later, and here we are once again," said the thin metallic voice that echoed inside Stefanie's head from long ago (Linz, 1907; Vienna, 1909). "From a most interesting perspective, I must say. Although how much less worth my while is this creature who is upon you, than the last one through whom we met, and thanks to whom my own redemption is surely at hand. Because even if he loses all, I have already won."

Sudden disgust overwhelmed her at these words, real or imagined; for once she had imagined hearing them, the presence that had spoken them disappeared, the lingering scent—of *burnt wool*—diminished, and she was squarely in present reality, being violated by a paunchy drunken SS private whose only claim on her was a combination of his own lust and their mutual misperceived past . . . and a tenuous connection with Hermann Goering.

Enough!

Hoarsely, she swore in the rich idiom of her (and his) Salzburg backalleys, more thoroughly than she had for years.

"*Fick dich, wichser. Mach es dir selber, du misgebürtlich hurensohn.*"

"*Ha,*" was his only reply.

She thrashed, pushed, twisted, and heaved, eliciting further wordless groans of resentment from Kohler who, even when it was becoming apparent to both of them that the alcohol that had provoked his desire was now preventing performance, persisted in tearing at her blouse and groping her thighs and making absurd faces of pantomime desire. There was no titillation in this; there was foolishness, and squalor, and sin. She needed to escape, but he was settling in on top of her like a blanket of snow on a meadow, and he'd get what he wanted, in his stubborn half-witted Salzkammergut way, if it killed him, or her . . . and speaking of that, she needed a weapon, in case he really did try to kill her. The SS killed people all the time. And who was she, after all? A teacher, a mother: a nobody. An honorary Jewess, in fact, therefore quite expendable. Indeed, some people might want to have her gone (this thought had taken root shortly before, as she was musing over her Obersalzberg romance and remembering others who had crossed into that same orbit whose existence had becoame inconvenient: Geli Raubal, Ernst Roehm, General Fritsch) . . . or maybe all this was the hysteria of the moment. Truly, she was *a nobody*. Truly, no one cared. Truly, this *scheißkopf* was intent on having his way, or else, even if he was impotent as a stone.

Some kind of dagger, she remembered, lay on the coffee table, next to a sword, either one of which would meet the case. She saw both weapons with a quick sidelong glance and grabbed at them from under the malodorous undulating weight atop her. She missed the knife and knocked the sword off the table and he grunted and snarled but she tried again and had succeeded in grasping the handle and was raising it in the air, willing and quite determined to drive it between his ribs, come what might, when suddenly he interrupted his abortive conquest, now in the stage of fully lowered trousers and raised skirt, next stop Orgasm, Win Or Lose, when with a loud "*Scheiße!*" and a series of staccato and violent coughs to the point of strangulation he clutched his chest and rolled off her and fell heavily onto the floor. For a second or two he sprawled there, trousers around his ankles, then he started feebly squirming, like a gigantic salamander, and coughed retchingly, gaggingly; then came a long purring release of intestinal gas and silence. He was immobile. He was dead.

She lay, panting, still holding the knife. It was so much like a bit of bad theater that she hardly dared breathe, much less attack him with the knife; even with him lying there, she was uncertain whether to risk it . . . but she still had the dagger in her hand, and her hatred of him was at its zenith, the vulgar, patronizing, ignorant *wappler* . . . blindly, she grabbed it, just in case . . .

"Just in case?"

A man's voice, speaking German-accented French. Standing next to the door inside the room was a man in an SS uniform; entering the room behind him was another, younger SS officer.

"Go ahead, Madame! Make sure! Stab him to make sure he's dead."

Both were smiling. The young one was no more than twenty-five or twenty-six; the other was older, with gray hair. Both walked with the arrogance of the Nazi age and the cachet of their uniforms.

"Simple, on the face of it," said the first man. "Kohler, our randy chauffeur, takes advantage of our absence to use the flat for his assignations, victimizing a buxom middle-aged French Jewess who, reluctant to be impregnated with Goyish sperm, decides to murder him."

His colleague laughed and proffered a packet of Muratti cigarettes.

"Smoke?"

He waved the packet at Stefanie. Ignoring him, she straightened up, brushed down her clothes and hair, and dropped the dagger onto the table. Then, calling on all her reserves of ancestral pride and dignity, she said in German,

"I am not French. I am an Austrian national by birth. My

name is Stefanie von Rothenberg." She did not volunteer whether or not she was Jewish, not wanting to so hastily claim innocence by virtue of religion, which seemed cowardly; her name by itself, she thought, was sufficient to disabuse them of the notion . . .

"Not *Rosen*berg . . . ?"

She ignored the interruption.

"I was invited here for luncheon with a man who has been of some help to me professionally but I consider the invitation was made under false pretences. I have been barbarously assaulted, and my assailant, as you can see, has suffered a fatal seizure, I expect the two of you, as honorable German officers, to take the appropriate steps to clear up this horrible business."

The two SS officers—the older one, according to his pips, a major, or *hauptsturmführer*, the other, lower-ranked, a lieutenant, or *obersturmführer*—sauntered into the room and stood over Kohler's body. The lieutenant prodded it with his foot; his colleague squatted and felt Kohler's pulse, with head-shaking finality.

"Dead," he said, and got to his feet. "No doubt."

"Well, well," said the lieutenant. "So! So Kohler's dead. Poor Kohler. He was a good chauffeur. What shall we do without him? More to the point: What shall we do *with* him? And whatever shall we do with you, Fräulein von Rosenberg? Sorry: *Rothen*berg? Sorry again: *von* Rothenberg, isn't it?"

With difficulty, Stefanie subdued a flaming rage and said nothing, but she could feel the blood rush to her face.

"We live here, you see," said the major in a conversational tone. "I am Peter Schneider; this is Arnim Stemmer, we are both of SS, of course; and, as we have said, Hans Kohler was our driver."

"*Ja*, we had no idea Kohler had a mistress. He was a married man with children, but clearly not a respectable one," said Lieutenant Stemmer with a predatory grin. "Mind you, he pretended to have business all over town but we knew he took the car out almost every night, looking for women."

"*Ja*. Usually girls from Pigalle or the Bois. Professionals, you know. Not, until now, such a high-class lady," said Major

Schneider. "If my assumption is correct, and you are not yourself a professional?"

"No, gentlemen. I am not a whore, nor was I that man's mistress. I am a teacher at the Haus der Deutschen Kultur and a theologian. And I will go now, with your permission," said Stefanie, seeing no reason to do anything else. But the officers had other ideas.

"Not quite yet, Frau Rothenberg," said Lt. Stemmer. "We have a corpse on our hands. A man of the SS. This is quite serious, *ja*?"

"Yes, but it was none of my doing. He must have had a heart attack," said Stefanie. "Look, he was in bad physical condition and overexcited and he'd been drinking and his heart couldn't take it. It happens all the time."

"But this precise situation doesn't happen all the time," said Major Schneider. "I enjoy a drink and I enjoy making love, but I haven't had a heart attack yet. Please. Do sit down."

The courtesy alarmed her, as a likely prelude to its opposite, which she then provoked.

"No, thank you. I will, if you wish, give you a statement. But then I must leave."

Stemmer crossed the room in two swift strides and with the back of his hand slapped her hard across the face, twice, cutting her right cheek at the cheekbone. She cried out and touched her face and looked in amazement at the blood on her hand, then, in wonderment, at Major Schneider, but he was casually watching her, no more moved by the spectacle of a middle-aged lady brutally assaulted by his subordinate than by the sight of a fly swatted. Well, they were, after all, SS, to whom the rest of humanity were indeed, no more than flies. And they had a defenseless woman—whom they presumed, or hoped to be, Jewish—as completely at their mercy as they had the city, the country, Europe, soon the world . . . She felt a coldness in the pit of her stomach as she realized how serious, not to say fatal, her predicament might be. If she never left the apartment, who would know? Who would care?

Who would help a nobody?

"Sit down now, Jewess, and do as we say," said Lieutenant Stemmer, in a testy, strident voice, heavily Saxon-accented— Leipzig, she thought, irrelevantly. "We will decide when, or if, you can leave. But first some questions."

"No," she said, hoarsely. "I am not alone, you know." One hand still cradling her bleeding cheekbone, she pointed with the trembling other at a telephone on a small occasional table next to the sofa and spoke through the fog of fear. "I want you to pick up that telephone and make a call."

Stemmer stepped forward, hand raised, smiling at the prospect of inflicting more pain; but Major Schneider intervened with a frown and shake of the head—more out of curiosity than concern, as the overly unctuous tone of his voice implied.

"And to whom would you like us to place a call, Frau Rothenberg?"

"To the Führer," she said. "He's an old friend of mine."

Stemmer swore and with a humorless laugh he lunged at her, but she darted behind the sofa. He ran at her; she sidestepped him. Major Schneider called a halt to the sadistic farce.

"Stop now," he said. "Madame, I am willing to give you the benefit of the doubt. But if we find you're making fun of us . . . Stemmer, first call the local boys and get someone up here to take care of this, then place the call Madame has requested."

"But you can't possibly take this seriously."

"Place the call."

"Yes, sir."

In the interim, while Stemmer spoke in a rapid undertone into the telephone, Major Schneider finished smoking his Muratti and looked down at dead Kohler with many a theatrical shake of the head and cluck of the tongue; and Stefanie balanced herself tentatively against the arm of the sofa, still patting her burning cheekbone, mind racing with half alternatives (run away? pretend to faint?) and mad ideas (Fritzl? Sami?), as the series of small disasters that had accelerated since the beginning of the afternoon threatened to take over not only her life but that of her mother, her cousin . . .

"So. The gendarmes are coming," said Stemmer, then

turned his back and muttered into the phone "*ja*, that's right, the Führer's office, it's urgent, from Major Schneider of SS GroßParis." After a series of short conversations he put a hand over the mouthpiece and said to Schneider,

"He's not there. They said he's at the new field headquarters in Russia."

"The *Werwolf.* In Ukraine. Near Vinnitsa. *Ja*, we were just told about it. It opens this week."

Schneider hissed through his teeth annoyance mingled with cigarette smoke and glanced at his watch.

"Well, it's only three o'clock, and we know he's a late riser. But he should be up now. Try the switchboard at *Werwolf,* Stemmer."

"Oh, come on . . . "

"Stemmer!"

"Sir."

For Stefanie the ensuing minutes, no more than fifteen, during which Stemmer tried to carry out what appeared more and more to be an absurd request, were longer than mere minutes; indeed, so malleable and subjective a thing is Time, so capable of being stretched or shrunk by individual mood and circumstance, that those fifteen minutes were one of the longest periods she had ever endured, seemingly longer than the years of her motherhood, or her life in Paris, or the years since the first war, and nearly as long as the thirty-five years since she and young Adolf Hitler had taken tea together in Linz, in the shadow of war and the devil. Long enough, in any event, for her to return to the source and origin of her spiritual life. Long enough for her to find the space within her for the presence of God and to think it—He—was there, suddenly; it seemed to rise within her and drift upward and outward, streaming suddenly into a penumbra of multi-colored energy, or, as she thought, light somehow invisible yet dazzling and containing the entire spectrum of colors—it surrounded her and contained her—and if this was God, it was also, incontestably, *her*. It was Mother Mary . . .

"Hallo? HAL-lo?"

Long enough, too, for the true answer to her query *Who*

would intervene to help her? to make itself clear. Hitler? No, no mortal man, least of all him. The answer had long been obvious, but she had turned her back on it, on her salvation, harried by the countless irrelevant things in everyday life, by her normality, her humanness, her weak-willed soul. Her suffering, she knew, had been postponed, but postponed only. It would come. It was willed, it would be, it was inevitable. It was part of the role she was destined to play in the world. This awareness—this certainty—gave her a near serenity to tranquillize her agitation. She felt sure of things, of life, of herself. She knew that no matter what they did to her body her soul would be intact, and that pain is transient, indeed, it transcends itself, and the body's existence ends only for the other, greater existence to begin, like a soaring butterfly born of an earthbound caterpillar.

Like Teresa of Ávila, she would offer her suffering: to God, to Mother Mary, and to Mary's holy son.

Like Paul, she would say "Are they Hebrews? So am I!"

Like Mother Mary herself, she would be bright, confident, unashamed, generous, full of love.

Like Moses, she would live to smash the idol.

The wait was long enough for her to feel a mocking amusement at her all-too-human response to the SS officers (she smiled; Schneider, noticing, raised a puzzled eyebrow), and finally it was long enough for her to hope against reason that Lieutenant Stemmer's phone call would not go through; and this was the easiest of her hopes to fulfill, because people didn't just pick up the phone and call the Führer.

"It's not getting through," snapped Stemmer. "Of course. What did you expect? I'm getting some *Schütze* on the front who's so afraid I can hear him shitting his pants, *ja*, he's too scared to interrupt his captain, who's actually in charge of official Führer-scheduling and who's busy somewhere else, of course. And anyway, *HE's* at the front, and I imagine he's got a little more on his plate than . . . well."

Stemmer held the receiver to his ear for another second or two, then grunted "*Danke*," put the phone down and gave Stefanie a calm and steady look. "So he can't help you, I'm afraid."

"Shall we try *Reichsführer* Himmler now?" inquired Major Schneider, jovially. "Or Reichsmarschall Goering?"

Yes, cried a voice within her. *Try Goering. For pity's sake. Call him! Ask him to save me!*

She was deaf to the voice.

"No," she said. "There is no one else."

"Then we must ask you to come with us," said Major Schneider.

Lieutenant Stemmer was smiling as they left the room.

Gustave
Eleven

A TENSE MOMENT indeed . . . poor Stefanie! And speaking of phone calls, when Martine finally called, what did I do? I ran.

When the beeping of the message machine woke me I was tucked into my old armchair with her book spread-eagled across my chest (the mealymouthed sanctity stuff bored me, I must confess, but the Nazis kept me going, as they tend to do) deep in a dream of an occupied Paris in which I was an aggressive Orthodox Jew in yarmulke and phylactery eating carrots and fearlessly striding down the Boulevard des Capucines past German soldiers on my way to a romantic rendezvous with Sarah Bernhardt. Just before being dragged from Dreamland to what we laughingly call reality, I was being arrested by Guy Gax in the uniform of an SS officer. Groggily, I rose to my feet, roaring through the phlegm like the mighty water buffalo of the Indus Valley, and replayed the phone message.

"Gustave?" It was Martine. Her voice sounded uncharacteristically timid and nervous. "It's me. Call me as soon as you get this. Please. Nine one nine," etc.

Instead of calling her (how poignant that "please"), fool that I was (and am), I ate a couple of carrots, threw on my overcoat, and went out, not entirely out of perversity or cowardice, although slowly and dreadfully I was becoming reaccustomed to my previous—pre-Martine—mode of existence and thought, as a heroin addict will backslide a dozen times before the cure . . . but it was Tuesday night and time to honor my appointment with Dr. Dürrenmatt at the Café du Temple in Carouge. It was too far to walk, so I took a 12 tram from the Plainpalais stop and sat listlessly in the rearmost seat and with combined relief and envy watched the homeward-bound on the street, the adolescents high on adolescence, the life-burdened oldsters, the relentless shoppers, the drunks, the city crowds that look so normal from the outside.

(And there could be a stray Hitler there. And God only knew how many Hauptsturmführer Schneiders.)

The Place du Temple was lively and well lit and from the tram seemed warmer than the city center, but once disembarked I felt the chill probing of the dying bise. Still, Carouge has always had a warmer, more Catholic feel than the rest of the Swiss-French metropolis, as Geneva's own little Montmartre—or rather, its corner of Aix-en-Provence, with narrow Mediterranean streets and houses with inner courtyards of restrained elegance and food stalls and quiet squares lined with plane trees and parasols. Once a byword for laughable provincialism, along the lines of Swindon or Issy-les-Moulineaux, like once equally risible Sachsenhausen (also on the south bank of a parent city's second river) it has turned into a ghetto of the city's most chic; indeed, in some parts it looks like an overly elaborate stage setting for some punk version of *Carmen*, boutiques, Leftist theatrics, ear-studded trendysexuals in leather, and all. But the cafés are well run and stocked with good wines, and one such is the Temple, into which I stumbled, rubbing chilled hands, and in the corner of which, diagonally across from the door, sat Dr. Dürrenmatt, behind that day's *Tribune* and a half-empty bottle of . . .

"Gamay du Mandement," he said, naming a local vineyard that produced wines adequate for boozing but insufficiently full-bodied for fine dining. "One of my favorite tipples. How are you, Doctor Termi?"

I noted the "Doctor." Of course, he was from Zürich, where they start calling one another "Doktor" at the age of five.

"Well enough."

We shook hands. Dr. Dürrenmatt made an expansive gesture that took in the café.

"I always come here when I am in Geneva. It's a nice little place, *hein*?"

In this, at least, the good doctor was right. The Café du Temple is a quiet, unpretentious haven. It had, and no doubt still has, a neat trick of being well-lit while seeming not to be; or more precisely seeming to be well-*candle*lit while actually spending a little more on a few flickering-candle lightbulbs to create an effect pleasing and restful and evocative of simpler times, and an atmosphere through which waiters can silently pass, like sailboats in the twilight. This dimness also has the virtue of ensuring that one's neighbors or fellow diners are shrouded in half shadow, thus simultaneously concealing all extracurricular relationships as well as unsightly blemishes and annoying ear-piercings, etc., a not inconsiderable virtue for such as I. As for Dr. Dürrenmatt, he was unblemished except for being crewcut, hearty, lantern-jawed, and very Swiss-German . . . if indeed, it isn't almost redundant to add that he was *very* Swiss-German, because he *was* a Swiss-German, and I have never known a group to conform so utterly to their *image d'Épinal*. They have (especially the Zürichers) a meticulously restrained heartiness and a passion for precision, even in radical politics and sexual mayhem. Hence, Dadaism and the banks. Hence, Jung. Hence, too, Dr. Dürrenmatt.

But there was one thing I wanted to get out of the way immediately.

"Nay, nay," he said, in his brusque Toto way, "I'm not related to the writer. At least, I don't think so. Although both of our families came originally from Thurgau. The town of Gullen, to be precise."

It was a joke: "Gullen" means "shit" in *schwyzerdütsch* and is the setting of one of Dürrenmatt's humorless stage farces, I forget which one.

"Gullen, *ja*?"

I chuckled dutifully then yawned, discreetly, at this feeble *jeu d'esprit*.

"Nay," the doctor continued, pouring me a glass of the Gamay, "I come from a family of psychiatrists and policemen, not playwrights. *Ja, ja*," he said, his *ja*s jarring me momentarily into the shadowy world of Stefanie and her Nazis, "I don't know why, but that's the way things have worked out. My brother-in-law is the police chief of Geneva, for example."

"Good God. Is he, now?"

"Yes. Your city's *superflic, hein*? The top cop, ha? Do you know him? Dieter Fegelein?

"No, I'm afraid not."

"And my nephew Andreas Ziegler is the assistant *commissaire* of Lausanne."

"Good heavens. Why don't you stay home and play führer in your own cities?"

"But these *are* our cities, Dr. Fermi. We are all Swiss, no?"

"Well, some more than others."

"Still, you'll be pleased to know that my father was a psychiatrist in Winterthur, and his father before him."

"Thank goodness."

"And his father was a student of the great Jung."

Him again.

"And your father, Doctor? If I may ask?"

Ah, the old father-son thing: I was onto him. Papa and I got along fine, I was going to say, but the waitress came to take my order and it wasn't until she had repeated everything I said—mushrooms, kebabs, couscous, carrots—that I became aware of a) a certain sensual scent and b) the Italian accent, and not until I peered closely in the atmospheric half-light that I recognized Giulia, law student and good-time-girl and my on-again off-again part-time *putana* these many months . . .

Mamma mia.

"*A-o, professore*," she said, also surprised, but, surprisingly, also (apparently) pleased. My, how winsome she was in the sub-aqueous light! Her slight inclination to plumpness rendered her face a sweet oval framed by tumbling curly locks jet-black in hue. Her olive dark eyes the eyes of the naiad in Pompeii's Villa of the Mysteries. Her arms warmly tanned a dirty gold. Her hips and bust . . . well, my pulses stirred; my mental fantasy theater threw together a brief lively skit featuring me and those thighs, a replay of foolish days past.

"Giulia! *Dio!*"

With Giulia I abandoned all Swissness and became utterly the descendant of my ancestors. Dr. Dürrenmatt was forgotten. So, I regret to say, was Martine Jeanrenaud—and of course in retrospect I can see that *that* was the point. I was digging ever deeper my heart's grave.

"*Che fai qui, cara?*"

She was working there three days a week, she explained, because she couldn't afford to live in this city otherwise, except with a great many more sources of income (wink). When she left with our order, Duerenmatt smiled blandly.

"Nice girl, eh? Italian? So! So, how are you, Doctor?" he inquired.

"Very well, Doctor. And you?"

"Oh, very well. Except perhaps a twinge now and again of the neuralgia—so!" He mimed a grimace. "Now. Perhaps we can discuss your epiphenomena of these recent days?"

"Of course. Where would you like to begin?"

"Well, why not with the angel. Yes, I think so. The angel, please. And no mention of this foolish porphyria illness. I have looked it up. Yes, it is definitely a disease of Southeast Asian peasants, nomads, and other primitive cretins. And you are not one of them, if I'm not mistaken. Or if you are you are very well disguised! Ha ha?"

But then Giulia returned, bearing a tray. As she and I continued in Italian, shutting off Duerenmatt like a tap, I found myself making vivid aerial gestures, like a Roman taxi driver, evoking in an obnoxiously loud voice the dramatic turn my life had taken: mysticism, professional anguish, inspiration, *l'amore* . . . Pompous fool, wallowing in the presumed adoration of a mere girl. But Giulia, who had rented her body to me on several occasions with no apparent ulterior interest in intellectual and/or moral companionship, now—on her way to an adjoining table, her tray heaped high with a triple order of *steak frites salade*—showed great, even indecent, interest in extending our previous conversations; and, wretch that I am, I rode high the tide of my petty power.

The steak-frites crowd next door was becoming impatient, with their victuals within olfactory distance. Giulia leaned over.

"I'm off at ten. *Ci vediamo.*"

Reluctantly (after glancing at my watch: ten o'clock was an hour distant) I turned my attention to Dürrenmatt, who was now quite drunk. His heavy glasses slid down his perspiring nose onto the table. He tucked them away in his jacket, after two or three wide misses of slapstick clumsiness, and leaned forward to make himself heard, as if the ambient noise, not he, were deafening.

"So Doctor Fermi," he bawled. "You have been having visions, I hear. Of God and angels? Ha ha! Perhaps you are a fucking saint, OK? Waitress! Some wine!"

We had another bottle, furnished by a blonde waitress who seemed to make an impression on the good Doktor.

"*Lieber Gottli*, she is quite pretty, *ja?*"

I wolfed my kebabs but Dürrenmatt largely ignored his *croque-monsieur* in favor of deeper and deeper swallows of Gamay. His eyes were skewed, comically (or tragically); after a desultory bite of his sandwich he made a grab for my cigarettes and popped one into his mouth.

"I quit last year, but fuck it, *hein?*"

"Absolutely, Herr Doktor."

He lit up and inhaled furiously, exhaling then in blasts of smoke through his nostrils.

"So!"

For him, the hour of masculine intimacy had struck. Like the Japanese, the Swiss-Germans are stiffly formal in offices unless they're being wildly juvenile in bars. He attempted small talk. Was I, he inquired, related to the great physicist Enrico Fermi? Well, I might have been, I suggested, had my name been Fermi. Certainly not as closely as he was related to the late playwright Friedrich Dürrenmatt . . .

"But as I have explained," he protested thickly, "that we are not. I mean, I am not. And nor was he. As far as I know. But is't 'strue, what you say? That we are relatives? No, no, not you and me, ah ha ha, although we might be, you never know, after all if you go back far enough we are all related through Lucy, *nicht?* Lucy, you know," he dropped to the floor, cigarette bobbing in his gob, glasses slipping to the end of his nose, aping apish behavior with knuckles trailing on the ground and comical grunts. From the neighboring shadows came giggles and hoarse whispers of "Look!" and "What the . . . ?" "From Africa?" thundered the mad doctor, creating a more than passable illusion of chimpanzeeness with his knuckle-grazing and tongue-engorged lower lip. "Lucy, of course. No, no, ha ha ha, I mean," he sat down again, fag in gob, brushing off his trouser-knees, "Me and him. Friedrich. The other Dürrenmatt. Ach, Friedrich. You have read him? I mean, met him?" He shook his head, dropped his cigarette, grabbed another and lit it. Then, gazing rapturously at his shoes (oxfords, well polished), embarked upon the rendition in a shaky tenor of a song in Swiss-German dialect, roughly:

> *O a ee danke füer de Anke*
> *Danke füer de Anke*
> *Wann wanke du*
> *Wann o wann*
> *Waaaaaaaaann*
> *Wunn wanke wanke du*
> *Mein Buschi Buschi Büüüü . . . "*

Et cetera, until the hoarse tenor dissolved into deep, heaving sobs. By that time I was on my dessert flan, and discreetly signaled the situation to Giulia and to M. Delon, the manager. M. Delon recommended coffee, and served it to the apologetic Doctor. At ten Giulia appeared at my side; Dürrenmatt, thanks to the coffee, had momentarily pulled himself together and was working on a stiff apology and perhaps, I thought optimistically, an offer to commit ritual suicide, Zürich style.

"I am deeply sorry, Dr. Termi," he said. "I apologize for everything. I apologize for drinking. I apologize for smoking your cigarettes." He was standing with head hung, like a scolded child.

"Not at all. Have another," I said, offering the pack. Disconcertingly, he threw back his head and laughed cavernously.

He was a man of sudden and mercurial moods; in a word, a lunatic. What profession other than psychiatry could he, therefore, logically choose?

"Ha ha, you have a most clever and unexpected sense of humor, Dr. Fermi, I mean Termi. Somewhat like Gerd Augustus von Hohenheim, the poet, mime and window-cleaner? Do you know him?"

"No."

"No? Why not?"

"Why the devil should I? Does he know me?"

"OK, that's a good answer. Now listen, so I will reschedule our appointment and discussion. Perhaps we should meet in my office, I mean the office the college has kindly put at my disposal. The café was a good idea but I got there too early and had too much wine. Stress, too, you know, and the artistic atmosphere of these places. Waitresses, prostitutes, painters, *ach du lieber Gottli* you might as well be in Montparnasse, or Montmartre, in 1897, or 1900, surrounded by men with beards and women with no clothes! Or vice versa! HA HA HA HA . . . " and so on *con gusto*, and even a backslap, directed at me but missing its target. Once he had pulled himself together again, he continued: "Anyway, I am stressed, yes. Very. I have been working on the case of Heinrich Halsingborg, the notorious Don Juan and false spy. Do you know this case?"

I did not. Naturally, he went on to describe it in tedious detail: The man from Flensburg in northern Germany who had tricked half a dozen women in the greater Hamburg area into believing he was a high-ranking secret agent in the BVS, Germany's spy agency, stashing one gal in a well-furnished cellar and tricking another out of her marriage and inducing her to live in his garage. The wretch Halsingborg had moved to Küssnacht on Lake Zürich and had acquired an unassuming identity as an urban planner until unmasked by a vengeful ex-girlfriend (the one in the garage). It was a sobering tale, and indeed by the time he had finished telling it Dürrenmatt was nearly sober, or at least less raving drunk.

We walked together through the streets of Carouge, now

moist from a fine rain sifting through the November mist. There were four of us: Giulia, me, Dürrenmatt, and Giulia's roommate, the other waitress from the Temple, a rather pallid girl from Bern who, notwithstanding her apparent insignificance, hit it off with Herr Doktor immediately, being a fellow Swiss-Toto and, unexpectedly, a bit of a flirt; indeed, it was as a quartet that we left the café, and as that same foursome that we arrived in Giulia's and Greta's (for that, as the great novelists say, was her name) artistic garret overlooking the Place du Marché, some ten minutes' walk from the café. Happily, the flat was arranged into separate living quarters, the ensemble being of such spaciousness that I fancied I detected the hidden hand of benefactors with deeper pockets than I had.

Believe me, dear reader (as the lesser novelists say, or once said), as soon as Herr Doktor Dürrenmatt and Greta from Bern had left the living room to "admire the view from Greta's parlor window" (delivered amid a blizzard of winks by the already-besotted Duerenmatt) Giulia and I were rapidly approaching intimate terms again. I was harmonious from the Gamay du Mandement and an all-encompassing randiness reinforced by guilt (Martine's little voice on the answering machine . . . well, I could hardly call her now, could I?). And Giulia? Ah, no fault of hers. She was just a love-loving, healthy young woman from the fertile abundance of Emilia-Romagna; and I truly believe she respected me, either as the traditional father figure of psychiatric mythology, or just as a good companion with a bit of money to spend and a deep admiration for her body. (Or perhaps *her* angel was the Blue one of that name whose mission was to deflate the vast, stentorian pedantic pomp of Professor Termi, played by yours truly with heavy-breathing fervor equal to that of Emil Jannings in his original number, ca. 1930.)

Around postcoital smoking time she turned on the TV at the end of the bed. From next door, or a couple of doors down, we could hear the raucous guffawing of Dürrenmatt and the birdlike peeping of his companion.

"Schnapps!" roared Dürrenmatt; then, "*kirsch*!" Greta giggled.

"*Che stronzo*, eh?" muttered my prone Giulia. She wore

nothing more cumbersome than a chiffon negligee that floated lightly above the white demiglobes of her bottom like mist above snowdrifts. "Never mind. We hope he's made poor Greta a nice present." We sleepily watched the parade of commercials. I traced the line of the gluteal sulcus that was sweetly scented of what had just transpired. My guilt was in abatement, such had been the delights.

After the commercials I was beginning to nod off, it being past my usual bedtime. There came a wrap-up of the late-night news, usually a boring affair of who said what in the Grand Council and whether the cows in Gruyères were down from the meadows yet or which Swiss sportsman had just been picked for this or that football club . . . but not that night. Instead, we went live to the upscale Parc de Budé and an earnest TV "action team" of one young woman and one young man standing in front of a police car with its blue rooflight rotating, behind which shadowy figures milled about. Both reporters were wearing red anoraks emblazoned on the shoulder with the TSR TV emblem. I idly, guiltily, wondered: Where's Martine, their star reporter? Then, suddenly quite wide awake, I realized that I was looking at Martine's apartment building on the television screen.

"The gunman or gunmen should be up there," said the young woman, pointing to an upper balcony, barely visible in the dark but faintly illuminated from inside the apartment, on the . . . ground—one—two—three—fourth floor. "As we have reported, he, or they, might have two hostages: our colleague Martine Jeanrenaud, and Martine's sister, Laure Descombes, who was visiting her from Paris . . . "

I spilled off the bed, pulled on my sagging Y-fronts, stumbled across the room ignoring Giulia's inquiring cries, and hammered on the door behind which groans and peeping could still be heard. They ceased as Dürrenmatt, quite nude except for a red thong and eyeglasses, opened the door and peered out.

"Now, Doctor Termi, really," he said.

"Yes, Doctor Dürrenmatt, really, you must call your cousin or brother or brother-in-law or whoever he is at once, do you hear. The policeman? The *commissaire*? The *polizei führer*? Now, please. It's an emergency, man."

He stammered and put on his trousers, but, given who and what he was, he instinctively understood the need for efficiency and promptness; so, bursting through the befuddlement, in short order we had a) summoned a taxi; b) contacted the Chief's wife at their (according to Dürrenmatt) elegant lakeside villa in Cologny and learned that the Chief was, in fact, at the scene; c) bidden bye-bye to the girls, with hasty and incomplete explanations (they shrugged, existing as they did by and for the vagaries of men); and d) gone to the Parc de Budé in the taxi, a crosstown journey of fairish duration, even at that hour, in the course of which I told Dürrenmatt, with some reluctance, why I was so barely able to contain my fear and frenzy . . . and my loathing, as I was quite certain who the gunman or gunmen were . . . or rather, *what*.

The terrible allure of doing nothing, of languidly waving the world away, competed in my heart with the urgent need for action, for a way to wrench myself from my groove of self-pity and inertia, to prove that I still existed, to declare myself to Martine. I knew that if I did nothing at that moment, however insane, I would never do anything, and would never see her again. Worse, if I did nothing now (however insane), I would never do anything worthwhile and would die deservedly unmourned.

Happily, it was no contest.

Full Speed Ahead

When the taxi pulled up behind the Intercontinental Hotel, Dürrenmatt pointed out a tall angular fellow in a raincoat talking on a mobile phone.

"Him. Dieter. He's my brother-in-law."

I hailed the man.

"Gustave Termi, Professor. Listen, *commissaire* . . . "

He chuckled.

"Professor Termi? The one who's been having visions?"

I was at a loss, momentarily. Dürrenmatt stepped in.

"Come, Dieter," he said, taking his brother-in-law's arm. "Now isn't the time."

Nor was it. I was annoyed at this evidence of Dürrenmatt blabbing behind the scenes . . . with, not a hundred meters distant, a drama unfolding with my lady love front and center. Yes: It was shameful to feel wounded pride at such a moment. I thought of my stern Italo-Scottish ancestors, pulled myself together, and asked for details. Police Chief Fegelein, having had his chuckle, referred me airily to an Inspector Nicod, his fiftyish, sad-eyed, and paunchy Sancho Panza, with—notwithstanding the sad eyes—the assertive stance of one who knows that his true place is higher than the one to which society (or the police force) has assigned him. A brief current of fellow feeling passed between us.

"Sorry about that, Prof," he said, indicating the Chief, who was now in his full glory, surrounded by reporters and toadies on the make, and utterly indifferent to the fate of the women in the apartment. In an old-fashioned gesture reminiscent of films of the 1950s, Nicod took out a packet of Gauloises and shook one loose for me.

"Smoke?"

We smoked. My heart paused, hovered, stumbled, galloped briefly, then recovered. I was under stress and it was past my bedtime, but an odd exhilaration tingled in my fingertips.

"Well, near as we can make out," said Nicod, narrowing his eyes against the smoke like Yves Montand, "some pair of Muslim jockey-jobbers took your lady friend and her sister hostage on condition that her mother, if I've got this right, or mother-in-law . . ."

"Her mother," I interposed. "That's right. She was married to a Pakistani. Then she decided she'd had enough and came back home. The mother, that is. But Martine, her daughter, received a threatening phone call from some nutter oh what was it, five days ago?"

Nicod looked at me with interest.

"How well do you know them then, Professor?"

I explained, haltingly. Discreetly, he looked down and away

while I attempted to fashion coherence from incoherence: I knew her slightly, but we were—well, I hated to go into details, but there was a certain minimal ah, ahem . . . She was an acquaintance, shall we say? When I'd finished he shook his head, whether in token of the seriousness of the situation or of my own foolish stammering it was hard to tell.

"I *am* sorry," he muttered. "What a mess. We'll get through this one way or another, you have my word." He called over a young officer who was speaking into a mobile. "Tschudi, come here, please." The young man was introduced; we shook hands.

"We're evacuating the flat next door, Professor," he said. "As you can see, Mademoiselle Jeanrenaud's flat is on the corner of the fourth floor, a good tactical move on the part of the gunmen because it means *we* have one less way in. So we're looking at the balcony as the main point of access."

Sure enough, the gunmen were both Pakistanis, and their demands were simple: Give Madame Suleiman back to her husband or they'd blow up her daughters and themselves with the neat plastique explosives and green ("for Islam") wiring they had strapped around their puny midriffs. The local authorities, despite much bending over backwards, had scant success, and were rebuffed when they tried to explain that Mme. Suleiman was a free agent and a native-born Swiss citizen in good standing and could do what she liked. Furthermore, she was in Paris consulting a divorce lawyer and refused to leave. These were alien concepts to the young fanatics. "We will kill!" was their only response. "Kill! Kill!" The police were at a loss and milled about, diverting traffic.

Outside the co-op market across the street, crouched over his mobile phone, was a television chap I recognized from the newsmagazine *Temps Futur*, a so-called expert in hostage negotiations who had succeeded in freeing the Algerian laundresses from the nine Bosnian Mullahs in Maubeuge last year (a case that had electrified all France and environs, notably Belgium). But for all the impact he seemed to be having on things he might as well have been—and indeed possibly was—talking to his wife about the week's grocery shopping. Indeed, as I watched he snapped his phone shut with a brisk *ciao* and, looking forlornly about as if hoping for company, he opened a notebook and made a show of consulting notes. Not a single policeman or camera crew was nearby.

As for Mister Suleiman, the ex-husband-to-be in Karachi, he was disavowing the whole business but allowed that he would welcome his wife back "on any terms in Islam." On the screen of his DVD-mobile, Inspector Nicod played me a recording of the man's scratchy telephone-amplified voice, heavily Indo-Pak.

"I never made any mistake, God knows I am telling the truth," hollered the idiot. "I was always kind and just. I don't know vhy she left. Maybe it vas my brothers, Ahmood and Ayrak. They're temperamental boys sometimes. But I don't believe in wiolence. I just vant her to come back and everything vill be OK. OK?"

Dürrenmatt wandered over, looking unsure of himself.

"I'm truly sorry, Gustave," he said. "About Dieter, I mean, saying what he did. *Ja*, I did mention your case to him, I confess, but only in passing, you know. Well," he spread his hands, "it's not every day a psychiatrist gets to treat a man who sees angels! But Dieter, no. He had no right to bring it up at such a moment."

I punched him gently on the shoulder.

"Don't worry, Herr Doktor. There are more serious things to worry about."

"Like the men from Pakistan?"

As if on cue, a Mercedes S-class drew up and a man from Pakistan got out. He sauntered over to us, redolent of cloves, peeling off limp leather gloves and slipping them into the pockets of his fawn Burberry.

"I say, Nicod, do let me talk to the little buggers," he said. "My goodness they need a talking to, I think."

This was, it transpired, the Consul-General of Pakistan, Mr. Sayyid Jaffrey. It transpired also—from a casual apology for having left the garage door open—that he was Inspector Nicod's tenant, pending security upgrades to the Consulate, which had been receiving steady bomb threats. Consul Jaffrey was a full-sized man boasting all the signs of a life dedicated to pleasure.

His small eyes sparkled and darted; he attempted without success to conceal his portliness under a full beard and the Burberry, which was at least a size too large. He carried a leather handbag and affected a crewneck pullover that clung lovingly to his undulating contours. The cloves were, I suspected, an olfactory disguise for whiskey fumes (Chivas Regal, no doubt). He, too, proffered cigarettes, Dunhills of course, but I declined. I was getting impatient with these smiling niceties, with Martine up there at the point of a knife, and said as much.

"Bugger it, I'd go in there myself if you let me," said Jaffrey, igniting a Dunhill with a graceful gold lighter. "I can talk to them. They're stupid boys. All they really need is a good fuck, of course. I doubt they've ever had one—with a woman, that is. Straight from the Sindh to Switzerland without a stop in between, all because of that diamond money from the old man. No, if these lads even know how to use a knife and fork, you can call me Barnum and Bailey. God, you wouldn't believe the level of ignorance in the Pakistani colonies, even with the kids growing up all over the place, Geneva, Paris, Rome . . . but it's all behind closed doors, for boys, too, you see. All Allah this and Allah that and When are you going to get married? So here they are, and they just want to make a noise and go on about God and the crusades and all that silly rubbish to feel important. Actually, I happen to know that one of them, Rustam, was smacked about a bit when he was a nipper. I knew his dad, you see. A real hardliner, ex-Army, Sandhurst and Rawalpindi and all that. So the lad's a bit brassed off at life, don't you know. I've no doubt the other little chap, Ali Soyuz, is the same."

"Sorry, Sayyid, we can't allow you to go in," said Nicod. "We're responsible for civilians."

"Nonsense. If I can't talk them out of this silly caper I'll offer myself as a hostage. They can cut my bloody head off. How's that for a scene-stealer? It's commonly done in these situations, I know that much from the movies. Al Pacino, wasn't it? Eh?"

He turned to me. I admired his bravado. Like the frilly shirt he was wearing, it was laced with pretension. But it was infectious. Before I knew it, I, too, found myself saying,

"I'll offer myself as a replacement hostage, too," and added, as a flourish fit for an Edmond Dantès, "by God, sir." When I'd said it I felt a starburst of emotion in the intestine, composed in equal parts of horror and incredulity—and a more settled sensation that it was the right and only thing to do, if I ever wanted to see Martine again. Nicod looked at us warily.

"Sorry to be bureaucratic about this, gentlemen, but the police department takes a very dim view of civilians getting involved in hostage negotiations, but if you both insist I'll have to get you to sign a waiver of responsibility, so if anything does happen, the Police Department, blah blah blah, you know . . . "

"Of course," said the Consul, briskly. "You don't want to be stuck with our funeral expenses, do you, Antoine? Well, I don't give a flying fig about that, how about you, sir? Now let me talk to these young Mughals." The young policeman, Tschudi, punched urgent numbers and reluctantly handed Jaffrey the mobile, from which emanated a loud squawking, as of angry macaws. The Consul returned fire with a hectoring in, I presumed, Urdu, consisting mostly of what sounded like and undoubtedly were insults, approximately: *"Boy? Boy boy bay waqoof. Buzdil waqoof. Bach cha. Cha cha cha. An nandeen narab ach. Cuss emah. Waqoof. Woof woof,"* or words to that effect—an effect entirely negative, as I could have predicted from the moment the Consul took the phone. I felt slightly vindicated when he punched off in frustration.

"Fools," he said.

But their rage was twice as righteous, and it was the rage of Allah. And it had to be confronted on those terms, not on the banal terms of those such as decent, plodding Inspector Nicod, who explained that, as per procedure, the police commando team was readying itself for action, either by storming the building from below or by dropping from the roof, one story above, onto the balcony; accordingly, we were all to step back behind a new cordon sanitaire thrown up by Geneva's finest. Shit to that, said I to myself, I'm going in. Why not? I'd already been enough of a coward by not calling Martine back, and by sneakily avoiding her and thereby avoiding responsibility, in the squalid circle of my selfish life, for another human being whom I loved—the only one I'd ever loved. Oh yes, I'd do it, and I knew how. I recalled my days as a slim young Casanova visiting my fiancée Françoise at the Argentinians' flat, via the old service lift to avoid the she-dragon of a concierge at No. 15, the next building down. I was certain all the buildings in the complex were built along exactly the same 1960s lines, so Martine's building, too, would have the requisite service entrance: The dim lightbulb, the cement-block basement doorway behind a wooden fence, the stacks of empty Cardinal and Knorr boxes at the business end of the elegant apartment blocks, adjacent to the cemetery next door and the ceaseless flow of the traffic on the Route de Ferney . . . well, then. There was no time to dither, to have another smoke, to consult the time or to make a phone call. In Bardic terms, if 'twere done when 'twere done, 'twere best 'twere done quickly. My heart flickered madly. Nicod and Jaffrey were conferring with much hand-waving and brandishing of mobiles and cigarettes. Fresh faces joined the crowd, some familiar: I saw Kia Dos Santos, my Brazilian or Amazonian student; another TV journalist known to all as "Tante Rosie," star interviewer; the Mayor, a bulky Italian-born lady socialist to whom I was distantly, distaffly, related; and others, all neighborhood residents (a movie star, long since faded; a chef, eased out of the Intercontinental for emotional incontinence; a test pilot; a celebrity dog trainer . . .). Dürrenmatt wandered about, not sure how or why he was there. His brother-in-law Chief Fegelein was now sitting in the back seat of a big black Opel, bawling into some electronic gadget, either a mobile phone or a tape recorder. The TV crew was hanging around next to the corner of Martine's block of flats, hunched into their red-and-white anoraks, smoking. It was a moment of stasis in the midst of turmoil—in short, everyone was clueless. An ideal time to pull off a surprise attack.

Now I, Gustave Termi, fifty-three, am, admittedly, bibulous; cantankerous; lustful; portly, not to say stout; foolishly opinionated on subjects of no consequence; and, last but not least, I was a twenty-a-day man—although, admittedly, milder Virginias now than my previous Caporals. I was not, in sum, the James

Bond of the hour, the dashing D'Artagnan called for in this script. Moreover, I was unarmed, except for my Army knife and a small aerosol of Mace on my keychain. But there I was; and I was all there was. And something within told me to be confident of support. And that same long-dormant spirit damned all the politicians and police departments and all their sterile exercises—in short, the predictable actions of those regimented by mediocrity, for it is precisely these exercises, this sterility, that predictability, that the toss-offs like my Martine's captors planned for. And one thing they certainly wouldn't be expecting was the arrival through the back door of an eighteen-stone fifty-three-year-old history professor and poet, with or without celestial companionship.

Yes, you see, I'd memorized my archangel's feast days: it was November 12.

The archangel split the rock by lightning and sanctified forever the waters which came from the gorge. The Greeks and Bulgarians claim that this apparition took place about the middle of the first century and celebrate a feast in commemoration of it on November 12.

Well, if it was good enough for the Greeks and Bulgarians . . . Midnight had come and gone, so, fueled by my own foolishness, and a fond belief in inevitability—if they shot me down, I'd have died in a good cause, and you can't beat that; if they didn't, well, I'd have tried, and that's a close second—I detached myself from the sundry clumps of cops and chumps and slipped soundlessly and exuberantly away, as cozily confident as a ten-year-old boy alone in his attic, with the grownups downstairs. And God, was I wide awake; and Christ, did my fingers tingle; and Blessed Michael, was I filled with Blakean righteousness and lunacy!

Lo, I was possessed by an Innumerable company of the Heavenly host crying Holy Holy Holy is the Lord God Almighty!

Excessive, yes, but the road of excess leads to the palace of wisdom, *n'est-ce pas*? Chuckling, with a dotty feeling that all was in its place, God in His heaven, and His messenger on the way, I bustled away from the throng through the quiet walkway that led past the co-op supermarket (fleeting ghost-memories from a hundred years ago of me traipsing sullenly in Mamma's wake along the aisles of that same market, once the city's best, as she weighed, sniffed, and kneaded the cheese, the bread, the fruit), and turned onto a leafy path that meandered between neatly trimmed hedges back to the main avenue about two hundred meters uphill from the nucleus of blazing police and camera lights which created a zone of illumination beyond which the darkness, in which I sought refuge, was the more complete. There were people on their balconies, despite the midnight chill. Of course, the Parc de Budé was a tranquil and cosseted enclave, and high theatrics, with the chance of being seen on television, were so unusual there as to warrant a late night. I glanced up as I crossed the street; a child saw me and waved. Go to bed, I scolded telepathically. Then, before anyone else noticed me, I was inside the lobby of No. 15, my old stage of love; and, just as in the old days, I hurried through to the back, past the letterboxes under the staircase—beneath which, like a troll, the dread concierge once lurked, and maybe still did, with a front-row seat for all the comings and goings signaled by the thunk and whine of the passenger lift. The cargo lift, however, was far enough at the back of the building, and encased in sufficiently dense concrete, to be inaudible to fire-breathing concierges or apartment dwellers. Indeed, Françoise had often commented on my arriving "like a thief in the night" via the servant's entrance, through which the tenants' Filipina or Portuguese cook would hump her shopping bags bulging with eggplant, mahi-mahi, and Rioja wine from the cargo lift into the kitchen without distracting the Ambassador from his concubine or the memsahib from her tea party. (With monumental irrelevance, I thought: *Well! Martine must be quite well off to live here!*)

I pushed open the rear door; it creaked. I stopped, then proceeded stealthily, with only minimal heavy breathing and no audible clicking of aging joints, and ducked behind a hedge as I slowly circumnavigated my way through the rear car park to the service entrance of Martine's building, No. 17. A lonely fly-specked lightbulb in a grate burned above the red fire door. No one was in sight, and the only sounds were the even flow of the France-bound traffic on the Route de Ferney on the other side of the wall and the eddying surf of the throng on the far side of the building, where the action was. I opened the long-unoiled service door and gritted my teeth at the resulting shriek of rusted hinges, but the distant clamor throbbed on regardless, and I stepped into a close, damp space that smelled of rotten vegetables, mice, and urine. Inside, another naked bulb shed its pitiful empty light on a wall upon which some spray-painting genius had daubed "Push Me Pull You Fuck." Behind and to the right was a small loading bay and the green metal door, with porthole, of the cargo lift. I pushed the button for the lift. Deep in the bowels came a Fafnir or Fasolt grumble and snarl and the lift lurched and clunked and rose with deliberate slowness and came to a halt in front of me with a tired *hsss* and sudden jerk. I stepped on board. A fluorescent tube; more graffiti on the unpainted walls: "Sex phone OK" and a number; "Gag *Mutti*"; "Fuck," the single favorite word of all graffiti vandals around the world. (My city was degenerating. When I was a boy there was not a single non-political graffito in any of Geneva's forty-five communes. After '68 the smart slogans proliferated —"The Future Isn't What It Used To Be," etc.—as Geneva strove to imitate Paris. Then came the sanctification of the ghetto, and now the blight was everywhere. I'd seen the word "caca" on the walls of St. Peter's, under Calvin's nose. On the Grand Theater. On the buildings of the College. And elaborately curlicued in purple paint across the front door of my apartment building on the Boulevard des Philosophes was the mysterious pseudo-English word "Funt." Was it any wonder, then, that I was resigned to my fate, if it only meant leaving such a world?)

(But it was a world with Martine in it.)

Martine's apartment was on the fourth floor. I pressed five, just in case the mini-mullahs had posted a sentry by the fourth-floor lift door. (Was I thinking that clearly? It's amazing. I was in a state of grace, or madness, or both.) The old lift had the same lift-smells I remembered from all those years ago, and the memory roused by those smells awoke a parallel shiver of anticipation: of sex then, of I knew not what now. On top of the general grubby stale-tobacco-and-puke pong was an odd overlay of armpit odor, concentrated, as if released in industrial-strength quantities. Or was it spilled beer? The two are olfactory cousins . . . grimly, then, the lift rose through the shaft, staggering a little with the effort. My exaltation started to wane with the ominous *clunk* of each passing floor. As the first floor went slowly by I thought I saw, through the frosted-glass porthole of the lift door, a waiting figure. I braced myself for the anticipated stop, but the lift groaned onward and upward. As the second-floor door came gradually into view, so did a human shape that, as the lift rose sluggishly ever higher, disappeared. But on the third floor he came into full view as an apparition of vibrant shining gold. To him, of course, doors were no barrier. He simply melted through them. This time he seemed all there, three-dimensional, like a human being, and he greeted me with a harder, deeper voice than before, in which there was the trace of an accent: mine. In the air was a scent of ozone. It was, I assume, the smell of an archangel, for he had no other smells.

"Hail, Gustave Termi."

I managed the correct salutation this time, despite a sudden stammer.

"Hai-hail to thee, great archangel."

He seemed quite pleased to be so addressed. The vanity of an archangel long ignored? Perhaps, I thought, I was learning the lexicon of visionaries. After all, these angels were ancient beings who drew upon sources of conduct and logic even more ancient, sources alien to computer-using, car-driving, DVD-watching, deeply confused twenty-first century Europeans. I was awestruck. I was in the presence of the one who threw Satan out of Heaven, the one whose name is mentioned in the Bible. (Oh, I believed it. I did. I do. And there's not a trace of porphyria in it, if you ask me.) And I was one of the very few ever granted the sight of him. Why was he there, then, in that squalid cargo lift, in the back of a Geneva apartment building lived in by people of no faith? Was it the anguish in Martine's heart that had brought him through the ether? If so, why had he not been at crucibles of the world's anguish such as Auschwitz or Rwanda, when he could have swooped howling upon the demons and put them and their works to the sword? Well, in the words of the poet James,

How many angels knew who Hamlet was
When they were summoned by Horatio?
They probably showed up only because
The roster said it was their turn to go.

He was there because he was there, and to be quite honest, this time I never had any doubt that he'd come. It was the closest thing to a genuinely religious sentiment I'd ever had (and it wasn't very close, being more instinct than anything else, like the feeling that it's about to snow, or that there's someone on the other side of the door) . . . and he was immense at first, as immense as his statue atop the Castel Sant' Angelo, too vast for the humble cargo lift, which simply disappeared, turning instead into a mere stage for our encounter as around us the outer darkness spun wide with the steady music of the cosmos. But the archangel's dimensions were under his own control, like the language he spoke or the vestments in which he was arrayed (gold, blue, white), and before we reached the next floor (and of course it took precisely as long as he decided it would take, a millennium or a second, and I couldn't tell you which) he was almost normal in size, about ten centimeters taller than I (a meter seventy-five in socks), and his wings, if folded, were well concealed; in fact, for a moment he seemed more of a man than he ever had before, more of the kind of man who might sell you a train ticket, or paint your house, or teach you a foreign language—but if he was a man, he was a man garbed in shimmering, aqueous light such as no mere mortal has ever worn. It was blinding, beautiful, magnificent. I had none of that sense of beholding an image that I'd had the last time, but rather of seeing a supreme work of art and an ideal example of the human form (and I'm no worshipper of the body beautiful, unless it's Woman's) at the same time. I had to speak, but felt tongue-tied (who wouldn't, under the circumstances?); still, I managed "I'm pleased you've come, Angel," sounding like the host at a cocktail party. "I knew you would."

He seemed content with this. He didn't smile exactly, but

there was a brief flare-up of *goldenness*, like a quiet fire in his eyes.

"I am from the Seraphim, the angels of courage," he said, matter-of-factly. "That is why I am here." His eyes were infinite in what they expressed. It was like looking into the firmament itself. I felt faintly nauseous. "In your road of life you are adored, Gustave Termi, as are all brave men, by the Most High."

I was flattered, of course, and felt the terrible nearness of God and all that meant to my topsy-turvy view of things, then I began to wonder if the finality of the angel's comments didn't mean I was about to die. I suddenly felt frail and feeble and mortal and very silly, and the tiredness I'd been holding at bay washed over me. My feet and head ached, and I needed a pee. All the while the Archangel was staring at me with those amazing blazing eyes, apparently expecting me to say something, but the best I could do was stammer out an old Italian proverb the *nonni* in Piedmont repeat on Michaelmas.

"St. Michael's rain does not stay long in the sky."

He laughed. Yes, he laughed. It was like the rushing of the wind through leaf-heavy branches . . . no, through the full late summer foliage of vineyards on a hillside, when the wind suddenly gusts upward from the valley below.

"True, Gustave Termi. That it does not, although it may rain with the force of a deluge for a while. As now. And now we are where I said to you we would be one day. Fear me not. Love me and love your God. And remember: *Lux in tenebris*, it is always darkest before the dawn." With an all-encompassing sweep of his arm (I saw then the glitter of his giant wings, which rose majestically, emerald green, into the air) he stripped opacity from the entire fourth floor of the building, changing walls and doors into the transparency of glass. The entire apartment was spread out in front of us. In the living room sat my poor Martine with her head in her hands. Next to her on the sofa was another young woman, no doubt her sister Laure, looking toward the window. The two gunmen, one holding a submachine gun, the other a pistol and a mobile phone, were conferring in the open kitchenway about ten meters left of where Martine was sitting. No one appeared to be aware of anything. Martine was wearing

her maroon dress, the one I had been privileged to remove on
our single night of love. This detail placed the scene squarely
in the gritty randomness of reality; and yet, standing next to
me and towering above me and swirling all around me was the
Archangel, now redolent of the upper air, of space, and purity
(like oxygen). With a magnificent undulation across various spa-
tial dimensions he grew immense again and drew his sword and
pointed it forward and downward, in the pose of his likeness
on the Castel Sant'Angelo. Then, speaking a language I did not
understand, with many harsh and guttural utterances, he filled
the scene before us with a quivering, blinding, dancing light in
which I hazily half discerned a frenzy of dancing figures, some,
it seemed to me, with a halo and a crown, others with horns and
a tail, others more than part animal from the waist down, all
of them frolicking and curtseying and spinning in circles, with
a bewildering babel of droning and harsh laughter and high-
pitched ululations. The air smelled strongly of ozone, again (it
smells a bit like the sea, with a pinch of diesel fumes, in case you
were wondering), then of hot metal, then of the earth (wet), then
of rain. There were screams, male and female, in Urdu or Arabic
or Pushtun or something incomprehensible, and in French, and
in I knew not what else . . . Angelic?

"Mikail!"

"*Oh bon Dieu bon Dieu bon Dieu . . .* "

"Get out!"

"Ras Ullulah!"

"Bass Wami! Ullah!"

Blue smoke swirled, and the light-figures suddenly vanished,
and a thunderous pounding started up amid cries and screams. It
was like suddenly finding oneself in an avant-garde discotheque.
I tried to make my way toward where I thought Martine was, but
I ended up in a darkened hallway, blundering about between a
bookcase and a wardrobe, coughing up fumes—not ozone this
time, but the raunchy, acrid stink of household combustibles
like rugs and cushions.

"Martine!" I bawled, then coughed, and retched quietly for
a few seconds. Figures loomed through the fog. One grabbed

hold of my elbow. I shook off the strange hand and blundered toward a sudden bright light, hoping to see . . . the Archangel again . . . but he was gone. I saw Martine instead. She was staggering blindly toward me, covered in soot and grime. Holding a blanket around her shoulders was a man wearing a leather jacket and a ski mask pointing into the darkness a torch that bobbed up and down and sideways. Across the back of the man's jacket was emblazoned the word POLICE. He motioned to me and pointed to the door, which was slowly becoming visible again. I shook my head and went up to Martine and touched her on the shoulder. She looked up, dazed, and weakly half smiled when she saw me.

"Gustave? *You* here?"

The entire place was becoming visible again. The fog was lifting, the walls were once again opaque, a fire extinguisher hissed and contributed its peculiar sweet-and-sour odor to the miasma. The two Pakistani gunmen were handcuffed and sitting side by side on the still-smouldering sofa in the living room and responding surlily to police questions. Broken glass was strewn all over a very fine, if slightly charred, Afghan carpet, and three or four more police commandos stood about. One was holding a rope, as if about to set up a lynching party. Martine was sobbing in my arms. I made an attempt to brush cinders and other shards off her hair. She looked up at me again, tearfully. She wasn't wearing her glasses. I was reminded of our night together and of how happy I was that she was safe.

"Gustave? My God, how did you get here?" she inquired, between gasps. "My God. Is it really over?"

"Perhaps you should accompany Madame to the Cantonal Hospital, *monsieur le professeur*," said the leather-jacketed policeman, reassured as to my identity and intention and clearly impressed, as are so many Swiss, by professorial status. "The ambulance is downstairs."

"It's over, *chérie*," I said, holding Martine tightly. "Let's go."

"God," she mumbled. "I'm alive. Laure's alive. It's a miracle."

"Oh yes, a miracle. Quite definitely."

She sighed and sobbed and nearly fainted in my arms and

slid to the floor before I got the young police commando to help her onto a stretcher. Soon the paramedics were on the premises, along with Inspector Nicod, whose pop-eyed expression of astonishment at seeing me there would have done credit to Jerry Lewis.

"Professor," he said, "you are insane to have come up here. Insane and misguided and in violation of a half dozen laws and ordinances. I really should arrest you right now."

"But you won't, eh, Nicod," I said.

"Not at the moment," he said. "Because it was a clean operation and no one was killed, not because you don't deserve to be arrested."

"A clean operation?"

"But yes. Immaculate. We are very proud. You see, the ladies are all right."

I watched as the paramedics affixed a glucose drip to Martine's arm and wheeled her out onto the landing. She turned and looked over her shoulder at me, and I nodded reassuringly. Two more medics followed with her sister, also on a stretcher, but asleep, or drugged, or unconscious.

"Our commandos did it all without bloodshed," said Nicod. "Which you especially should appreciate, Professor, as they're instructed to regard any intruder on the scene of an operation as a potential target. So you're lucky they didn't shoot you. But they're highly skilled—and by God they did a good job here, didn't they?"

With the memory of that heavenly ozone scent still fresh, I gave him the luxury of his illusion; but had he not, I asked, noticed anything else? Any*one* else . . . ?

"Anyone else?" He looked at me sharply. "Please don't tell me you brought someone else along."

"Well . . . " In a manner of speaking, I had, but how could I tell this good, stolid, down-to-earth Geneva policeman that the companion I had brought with me, or who had brought me with him, was the Archangel Michael, scourge of Satan? And that it was he, with his mighty sword unsheathed, who had struck terror into the hearts of the cowardly gunmen, who had then been left defenseless and gibbering when the commando team swung down from the roof? I contemplated Nicod's face: lined, jowly, tugged downward by gravity, the face of a man more accustomed to angel dust than angels . . . on the other hand, was it not the great eighteenth-century phrenologist Franz Joseph Gall who believed that the mental organ for problem-solving, i.e. detection, was the same as the organ for creativity and religious belief, i.e. hallucinations . . . ?

But perhaps it wasn't the time to mention it.

"No. I just thought. Of course, in all the confusion . . . "

"I'm very glad to hear it, Professor. Please excuse me, and give my regards to Mademoiselle Jeanrenaud. I'm very glad she's safe. I've watched many of her broadcasts over the years." The Inspector then excused himself for the myriad administrative duties that faced him. And Chief Fegelein soon faced *me*, downstairs in front of the building, waving a finger in very Swiss-German token of mock-irritation.

"Professor Termi!" he exclaimed. "I should have kept a closer eye on you! Maybe we will bring you to court, *hein?*"

Dürrenmatt soon materialized at his side to assure me that such a thing would never happen, against the backdrop of the loud neighing "nay, nay" of his brother-in-law, who soon lost interest in me, again, being easily lured away to give an interview to a TV reporter. I accepted Dürrenmatt's offer of a ride in a taxi as far as the Cantonal Hospital. As we sped across the Place des Nations, empty at that hour (it was now one twenty a.m.), Dürrenmatt placed an amicable hand on my shoulder and said,

"*Ja.* You know, Gustave, I saw him too. With the sword? *Mein Gott.*"

He was lying, I was sure of it: the shrink's ploy, to forge false bonds. At the Hospital I bade him good night, with considerable relief. A young doctor with red hair and freckles informed me that Martine was resting and that Laure was undergoing a CAT scan and that neither was to be disturbed until morning and anyway their mother was due from Paris shortly, and as I was no kin, would I kindly leave and check up by phone on the morrow?

It was drizzling as I walked the three blocks downhill to my

apartment house. My legs ached; my head throbbed; my stomach grumbled. Traffic was sparse. At home I fell across my bed
and plunged into the dreamless sleep of the dead for four hours;
then, wide awake at five a.m., I had a coffee, then a croissant,
then a smoke, then a slice of Bleu de Gex, then I played a recording of Géza Anda interpreting Mozart's 26th Piano Concerto on
a Steinway in Stefanie von Rothenberg's native town of Salzburg.
The music glimmered with understanding of the incomprehensible. Pain was transformed into beauty, then back into pain again,
in the melancholy perfection of the Adagio. I shed a tear, briefly,
as I listened, while thinking back over the previous evening, and
over my life as I'd lived it up until then. Worthless, I thought.
So I'd almost thrown it away. Christ, it was true, I *had* taken my
life into my hands, madly, suicidally, to save Martine's; true, I
loved the woman, and Guilt idly picked nits from my conscience
at insistent memories of the night's boozing and Giulia, but it
was inconsequential, Giulia was ephemeral, Martine was Love,
I was still alive. So I'd risked it all. Brave, was I? Not really. As
fed up with life's inadequacies, and mine, as anything else; I
suspect this lies at the root of much heroism. Anyway, I knew
from the outset that the Archangel would appear. How had I
known, apart from the date? I knew not, truly. But I trusted my
direct line up there. And by the way I thought one or both of
those Pakistani would-be terrorists had also been granted a vision
of the avenging angel, whence the cries, in Arabic or Urdu, of
"Mikail!" After all, the great Archangel was a star in the Islamic
firmament, as well.

So were both religions right? Or neither? What about the
Jews? Could I see Abraham? Would I ever see Michael again?

After this wild brooding I was too frenzied to sleep. Until
weariness took me, therefore, I sat by the half-open window
and breathed in the frosty night air and resumed reading about
Stefanie and occupied Paris and the frenzied circumstances of
her life.

Life and Transfiguration

At first sight the Gestapo office on the Avenue Foch, near the
Étoile, was just another office. In the courtyard bicycles leaned
against the wall like weary travelers. Cats dripped over the wall
from the Peugeot garage next door, now a service station for
the Wehrmacht motor pool. A glowering concierge sat smoking a cigarette at her post behind a glass door on the *rez-de-
chaussée*, listening to a radio from which the throaty voice of
Maurice Chevalier was rendering "*Ça sent si bon, la France.*" The
entranceway smelled of chicory, cheap detergent and cheaper
tobacco. The lift, behind a brass-and-glass door that squealed
when opened, creaked its way in typical Parisian-lift fashion up
to the third floor, where, behind an oak door with gleaming brass
handle and in front of worshipful poster-icons of the Führer
and the Maréchal in their respective languages—*Adolf Hitler Ist
Der Sieg* and *Maréchal, Nous Voilà!*—there was a reception desk
at which bright and chirpy German girls of the secretarial type
but in crisp uniforms chirped brightly to each other but said
nothing to Stefanie, who was flanked by SS Lieutenant Stemmer
and SS Major Schneider as they brought her in and courteously
stood aside for her to precede them into the den of the wolf,
Gestapo headquarters for Greater Paris. Typewriters clattered;
doors opened and closed; pungent clouds of cigarette smoke
drifted from room to room; telephones jangled. The business of
torture, efficiently and tirelessly executed, was apparently booming, without even any screams to disrupt the surface normality of
things. The torture cells were in the basement, supposed Stefanie,
resigned to finding out sooner rather than later. The activity of
the moment lessened her dread at what awaited her. In an odd
way she felt no worse than she had when sitting her final theology exam, or going out with Arthur the first time: apprehensive,
eager, but all too willing for time to pass.

But the courteous treatment continued. Stemmer and
Schneider excused themselves and left to report to a superior on
the circumstances of Kohler's death. An SS corporal deferentially
("*Mein Frau, bitte*") showed Stefanie into a comfortable waiting

room with pink wallpaper and a Hitler portrait (the prewar suit, coat slung over his arm, glaring into the gloaming) and a second-rate landscape painting (cows, a meadow, wispy clouds) and offered her coffee which, in her surprise, she accepted. Copies of *Signal, Pariser Zeitung, Der Stürmer* and *Je suis partout* lay on a side table. Like the dentist's, she thought, with the prospect of the agony of the dentist's chair, only much worse . . . and yet. There was nothing but the distant clack of typewriters. Conversations, in French and German, faded away. A telephone rang; a French voice answered. This waiting, too, was a velveteen form of torture. Feigning calm more for her own benefit than that of any potential witnesses, Stefanie picked up *Pariser Zeitung*, the sycophantic newspaper issued by and for the occupation forces, and browsed the comic strips and advertisements for ersatz groceries and the social doings of *Brigadeführer* Abetz, the Reich's Ambassador in Paris, only to look up at the sound of the door opening. A man with a handsome if somewhat weather-beaten face stood in the doorway, a raincoat draped over his shoulders, a pair of gloves in his left hand, giving every sign of pleasure at seeing a woman who to the best of her knowledge had never seen him before.

"Frau von Rothenberg? *Oder* Lebel?"

"Yes."

"Do forgive me, *mein Frau—oder Fräulein?*" The precision was a very German footnote. "Frau Lebel, *ja*? What a coincidence!"

"A coincidence?"

"I am Karl Epting, first attaché at the Embassy. I believe you know my wife? The director of the Institut des Deutschen Kultur?"

She then underwent the ritual of having her hand kissed, scrutinizing the pate of his head as he bowed over her hand and clicked his heels in the age-old German-Austrian bourgeois tradition: hair moist and brushed severely back from his forehead, like an old lady's—like, in fact (she couldn't help thinking), her own mutti's hair, blonder, of course, and minus the bun . . .

"Yes. A pleasure. You know, we are having some trouble with

malcontents these days, and for everyone's benefit . . . in any case, I checked your name in our files, and good heavens, *mein Frau*, you *have* been through the mill. Please accept my regrets."

"Thank you."

"You are not Jewish, are you?" She said nothing. "No, I know you aren't. Although you do keep some rather Jewish company." Epting sat down across from her and took out a cigarette case. She declined; he lit up and exhaled with much to-do (teeth bared, smoke flaring forth, free hand brushing away invisible ashes from knife-creased trousers). He was a man with more polish than handsomeness, but both, she was sure, conspired to have an effect on susceptible women, starting with Frau Epting.

"You must know," he said, "that Johann Kohler, who was officially just a chauffeur for officers of the SS, was in reality playing a dangerous game. In fact, it would not be too much to say that you have done us a favor by hastening his death, so to speak."

She stared blankly.

"We were planning to turn him and use him for our own purposes, and of course the Gestapo were to have had a hand in this."

"Turn . . . ?"

"Yes. Into a double agent?" His face wrinkled into an expression of real or feigned distress. "But surely you realized he was a spy? Did he not ask you—you can be quite candid with me, Frau von Rothenberg, I can assure you you are in no danger, nor your family—did he not ask you to smuggle things to Switzerland for him? Or people?"

"No," she said, with strict truthfulness. "He did not." Herr Epting looked at her through the upfurling curls of cigarette smoke. "But he did mention something about Switzerland, yes," she added, scrambling for the high ground of verisimilitude. "Not smuggling, though. Perhaps he was planning a trip there and wanted me to go with him." Again, this was perfectly true, in a strict sense, although one far stupider than Herr Epting would have detected the illogicality of such a man—a smuggler, a spy: she wasn't that surprised; in fact, it raised her opinion of Kohler from the ridiculous to, if not quite the sublime, at least to the respectable—inviting an innocent woman to go to Switzerland with him in the present circumstances of the world. (And one much less intelligent than she would already have tumbled to the direction Kohler's proposal about a make-believe wife would have taken, had she encouraged him.)

"I see," said Epting. "Well, I can tell you he was the very small tip of a very large iceberg whose dimensions we are only just beginning to appreciate, and it is only his potential as a double agent that would lead any of us in the Occupation Authority to regret his untimely demise. Still, it can't be helped, and I am quite sure I can get the French police to see it as the mere accident it was."

"I am happy to hear it," said Stefanie, unsure. Epting inclined his head in acknowledgment.

"But speaking of Switzerland," he said, genially, "You do have a son there, I believe?

"Well, since you know. Yes."

"We do know, Frau von Rothenberg. And we need help here and there, a bit of collaboration, *ja*? So, if it isn't too much to ask, perhaps you can be of some service, as a patriotic German."

"I am a patriotic *Austrian*, Herr Epting," she said. "And loyal French national, by marriage and long residence."

"Indeed, I know that. But a patriotic Austrian and loyal French national is now by definition a follower of the Reich, *nein*? Or at least of Le Maréchal?" He paused, smacked his lips, and sat upright, index finger held high, like a schoolboy preparing to recite a poem. "*Car, comme Carthage, l'Angleterre sera détruite!*" he declaimed, quoting the words spoken by a prominent collaborationist radio personality at the close of each broadcast. Herr Epting's French had the pedantic German's fractured jauntiness. "*N'est-ce pas?*"

Stefanie shrugged.

"*Je ne suis pas politique,*" she said. Epting chuckled and reverted to German.

"Well what about your marriage? That is more or less theoretical, *nicht wahr*? What with Herr Lebel in America?"

The questions continued, labored and predictable, forming

part of a one-sided conversation which to Epting was no doubt a masterpiece of subtle manipulation, but which to Stefanie was a masterpiece of the obvious that thudded forward with the blind clumsiness of Nazi propaganda, or a marching band bleary from beer. Right from the start she had deduced the outcome of this interview: an offer to continue and expand the work of the late unlamented (except, oddly, by her, slightly, now that she knew) Kohler, but also to . . .

"Keep us informed," as Epting put it . . . as Kohler had put it.

Stefanie was incredulous. Having given up any efforts at salvation by human agents, having at last steeled herself to resist the harshest torture and to consign her soul into the care of Mother Mary, having in fact prepared herself for her martyrdom, she had discovered instead a waiting room with pink wallpaper and newspapers and the banality and pleasant chit-chat of a cocktail party. And an invitation to extend her work for the Reich from teaching German to spying. Thinking only of the opportunities for protecting Mutti and Ignace, she told herself that there would be time enough to square it with her conscience. If only she could talk it over with Sami.

Well, said Epting, they would, she could be sure, be in touch very soon, and he departed in a whirl of self-importance after returning her belongings to her and instructing his driver to take her home, with further, murmured apologies.

The first contact came within twenty-four hours, heralded by a beaming Frau Epting, for whom Stefanie was now a prized colleague.

"The office of Ambassador Herr Doktor Brigadeführer Otto Abetz is on the telephone," she said, interrupting Elementary German. "For Frau von Rothenberg." She looked around, as if to make sure everyone had heard. "*Abetz*," she repeated. The French black-marketeer mimed an embrace.

"*Otto, mon amour*," he said.

In fact, it was Herr Epting, requesting a meeting at the Embassy the next day. Stefanie told her mother that evening, after complimenting her on the eight grams of *andouille* she had managed to procure from the new butcher outside the official perimeters of her V card. Outside, on the Rue Soufflot, there was a military parade to honor someone's birthday—Horst Wessel? Goebbels? It hardly mattered anymore. Parisians lowered their heads and went about their business, most of them doing their best to ignore, and be ignored by, the strange alien presence in its multitudinous feldgrau uniforms and kubelwagens, and its loud harsh language and exotic love of marching bands. This one came to a halt just under Stefanie's window and played *Deutschlandlied, Alte Kameraden, Lorelei,* and—as the publicity brochures have it—much, much more. It was a sultry evening, so the windows were open, admitting the annoying thumping and drilling of the band and mingled whiffs of coke-driven engines and woodsmoke, the new signature scent of Paris.

"The German embassy? Don't go, *mädl.* Leave them alone. Somehow we'll get through all this. Ahack."

Mutti had developed a cough and argued it was caused by the coal smoke and the filthy air; but Stefanie smelled the cigarettes. They were, after all, her own, stolen by her mother late at night.

"I must go, *Mutti.* For you. And Ignace."

"You mean for *you.* Ignace is fine. He's *in* Switzerland, for heaven's sake. And me? Pah. When I go I'll go fast, don't worry. And that won't be long now. So please don't give these monsters the time of day."

She rose and went into the bedroom and coughed a while before falling asleep. The German band oompa'ed its way down the Rue Soufflot to the Luxembourg Gardens, from where snatches of their efforts were still being magnified by errant breezes an hour or so later.

Events developed thereafter with the swiftness a sudden change in life's course usually brings in its train: a meeting at the Embassy at which Herr Epting presided; a meeting at the Institute with an officer in the Abwehr, German counter-intelligence; yet another meeting, this one somewhat more clandestine, with a sullen Spanish "border runner" at a café on the Champs-Élysées, to make arrangements for Stefanie to do a dummy smuggling run across the Pyrenees . . . then came a telephone call from Sami, the first since his disappearance. He was breathing heavily, and in the background Stefanie heard a regular pounding sound like a woodsman's axe, or a steam hammer.

"Madame? This is football coach Paul," he said. "Your international match is cancelled because of dangerous weather conditions."

The absurdity of it caught her in the throat, but at the sound of his voice all the warmth and generosity of their long-ago love swelled within her, and she fought back a cry of despair.

"A friendly match will be arranged in another place, with all the former members of the team."

He hung up.

The next day Herr Epting told her the Spanish jaunt was off.

"Bad weather conditions," he said, with a straight face. "You'll be going to Switzerland instead. More information forthcoming."

Stefanie wondered who was getting weather reports from whom. The temptation to say something was great, but there was a thrill, too, at the imposed secrecy. Still, she wished, for more reasons than one, that she could talk to Sami. There was a feeling in lies, or half-truths, from others, of being excluded, of not being trusted—of being thought stupid—and she had to overcome a lifetime's pride to accept it as part of the new world to which she now reluctantly belonged, after so long away.

And she reminded herself the stakes were high, the combat relentless, and her time was coming.

Tartuffe in Annecy

The journey south was one of the worst Jean-Xavier ever taken, and he'd made the Paris-Annecy trip a good dozen times over the years. But last time there hadn't been the Occupied and Free Zones, and entering the Free Zone was a nightmare of being shooed off trains at some dingy depot just beyond Châlons by one group of *flics* and lugging bags hither and yon in the pouring rain and getting onto other trains only to be forced to get off again ten minutes later at some abandoned *bled* of a country station with an unmade bed in the office of the Chef de Gare and alarms ringing incessantly on the platform and more flics everywhere, then having to shuffle from one dimly lit shed to another and being barked at by all the *poules* and the new Intelligence Service guys and having to show total deference to those *connards* as well as producing on demand like a magician a thousand different specimens of identity card . . .

"Too bad they weren't this efficient on the Somme and Aisne in '40," Jean-Xavier muttered to himself. A policeman in a cape called him over and held up his identity card and driving license.

"Durand?"

"*Oui, monsieur*. Jean-Xavier Durand. I'm going home to . . . "

"You are an employee of the Grand Hotel Rastignac, Avenue de Maine in Paris?"

"Not any longer, monsieur. You see, the hotel has been taken over by the German Army and they have their own porters."

The man turned to a colleague and both guffawed at the notion of the German Army's "porters."

"And your wife owns a patisserie in Annecy?"

"*Oui, monsieur*. I am hoping to work there."

"Well, perhaps if you are very nice to her, she will offer you a job," said the first gendarme, who turned again to his colleague and added, "but don't expect much of anything else, *hein*, after you've been away so long!" More guffaws. Durand joined in, apathetically. He'd heard all the *cocu* jokes before and he'd usually joined in because he'd never taken them seriously. Only this time he'd heard from neighbors back in Annecy, the Wengers, good Swiss, about this fellow from Paris, this Monsieur Paul with his flash Delahaye, this supposed master pastry chef, moving in and virtually taking over; so he, Durand, was on his way home. His wife knew he was coming, but not his specific time of arrival, so he could see what he would see as it were . . .

Finally his identity papers were returned and he was directed to another train with the admonition to re-register with the *Police Judiciaire* in Annecy for a whole new set of ration cards and permits for Pétain's new French State in which Liberty, Equality and Fraternity had yielded to Work, Family and Fatherland.

"*Et vive le Maréchal*," said the policeman, apparently in all seriousness, waving him on. Durand echoed the exhortation,

mechanically, and boarded another train, which eventually rattled sluggishly south from Dijon and through the woods and
meadows of the high Jura where the lonely *mas*, the cowherds'
sheds, sat out the long winters under their mantles of snow. At
Bellegarde, a small town tucked into a cleft on the Rhône near
the Swiss border, Durand changed trains again for Annemasse
and Annecy, this time to a modern *micheline* of the type recently
introduced. As the train rolled along, Jean-Xavier thought of
his wife, Amelie, with affection, nostalgia, jealousy, and a nervous anticipation. He smoked and recalled incidents of the past
incredible months in Paris and the upheaval at the hotel and he
remembered seeing Hitler and the marching Wehrmacht.

"*Quel bordel*," he said to himself.

He turned his gaze outward and saw the familiar gorges and
waterfalls and abrupt limestone cliffs of the Jura give way near
Cruseilles to high pastureland and larger farms and the distant
wall of the Savoy Alps glinting white in the sun. Coming into
Annemasse, on the frontier, he caught a glimpse of the great
placid sheet of Lake Geneva: Switzerland, more of a haven than
ever, but no longer the place to go for a weekend's shopping or
a higher-paid job. The Germans were on the other side, and the
border was closed off.

At six, after another flurry of identity checks, this time by
Vichy "armistice" troops, he arrived in Annecy. He saw no one
at the station, and decided to walk: It was only a few streets
away, just off the Rue Sommeiller. The air was clean and bracing
after the train's smoky fug. Clouds sheered off the jagged peaks
of the Dents de Lanfon across Lake Annecy. The chateau of the
Dukes of Savoy, now occupied by a brigade of Pétainistes, part
of the "Armistice Army," loomed familiarly above the canals and
alleys of the old town. It was good to be back. Durand nodded
to passersby.

"*Salut, Durand*," said his wife. She was standing expectantly
outside the bakery, arms folded. They kissed somewhat formally,
like generals. On the shop window was a sign hand lettered in red,
white and blue characters: *Spécialités d'Alsace! Rouleaux d'Alsace.
Pépites de grès rose des Vosges. Gateau Elise. Tartine de Mirabelles.*

"What's this?" inquired Jean-Xavier.

"Monsieur Paul," said Amelie. "He's from Strasbourg. He's a wonderful baker, Durand. If it hadn't been for him, we'd be bankrupt now. Everyone wants to buy Alsatian specialties to show their support for the poor people up there who were taken over by the Boches."

"Where does he live, this Monsieur Paul?"

"On the Avenue d'Albigny," she said, naming Annecy's elegant lakefront boulevard.

Jean-Xavier was less than charmed, although Monsieur Paul, when he was introduced, proved to be a thoroughly charming gray-haired, heavily mustached gentleman on the far side of middle age and, one hoped, well past the seduction of plump forty-year-old *patissières*; but there was a dapper knowingness to him that Jean-Xavier, ex-communist, ex-porter, man of the people, recognized as upper-class or cosmopolitan or Jewish or something and instinctively distrusted. After dinner he went next door to see Arsène Wenger, the Swiss neighbor who'd roused his suspicions in the first place.

"Oh, I don't know," said Wenger, an electrician. "I'd keep an eye on him, that's all."

"But you said."

"No, *m'sieu* Durand. I said I *thought*. Not that I knew."

"*Il est juif, hein?*"

Wenger nodded and reached for a cornpaper cigarette.

As for Sami (for of course it was he), he sensed Jean-Xavier's distrust, his suspicions, his potential for anti-Semitism, the limits of his intelligence; such men had once been the backbone of the Radical Party, however, and he had vast experience in charming them into compliance.

"I can understand your surprise at finding a total stranger in your home, Durand," he said to Jean-Xavier over a placatory *renversé* and cognac. "But it's simple, really. *C'est la guerre, n'est-ce pas?* I was forcibly evacuated from my hometown of Strasbourg by, ah, recent events, as you can imagine. Annecy was mentioned as a candidate for capital of the new state, so I came here for the probable opportunities, and your wife's bakery needed a little shall we say pecuniary infusion? So I've been helping your lady wife with my expertise, mostly in Alsatian pastries, and a little capital here and there."

"Capital? How much?" Jean-Xavier's cup paused halfway to his mouth.

"Don't worry, *mon cher*. No question of repayment. It's an investment for all of us, you see. *Santé*."

They drank their cognacs.

"Anyway," said Sami, "the climate here is superb, *n'est-ce pas*? Here, try one of my *rouleaux*. That's nutmeg you taste in the middle. And ground cinnamon. Both very hard to come by these days."

"Not bad," nodded Jean-Xavier, munching appreciatively. "Not bad at all."

When Jean-Xavier started behind the counter, Sami stood aside and let him make a fool of himself with batches of runny, flavorless chicory *escargots* and limp croissants with margarine instead of butter. But the man slowly grew more competent, and by the time he was fully in charge of the morning shift, with his wife taking over in the afternoons, he was worked so hard and had to rise so early, even with the wartime rationing, that he had no time or energy left to spy on Sami's trysts with his wife—for of course the rumors were true, how else could Sami have found such a haven?—and his after-hours meetings in the "annex," a disused Renault service station across the Rue Sommeiller whose former manager, before it had been requisitioned in '39 by the Army and since closed down, was Henri Max, now officially the owner of a ferry service on the lake and unofficially the regional commander of a dozen embryonic *Franc-Tireurs et Partisans* resistance units, none of which was officially aware of the others' existence. Only Sami, with his bankroll, his Jewishness, his Socialist credentials—although all the FTP units were communist—and his native panache, managed to get in on the secret. Mondays they met after midnight while Annecy slept. They smoked and chatted and drank pastis. Max had once run a *tabac* on the Place Blanche, and knew the clubs and backstreets of that seamy Paris neighborhood as a mountaineer knows his peaks.

They examined maps and listened to the BBC and made plans to smuggle in more radio transmitters and drew up lists of enemies and potential friends. The former was longer than the latter and growing longer by the day. After the collapse in '40 most French, stunned, at first only wanted to curl up in the great cozy land of make-believe that was the Vichy state and quietly get on with their lives, but the cruel and clumsy tactics of the Germans and, especially, their Vichy stooges, made more active resistance probable. After the Germans massacred a group of FTP *résistants* at Châteaubriant in '41, it became inevitable.

"The realities of the situation have penetrated even the incurable egoism of the French peasant," said Sami.

"And the even more monstrous egoism of the Paris *boulevardier*," retorted Henri Max.

By '42 the entire southeast was in ferment, although the Italian occupation was benevolence itself compared to the German, itself a blessing by contrast to that other German occupation in the devastated Slavic lands farther east; still, it was the Nazi jackboot, it was on Marianne's neck, and it was a sickening humiliation for great France.

"Communist, socialist, bloody royalist, or whatever you call yourself, you're a Frenchman, Jew or Christian," said Henri Max. "That makes two of us. France needs us."

Sami was put in charge of escape routes for the Haute-Savoie region and assembled a team of six—two auto mechanics, a priest, a Latin teacher, an alpine guide, and an aspiring novelist. They crossed the border regularly, either as "passeurs," with Jewish refugees on forest paths by night, or as smugglers, brazenly in daylight, via the "Annemasse hole," through which regular services of SNCF trains still went back and forth from Switzerland to the Free Zone. The team's first assignment was to get a pair of stranded British airmen off the Plateau de Vercors and into Switzerland. Pleasantly joshing and flashing banknotes and organizing card games with the French and Swiss police and border patrols, Sami deftly smuggled the Tommies across in the guise of visiting Swedish football players. The next time, three weeks later, he got two downed Canadians across by holding a soccer match on a pitch that straddled the border; at half-time, the teams switched, three extra players were brought in on the French side, and the Canadians were in Switzerland. Sami's escape route was dubbed the Football Line. It faltered when, during another cross-border mock football game the third group, a pair of Britons and a Pole, ran into a Swiss patrol at the Swiss end of the pitch and, mistaking them for Germans, took to their heels in the undergrowth along the border. Reports soon came in of sightings of the three as far away as Perpignan, heading south, then of their arrest, near the Spanish border. Sami cashiered two of his underlings after that and led the next group across himself, posing as a Swiss-German soccer coach with his amateur players, homeward bound from an exhibition match in Arles . . .

In Geneva on that occasion he met Ignace, who demanded news of his mother.

"She's well."

They sat indoors at the Café du Commerce on the Place du Molard. The lake was stern and choppy that day under a wind-whipped sky of Watteau blue. Ignace had a beer. He was eighteen, and old enough to drink. There was an embryonic mustache on his upper lip, and his voice was abnormally deep and dark, like that of a man seriously hungover.

"And you, uncle?"

"I run risks. I don't deny it."

"You're crazy. You should stay here."

"I can't live with my thumb up my arse. Our country is occupied. We have no choice. We're men."

"Bah. You mean you'd be bored otherwise."

"Bull's-eye. You're growing up, boy."

They embraced long and hard when Sami left and slipped back into France that night near Collonges and drove Max's van back to Annecy by the back roads. It was three a.m. when he arrived at the bakery. Not yet ready for bed, he yielded to his oldest impulse and paid a visit to Amélie upstairs while Jean-Xavier was cleaning the ovens in the kitchen in readiness for the 4 a.m. shift. The rhythmic pounding of the cleaning brushes drowned out all other sounds upstairs, but the sounds of another kind of rhythm coming from his wife's bedroom confirmed Jean-Xavier's apprehensions when he came up to look for a recipe for ersatz *tarte à l'oignon* in his wife's copy of Demoilu's *La Patisserie de la Guerre* . . .

Jean-Xavier listened for a while to the industrial-strength panting and gasping, then shrugged and returned downstairs, where his first customers, the SNCF yardmen and guards from the station, were already lining up for their morning margarine croissants and acorn baguettes. One of them, a certain Monsieur Sismondi, also happened to be a member of the auxiliary police force, the Groupes Mobiles de Réserve (GMR); and when Jean-Xavier took him his *thé au lait* and *tartine sans beurre* and confided his suspicions—that the man upstairs was certainly an adulterer, almost certainly a Jew, and very probably a *résistant*— he proved most eager to collaborate.

"Lead the way, monsieur Durand," he said. "Or shall we allow them a more diplomatic moment?"

"*Mais non*," snapped Jean-Xavier. "*Allons-y.*"

The Road South

There was a new poster on the corner of the boulevard and the Rue de Seine. It was another of the countless warnings issued by the Occupying Forces, but this one was outlined in bloodred and black, with especially large print intended to draw the eye, as it drew Stefanie's. She crossed the boulevard to read it.

WARNING

I have observed that the majority of the French population in the occupied zone continues to go about its business calmly, in an orderly and respectful way. However, it is precisely this very order, this calm, this peace enjoyed by the majority of French citizens, that is gravely endangered by the attacks and acts of sabotage and destruction undertaken by the British and the Soviets and their agents and directed against the Army of Occupation. I am determined to guarantee the French populace, amid war and upheaval, that the continuance of their calm and peaceful existence is my highest priority; but I could not help remarking that it is the close relatives and friends of those committing these acts of sabotage and destruction who have helped them before and after the attacks.

Consequently, I am announcing the following penalties;

1)All close male relatives in ascending order, as well as brothers-in-law and cousins over 18 years of age, will be shot.

2)All close female relatives of the same degree will be sentenced to forced labor or shot.

3)All children, of 17 years of age and under, of all men and women affected by these measures will be taken to reform institutions; those over 17 will be shot.

I therefore call on all law-abiding citizens to prevent attacks, sabotage and other disturbances by promptly notifying the German or French police of any suspicious activity. Great consideration will be given to this patriotic duty.

Paris, 10 March 1942

DANNECKER

Der Höhere SS- und Polizeiführer im Bereich des Militärbefehlshaber in Frankreich

This was not just another in a series of pompous proclamations. It was a declaration of war on the civilian population. In the summer of 1942, especially after the Vel' d'Hiv' raid when 1500 Jews were forced from their homes by Paris police, the number of families without a relative either interned or in the resistance was dwindling by the day. Under the terms of this order, with Sami a member of the resistance Stefanie and Mutti were subject to the ultimate penalty, enforceable at any time, anywhere. But like the expression of an age-old geological fault, the earth under the Germans' feet was beginning slowly to shift. People were beginning to think that there was no longer any excuse for turning a blind eye, not with this open threat, and most definitely not in the face of the devastating reports of "resettlement"—extermination—coming out of the East. Stefanie's former paramour was opening the gates of Hell, not just for Germans and Poles, but for all Europeans.

To be precise: *Jews first, then everybody else.*

The time to act had arrived. The Devil had locked the door, but God had shown the way. The fiend must be destroyed.

That same evening Stefanie was accosted on the Rue de Sèvres, coming from the Duroc Métro station. On the corner of the Rue Dupin a broad-shouldered man with thinning hair and round spectacles contrived to bump into her and drop his spectacles, and while retrieving them introduce himself with charmingly insincere effusiveness as "Luc," an old friend of "Paul—the rugby coach?"

She was swift on the uptake. It was Jean Lussac, Blum's man, former minister in the Popular Front government. Except for the round spectacles and the sad eyes, now even sadder, as if a veil of weariness and anxiety had fallen over him, Stefanie barely recognized him.

"I am so sorry that the match was cancelled, Monsieur . . . *Luc*," she said. "I was looking forward to it. How is dear Paul? Is he still as keen a *footballeur* as ever?'

"All right, Madame," muttered Lussac. "No need to overdo it. No one's listening. Café Banco, Rue Monsieur-le-Prince, in two hours. Six o'clock *pile, hein*? I wait five minutes, that's all."

Lussac shook her hand and disappeared into the Métro station. Two hours later he was checking his watch when Stefanie entered the Café Banco on the Rue Monsieur-le-Prince in the heart of the 5th arrondissement. It was a neighborhood of narrow streets, isolated courtyards, a network of escape routes, numerous clubs and secret societies, and a population traditionally anarchic and subversive. But in the event of uprising the district could be sealed off from the adjacent boulevards, so patrols were few, and the Wehrmacht tended to avoid the area, which, in consequence, still retained something of its *avant-guerre* bohemian atmosphere. Stefanie saw nothing in the faces of the other customers in the seedy, boozy Banco but the glow of youth's self-love, fueled by alcohol and lust. She had a *blanc*; Lussac declined. He had little time, he explained. Indeed, he was perched on the edge of his chair, very much a man in a hurry. He smoked, too, like one pressed for time: quickly, jerkily, in short, sharp gasps. He apologized, but first . . . and of course it seemed quite absurd, as they had met already, *mais à la guerre comme à la guerre* . . . he had to make sure she was who she said she was. Stefanie showed him her ration card and national identity card. He peered at them and at her. Very well, he said. Of course she was herself. Who else could she be? Now they could talk seriously, but he had to be sure she was trustworthy. If she was, she would be an ideal agent; Sami said so. If not, well . . .

"Sami doesn't trust me?"

"But madame, of course he does. But we feel he may be moved by, ah, sentiment. Personal feelings. As for us, *eh bien*, how shall I say it? You and I have met, *certes*, and M. Blum has a high regard for you, but he is now a prisoner of les *Boches*, and therefore probably doomed. And we know that you have been seen consorting with members of the occupying forces, an SS trooper named Kohler . . . "

"In the café downstairs from my flat, yes, I don't deny it, we met for dinner, I knew him in the old days, but he was working for the other side, your side . . . "

"Ah yes, the other side, well you can't believe everything the Boches tell you. And you, you have a certain background, and certain connections, that we cannot ignore. Even if Sami says they would be great advantages to us . . . "

"Where is he?" she interrupted, avid for news. "How is he?"

"He's well. He's in the south. I can't tell you where, in case . . . well, I'm sure you understand."

In case the Gestapo tried to torture the information out of her. Well, well, she thought. Perhaps her Calvary had merely changed address. At the thought, a furious joy flared in her heart, reminding her that she truly did believe, in spite of everything; and she offered a silent prayer to Mother Mary.

"Anyway," said Lussac, looking down at the cigarette between his yellowing left index and forefinger, "Paul—let's call him Paul—yes, it's ridiculous, but you know—has a friend in the embassy in Madrid who is working with us. Now, this person has a contact in the German embassy here with incomparable access to important information . . . "

"Yes. I just had a demonstration of that." Stefanie described

Sami's telephone message and Herr Epting's echo thereof. Lussac seemed momentarily upset, but quickly recovered his equanimity.

"A bit obvious, I fear. Perhaps to reassure you? Paul's idea, I'm sure. Anyway, our contact has access to documents concerning German troop movements, plans of attack against resistance targets, names of Allied prisoners held in France, where they will be moved to, the exact location of French concentration camps, and so on."

He blinked expectantly. She shrugged.

"*Et puis alors . . . ?*"

"*Et puis alors*, we need someone to take these documents for us to the Allied embassies in Switzerland." He flicked his cigarette onto the floor and extinguished it with a quick heel-twist. "Urgently. Our previous courier lost her nerve at the last minute. Believe me, I understand, the nerves can go. Especially in a lady."

"In a lady and not in a man? Oh no. I'd say *merde* to you, Lussac. If I take the assignment it's because I can do it."

This was as much bravado as truth, but it made an impression. Lussac inclined his head respectfully.

"I'm glad to hear you say it, Madame. As you will be posing as an agent for the Germans, you will have the ideal camouflage."

"Now for all you know I could leave this place and directly go and tell my German friends . . . "

"And then you know what would happen?" He grimaced and chopped at his throat with the side of his hand. "Or your mother . . . ?" He repeated the gesture, then shrugged. "I know it sounds barbaric, but when you're fighting barbarians . . . "

"I understand, Monsieur."

"So you accept?"

"I accept."

They parted. She heard nothing for a week or ten days, during which time she assumed "they" were confirming her trustworthiness, one way or another. She was certain, for instance, that she was followed, once or twice. One night the telephone rang and she heard a muffled muttering on the other end of the line. And on another day there was a strange man looking through the window of her classroom. Then, in early May, instructions began to arrive in the piecemeal fashion in which clandestine communication took place under the Occupation: a note slipped into her hand at the newsstand on the Place du Châtelet; a brief re-encounter with Lussac at one of the bookstalls on the Seine ("I'll be browsing the German novels," he said over the phone); phone calls received and made, one, perilously, under the nose of Frau Epting, the others at public call boxes in cafés on and around the Place Edmond Rostand, near Stefanie's flat; a coded message over the radio, written down by Mutti, who listened eagerly in the kitchen to the forbidden BBC broadcasts from London every night at eight; a stranger in the doorway one blustery Saturday night, requesting a match and revealing himself in its light to be horribly scarred, like a villain in a Hollywood film . . .

"Be careful," he said in the hoarse baritone of such a character. "You may have enemies where you think you have friends. Be very careful, *madame*."

The next morning she was walking to the Métro and saw the man again, being escorted by gendarmes into a horse-drawn prison wagon, gesticulating wildly and crying "*Aidez-moi, Madame! Aidez-moi!*"

Stefanie, not sure whether she was the "madame" being addressed, stopped and looked, but kept on walking when she noticed one of the gendarmes watching her. In those days Paris was a stage set for morbid and unreal dramas. Great mob surges that momentarily recalled the happy bustle of the prewar years would suddenly part like the Red Sea for Moses and melt into nothingness, revealing a man shot lying facedown on the pavement. Or in an empty square a crowd might suddenly coalesce from nowhere—from unnoticed doorways, alleyways, and courtyards—around a suspected stool pigeon or German agent or resistance fighter on the run and sweep him (sometimes her) away to safety or doom down side streets along which the throng would flow like a river, then vanish. Or an air raid siren, ignored, would reiterate its jagged wail above the rooftops in the morning sunshine while people lined up with their ration cards in front of a *boucherie* or *patisserie*, exchanging rumors and gossip as if they were in the main square of a happy village in the Orléanais or Anjou, obstinately oblivious even when the British bombers appeared in the sky, sneaking forward with their steady, snoring drone, like giant bumblebees. Or the sound of running footsteps and police whistles in the depths of the night in the street outside would wake Stefanie, and she would lie listening to Mutti's breathing and staring at the dim outline of the blacked-out window and feeling the surrounding universe of sorrow, the anguish of the war's victims, individuals every one, multitudes across the continent like millions of atoms whose separate identities would forever remain lost to history but whose total numbers contained more tragedy than a single person could ever imagine or bear: that crushing burden borne by millions, each of those multitudinous griefs an individual, particular, unique lament, a tale of misery and sorrow that should have turned out differently . . . as she lay there, she sensed the enormity of the catastrophe all around her in the infinite collective expression of those unique lives and undifferentiated undeserved deaths and all the mourning in dark corridors, dimly lit houses, half-empty churches, dull kitchens, narrow beds, windy empty fields, and unbearable memories. The suffering of the city, the nation, of Europe, like a herd of frightened sheep pressed in upon her soul.

So the mission was paramount, and she knew what her Mother required her to do—what all of suffering humanity required her to do. For she, of all people, knew the Antichrist, and she of all people could strike the blow that freed the world . . . or she thought she could. Certainty was at a premium in those days, except for certainty of suffering. But she was confident that her Mother would find a way.

And at least she knew (at secondhand, admittedly), that Sami was still alive; but she had heard nothing from Ignace in several weeks, nor from Fritz; and Mutti's enfeeblement continued apace, although Madame Nysgard, a Danish widow who lived on the rez-de-chaussée, had taken to stopping once a day. The two shared a certain cosmopolitan outlook and nostalgia for the past both were realistic enough to know had never existed. Both, too, were in love with their dispossessed homelands and, therefore, deeply anti-German; and Stefanie, as she embarked on her journey, was concerned that they might take a glass too many of Algerian wine and turn up the volume on the radio during the BBC's nightly broadcasts. But she went ahead with her mission, which she regarded as the preamble to her true mission. The reasons for not doing something, after all, are usually several, compared to reasons for doing it. Accordingly, on the morning of July 20 she set off, just minutes before the gendarmes, acting on an anonymous telephone report (in a distinct Danish accent) denouncing a clandestine BBC listener, arrived at the Rue Soufflot to take Mutti away, first to the Vel' d'Hiv,' then to the transports, then aboard a train bound for Auschwitz.

But Stefanie knew nothing of this, nor of the wider net that was being cast everywhere. At the Gare de Lyon the train was crowded with ailing relatives being sent out of Paris, children going to stay with country cousins in the Free Zone, taciturn policemen in uniform, smooth-talking "salesmen" in Borsalino hats and trench coats, and anonymous solitaries in nondescript clothes well concealed behind uncontroversial newspapers—*Le Figaro*, not *Le Petit Parisien*; *Signal*, not *Der Stürmer*. The train crept out of Paris under a sky of mindless blue. Stefanie's nervousness alternated with elation. She carried false identity papers provided by the Germans in the name of Sylvie Vautour, native of the Jura; a Swiss passport courtesy of the Resistance in the name of Birgit Frauenfeld; five thousand occupation francs from the Germans, two from the less-well-heeled *maquisards*; three "top secret" German Embassy files from the mysterious "contact," via Lussac at the Café Banco, folded and tucked under her brassiere (she had considered stockings as a hiding place, but such luxuries as nylons would attract too much attention at a time when even elegant Parisiennes were reduced to painting their legs an imitation-stocking brown); and a book of Theodor Mommsen's essays on the Renaissance, containing in a false cover the equally false German Foreign Ministry documents Herr Epting had given her as a raison d'être for her maiden voyage as a courier.

"You will no doubt be approached, either on the train or in Switzerland," he said. There were passwords, or passphrases.

Hers, quite absurdly, was *"Kaffee mit schlag und zucker, bitte."*

"These passwords are changed frequently and transmitted to all agents. If one should not recognize it, exercise the greatest caution. Remember at all times, please, the perils of your situation, and for whom you are working. Contact me only in the event of extreme emergency."

Herr Epting was being didactic and professional, befitting his nationality and station, but Stefanie needed no reminding— although the emotion bubbling in her breast was more akin to a child's anticipation of summer holidays than that of a woman risking her life for a cause.

The train was on time at least, not a usual occurrence in those days. In the compartment were a frowning priest, two eight- or nine-year-old girls deep in conversation over an album of old family photographs, an old lady in black, and a silently smoking man with a heavy jaw and tinted spectacles. As there was something inherently suspicious about crossing the armistice line, no one (except children) gave anyone else more than a casual glance. To cool her anticipation of she knew not what, Stefanie read Mommsen and made confession of her distance from God, like the least of sinners; but she felt herself to be the worst of sinners, if not in deed, then in thought—or in omission.

The train picked up speed in the luxuriant countryside beyond the canals and rail yards and factories of Charenton (and, atop a delirious hill, the world-famous madhouse) and settled into a soothing rattle-and-click rhythm until Sens station, where French police got on and went rapidly from one compartment to the next, barely glancing at the travelers. More police boarded at Auxerre; and at Dijon, the last stop before the Free Zone, a coalition of the Wehrmacht, the French police and the French and German Gestapo climbed on board and in uneasy partnership undertook a thorough border control, the French stepping in whenever a word was needed, or when their German counterparts seemed confused. Stefanie was giddy with the danger of her enterprise and bantered gaily with one of the Gestapo men, a native of Graz who sized her up as a dotty middle-aged lady, a reader of books, an Austrian aristocrat at loose ends; then, brightly, she looked at him and blurted, "*Kaffee mit Schlag und Zucker*," and he suddenly became furtive and conspiratorial and conferred with his superiors, who sized Stefanie up quite differently and asked her to please get off the train.

"But I have urgent business."

"Of course, *Frau*. The train goes nowhere until we say so. Please."

She followed, embarrassed in front of the priest, the old lady, and the two young girls, all of whom looked up and stared as she was led away; but the smoking man kept on reading his newspaper, oblivious. The formerly smiling man from Graz looked at her coldly, as if she naturally deserved what was coming to her, which turned out to be a quick march across the tracks to the stationmaster's office for orders from Paris. She resisted the temptation to touch her rustling brassiere as she walked. In charge was a Wehrmacht officer named Captain Schmidt, clearly bored with his secondment to a stationmaster's office that smelled like hot axle-grease and cigars, one of which was burning in an ashtray, sending up a long blue curlicue of smoke. He looked her up and down as if she were a display in a department store, took a pull of the cigar and said,

"Abwehr sources have learned that the so-called *résistance* has recruited an agent or agents for the Switzerland run."

"And?"

"And has anyone approached you?"

"Only you," said Stefanie. The man glowered.

"I mean anyone of the so-called *résistance*."

"Not that I'm aware of."

"And what are you carrying?" He signaled to subordinates, who took the book out of her hands. Expertly, Captain Schmidt flipped open the back cover. Documents tumbled out. Schmidt snatched them up.

"Ha! Ground plans of new tank factory in Denmark? Minutes of secret meeting between *Generalleutnant* Adolf Galland and Admiral Darlan? Map of naval base at Portsmouth, England? These are classified documents, very important."

Stefanie protested.

"Call Herr von Epting at the Embassy," she said.

But Schmidt refused. He was chasing his dream. His sour lupine face lit up as he went through the documents, repeating "But these are classified, *ah ja*," and nodding in agreement with himself. Stefanie tried to explain the papers were fakes, and once more requested a phone call to the Embassy, but he shouted "Silence!" and motioned to his corporal to take her away. She was escorted to a small holding cell at back of the station by the apologetic corporal, who bowed slightly before locking her in and said, in a *Plattdeutsch* accent, "*Gnädige Frau.*"

As in romantic stories of the Dumas school, her first thought when the key grated in the lock was the "terrible finality" of the sound; her second, "*Scheiße*. You've done it now, *Gans*." The corporal hummed as he walked away: *Lili Marleen*, of course. Inside the cell were a cot, a washbasin, and a toilet. Everything was scrubbed clean, as if in expectation of a resident. The walls were painted a pale snot green and adorned with scratched and scrawled inscriptions: "How much Pernod is too much? Jean, 15/3/40"; "The stationmaster is impotent" or "Antoine Leduc was here, 14/7/41, *vive la France*." The window was stained and cracked in one corner and anchored on the outside by three bars. A meter or so away was a young sycamore tree, through the gently swaying branches of which Stefanie could see an alleyway where dustbins slouched and a car, a Citroën Leger 11, was parked. Through the tree branches was the blue sky, in which birds wheeled and tattered clouds drifted. Stefanie gazed out for a minute, then slumped onto the cot in sudden despair.

"*Ach du lieber Gott.*"

So her career as a courier for the resistance was over before it had begun. Indeed, the whole arrest—that was what she assumed it was, although in those days it was hard to tell—had taken place with the greatest dispatch. But it was all quite ridiculous, being thrown into jail just three hours after the beginning of the mission. Had she not the authority of the German Embassy and Herr Epting behind her?

Perhaps not. Perhaps she had trusted too willingly. She remembered the scarred man's hoarse warning, and his abrupt removal in the street the next day.

Perhaps she should trust more in Her, Whose will would be done.

"Fool," she said, shaking her head at her own gullibility. The phone call from Sami, the same words spoken by Epting—how could she not see it . . . ?

Not to mention the real documents hidden about her person.

And never mind this insignificant Captain Schmidt (a joke name for the fool in many a Salzburg Christmas pantomime). He only saw his major's pips. And a post somewhere more important than Dijon.

But how could they have found out? *What* had they found out? That she was carrying ostensibly secret documents in her briefcase? Well, that was part of the plan, as arranged by Epting with his superiors, to deceive spies and agents from the "other side" in case she needed to . . . but had they found out about her dual purpose?

And how did she know that she could trust Epting?

Had they captured Lussac—and Sami?

Most importantly, she needed to destroy the genuine papers. But how? Eat them? Tear them up and flush them down the toilet? There was hardly room, and anyone could look in at any minute.

And if they let her go after all what could she do, having destroyed the papers, and with them the entire mission?

Too many questions, no answers. Now she was worried. Now it was time to pray. She knelt by the side of the cot, upon which was a well-worn blanket with faded stains and the bleached-out letters "HOTEL DE LA GARE," and she gazed upward at the small patch of Burgundian blue heaven and recalled a verse by Paul Verlaine written under conditions of imprisonment that were suddenly no longer the abstract experience of a long-dead stranger.

> *Le ciel est, par-dessus le toit,*
> *Si bleu, si calme!*

Un arbre, par-dessus le toit,
Berce sa palme.

Hardly had she begun praying when Captain Schmidt appeared at her cell door.

"Come."

Stefanie stood up. "Do you mind, Captain?" She pointed to the toilet. "A minute, please."

The captain frowned.

"All right. A minute."

He left, muttering. Stefanie deftly slipped from her brassiere the documents, which were of light onionskin paper, and quickly folded them together into a tight cylinder with makeshift wings, like a child's paper airplane; then, after a second's hesitation, she opened the window and sent the tiny plane into the freedom of the great outdoors. It swooped upward, hesitated, and plunged into the branches of the sycamore, where it lodged, just visible as a little white tab at the base of the tree.

"Come."

She followed Captain Schmidt and the corporal down the hallway, back across the platform, upon which people were standing as if posed, awaiting the arrival of the delayed 13:25 to Paris-Gare de Lyon (she noticed the time with a little pang, noting its ordinariness, what she was usually doing at 13:25 every day, and feeling the yawing of panic as she briefly contemplated a future of 13:25s in places unknown and unimaginable).

This time it was the Wehrmacht and the SS, and the news was bad.

"We know everything now, Frau Lebel," said the smugly delighted Captain Schmidt, smiling for the first time, more like a wolf than a man. "And I would rather urgently request you to provide us with the real documents."

"You have them," she said.

"These . . . ?" He had the contents of the Mommsen book spread out on his desk in front of him. He shook his head. "*Nein, Frau.* These are deliberate hoaxes, as we know from the Embassy in Paris, *ja*? But what we learned from this man, this . . . "

He flipped through the pages of a notebook. "Ah. This Johann Kohler. You knew him, *ja?*"

"Only as an acquaintance. He was from Salzburg, too. We worked together once."

"More than once, I think. And Jean-Xavier Durand. Do you know him?"

"No."

"And this . . . Jean Lussac. Him?"

Her second "no" was unhesitating, although her heart gave a lurch.

"Hm. Strange, because according to Lussac, he recruited you two weeks ago."

"He is a liar."

"Or you are, *ja?* However. We will soon find out. And this Durand person . . . ?"

"No."

Schmidt sighed.

"Very well. I admit there is little reason for you to have met, but you never know . . . he is a former porter at the Grand Hotel Rastignac in Paris. After the Armistice the hotel was billeted to our troops and he went home. Well now, it seems that he is a jealous type, like so many emotional Frenchmen. Latins, you know, not much good at fighting but lions in the bedroom, *ja*, ah ha ha? Like your *mensch* Samuel Lebel, or should I say Shmuel Schoen?"

Stefanie despaired. Schmidt noticed.

"*Ja*, well, you won't be denying you know him, will you? A Jewish member of the so-called *résistance* and quite a ladies' man, it seems. So. When this Durand went home to Annecy, he found his wife and Herr Schoen . . . well how shall I say? *In flagrante delicto* . . . "

He went on. Sami had been turned in to the local police by Durand, husband of the woman who ran a resistance cell in Annecy . . . Stefanie's heart took another cold tumble. She felt, as if he were in the room, the aura of Sami's suffering.

She felt another presence, too, one that had long been absent.

"Enough said. The man—the Jew Schoen—talked. When

you are his age—sixty-two? Three? You cannot stand up under interrogation." Captain, soon-to-be Major, Schmidt, folded his arms and smirked. "He did not. So you see, Frau Lebel. We know you were recruited by the so-called *résistance* and we know you were traveling to Switzerland to meet their agent there. We need that agent's name, and the names of your contacts in Paris. We need the documents you are carrying. Need I say more?"

Technically, this was wrong—she had been instructed to go to embassies, not to meet an agent—but Stefanie's swooning soul gave her no quarter.

"I have no documents except those you have."

The captain stood up and snapped his fingers.

"*Los!*"

Men came in; she was dragged, stumbling, into an interrogation cell, with a bare lightbulb and a smell of vomit and detergent and, unexpectedly, well lit by the gently swaying lightbulb, a poster showing a sheet of music and above it the jaunty words *Encore un Dubonnet*! It was an involuntary link to the normal world of bustle and crowds (or perhaps deliberate, as a token of Gestapo humor, the infinite perversity of the sadists to whom the devil had temporarily entrusted Europe). She was forcibly seated, partly undressed with brisk dispatch, slapped with evident relish. It was beginning. Where were the papers? Whom was she meeting? Whom did she know, in Paris, in Austria (Ostmark)? Names, please!

"Will you sign this?"

A document was thrust at her. It was a *Schutzhaftbefehl*, swearing under oath that she desired above all things to be sent to a concentration camp as an enemy of the Reich.

"No."

"You will."

With the help of the Dubonnet poster, as the pain began she forced herself to think of the Métro and the other normal things of her normal Paris life: The Luxembourg Gardens on a warm May Sunday; the terrace at the Café de Cluny on a rainy evening; Ignace riding a pony in the Tuileries when he was a boy; Arthur playing the piano at the Salle Pleyel; the movement and high promise of the early inter-war years; lunch with Léon Blum; lovemaking with Sami, and Arthur, and Sami, and Sami, and Sami again . . . *and Adolf*. . . . Above and in and around her flowed the waves of pain, but they led to a vision of holiness; through the misty dusty window behind the officer's back shone the purest light of heaven, and swirling in Stefanie's brain were the voices of all her loved ones. Above them all soared the dove of peace, and Mother Mary rose from an unseen place in the darkest corner and turned it into light. She came toward her, arms outstretched, speaking in the dialect of the Salzkammergut.

"*Steffi, mädl*," she said. "Your life is with me."

And through the blows that fell on her and the anguish of the thrashing they—the corporal, an SS man from nowhere, a Frenchman—gleefully gave her, dappling her shoulders and back with her blood, she heard the voice, soft and mellow, the voice of a savior, of a friend:

"*Steffi, mädl*, here I am," and it was as if she were herself soaring above the towered fortress of the Salzkammergut—the Attersee—the Wolfgangsee—the tumbling Salzach river— the meadowlands around Ingolstadt—the plunging cliffs of Obersalzberg—the serried streets of the Altstadt—and through the golden misty infinity to Heaven itself, which was little more than a replica of Stefanie's native land; and through it all, except for an intrusive pain that, being more ache than pain, returned her momentarily to the reality of that cell, those sweat-streaked walls, that smiling face with the faint and nauseating scent of stale garlic, the cane . . . but when the pain arced beyond what was normally bearable it attained a kind of purity that melted into unconsciousness, or consciousness of a higher order, and it was then that she heard Her voice, and felt Her touch . . .

"Come with me, now, *kleinchen*."

Rittlings der Welt

Bormann, standing at the door to the terrace, waiting to be noticed, was holding something in his hand. Good old Bormann. A man of sterling qualities, not the least of which was a keen awareness of his own insignificance. He'd stand there until doomsday, silent, hovering, passive.

"*Jaaa?*"

"A letter, *mein Führer*. An unusual one. From Paris."

"A letter?"

But . . . he was *busy*. He'd just been looking over the new map of Russia. He had vital decisions to make, and soon. The generals were due in an hour. When they'd finally taken Moscow and Leningrad and the Caucasian oilfields and chased the old devil Stalin out of the Kremlin straight back to hell and razed the Kremlin and sent in German colonists, then they'd move outward to the periphery and designate the Urals the eastern-most boundary of the Greater German Reich and there you'd have it, German lands all the way from Elsass-Lothringen to the very threshold of Siberia. That would be enough, he'd retire, the Yankees would sign an armistice, no one would bother him at home in dear little Linz. This would all happen; it was only a matter of time. Russia was falling. One more offensive push and the Red Army would melt away. Look at what was happening in the Caucasus, in Crimea. Kleist, Paulus, von Weichs, they'd pull it off, oh no doubt at all. The Russians were no match for those old *jaegers*. Russians had no food, no reason to fight, no culture, and they all hated Stalin. Millions of the wretches were surrendering like flies to insecticide. Now—*vorwärts, jeder vorwärts!* Onward to the oil fields of Baku!! Onward to the Caucasus!!! The Caucasus was wide open. Oh, they'd fight. But so had the French in '40, good God they'd lost a hundred thousand men, and look at them now: Pétain, Darlan, that dreadful crawler Laval . . . Sporadic resistance did not an effective defense make, and sporadic resistance was all they'd encountered so far in Russia, really. It was France all over again, on a bigger scale, and much more useful, with all that empty land; you couldn't get rid of all the French, or their culture. You could just put them in their place, for a while. But there was no reason why they shouldn't eliminate the subhuman half-Asiatic Russians lock, stock, and barrel. Bolshevism! *Gott* what barbarism. No love of country, no race loyalty, no culture . . . no wonder so many of them were Jews.

Exterminate the biological basis of Bolshevism and you eliminated the problem itself. And as for the so-called Old Russia—
vodka? Bearded monks? Hideous onion-domed churches painted
ghastly colors, like whorehouses? More Jewish beards inside? *Pah!*
At least the Catholic Church was a clean-shaven church—and
speaking of the Church they were cooperating quite nicely, all
in all, bar a couple of hardheads like that Bishop Gaben, well,
all in good time . . .

Then, for relaxation after the maps he'd turned to his architectural blueprints for designing the triumphal *Walkyriebrücke*
in postwar Linz, Linz the Great, capital of *Hitlermark.* Only
question was: should there be four lanes, like an autobahn, or
should he restrict it to two, for general weight-bearing and structural considerations?

Four, definitely. Structural questions could be worked out
later. He'd ask Speer.

Meanwhile, Bormann was still standing there, squat and
immobile, like a giant garden gnome.

"What is it, *Reichsleiter?* Why should I read that letter in
particular? Do you know how many letters I get every day? Of
course you do, you read them all."

"Yes, *mein Führer.* Forty a day, on average, from the Adolf
Hitler Endowment Fund of German Industry alone. Another
sixty or so from the Adolf Hitler Architectural Guild and the
Adolf Hitler Shepherds' Fund. And more from all over. I read
most, but not all. They're from lovesick women, usually, wanting
to marry you, you know the sort of thing. The others I send to
the *kettenhunden* over at Sipo. You know, poor Heydrich's boys."

The "poor" dangled there provocatively; Bormann never felt
inclined to pity anyone.

"*Ja.* Poor Heydrich, eh?" Well, a remarkable young man
indeed, but a romantic fool, riding around in an open car, just
like Franz Ferdinand surrounded by all those Slavs seething with
hatred . . . briefly, he remembered Linz, 1907, but only briefly,
for the past was mere window dressing for the world he was making anew . . . So: Heydrich. Even with our best troops you knew
it had to happen. Silly young fool. That a man as irreplaceable as

Heydrich should expose himself to unnecessary danger is stupid and *idiotic*. So many idiots. And let's face it, he'd exaggerated for effect, no one was truly irreplaceable, not even the Führer himself.

But! At least we eliminated a whole nest of those miserable Slovaks or Czechs or Moravians or whatever they called themselves—Slavs anyway—in that miserable *scheissendorf* of Lidice, which he imagined in terms of wayside squalor of the kind he'd glimpsed in Ukraine: mud, sagging fences, lopsided wagons, pigs indistinguishable from their human co-residents . . .

Bormann was still holding his letter.

"Go away, Bormann. I don't want to read your damned letter."

"Well, this one's a bit unusual, being from Paris and all."

Paris? He was no longer in interested in Paris. Once, yes. But once it had been the capital of a proud and intimidating nation, a great rival to Germany, the source of much learning and art as well as corruption and decadence and Jewishness, but now it was a mere pseudo-Vienna, a giant Prater, a dilapidated provincial town too big to be of any use except for the circus and café life and artists and their whores. To the devil with Paris. Its time was over. Besides, he'd seen it, seen the Opéra, seen the Panthéon, seen the tomb of the Corsican. Even the ghastly Tower. What more was there to Paris? The Arc de Triomphe? Passable, but a mere model of the future one in Berlin. The Rue de Rivoli? Ah *ja*, that was nice, that would look even better when it was recreated as Strasse des 20. April, leading from Adolf-Hitler Platz to the new Walkyriebrucke in Groß-linz.

"Paris? From OKW? Or one of those French *arschküssern*?"

"Haha. Probably one of them, yes, *mein Führer*. Although it was written by a woman, not one of your many anonymous admirers, but one who actually claims to know you. The name appears to be French. Lebel. But we have determined that the woman is a German. Stefanie von Rothenberg. She married a Jew, and . . . "

Bormann paused just long enough to remind him that he knew the name and knew what it had once represented. Right here on the Obersalzberg. He glanced around with obvious significance. Hitler bridled.

"*U-u-und?*"

"And it's taken over three years to get here. Posted in '38, then sent to dead-letter files for a few months, then brought back to life after our victory and routed through French intelligence and finally send along to Canaris, who attached this note."

Hitler took the note and read, in Canaris's *ancien-régime* copperplate cursive:

Mein Führer!

The writer of this letter claims acquaintance with you. I would not have bothered you if it were not for the fact that the letter is most unusual by virtue of having taken so long to arrive and having been intercepted by an inordinate number of intelligence agencies, both French and German. Also, the writer makes mention of certain events in your past, including a portrait . . .

He glanced through the letter, saw the signature: Stefanie Lebel, felt his heart turn over as if he were once again that young man on the Donau in Linz in 1907 but quickly dismissed the thought and as quickly dismissed Bormann, to read the letter in peace.

He walked out onto the balcony. The mountains greeted the *Grösster Feldherr aller Zeiten* with indifference. It was a calm day with no wind, just the faint haze of midsummer floating above. In the valleys the cowbells clanged. He put on his reading glasses. The writing was thin, cramped, as if done in haste.

For a minute he was his old self, worshipping at the distant flame, hoping against hope for a word, a glance . . .

But now it was almost impossible to believe that there had ever been such a person with such hopes. He raised his eyes and gazed out over the jagged ramparts of his domain. Stefanie von Rothenberg. And to think, as recently as his visit to Paris he'd planned on seeing her, mostly to show off, yes, but partly also because somewhere deep inside he still wanted to see her, all woman that she was, sum of all women.

He read to the end. It was a short letter, just a page, mostly about the old Jewish uncle in Vienna. (He remembered, reluctantly. The small palais, its chilly anterooms, the feeling of inferiority.) On the margins of the letter were the blue stamps and seals of the various French and German intelligence and counter-intelligence groups into whose incompetent hands the letter had fallen on its long and leisurely way from the Bureau de Postes de St. Michel to the Obersalzberg . . . Bureau des Renseignements; Sicherheitsdient; Abwehr . . . Two years it had taken the idiots to get the letter from Paris to Berchtesgaden!

Had they taken her in for questioning? He wondered. Had they used extreme measures? He imagined, with a tiny shiver that was not entirely unpleasant, her body, tortured.

He reread the last paragraph.

" . . . *can the life of Dr. Freud be worth so much more to you than the life of my beloved uncle, who never harmed you; on the contrary, don't you remember, he once gave you a painting commission when you were near starvation? . . . "*

That painting again! *Gott verdammt!* It had never been recovered. It was one of those things that he'd long intended to do, but with one thing and another . . . *ja*, he remembered, he'd put through a call to Vienna years ago, or just after Anschluss; Seyss-Inquart had done nothing, nothing, and the new man was worse. But he simply couldn't allow that painting to be seen. For the Führer of the Greater German Reich to tip his hand to the world, just as he was on the point of conquering that world, as a love-besotted bohemian artist who'd painted, out of sheer panting puppy love, a portrait of his little Viennese *Schnitten* when his artistic reputation such as it was reposed solely on landscapes, buildings, designs, all impersonal, dignified, detached, and formal, like his image for the German people; architectural drawings you'd expect to find in the workshop of the master builder and quasi-divine designer whose sole and unique mission was to redesign an entire city, an entire nation, the world . . . no, to expose that sentimental portrait to public view was unthinkable. He imagined the sniggering, behind his back of course, but it would be there, he knew, starting with Goering (who would as always, be excessively polite to his face); the ignominy of suddenly being on the same moral level as Arno Breker and his comrades, roistering in some insalubrious Parisian bistrot with their whores and fast Chanel girls . . . not that Breker was a bad artist. But that was all he was: an artist of paint and stone. Whereas he, the Führer of the Greater Reich, was an artist of *nations*. Of *souls*. Of an entire *race*.

So it was impossible. The picture had to go.

Failing that, those who knew about it, or knew its whereabouts, had to go.

Funny, *ja*. How he'd almost gone to see her back in '40. Crazy, too. It must have been the combination of Breker and Paris and memories of a time when . . .

"Bormann."

Alone as he was, he knew he had only to speak the name in conversational tones and the man would appear, like a djinn from Ali Baba.

"*Mein Führer?*"

"I want you to find this woman."

"*Jawohl, mein Führer.*"

"Bring her here."

"Bring her . . . back here. *Ja, mein Führer.*"

He caught that "back." The devious *fetznschädl*.

Pah! Who cared?

The OKH phone rang. Bormann heard it through the window and hurried inside. He answered, bowed, nodded, beckoned to his master.

"News from Russia."

"Good news?"

Bormann spoke more, then, cupping the mouthpiece with his hand, smiled in his wan unhappy way.

"*Ja, mein Führer.* We've taken Sevastopol."

On impulse, Hitler stamped a jubilant foot; then he threw the letter into the air and watched for a second or so as it was whisked upward on the warm thermal winds of early summer; then he went inside and picked up the phone, still looking through the window as the letter rolled and tumbled on the up- and downdrafts until it was barely visible, a tiny white speck fading into the distance; then it was gone.

Intermezzo

But she did not die. Oh, that she had! But like the tide the agony crested and retreated and sought its level, and in those tidal pools of pain it reminded her she was alive. Alive, after two days' interrogation in a room in the Dijon police headquarters, during which she said nothing they wanted to hear, because she had nothing to say. Like most of the hapless and the innocent dragged into the hellrooms of the Gestapo, she knew no secrets; she only provided her tormentors with her helplessness and the pleasure of their dark art. She screamed and whimpered, hating herself for so doing, for giving them that much satisfaction; and she repeated to herself the one and only name of Our Lady and her Son, and she heard Her voice at her side.

"I love you, my *mädl*, for now and for always."

After the second afternoon of the immersion treatment in a metal bathub the Gestapo abruptly handed her over to the somewhat abashed French police, who promptly sent her back to the station and the holding cell, which by now seemed to her like a second home; and as she looked through her swollen, streaming eyes at the blurred outside world—the blue sky of Burgundy, the young sycamore cradling its Verlainian branch—she saw the black Citroën drive away. Then she slept and awoke to the hard bed and the harder necessity of continuing to exist when so much of what made her life worth living was lost to her. Mutti, they said (Schmidt had said), had been sent to a place called Auschwitz, a name she had heard with increasing frequency in her last days in Paris.

"Take me, Mother Mary. Or let me take my own life."

But there was no answer, as the holy ones do not countenance suicide.

The guard fed her—not forcibly, for a change. But she couldn't eat and was violently sick, much to the annoyance of the joint Wehrmacht—Gendarmerie command in whose charge she was. She passed out; and when she came to, the cell and her

increasingly ragged dress had been cleaned, and it was night.
Captain Schmidt was no longer in evidence. The young corporal from Hamburg or Bremen, whose name was Kranz, sat
behind the desk. At first, from some hopelessly *bürgerlich* place
deep inside her flickered the hope that because of his youth, his
awkwardness, and the fact that he had once called her *gnädige
Frau*, he would be more humane and civilized than the odi-
ous Schmidt; but then Power did the inevitable and became
absolute in his tiny domain, and, being young, Kranz had no
defenses. He turned cold, indifferent, and entirely officious. He
had apparently been promoted; the corporals addressed him as
Feldwebel (Sergeant). He was in charge of the papers that would
send Stefanie away. At midnight on the third day after the interrogation he summoned her to him. A guard woke her, roughly.
She had only just found a comfortable position to lie down in,
but not for long, and sitting was still difficult. She stood, therefore, tired as she was.

"Your man is dead," said the Sergeant, with no preamble. He
did not smoke, but the rank ghosts of his predecessor's cigars
were still in the air. "The Jew Schoen, that so-called *résistant*.
Your mother, too."

She knew. Why was he telling her?

Yes, but . . . her mother? And she thought she had no tears
left, no pity for the world or anyone in it. But . . . her *mutti*?
Tears blinded her, and she sat, unaware of the pain in her lower
spine. She didn't care. The Sergeant did. He was relishing the
sordid romanticism of his role, the ruthless time of night, the
suffering of the woman under his control. He had further tid-
ings to impart.

"And your cousin with one arm, he was taken by the French
at Porquerolles, trying to board a ship for Portugal. He has been
sent to the East."

Portugal? A ship? Poor Fritzl?

"The East?" Not paying attention, she imagined
Constantinople, Samarkand, the Spice Islands . . .

"Auschwitz?" That name again, like a handful of ice crystals
dashed in the face. But the Sergeant corrected her, in the even

tone of voice of a car salesman discussing different models: a coupe, a saloon . . . "No. To Theresienstadt, in fact. In Bohemia. It's a place chiefly for half Jews and French and so-called 'eminent citizens.' Yes, he is possibly on the way to Poland, but possibly not. I've heard it's one of the better ones, this Theresienstadt." He frowned, catching himself in a humane moment, on the edge of sympathy, so he backtracked and added, in a tone of manufactured contempt, "Anyway, he's a Jew, so you know," and shrugged. As if she should have known better, and as for him, the half Jew, what could he expect?

Stefanie laughed. The Sergeant stared, surprised.

"You think this is funny, *frau*?"

"*You* are funny," she said. A dark, brilliant rage rose in her. She dried her tears. "Well, not really, not funny in the sense of humorous. Stupid, clumsy, boorish, pathetic. Funny, like a clown? No. Laughable but not amusing. In fact, you are awful." She was gasping for breath. There was a stabbing pain in her right side, but she had to speak. It gave her an almost erotic satisfaction. She glared at him, tasting her contempt. "But you and all those like you—and you are all the same—are so pathetic, which, yes, makes you funny, in your way. God's laughter will echo in your ears when you're lowered into your graves. Kohler, Schmidt, Epting, Kranz, whatever your names are, it doesn't matter. You're all the same. You've all traded your immortal souls for a shabby illusion, the illusion of superiority of the mediocre, and a tiny moment's power over the weak and defenseless. Does that make you feel good, *ja*? Does that make you feel like a man, junior *Kranzl*? *Du schleimer*? *Du schnorrer*? *Du seicherl*?"

He waved a hand in annoyance.

"Be quiet," he shouted. "You are talking treason now, and we have our means." But she went on.

"*Ja. Ja, du lauser*. I'll be quiet. I'll stop telling you the truth you can't stand to hear, how you and your friends have squandered your personalities, your character, the respect due you as Germans, as Europeans, as members of the human race. You've betrayed Christianity, humanism, your families, and the West. Morally, you're lower than dogs. Much lower than dogs, because you have the ability to reason and to change. But you choose not to. You're slaves to the lowest and most bestial motivation. You're nothing." She repeated the word, rolling it around richly. "*Nichts*."

"*Los*." The Sergeant was pale. He beckoned to his successor as corporal, who was waiting in the hallway. "Take her back to her cell."

"Tell me something before your cowardice forces you to remove me from your hearing, Kranzl *knabe*."

He said nothing, but stared at her blankly.

"Do you actually believe this racial idiocy?"

"I am a loyal German."

"Which means no. Otherwise you'd have to believe that you, an insignificant little *wappler* from, I'd guess, Hamburg, by your accent . . . ?"

"*Ja*. Altona," he replied automatically, then, snapping his fingers in impatience, or desperation: "*Schütze! Herein! Schnell!*" The corporal hurried over.

" . . . that an insignificant little Hamburger like you is superior by mere virtue of your race to the kings of Israel, or the Christ, or mere *Jews* like Dichter Heinrich Heine, or Dr. Sigmund Freud, or Meister Gustav Mahler, or Professor Doktor Albert Einstein, men who have enhanced civilization as immeasurably as you and your kind . . . "

The corporal placed a heavy hand on her shoulder. She shook it off. Her voice rose.

" . . . as immeasurably as you and your kind have *shat on it*?"

She stood up and winced, reminded for the first time of the lingering pain. He noticed; he smirked. She noticed him noticing; she nodded. "Oh, indeed, that's your only strength, the weapon of the sadist, the schoolyard bully, the sneak, the coward, the fool . . . "

She allowed herself to be taken back to the cell, expecting the worst (but how much worse could it be?) . . . but for an entire day and night she was left alone, except by the corporal who, wordlessly, brought her food. She slept a light and fitful sleep. In her wakeful moments she wept. The thought of how her mother must have suffered was as nearly unbearable as anything she'd ever felt.

"Ach, *Mutti*."

On the morning of the second day she looked out the window, hoping to see the patch of blue Burgundian sky that was becoming a friend to her, so like a glimpse of her mother's heaven, the heaven where both her mothers now dwelt; but that day the sky was iron-gray and a steady rain was falling. She looked at the sycamore tree, darkened and listless, its leaves drooping under the burden of the rain. At the bottom of the overhanging branch a small square of whiteness declared itself vividly against the gloom: The documents she had tossed through the window before the interrogation began. Still there? It seemed like a year at least since she'd sent the paper airplane on its way, but of course it had only been five days, if that . . . Time's infinite malleability, again . . . were the documents still legible? Were they real? Was it worth letting someone know, somehow?

Real or false, it hardly mattered now.

Her breakfast arrived: a bowl of chicory coffee, a dry roll, a *tartine*, some surprisingly edible cheese. It was good. She ached all over and there were nodes of pain whenever she stood up. No doctor was available, but she put her faith in Mother Mary and was rewarded with a strange experience. She had finished her breakfast and was sipping her ersatz, wishing she had a cigarette, when the door to her cell, a paneled, ironbound affair dating back to the last century, silently swung open (it had always creaked before) and a mystic's utmost vision appeared in the doorway: God-encircled, ablaze with light, caparisoned in celestial blue, crowned with heaven's gold, holding out her arms. She entered, and the door swung to silently behind her. Stefanie had the impression the clouds cleared up and a blinding deep blue filled the sky. Then Mother Mary was standing over Stefanie, looking down. She was small and plain, with black hair and a long nose, and the innocence on her face was that of a very young child, but great age was in her eyes, from which all her beauty came: honey-colored they were, shining, multi-dimensional, as if they looked inward upon an infinity of doors opening into long, long corridors of endless time.

She spoke, as she always did, Stefanie's own Salzburg dialect, in a soft voice.

"Truly, my Stefanie, you have borne much," said she. "Yet there is more. He will call for you again. You must go, *mädl*. You must go. Only you can bring the love of God to this man who is now so close to the nameless one."

"Whom I have also seen," said Stefanie. "Why, my mother?"

"But you have seen so much, so many!" was the enigmatic reply.

"But why?"

"The very question not to ask, my daughter. Never why, only how!"

"Then: How?"

"Listen carefully, for we will meet again only once. They want you to join him again."

Stefanie, with a start, realized who the "him" was: The warlord of the world. Her ex-painter.

Him.

They?

"And do you also want me to join him?"

"I do. Then I will welcome you. For your duty is clear, your mission mine, my mission God's. To build for me the holiest of shrines, atop the highest places on earth, by first destroying the nameless one's works. This only you can do. Then build anew, with your faith and your hands. And the hands of men."

The shimmering vision began to fade. First the outer rings of golden light dimmed and went out, like lights in a shopwindow at closing time; then the inner, silken glow darkened at the edges and was slowly eaten away by the surrounding darkness, in which the diminutive holy figure still doughtily shone out, a lighthouse on a dark night; then as abruptly as a *guignol* she was gone, leaving behind her the afterimage upon the retina of something shining and wonderful, and in the air that same scent of roses or rosewater or fresh-cut tulips in the spring, that all visionaries spoke of, and that Stefanie recalled . . .

The sky was still overcast, she noticed, and it was raining sheets.

"Madame Lebel?"

A young man in a suit stood in the doorway through which Mother Mary had shimmered into the ether. Stefanie wiped her eyes and tried to focus. He was familiar, but she couldn't place him.

"Yves Chatillon, from your German class in Paris."

It was the young intelligence officer, the cynic, the one who'd assured her he'd be studying English within a year or two, the one with the proudly proclaimed black market connections. Pleasant as he was, and he was something of a cool breeze after the Kranzes and Schmidts and Kohlers, she reminded herself that he was just another one of Them, just a Kranz or Kohler in a French suit. But he came in and sat down on the bed and frowned at its hardness, and offered her a cigarette—a real cigarette, an American Virginia, not one of those wartime substitutes half made of cabbage. She smoked gratefully.

"I had to find out where you were from *nos amis de la Gestapo*," he said. "Thanks to the German you taught me, Madame, I managed to get an *ausweis* for a day's journey to the Free Zone. Such a pleasure to get out of Paris! I have news for you, and a proposition."

He spoke as if he were visiting a relative on a brief walking holiday in the mountains and made no comment on the bruises on her face, or her swollen eyes. Snake, she thought. Just like the rest.

"What about . . . ?" She indicated the corridor outside: the surly Feldwebel and his Germans. Chatillon shrugged.

"Never mind. I have superior authority. I can get you out of here right now. IF." He held up a warning finger. "IF you agree to one thing, and it is a bit unusual, Madame."

Could anything be so described in the present circumstances of the world and her life, such as it was? She thought not. However, when he explained, she was surprised; then she remembered what the Virgin had said.

"Go to Salzburg?" she repeated.

"Yes, Madame. Where you were born?"

"Yes. But Paris is my home now."

"I understand. But it is easier to get you out if I can claim to be repatriating you. Essentially, claiming you are a German national who has been held by the French all this time."

"Oh. I see." She had nothing further to say. Salzburg? With no *Mutti*, no *Pappi* to greet her?

"Also," Chatillon flexed his limber fingers, "I have had a request that you make a brief stop nearby, en route as it were. I am led to understand, you have already been, as a—shall we say—privileged visitor to Berchtesgaden? The Berghof . . . ?"

"Yes?" Numbed as she was, possessed as she was by the spirit of her earthly and divine mothers, she felt only mild surprise; yet she felt satisfaction, too, a vindication that things were coming to pass as She had predicted . . .

"Well, you see," said Chatillon, "apparently a letter was written, sent some two years ago or more, and only just received. I know, it says little for the French post office! However, I think the events of the past two years are some excuse for this tardiness. In any case, the information was forwarded to us at Intelligence Services. We, or rather our predecessors under the Republic, were the first to see the letter, so it came back to us, *via un très grand circuit*. Knochen over at the BdS let us in on it, so that is how I found out that . . . what do you call him, Gröfaz?"

It was the ironic acronym she'd heard, short for *Grösster Feldherr aller Zeiten*, greatest warlord of all time.

"Anyway, *he* wants to see you."

Then she remembered the letter. Uncle Ernst, that desperate last-minute plea, the feverish days after the Anschluss, before the Fall. Her memory-cinema replayed the moment when she stopped at the corner of the Boulevard St. Michel and slipped the letter into the little yellow mailbox. Her emotions of the moment returned in a brief, violent wave: restlessness, anxiety, the still-living hope of a then-free France. With the mission given her by her heavenly Mother, this hope washed again through her soul, for it was indeed a mission, a sacred trust, a pilgrimage toward her destiny; and that destiny was in sight at last. This was no impossible deed of resistance doomed to failure at the first checkpoint. This was a confluence of intentions, human and divine.

Yes, at last it was clear. Everything had been leading up to it ever since that day in Linz. It would close a circle, her taking the liberation of half Europe upon herself and removing from among men the agent of the Nameless One. God be praised.

The Great Gamble of SS-Oberführer Kiesinger

So Mutti died, along with millions of others, but in the foul conditions of the transports, long before reaching Auschwitz, or Poland, or even the frontiers of the Reich. And all because the Danish woman downstairs, for the promise of a better ration card, denounced her as a Jew (many generations of Mutti's staunchly Catholic forebears would be turning in their graves) . . . Madame Nysgard got her card, but justice awaited her at the Liberation, when she was shot as a traitor for having also denounced an entire family on the Rue Soufflot as *résistants* (they were; two escaped; one went on to become Colonel Pollux, a hero of the 1944 Paris uprising, who commanded her firing squad). Her body was sent back to Denmark; her grave in Copenhagen's Assistens cemetery is marked with her initials and a simple year of death, 1945. But Mutti's grave is nowhere and everywhere, like those of her martyred fellow millions. In respect and deference to the unimaginable, we pass over her final moments, somewhere between Karlsruhe and Koblenz, mercifully attended by sweet memories of her long-dead husband and the Salzkammergut and her dear Steffi *gans*.

But Sami Lebel was alive and free. His arrest and/or death was a lie told by the Germans to persuade Stefanie to reveal secrets she never knew. True, after the denunciation by the outraged cuckold Jean-Xavier Durand, Sami (while leaving the Durand house by the side door at half five in the morning) was taken into custody by M. Sismondi of the Groupes Mobiles de Réserve, the reserve police force, but this turned out to be more of a shakedown than an arrest, and the subsequent interrogation, such as it was, took place in the Café Rousseau, in Annecy's old town. Sismondi, an Italian by birth and therefore less inclined to take sides in France's burgeoning civil war, claimed to be on no one's side but his own, and fully intended to come out of the war richer than he was when he entered it. Sami, with his investments in Cuban sugar stocks and Swedish match factories, had an appeal that was far more serious and wide-ranging than the mere putative offenses of Jewishness, or resistant activities, to both of which Sismondi gave, or affected to give, the mute blessing of looking the other way. Sami, scenting a pragmatist, used the proceeds of a substantial cash transfer to buy his way free.

"But stay out of France," warned Sismondi. "If I catch you again I might be more of a policeman, less of a capitalist."

"*Mais non*, Sismondi, I can tell your appetite is whetted. When I come over again I'll just bring my checkbook."

Sismondi was given "custody" of Sami's old but trusty Delahaye, in which he drove Sami to the frontier post at St. Julien-en-Genevois. He handed him his suitcase and a temporary exit permit before driving off with a merry toot of the old car's horn and earnest wishes of "*Buona Fortuna*."

"And stay in Switzerland, Lebel. Stay safe, at your age. Learn to recognize luck when it comes to you."

In Geneva, Sami telephoned Ignace. All but married by then to a wide-eyed young woman named Marie-Claire, the young man was living in a small apartment in the city center with his fiancée and their university textbooks. A balcony looked out onto a small square off the Rue Terreaux-du-Temple, one of the narrow streets down which hourly resounded the solemn dongs of the cathedral's great bell Clémence.

Ignace wanted to know only one thing.

"How is my mother? I've heard nothing."

"I don't know, *garçon*. I'm going to find out."

"Did they torture you?" asked Marie-Claire. She had been staring at him, like an excited child.

"*Non, ma belle*. Not yet."

"Don't ask such questions, Marie-Claire," muttered Ignace. "It's not a joking matter."

Sami settled in at a hotel-pension nearby. He visited his old friend Julie Schwab at her farm at Chancy, hard by the border. Geese honked; cows lowed; the breeze blew down from the Jura summits in occupied France.

"I'm bored, Julie. And I worry for Steffi."

"The woman who loved Hitler? Surely she'll be all right, of all people."

"On the contrary. I believe she's in deep trouble."

Julie squeezed his shoulder.

"You can't possibly know that. *Tiens.* Come and see me in that new Brecht play," she said. "It'll take your mind off."

"It's a laugh from beginning to end," interjected Julie's husband, Schwab, a small stout man with mischievous eyes and a mustache yellowed by nicotine. "If you like that kind of thing."

"All right. I'll come. It may remind me of the good old days."

"Old, perhaps. But good?"

But Sami did not want his mind taken off things; he needed action, decisiveness, purpose. Bored by Geneva, he was impatient to get back into the fight in the French mountains he could see from his window. Then came news of Stefanie, and his will, and his world—and the world—changed, again. The news came from "Mireil," one of the men on the Football Line.

"Mother Goose is in the kitchen," said "Mireil" over the hotel's telephone. Sami recognized him as the ex-Latin teacher.

"Whose kitchen?"

"Where mustard is the favored condiment."

"In which house?"

"Southbound."

"Going where?"

"The big house."

In this cryptic code "mustard" meant Dijon; "southbound" was a reference to the southbound lines at that city's railway station. "Mother Goose" was Stefanie, from her girlhood nickname, *Gans* (Goose); "the big house" the Reich. Later that night, after more prearranged codes—a phone call returned, a purported consultation between doctor and patient—Sami met "Balthus," "Montaigne," and a third man who used his real name, Armin. "Balthus" and "Montaigne" were "*passeurs*," or refugee-smugglers along the Football Line, based in La-Roche-sur-Foron, in the Haute-Savoie; one was a priest, the other a writer, but which

was which, Sami neither knew nor cared. Armin, a Bernese with
watery eyes and a receding chin, was the main contact for all
the resistance groups in Geneva's French hinterland. As a Swiss,
and, as it happened, an employee of the International Red Cross,
Arnim's ability to cross borders closed to others was of paramount importance; as a forger, he was, quite simply, the best
in Europe. The meeting took place in Armin's small apartment
on the heights of St. Jean, where the silence was broken only by
birdsong and the occasional train whistle from the Cornavin
marshalling yards far below. Armin's services would be required
if Sami's alias had any hope of succeeding, as the committee, in
consultation with Henri Max in Annecy, had decided to inter-
cept the train taking Stefanie to Germany and for the intercept-
ing to be done by an SS Senior Colonel, or *Oberführer*, played
by the former star of the Comédie Française, Samuel Lebel,
who was fluent in German and, said "Montaigne," "reputedly
quite convincing in a variety of baroque roles, according to the
drama critics." Oberführer Sami would requisition the prisoner
for questioning and a unit of the local Communist resistants
would then dynamite the railroad tracks, impeding arms shipments from the Dijon area to the Reich, at least for a time. Sami
and Stefanie would then fly to England on an RAF plane that
would have just delivered radio transmitters at a clandestine air-
field near Sorbet-lès-Dijon, departure time 2115 hours.

"England? I was hoping to come back here, to Switzerland.
Her son lives here."

"In good time. But for now it's easier to get you to England."

"*Bon Dieu*. What a caper. But an SS colonel? For me it's the
role of a lifetime," said Sami.

Arnim stared at him.

"Don't overplay it."

"No, no, a master of artistic subtlety am I. You should have
seen my Ruy Gomez in Hugo's *Hernani*. Even LeGros conceded
I conveyed the essential character of the poisoner with a mere
gesture." Sami made the gesture, a wave of the hand suddenly
arrested in mid-air. The others looked on, unmoved. Balthus
resumed:

"Ah—can you drive?"

Sami snorted in contempt.

"Drive? As well as I can breathe. I was doing the Paris-Turin when you were still wetting your nappies, boy."

"Good. Because we will have a car waiting across the border. You will drive yourself to Dijon, from which station where the train would be departing."

"Drive myself halfway across France? Dressed as an SS colonel? It's madness!"

"So is everything these days. If you avoid resistance cells, no one will dare question you. It's all right: we've ascertained there are no high-ranking SS officers currently in the region."

"Madness, truly. I love it!" exulted Sami, who had been away from the stage for too long.

"Anyway," said "Montaigne," "we can't get hold of a plane, not until the RAF makes its radio drop. And a senior officer of the SS would likely not subject himself to the unreliability and tedium of changing trains a dozen times."

"All right. Who's the contact?" A contact was always needed before the next phase of any operation could get underway, in the not-infrequent event that everything went wrong.

"A man codenamed Renard. A double agent. Paris Gestapo by day, *résistant* by night. And by conviction, which is not always the case. He arranged for the lady's repatriation and got in touch with Mireil. Very useful to us."

Montaigne gave Sami an envelope containing SS ration cards, letters from the SS *Kommandantur* in Paris, and instructions in code.

"And how do you know we can count on him?"

"I don't, of course. But he's worked out before. And how much can you be certain of, in this world of ours?"

"Only that the Nazis will continue to be bastards."

Armin the forger was given his task. Not a few Jewish escapees to Palestine and downed RAF pilots owed their lives to his talent with inks, paper, photographs, and rubber stamps. "Balthus" and "Montaigne" left without a word and, although they were in a neutral city, it was a city with suburbs in German hands, so they took pains to leave by separate doors, heads down, engaging no one and nothing, pausing to read newspapers in mock-casualness.

Sami dined with Ignace and Marie-Claire but said nothing of his mission, only that he would be away "for a day or so." He could tell that his meaning was clear—at least to Stefanie's son, who, when they parted, gave him a painfully direct stare and said, "*Adieu, Papa Samuel*," and they embraced.

Once again, then, into occupied France. Sami was as excited as a small boy on a treasure hunt. Self-conscious in the SS uniform provided by Arnim, but somewhat reassured by the snug bulk of the standard-issue Walther P38 (obtained from a German guard via cross-border barter against a promise of access to Swiss bank accounts) and the forged documents in his breast pocket, he cycled to within a kilometer of the border, then took a drover's path through the woods to a forest footbridge over the Allondon river. Mireil's unit—Mireil himself and two younger men dressed like farmhands in corduroys and jerseys—met him beyond the German checkpoints at a crossing in the forest between Prévessin in France and the Swiss hamlet of Meyrin. Mireil gaped when Sami dismounted from the bicycle.

"*Dieu*, it's too good, that uniform," he muttered. "You look the part."

They shook hands and Mireil gave Sami the keys of his borrowed Citroën Léger. It had an SS flag on the right front wing that would give any curious gendarme pause. Sami walked around the car admiringly.

"Where did you lads get hold of this beauty?"

"My brother's a mechanic," said one of the younger men. "He used to sell Citroëns. This was the last of the '39s. He decided to put it to good use."

"We put the flag on this morning," said the other youth. "It might not look so convincing in the daylight."

"*Bof*, don't worry, *les gars*, that's my job, to be convincing," said Sami.

The car, said Mireil, was full up, but there was a canister with extra petrol in the boot, should Sami need it.

"*Peuh.* I can smell it."

"*Bonne chance*," said Mireil, with a smile. He had a permanently sad face, further saddened by events, which made his smile faintly comical. "Keep your eyes open. And make sure you know whom you're talking to—friend or foe, I mean. The communists up around Dijon shot a Wehrmacht captain only last week. They would regard an SS colonel as a real trophy."

"*Merci, mon brave.*"

Mireil and his boys disappeared into the forested darkness. After poring over the coded instructions in the light of the car's headlamps, Sami drove slowly down a rutted trail until he was well beyond the border zone and police and Wehrmacht checkpoints; then, with on his lips the only prayer he ever uttered— "*Eh bien merde, mon grand, allons-y*"—he made his way to the main highway, the Route Nationale 5, that led from the Swiss border across the mountains to Dijon. Beyond the narrow beam of light cast by the car's slotted headlamps, the highway lost itself in the onrushing dark. Hamlets and villages less than twenty kilometers from Geneva's bustling boulevards might as well have been two hundred kilometers away and as many or more years in the past. Gas lamps glimmered behind half-hearted blackout curtains. Cows mooed and rustled in their stalls. Dogs barked. The wind blew; shapes moved, shifted, diminished. Sami glimpsed a dim light outside a looming shack; a figure lurched into the road, swerved, melted into the darkness. In Gex there was a light on in the Hotel du Jura in flagrant disregard of the blackout, a bare lightbulb, suspended from the ceiling, illuminating flowered wallpaper and casting the ideal silhouette of a man in braces and shirtsleeves smoking, elbows on the windowsill. Sami briefly imagined the mission that had brought the man there, the thoughts possessing him as he smoked and gazed out into the inky night of Gex—and saw a black SS car drive by. The light went out; shutters closed. Farther on, in the instep of a bend in the road, a café was closing for the night, chairs on tables, a mop in a woman's tired hands making the rounds. In the high mountains wind whispered in the pines and waterfalls hissed faintly, in their timelessness spared the idiocies of man's rule.

Sami drove fast, expertly, eyes fixed on the road ahead. He was grateful for the driving; it cleared his mind, for the moment, of other thoughts. The road was empty. Between Ferney-Voltaire and Morez, thirty kilometers away on the other side of the Jura, he passed only two other vehicles, a coal delivery lorry and a wheezing old Renault with two men on board. The first manned checkpoint came just outside St. Claude: a Wehrmacht company sergeant with his Alsatian dog next to a red-and-white striped barrier and a red-white-and-black booth. The arrival at three in the morning of a gleaming Citroën was unmistakably a major event; the presence behind the wheel of a Colonel in the SS doubly so.

"Herr Oberst." The sergeant stood to attention.

"Oberführer, *hauptfeldwebel,*" snapped Sami, in impeccable Strasbourg German. "I am of SS, *junge.* On my way to Dijon for an inspection tour of race facilities. Stand aside."

"I'm sorry, Oberführer, I had no notification that any high-ranking officers of SS were in the vicinity. I must ask for your papers."

"Papers? I have no time for this idiocy. Your name, *hauptfeldwebel?*"

"Tanz, Herr Oberführer. Gottfried Tanz. Thirty-fifth Hunding Regiment, Allgäu Division. And yet I must still ask to see your papers. Orders."

Sami had to strike a delicate balance between the exigencies of the situation and the native arrogance of the SS species. He had also to redirect his mind to the awful priorities of the German soldiering class, priorities that were diametrically opposed to his own: Submission to a creed; unquestioning devotion to superior rank; subjugation of individuality and decency in the name of the Cause.

"You are delaying me, *hauptfeldwebel* Tanz," he said. "But I recognize it when a man is only doing his job."

The papers passed their first official scrutiny, a cursory one, as Sergeant Tanz had frightened himself with his own boldness. He handed them back with a trembling hand through the window of the Citroën, then stood back and saluted while the dog, as if suddenly aware of the deception taking place, launched into a furious tirade of barking as Sami drove away. Tanz's remark that no SS colonels had been reported in the vicinity, although confirming "Montaigne"'s intelligence, was somewhat ominous, too: Stuck as he was in a dull job in a dull mountain town, the man would no doubt seize any excuse for diversion and lose no time in checking up via telephone and telegram on Oberführer Kiesinger, that was certain. And it was only a very short while— hours rather than days, if not minutes—before the word came through that there was no Oberführer Kiesinger in the Western sector, no "race facilities" in Dijon to be inspected, no SS colonels at all in the Jura-Burgundy region . . . why hadn't he chosen a less visible rank, say captain or major?

His jauntiness had worn off, and it was as a sixty-three-year-old and a tired one that Sami resumed his journey, broken by a pause at the roadside in the early morning light for a *tartine beurrée*, two boiled eggs packed by Ignace's fiancée in brown wrapping paper, a cold coffee, and a smoke, but the longed-for nap had to wait. From St. Claude to Dijon it was two hours on mostly deserted secondary roads, although as the sun rose more traffic appeared: men on bicycles, a priest in an old Peugeot, horse-drawn carts and milk wagons from the farms and dairies of the Jura meadowlands. All pulled off to the side, or came to a halt, as the imposing Citroën raced by. A lorry rattled across the road, carrying milk and cheese no doubt destined for the conquerors: churns and wheels of cheese that shifted about in the back like huge playing pieces. Such a bounty was this fertile land of France for her Aryan warlords to ravish! The driver raised a hand in faint salute. Sami ignored him, preserving the dignity of an SS Oberführer. Not that he had any idea how an SS Oberführer would react in any given situation. His tiredness underscored the perils he faced; but it sapped any fear he might feel, and kept him going, with an acquired momentum of its own. He swore to himself, as he swerved to avoid a line of schoolchildren following their schoolmistress just outside of Gray, that if he succeeded in this mission—essentially, to snatch Stefanie from under the noses of the German Army and its French goons—he and Stefanie were leaving, not for England, certainly for Switzerland (he had learned of any number of secret ways in and out along the Swiss border in the Jura and Haute-Savoie, across moss-stained foot-bridges or shepherd's fords, through drainage ditches and tunnels), possibly for Palestine. The raging anti-Semitism of the age had had its effect on him, he who had once scorned the very notion of a Jewish identity: "I am a Frenchman" had been his proudest boast. Now it was, he thought, a shameful declaration. Now to be a Jew was to be a hero; to be a Frenchman was to be a coward. Pétain's armistice would stain France's name forever. It was the death knell of the France of Louis XIV, Napoleon, and Foch. The France of Diderot, Voltaire, and Hugo. The France of Bernanos, Mistinguett, and the brothers Lumière. The jaunty, proud, bellicose, magnificent France Sami had so adored. Now, and forevermore, France's enemies would characterize her as the country of surrender, of abject subjugation, and of cowardice, never mind if Pétain called the thing an "armistice" and the Nazis went along with the old man's nomenclature. The subtleties of its coming to pass would be lost on future generations; the nation's weariness of war, its dread of more Verduns, the millions of refugees interfering with the army's last-ditch maneuvers, the sheer bled-dry exhaustion of it, one hundred thousand men killed in six weeks: all those considerations would be forgotten. Nothing would palliate the cringing shame that the armistice inspired in Sami and, he knew, in millions of others. France was his France no longer. He'd be happier as a Jew first, or a Jew only. He heard they were building a new Jewish nation in Palestine, or would be when the war was over, and he wanted to see it.

And the war *would* be over some day, he felt, for the first time. He actually allowed himself to envisage such a thing: The defeat of Germany. Not that the relentless successes of the Germans across Europe from the Atlantic to, almost, the Urals and Caucasus, gave any cause for optimism. It was his knowledge, acquired admittedly at secondhand, of the psychology of Adolf Hitler, that convinced him that the mad ex-painter could never sustain success, or live at peace with himself, let alone with the rest of the world. His was the temperament of the sexual

failure, the masturbator who must repeat his compulsion end-
lessly; the lifelong loner, self-raised in that solitude that is the
playing field of Satan. Yes, and apart from all that, Hitler's innate
restlessness and intellectual inadequacy and monumental selfishness would doom him sooner or later . . . and then there were
the Yankees. Gum-chewing hordes of comic-book readers. But
anyone mad enough to pit his medium-sized central European
entity against the continent-wide vastness and unlimited potential of *both* the USA and Russia was, quite simply, a lunatic.
Sami knew enough history to know that most conquerors, and
all lunatics, eventually fail, and it gave him pleasure to think
that the collapse of the colossus might come about in small part
because of his, Sami's, tugging at the guy ropes, and that of his
courageous resistance colleagues . . . his *comrades-in-arms.* How
he would have scoffed only three years ago! He, a cynic, had
embraced a cause.

And a woman, the most damnable and infuriating and elusive
woman ever embraced by man. Even now—now, in the middle
of the rolling dew-glinting pre-Jura pastures, in the tentative
beams of the rising early summer sun, in the dawn of a day
the end of which would see him victorious or dead—his heart
skipped a beat at the thought of her, and he realized he still didn't
know for sure, even after twenty years, if she had ever really loved
him; and he firmly forbade his mind to penetrate the realms he
had so effectively sealed off for so long. Imagination, and the
reality of what he'd heard about Gestapo methods, the camps,
and the whole monstrous edifice of evil that the ex-painter was
constructing . . .

God, it was enough to make you believe in the devil.

Yet it might be a consolation for some that there were still
Frenchmen like Henri Max, and "Montaigne," and "Balthus,"
and all the lads in the Haute-Savoie units, and Swiss like Armin,
and all the decent unsung ones trying to relight the lamps of culture. This Renard fellow, too, whoever he was: there was another
one willing to risk his life in the game of patriotism. Working for
the French Gestapo, and under the long noses of the enemy, he
had transmitted Stefanie's whereabouts to Mireil, via couriers in

Lyon, thanks to which Sami knew exactly where and when: That same day at ten thirty, the train from Dijon heading south and east, ostensibly to take her home to Salzburg, of all places, but they often made up benign-sounding destinations because even in the midst of their mad carnage they couldn't bring themselves to admit they were inflicting it . . .

It was nearly eight when he arrived in the Chevreul suburb of Dijon, a long narrow street bordered by telephone poles and two-story houses, some of which boasted lace curtains, others the signs of businesses—*Quincaillerie, Boucherie, Patisserie*—or the little red metal sign denoting a *tabac*. People were on the street, mostly women carrying string shopping bags. The traffic was heavy for the times. At an intersection Sami braked for a coal-powered smoke-belching Renault lorry and a motorcycle ridden by a gendarme, who saluted when he saw the SS uniform. Sami nodded distantly, as an SS Oberführer might. Buses, most of them still running on petrol, prowled the outer boulevards. Bicycles were everywhere, as in Indochina, or the France of yore; even velotaxis were common, a distinctly Asian touch. A lovely vintage Panhard 12 CV drove by, an old gentleman wearing white gloves at the wheel. It awakened a memory of Sami's lost youth; just such a car had taken him and his then truelove to the soft sands of blue Arcachon, one glorious summer's day in . . . 1913? More lorries chugged by, one of them towing a trailer on which sat a small rusty tractor. Just beyond the intersection was a hole in the road surrounded by traffic barriers and a sign that read "Déviation/Umleitung" above an arrow pointing right. There was no one about: Too early for work crews. Sami turned right, yawning, yearning for sleep. The road dwindled into little more than a dirt driveway curving away into an unknowable distance, overhung with heavy trees that drooped over a high gray wall along one side. There was no other traffic. Sami slowed down and stopped. He glanced at his watch: 8:05, nearly two hours before he had to be at the Gare. Perhaps a nap; he needed to rest . . . he chastised himself with a brisk slap on the jowls and was making preparations for a nice quiet smoke and the dregs of Ignace's cold coffee when he gave a start, suddenly aware of a round face rising like a pale moon at the passenger-side window.

"You are of the SS?" inquired the man through the window, in French-accented German. "*Sie sind von der SS?*" He was flaccidly plump, of medium height, with blotchy skin and pale blue eyes and wearing a *motard's* leather jacket. He rapped on the glass with an impatient knuckle. It was a bold approach for a civilian to an officer of the SS; unless . . .

Sami sat up and looked around.

"As you can see," he said, curtly. "What do you want?" With his left hand he fondled his Walther P38. Out of the corner of his eye he caught sight of a rapid movement from side to side, behind the car. He half turned, but saw nothing: The wall, the slowly stirring tree branches, a cat . . .

"Only to give you this, Herr Reichsführer. On behalf of the guys and girls at Drancy."

Whatever it was, it was half expected. Sami knew the man was resistance. Communist, *Francs-tireur*. Someone had been in touch with someone else with wrong information; it was a *risque de métier*, in the haphazard, dangerous world of the partisan underground. But Sami could do nothing. If he told them who he was, his mission was in jeopardy. If he said nothing, they would try to kill him. And so they did: shots went off; the side window of the Citroën exploded into shards, another man appeared. Sami fired the Walther, which recoiled violently. The second man ran across the road, pointing a gun. Sami threw the car into reverse and accelerated backwards away from the gunfire—the irony of it, running for his life from his own side! But it was a very unamusing irony. Because he had no choice; it was shoot or be shot. As he gunned the car he fired his Walther again once, twice, three times, like an inflamed roué at a duel, firing wildly, and having just enough time left to regret vividly never having had real target practice; then one of his shots hit its mark. The moonfaced man doubled over suddenly, but this merely caused his comrade to fire his revolver with greater ferocity, running down the driveway after the car as its tail swung wildly into the street and Sami, grinding the gears, threw it it into first and stepped on the accelerator just as his second assailant—to whom he was about to shout, heedless of the multiple possible consequences, "Stop, *les gars*, I'm one of you"—aimed and fired and scored a direct hit, through Sami's brain, taking away, with the soft pulpy gray tissue, Sami Lebel's life, and with *that* a character out of Maupassant, a boulevardier of a bygone era, a good friend with a unique sense of irony, a dapper dresser, a fine pastry chef, a great seducer, a lover of the good life, a fighter for the oppressed, a man who could have been a leader, and a now-proud Jew in SS uniform.

"*Sale boche*," said the communist *résistant*, and spat at the dead Nazi before throwing away his gun and heading down the road, followed by his limping companion.

Gustave
Twelve

I COULD READ no more after Sami's death, not because of it, dismaying as it was—a good life cut down, mistaken identity (or was it?), a dirty end, bitter irony, etc.; indeed, I'd become quite fond of Sami, even identified a little with him in the jejune way a second-rate reader seeks to identify with an author's characters. Nor was I prevented from continuing by the creeping presence of my native city in the narrative: Ignace, his fiancée, the university, the actress Schwab. No, it was the city itself outside my windows, the first faint gray light of another Geneva winter morning dribbling through my dusty drapes, that did me in, for I was suddenly as utterly exhausted as if I'd just waddled up and down the Salève in my slippers and then gone for a good run. I slept a deep, black sleep. When I awoke, face down on my bed in a warm pool of dribble cooling at the edges, it was noon. On the answering machine was a message from Martine assuring me that her sister Laure was all right (although I didn't even know the woman, and could therefore cheerfully skip the info) and that she'd be out of hospital later and would call me. How I hated, and hate, waiting for the loved one to call, when every minute without the call is potentially an insult, possibly the end of the affair! So say the insecure.

But I, the man who had seen an archangel, sallied forth and crossed the car-teeming Boulevard des Philosophes and had a dish of air-dried beef at the Café des Philosophes and with it drank a crisp Cardinal, then another. I ordered no carrots;

indeed, I haven't had one since. The waiter, a vulpine grinner from Pescara named Alfredo, complimented me in his standard insincere way: apparently my presence on the scene of the hostage-taking had been commented upon in one of the papers . . . !

Guess which one?

I looked at them all, nonetheless. "Triumphant Raid by City Police," burbled *Mon Temps*. "Commandos 1, Terrorists 0," brayed the *Tribune*. "Armed Police Viciously Assault Outnumbered Insurgents," ranted *Chez Marx*. And (roll of drums) . . . "Helium-Filled Professor Floats Into Woman's Apartment," wisecracked *Le Procope Helvète* on its front page, above a cartoon of simian-looking bomb-toters gazing up at said human helium balloon, complete with mustache and stringy hair, adrift in a sky peopled by vague saintly figures, a visual allusion no doubt to certain celestial apparitions.

"The moribundity of the sterile UN suburb named the Parc de Budé, where nothing ever happens except for visits to kitchens and toilets and bedrooms by the underpaid Third World cleaning staff of the idle and overpaid United Nations functionaries who spend their lives rutting and swilling there, was violently torn asunder, like the veil of Bashshar, by the sudden intrusion into the apartment of a TV personality and her sister of two armed Pakistanis . . . "

I reread this garbage. *Like the veil of Bashshar?* This referred to an old Persian legend, I dimly recalled, involving a woman's disguise at her supposed funeral and subsequent huzzahs or yells of bloody murder when the disguising veil is torn off and she is revealed to be alive and soon becomes dead . . . all in all, a quite distinctive simile that wouldn't occur to just any old jaundiced left-wing newspaper reviewer who happened to hate a certain overweight professor. Mental bells clanged loudly, then:

"I've got you, you bastard."

Not that it took much high-level detection. For none other than one Guy Gax was the author of a failed collection of short stories entitled *The Veil of Bashshar*. In fact, the last time we had dinner he'd been complaining, as you may recall, about his publisher's understandable reluctance to print a second edition when the first had sold less than a hundred copies throughout the Francosphere, from Quebec to Ouagadougou. My oh my, but he'd overplayed his hand this time, hadn't he? The traitor, the popinjay, the spider in the lawn chair! Of course, I'd known it all along. Yes, he'd done the dirty on me, for reasons of lifelong bile and resentment and the paltry local renown acquired from appearing in the pages of *Le Procope*, bumwipe of the congenitally malcontent. And no doubt he took advantage of the opportunity it gave him to prong, or at least hover around, Left-leaning and therefore sexually available young women. Masochistically, I read further.

"At stake at the business end of the twin barrels of these two Armalites was not only the life of a TV announcer, a small thing in itself, but the even less precious life of our favorite voluminous clown and gaseous mountebank, who for no known reason save perhaps the prodding of his favorite archangel entered the lists on behalf of his (get ready for it) (are you sitting down?) (hold onto your hats) lady love, the forenamed TV reporter . . . yes, the eminent Professor of Ancient Gas has somehow, perhaps with the assistance of those divine agents with whom he hobnobs, maneuvered his vast unlovely bulk into the good graces (and no doubt elsewhere, but there we draw the line) of said TV personality . . . "

That was enough. I returned to my apartment to compose a stinging reply, only to plunge headlong into hiccuping helpless teary laughter the moment I sat at my desk and turned on the cawing and grumbling old computer: Behold, the Professor of Ancient Gas, floating through the firmament! Maneuvering his vast (here was the Gaxian touch) *unlovely* bulk into that welcoming haven, the sheets, arms, breasts of his lady love. . . !

I wiped my eyes and allowed the computer to doze off again. Oh, it was all Gax, through and through. The man was envious; it was writer's spite in the grand tradition, and in all the years I'd known him I'd never seen it so clearly. He envied me the Archangel; he envied me Martine; he envied me my ancestry and my education; he probably envied me my car and my job and the silly title of "professor." Good God, he even envied long-dead Mallarmé. Gax was a man burned up by the acid of his own jealousies, a man incapable of forming friendships on an equal footing. He was a Hitler in embryo.

No, this was no mere case of an outraged letter to the editor, or even a ribald sonnet. This was war, and it called for . . .

"A novel?" inquired Martine, unknowingly finishing the last line of the paragraph above (a clever touch; I'll have to use it again in the novel) later that day, after she had taped an interview about her ordeal with her colleagues at the TSR building (and absurdly given me credit for doing what I hadn't done), and given a statement to Chief Fegelein and Inspector Nicod and a police stenographer (also gratuitously endowing me with undeserved heroism), and come with me to the Lyrique for dinner— and sat through my tirade anent Gax. (I scanned the horizon: he was nowhere in sight.)

Alphonse poured our Fendant with his usual palsied hand.

"I saw you on the television, *mademoiselle*," he said. "You too, *monsieur le professeur*."

"Ironic," said I. "Or do I mean idiotic?"

"Because it's television we're discussing, I think the latter, *monsieur le professeur*."

At first, in my self-smitten way, I could talk only of Gax and the form my literary revenge would take.

"Yes, a novel. A satire. The Misadventures of Guy Hack, a parsimonious, henpecked, envious failure of a café-table scribbler who derives his only pleasure from the spectacle of his friends' humiliations. A lecherous, malodorous, ill-nourished man suffering no doubt from chronic anal fissures and indigestion, reduced to bitterness by his recent brush with cancer and unable to keep his bulging red-veined goose-egg-sized eyes off the lush bodies of barely pubescent girls. (I'm fairly certain he's shagging one of my students, by the way.) A failure as husband and father, a not so secret drunk, a . . . "

"I think you over-egg the omelet somewhat, Gustave," said Martine. "I would start this way." She cleared her throat. I glanced at her sweet tired face; the tumbling russet hair; the half smile . . . *happiness!*

"My father," she intoned in her best TV reporter voice, as if quoting—which I promptly realized she was, and verbatim: *"Blas of Santillane, after having borne arms for a long time in the Spanish service, retired to his native place. There he married a chambermaid who was not exactly in her teens, and I made my debut on this stage ten months after their marriage . . . "*

I was honored to be sharing my table and my life (at least in part) with a woman who could not only write the life and incredible times of Stefanie von Rothenberg, but also quote the opening lines of that forgotten masterpiece, *Gil Blas*, without a stammer or hesitation.

"Gil Blas," I said. "Very good. You and I must be the only ones in Geneva who ever read it. Yes, the picaresque tale of a modern hack. A moral lesson drawn from the ruin of a soul. It will do. It must." And I fell upon the appetizers (*duxelles* with Périgord mushrooms) with renewed gusto.

"Gustave," she said, halfway through the *soupe à l'ail*, "why did you come? To the apartment?"

"Because I'm crazy about you and I didn't want to just hang about outside with that useless gang of drunks and poseurs while you were in danger. And because I'm just crazy."

"I believe you are. But not in a dangerous way, like those two little horrors who kidnapped us." She briefly sketched the horror of those horrors: The ignorance, the insults, the misogyny, the smells; then she sighed and cradled her chin on her hand and gave me her direct, sincere gaze. "I mean I think you're crazy in a generous, creative way. The way of the artist and the lover."

"Well, that can be dangerous, too."

"But it's my way."

I saw the moment, and it could wait no longer.

"All right, my dear, it's now or never. Try this on for size." I dabbed my mouth and mustache with my napkin and took a deep breath—and dove in. I told her about my first vision, on the Corraterie. I described the second, in the classroom. And when I came to the third, in the cargo lift of her apartment building, she gasped.

"It sounds mad, I know. That such a vision should appear to

a totally ordinary average modern semi-intellectual freethinker like me, I mean I've never had a religious emotion in my life. I never even went to church. But I've always believed in ghosts, like a good Scot."

I mentioned the diagnosis of porphyria. And then there was John Calvin, I said, and told her of his miraculous vision of the beast-carriages—although admittedly, with that I wondered if I hadn't gone too far. But she, good reporter that she was, was sitting back and listening with apparent neutral concentration. Her eyes wandered only slightly, and then only to the table between us, not to other, potentially more interesting sources of entertainment, as the eyes of a flirt might, or those of a politician or social climber (or Guy Gax). (I glanced around: still not there.) She did, however, etch a series of deep lines in the tablecloth with her butter knife, a gesture I interpreted as symptomatic of uncertainty, or nervousness.

"Well."

With Calvin, I'd done.

"I mean, I know it sounds like raving of the nuttiest sort."

She frowned down at the lines she'd carved, then sliced across all five with a deep horizontal incision—I was wrong, her fidgeting was a sign of decisiveness—and looked up.

"Raving? Not at all. Do you remember Hamlet?"

"The 'there are more things in heaven and on earth' speech?" I said, hopeful that she wasn't thinking of the "angels" bit.

"Precisely. It's my deepest belief. So you can rest assured that I take you quite seriously. The world's neither as boring nor as logical as it seems—thank God. By the way, have you finished my book?" she inquired.

"Almost. Sami's just died, poor bastard. I've one more chapter."

"Finish it, then," she said. Not wanting to seem too didactic, or overbearing, she smiled. "I mean, as long as you've read that far. No, quite seriously," leaning back to allow Alphonse elbow room for her plate of *oeufs brouillés aux truffes*, "you can rest assured that I won't consign you to Bel-Air asylum. You know, I knew all along."

Alphonse chuckled drily, receiving a glare from me.

"Knew?" I said.

"Well, really, yes. From the start you were fascinated by Stefanie's visions in a very personal way. I mean, I flatter myself that I'm not too bad for my age, but I had the distinct impression your primary interest was in the apparitions rather than in me. At first."

Ah, God. In a lesser woman this would have been the moment for a coy moue, or bashful glance. Not her. She was looking me straight in the eye, frankly, her face almost expressionless. "And of course as part of my job I see the local papers . . . "

"Ah, God. *Le Procope.*"

"I'm afraid so. And do you know what? It's beneath contempt. Juvenile pranks, no more."

But . . . I protested. Petitpoix was using it as an excuse.

"An excuse to do what? Dismiss you? No, I'd take the high road and forget the whole thing. They can't fire you for having visions. Nor can they require you to see a psychiatrist, any psychiatrist, least of all that buffoon Dürrenmatt. You can tell *that* to Monsieur le Directeur Petitpoix. And I'd be happy to consult our company lawyers. After all, which one of you was privileged to see the Archangel Michael?"

"No, no," I grumbled, "I'll write that book, you wait and see."

Meanwhile, I finished hers.

Recessional: 1949

The Convent of Sacro Monte della Beata Vergine dell'Ossola (Holy Mountain of the Blessed Virgin of Ossola) of the order of the Sisters of Dorothy, in the village of Elvetica Inferiore, sits on a spur of the Lepontine Alps in Val Lungo, a tributary of the Val d'Ossola in the northern Italian province of Novara. Ten or so kilometers away is the border town of Domodossola, which has provided an introductory glimpse of Italy for first-time travelers from Switzerland ever since the Simplon Rail Tunnel opened in 1879. Marie-Claire Lebel, wife of Ignace Lebel, lecturer in mechanical engineering at the University of Geneva, was one such traveler. She had never been to Italy, although born a scant fifty kilometers away, in Montreux, near the rail line that parallels the gentle thigh-curve of Lake Geneva's northern shore and runs straight and true through the Rhône Valley of the verdant Valais before turning abruptly southward at Brig and diving under the mountains to emerge in Italy; so when she and Ignace stepped onto Italian soil, having taken the train from Geneva-Cornavin earlier that morning, she was excited and happy and hoping for Italian scenes of Renaissance drama and vivid color. And indeed it was an ideal Mediterranean day beneath an enameled-blue Tiepolo sky into which the train burst from the Italian end of the tunnel. Ochre and russet tinted the high palisades of the mountains across the valley. The houses along the rushing river Ossola were freshly painted bright yellow and red, as if daring to put on makeup again after the long drabness of the war years. The customs guards of the new post-Fascist, post-Royal republic saluted with an operatic flourish that delighted Marie-Claire. Above everything, above the gaily decorated shops and brightly colored houses, above the crumpled ridge of the Alps, in the booming cerulean the eagles soared.

Husband and wife registered at the Hotel Corona on the Via Marconi, five minutes' walk from the station. They were welcomed by the owner, Signore D'Ettore, who had a slight acquaintance with Mother Filippa, mother superior at the convent Sacro Monte who came into town twice a month for supplies and who had written to Ignace proposing this visit. In an alley behind the hotel, a shiny Fiat Topolino provided by the local car-hire service awaited the Lebels. Ignace had looked at the map, and it was clear that they'd need a car to get to Elvetica Inferiore when they made the journey early the next day. A bus ride along that road, he said, would make them both seasick, if it didn't plunge them into the void.

Their room looked out onto the cozy bustle of the Via Marconi, from which the errant sounds of scooters and lorries and Italian conversations drifted up. Somewhere nearby a radio played sentimental songs, a hoarse tenor accompanied by an accordion. Garlicky cooking scents wafted in.

"How marvelous," said Marie-Claire. "Italy at last."

"Yes," said her husband. "Italy at last." It was not his first trip; he had been with a group of students to Turin once, to visit the Fiat plant. But this June of 1949 was a historic month for the little Lebel clan. Not only was it his wife's first visit south of the Alps, it was the occasion of two long-despaired-of reunions.

After washing up, they went down to the restaurant. It was a quarter to one. Ignace glanced at his watch.

"He was supposed to be here forty-five minutes ago," he said. "I bet he's never late for his concerts."

"*Eh bien*, he wouldn't be, would he? They pay him for them."

"True, *ma chère*. Very true. And I'm sure they pay him very well over in America."

When he was exactly one hour late, Ignace's father, Arthur Lebel, once-fashionable, now little-known composer of operas, musicals, and film scores, entered the restaurant. There was a spring in his step and a cigar in his mouth. His temples were gray, his suit well tailored, his tan elegant without being excessive. His apologies were well rehearsed but insincere. Still, Ignace was happy to see him; and Arthur Lebel was delighted, and taken aback, to see his tall, bearded twenty-five-year-old son, complete with winsome wife, rise from the table to greet him.

"Terribly sorry to be late, I . . . "

"Forget it, *Papa*. This is Marie-Claire, your daughter-in-law."

"Oh my goodness. Is it, indeed. Such a beautiful young lady. *Enchanté, ma chère*."

They embraced. Arthur perused first his daughter-in-law, admiringly, then a menu, thoughtfully. He ordered *osso buco* and a bottle of Sizzano.

"It's the right part of Italy for both," he said. "It's good to be in Italy, even just barely. It looks quite Swiss around here, doesn't it? God, how good it is to be back in Europe, though, even with things the way they are. I'm home again. Now, Marie-Claire. Tell me about yourself."

"Well, there's not much to tell. I'm still young, I haven't done much."

"You married my son. That's something."

"Yes, but I think you have much more to tell. How's America, *Papa*?"

"Ah yes: *Papa*. Ah yes! *America*. Well, America is all very well for those who want her, but I do not. America lacks texture. Not that I do not recognize her many virtues. She is bountiful and generous and free, and she has extended her hand to me in my time of need. And she and Russia have saved the world from the Nazis, and now she must save us all from the Russians. But I have had enough of the thinness of her history, the inwardness of her interests. Of the money madness of her impresarios. Of her provincialism—yes, even in New York, which manages to be at once the worldliest and the most provincial of cities. No, I'm moving back to Paris. I have a new opera in the works, about the founding pharaoh of Egypt's Third Dynasty, called by some Nepka, by others Shanakhte. My opera will be called Nepka of Thebes. Oh, *les enfants*, you must come. There's a procession through Thebes that I'm especially proud of. The Pharaoh carried high in a throne by bearers, the massed woodwinds calling, augmented chords on the double basses in the background, the chorus alternating with solo voices, all as I imagined ancient Egyptian music *might* have sounded, with the octave . . . "

Ignace stifled a yawn. He had not inherited his parents' love of the arts. But he was still interested in what his aging roué of a father had to say. Arthur Lebel had the attractive naivety of a man entirely possessed by his own interests and oblivious to all else. Like a child. Uncle Sami had had that same appeal, an appeal that had descended directly to him too, Ignace knew; he had no illusions, he knew women liked him for it, he'd known it since he could remember. It was the Lebel legacy. Yes, they were more alike than they appeared, father and son. The principal danger in their relationship was that the two of them would come to see each other as rivals, or buffoons, or rival buffoons, but for Ignace's sake, and that of his mother, they must deal with each other man to man. Happily, Arthur, in those first moments, did just that. He showed no signs of condescending to the son he hadn't seen for nine years (and not very often before that);

on the contrary, he treated him with gravity and respect, and seemed genuinely interested in his answers and opinions—to a limited extent, at which point the affairs and doings of Arthur Lebel took over. The premiere of *Nepka of Thebes*, for example. It was scheduled for the autumn season in New York, after which Arthur hoped to move it, and himself, back to Paris.

"To the apartment in the Rue Soufflot. Some Nazis took it over, I heard, but it's mine now, as it was then, in theory, even if I hardly lived there after '26. Your mother won't be needing it again. But of course you two are most welcome to use it whenever you want. There's that old café downstairs too, I understand it's reopened . . . the Gueuze, do you remember? It went *collabo* early on, but they should have fumigated the scent of cheap German cigars and exorcised the spirits of dead SS officers by now."

The war, the Germans . . . this line of talk led naturally to the reason for the family reunion.

"She won't write, you know," said Arthur after lunch, over sambuca and espresso. He lit a small cigar and inhaled deeply. "And I really wanted to hear from her, for a while. For the purposes of greater honestly between us, if nothing else. But later . . . I don't know. Now the plot thickens somewhat. I got a letter from this Mother, this Mother ah . . . "

"Filippa. Mother Filippa Giuseppina Storace. She wrote to me, too."

"Saying that Stefanie, that your mother, well . . . "

"Well, we'll just wait and see, won't we, Father," said Ignace, severely, lighting a cigarette off his father's cigar. Arthur, chastened, saw in his son the no-nonsense spirit of Sami; the young man's face, too, with its deep-set eyes and fleeting expressions of contempt, reminded him of his wayward uncle's.

"There's Stefanie's spine in the boy, and Sami's arrogance, and damned near nothing of me," he thought.

Their appointment at the convent was for ten the next morning. In the meantime they strolled the streets of Domodossola. At the memorial to the Partisans they stood and meditated and leaned on the parapet of the bridge above the rushing river Toce.

Arthur, who had flown from New York to Milan via Gander, Shannon, and London over the previous two days, walked as if in a dream. Dreamily, he admired his son and daughter-in-law and the wispy clouds shed by the peaks of the Simplon. Dreamily, as they walked, he recounted his war years: The voyage across; the Russian couple who behaved like nobles from the Tsar's court and from whom he'd heard nothing since he lent them money; his first attempts to make a living in the traditional way of educated immigrants, teaching private lessons; the immigration authorities and their unexpected suspiciousness of Jews; the apartments, one on Patchin Place in Chelsea, the other on Middagh Street in Brooklyn; the just-in-time sponsor, a fellow Jew from Alsace via Vienna . . .

"At any other time I would have thought myself hard used," said Arthur. "But not with the war going on."

Ignace detected a note of guilt in his father's voice at the relative ease and comfort of New York while so many others in Europe were being deprived of everything, notably their lives.

"Still, it was hard work," said Arthur. "I don't want you to get the wrong impression. I wasn't living the high life . . . well, not the whole time. After a couple of years, I began to get more engagements, a master class here, a concert there, and things improved."

"Did you meet any actresses?" inquired Marie-Claire, with put-on innocence,

"Oh yes, and one genuine film star." He named her; Ignace's eyebrows shot up. Marie-Claire gasped. "Really?"

"*T'as couché avec elle?*" Ignace inquired, with an academic's detached interest.

"Ah, Ignace, *mon fils*, the things I could tell. And may, some day, in my memoirs. And far more interesting things than mere movie stars. How I met your mother, for instance, in a girl's school in the Wienerwald, in the dying days of the Habsburg Empire. How we courted, and married, in the shadow of the Great War. I remember in particular an excursion to Baden bei Wien, where we ate ice cream and caught a glimpse of the old Emperor's mistress, Frau Schatt, walking in the gardens. *Bon Dieu*, it all seems about as far away as, well. The Third Dynasty of Egypt. How many lives can one man live?"

They were standing outside a café on the south side of the Piazza Matteotti, across from the Palazzo San Francesco. It was a convenient moment for Arthur to sit down and order an espresso preparatory to resuming conversation about himself; but Ignace intervened with thoughts of his mother.

"She's a recluse. A near saint, they say, you know, *Papa.*"

"A saint, eh? So I've heard. But all that's nothing new. She was a damned saint when I met her. That was one reason we had to separate. We could never divorce, of course, with her beliefs. As for me, I never had any ambitions to sainthood. Which is just as well, given my character."

"No, I mean really. They call her Honored, or Blessed of the Church, or some such."

The waiter brought two double grappas with the coffee. Marie Claire, in demure Swiss-girl fashion, had a hot chocolate. Arthur contemplated the notion of his wife as near saint while, overhead, red and pink cirrus clouds streaked the evening sky. Flights of starlings swelled and soared.

"They?"

"Oh, rumors only, of course," said Ignace. "I had no word of her at all until a few months ago, you know. Like everyone else, I assumed she'd died somewhere along the transport routes, like Grandmother. Then in a café in Geneva I went to a meeting of one of Uncle Sami's old resistance groups, the Football Line from Annemasse . . . "

"Football Line?"

Ignace explained the fraudulent football teams, the trans-border playing field, the pseudo-coaches.

"All Uncle Sami's doing. He was in his element, then, in the early war years. It was still a game, more fun for him even than football."

"And your mother . . . ?"

"Well, an *ancien résistant* at that meeting, when he found out who I was, told me he'd heard *Maman* had been living in an Italian convent, kept incommunicado by former Fascist elements . . . "

"Dear me. Fascist elements, in these days?"

"Oh, they didn't all go away when Il Duce was strung up, you know. After all, twenty-five years of rule is a long time."

"Of course. In Germany, I hear, they couldn't function if it weren't for the leftover Nazis."

"But so much of it was rumors, just rumors. And here's the strangest thing."

Ignace leaned forward. Marie-Claire and Arthur did likewise, conspiratorially.

"'She saved the world,' the old fellow said. 'She saved the world.'"

"What did he mean?"

"He wouldn't say."

They fell into a pensive silence. Marie-Claire took Ignace's hand and held it, examining it as if it were a scientific specimen. All around them came the gentle conversation of passersby and the put-put of small cars and lorries and the Vespa scooters that were beginning to appear everywhere on the freshly paved roads of newly rising Phoenix Italy.

"And Sami?" inquired Arthur, at length. "I mean, he died in the resistance, I know. But I know none of the details."

"Ah yes," said Ignace. Frowning, he looked down at his espresso. "*Eh bien*, it's a bizarre story, like so many from the war years. Sami was betrayed, as I found out from the same source who told me about *Maman*, the *ancien résistant* in the café. Betrayed by a man he trusted, apparently, a man named Sismondi, who sold him out after blackmailing him . . . an Italian by birth, in fact. Odd," he said, turning to Marie-Claire, who smiled in bright anticipation, "we have a street named Sismondi in Geneva, I wonder if it's the same family . . . ? Anyway, this man Sismondi was connected to the Vichy hit squads, it seems, and was assigned to infiltrate the resistance network in the Ain and Haute-Savoie departments. He succeeded all too well, *hélas*."

"Yes," said Arthur, vigorously nodding, "Uncle Sami was always a little too trusting, for all his surface cynicism. Look at his membership of the Radical party, that bunch of poseurs. Look at his love for your mother. Look at his naïve faith in Léon Blum and that ridiculous gang of incompetent dreamers thanks to whom, if you want my frank opinion, France was completely unprepared for war."

"Perhaps. But not really more than anyone else. No one was prepared for *that* war, *Papa*."

His father looked stern and said nothing.

"But you know," Ignace continued, "this Sismondi wasn't the only one who betrayed Uncle Sami; it was a dangerous game he was playing, after all. There was also a man named Lussac, a former minister in that Popular Front government you love so much. He'd been imprisoned and tortured by the Gestapo and released on condition of spying for them. It was he, I believe, who was also instrumental in laying the trap for *Maman*. But he was executed at the Liberation." Ignace finished his espresso at a gulp. "Anyway, as far as I know, Uncle Sami died just outside Dijon at the hands of real *résistants* who'd been misled by Sismondi's agents to believe that a high-ranking German officer was traveling in the vicinity. I believe there's a plaque at the place it occurred . . . you knew, of course, Papa, that he was in the uniform of an SS officer when he was ambushed?"

Arthur had not known it, and had from then to live with the mental image of his suave Uncle Sami in the black-and-silver executioner's uniform. A Jew in Nazi camouflage.

Uncle Sami, shot dead for being an SS officer.

Did he ever say *Heil* in honor of his ex-lover's ex-lover?

Sami Lebel, *né* Shmuel Schoen, *mort pour la France!*

The family had dinner at a *trattoria* and retired early. Ignace and Marie-Claire lay in bed in each other's arms, listening to the gradual diminuendo of street sounds from the open window through which a warm summer breeze blew, scented with flowers and cooking.

"I'm nervous at meeting your *maman*," said Marie-Claire. "She sounds *formidable*. I hope she isn't too impatient with me."

"*Chérie*, I'm nervous too. I thought she was dead. Then I heard she wasn't, just very ill. Now I find out she's living in a convent, hidden away in some remote mountain village. I don't know what to make of it all."

At the same time Arthur, whose travel-weariness had attained a transcendent state of euphoria, was sitting at the window of his hotel room. Above the mountains the azure of the sky had faded into evanescent gold, and in the piazza below was the busy coming and going of small cars, motor scooters, and strollers engaged in the ritual *passeggiata* that was one of the few things that united the Italian nation from its northernmost reaches, as here, to the distant Magna Graecia of the Mezzogiorno and Sicily. Arthur reflected on this, smoking, despite a touch of his recurring asthma that mostly manifested itself in the occasional fruity cough. In his hand was a Scotch: Walker Black, not bad, not quite the Macallan he had come to savor in Manhattan, but this was, after all, Domodossola.

Passing voices echoed from the street.

"*Ciao. Come stai?*"

"*Ciao, bella.*"

"*Ciao, bella,*" repeated Arthur, unthinkingly transforming the greeting into melody: a flattened fifth, a sensuous bent seventh . . . He hummed a few bars and thought of the meaning of "bella": beautiful. He thought then of his imminent reunion with his wife and how beautiful she'd once been and how little he knew her, how utterly foreign they were to each other now, how the monstrous events of one war had swept them together and those of another, apart . . . how his own selfishness, the inescapable self-centeredness of the artist, had played its own part in separating them, although he had once loved Stefanie more than he'd loved any other woman before or since. But it was now 1949. He had made love with other women a hundred times or more, usually in one-night stands after a premiere at the opera, or a middling performance at the keyboard fueled by too much Scotch and self-esteem (or self–loathing; sometimes it was hard to tell the difference). Stefanie, with Uncle Sami, had no doubt (he surmised) had her own sensual enjoyment, such as it was, with the old goat . . . and yet here she was, some kind of cloistered semi-saint, or hermit, or sibylline mystic (a good subject for an opera that, if he could ever get around to it, and persuade anyone to put up the financing) . . . he remembered his early opera *The Mystic*, a glittering success for all the wrong reasons (commercial, anecdotal), albeit heavily derivative of Debussy and inspired even then by Stefanie's strange urges and visions . . . the Virgin Mary, as he recalled . . . silly nonsense . . . not that he was unsympathetic to Catholicism. It was just that, as a secular Jew, he had no interest in or need of religion apart from Art, which was religion enough, and usually made sense, and was worthy of admiration. And anyway, as a Jew, especially a very unobservant one, he was hardly likely to embrace the religion of those who had only recently sheathed their bloodstained swords after an orgy of butchering his kind.

The sky was purplish-black above the slumbering rooftops of Domodossola and the piazza was quiet when Arthur finally collapsed onto the soft hotel bed and plunged into restorative sleep. Behind him lay six thousand miles of traveling and exhaustion and nine years of exile; ahead, as always, the dark unknown, leavened with expectation.

The family met at eight the next morning. After a barely adequate breakfast of *cornetti* and espresso, consumed rapidly in an atmosphere of silent nervousness, they left the hotel in the hired Fiat, Ignace driving, heading northwest toward Val Lungo. New construction was evident on the outskirts of the town, signs of Alcide de Gasperi's burgeoning New Italy, in which democracy had been rediscovered and dictatorship returned to its cage. As Ignace drove, with much downshifting and groaning of overtaxed springs from the little Fiat, Arthur told tales of the legends of the Alps, of icemen and goddesses and the ghosts of Roman legionaries and princesses disguised as eagles and winged monsters roaring out of caverns. Any one of these tales, he said, might make a fine theme for an opera; then, opening a guidebook he had brought with him, he read aloud a passage about the Convent of the Sacro Monte della Beata Vergine dell'Ossola, written in prose as densely Italianate as the convent's name and which Arthur read in an exaggerated Italian accent:

> *The convent, one of the most important of the area, is made of a rectangular chamber and of pre-existing structures such as the crypt with square plane and central pillar. The colonial house*

of the Sisters of Dorotea, born afterwards around the court, has
occupy the large environments that were originally hosting the
workrooms of the convent. In the village of Elvetica Inferiore
there is a chapel from pagan times, originally dedicate for the
god Genio, who is a Genius, and now to the Holy Mother, the
Compassionate Comrade of us. We have, indeed, documentaries
dating back to the beginning of the fourteenth century, but pre-
sumably even more antique, that testify about the place, as well
as the near existence of the castle of Val Lungo, which is the house
of the Duke of Ossola; the castled position and the extension of
the view over the valley, up to the road, facilitate his function of
protection of the area and imposition of control on roads from
Switzerland into Lombardy and Piemonte. Nowadays are still
in a good state of preservation the boundary guelph crenel walls
and the Maestro tower.

Arthur chuckled.

"*Ecco, bellissimo.* The Maestro tower is where they lock up bad
maestros, of course."

"Maestr*i*," amended Ignace, ever the academic, with mock
severity, aware that his father was merely babbling to cover up
his nervousness. Indeed, Arthur smoked two small cigars con-
secutively and broke into a sweat when the road evolved into a
series of hairpin bends above a chasm on one side and a river on
the other. Ignace exchanged a glance in the car's rearview mirror with Marie-Claire, who sat in the back seat, smiling, alternately admiring her husband's driving skills and the plunging
Alpine valleys on either side of the ever-narrower road. Clouds
streamed off the nearby peaks and parted to let in shafts of the
sun that patchily illuminated the emerald green of alpine meadows and the cobalt-blue of streams untainted except by the urine
of the chamois that clustered at higher elevations, watched by the
morning eagles gliding in lazy circles in the upper air. Perched on
a rocky crag across the valley, a squat, gray-stone castle came into
view: "Val Lungo!" brayed Arthur, with a dip into his guidebook
and the discovery of a photograph taken from the same vantage
point. The convent must be near, remarked Marie-Claire. This

observation reduced Arthur to meditative silence and the feigned perusal of the same paragraph in his guidebook.

The road, although barely wide enough for a single car to pass, was paved all the way to the village of Elvetica Inferiore; fortunately, for Arthur swore he would have been sick otherwise. The village itself was little more than a scattering of gray deep-eaved granite buildings around a sloping piazzetta, marked off by a diminutive church, a café-cum-tobacconist's, the local party headquarters of the Christian Democrats, and a small garage specializing in Vespa scooters. A sign pointed away from the square to the Santuario Sacro Monte, towards which another, steeper road wound upward out of the village and snaked around outcroppings of granite and miniature meadows of blinding green and small silver-blue lakes reflecting the sky. At the top of the mountain was the convent. It was a modest place from the outside. Built of the local granite and slate, and shielded from heavy snow and wind by long deep roofs, it was well camouflaged among the rocks and scree of the mountaintop that hemmed it in. A crenelated tower stood aloft from the chapel; atop a flagpole, the Italian tricolor fluttered busily. The sisters' quarters were in a long low building that faced inward onto a central cloister: the "large environments" of the guidebook. The little Fiat Topolino was perilously close to overheating by the time Ignace switched off the ignition. The three of them got out and breathed in the chill and pure air of a higher climate. The guidebook, said Arthur, said the convent was one of the highest in Europe: 1766 meters above sea level. Ignace glimpsed a courtyard in the background as soon as the main gate opened and a pleasant round face, enclosed in a wimple, peered inquisitively out.

"*Buon giorno, Sorella.* We are here to see ah," began Ignace. "My mother." He resisted the impulse to say "*mamma mia.*" Arthur stepped forward.

"Yes, his mother. My wife. *Mia moglie.* My wife lives here," he said, appreciating the surprised upward twitch of the nun's eyebrows. "As a sister," he added. "*Como sorella. Como lei. Se chiama Stefanie . . .*"

"*O, si,*" said the nun. "*Ci aspettanno.* They are wait for you.

Come, please. You, too, *signorina*," she said to Marie-Claire, who hung back, suddenly uncertain, daunted by the hidden medieval world of God's virgins, by the strange austere power of places girded by stone and hidden away in high mountain valleys. An ancient magic that predated cities seemed still to dwell there. In a way, it was a welcome thought, an escape from routine. In another way, it was terrifying, and she'd far rather be at a trattoria in Domodossola, eating *gelato*.

"Come, *chérie*," said Ignace. He took her arm. "I feel it, too."

The nun led the way across a courtyard of broad flagstones. Bicycles leaned against the wall and a vegetable lorry sat at the end of a short path on the other side of the courtyard. The path led to a gate; beyond the gate was a vegetable garden, in which bent backs implied toil. The young sister motioned for them to wait as she went into the garden and consulted in whispered conversation with a tall nun in a white habit who, as it turned out, was Mother Filippa. Her French was excellent, as were—she confessed without false modesty—her English, her German, and her Spanish.

"Many years, many missions," she said. "We are a well-traveled order." She had a long lined face like a face in a Dürer drawing: lined, angular, and slightly anxious, if not weary. But her color was good; there was ruddiness on her cheekbones, and her eyes were a clear, healthy blue. Her visitors had ample opportunity to appreciate those eyes, as she stood and stared with great interest for some minutes, asking banal questions—"Was the drive hard?"; "How far have you come?"; "Have you had any breakfast?"—as she looked hard at each person, as if trying to elicit the essential soul through its eye-windows . . .

"It will be quite wonderful for our honored Stefanie to see you," she said abruptly. "Her family. You are her son?" She touched Ignace gently on the elbow. "And you, her husband?" She repeated the gesture with Arthur, who smiled and bowed, and bowed again when she said, "The famous composer?"

"Famous? You flatter me, Mother."

"Oh but I went to one of your operas, in Milan, many years ago: Bel-Ami? I greatly enjoyed it." Arthur was surprised; it was

his most libidinous, cynical work, based after all on the work of
the libidinous, cynical Guy de Maupassant.

"*Mais oui— mais Bel-Ami? Vous, ma mère?*"

"Oh, that was before I came here." She smiled. "Not that I
wouldn't enjoy it just as much again. Perhaps more."

"And how do you enjoy it here?" inquired Ignace.

"Well, enjoyment is of course not our principal reason for
serving God." As they crossed the courtyard and ascended a long,
shallow flight of steps, she explained the convent's way of life: the
Masses every morning, the Rosary, the spiritual reading times,
the times for personal prayer before the Eucharist, the Office,
the silent mealtimes, the feast days . . .

"Extraordinary," muttered Ignace to Marie-Claire. "They
don't care a fig for the world we live in."

"Oh no," said Mother Filippa, who had overheard. "We love
the world. We only love God more."

They came to the top of the stairs and followed her along a
passageway to a low wooden door, on which Mother rapped her
knuckles smartly.

"*Avanti,*" said a voice that Ignace instantly recognized as his
mother's. He held Marie-Claire's hand tightly as they entered a
long, low-ceilinged refectory. Sunlight from the valley and ter-
races outside splashed off the whitewashed walls and lit up the
room and its occupant, introduced as Sister Stefanie by Mother
Filippa, who then quietly slipped out.

Stefanie was wearing a gray habit which, by concealing her
hair, made her seem younger, or ageless. There were tears glistening in her eyes.

"*Gruetzi,*" she said. "*Grüss Gott.*" Her voice shook. Ignace
rushed to her and they embraced violently and let go and stood
back to inspect each other, then embraced again, gently. Then
she turned to Arthur and offered a cheek, which he kissed.

"My Schubert, *à ses heures,*" she murmured. "You came too?
I never thought to see you again."

She held out a hand to Marie-Claire, who found it quite
natural to call her "Maman," and kissed her solemnly on both
cheeks. Then, after a minute or so of mutual headshaking

contemplation, they all abruptly sat down at the table, as if exhausted.

"*Himmeldonnerwetter*," said Stefanie. "And so here you all are. And here I am. Sometimes I wondered if we would ever meet again."

"Well, I, my dear, or rather we—although I can only speak for myself, of course," said Arthur, in between elaborate throat clearings, "had lost all hope." He sniffed. "I mean, we thought you were dead."

"I have to agree," said Ignace. Stefanie gazed at him, unaware of his words, awestruck by the sight of her son as a full-grown man. She wiped tears with a trembling hand. "But you look good," Ignace added, flatly. "I mean. Under the circumstances."

"You mean, not being dead?" Stefanie's shoulders shook with sudden laughter. "I know, *liebling*, how strange this is for all of us, especially you who had said your goodbyes to just one more victim of the war, as I had to my dear *mutti*, my cousin Fritzl, and others, too many others . . . but for you it was your *maman*, Ignace . . . your wife, Arthur, my dear, although I am surprised that you still feel such attachment as to make this long journey."

Arthur, at a loss without a cigar to light, fidgeted uneasily, with a self-conscious smile on his face. Ignace found himself momentarily disliking his father, wondering if a mere façade was all there was to him.

Stefanie went on, now in French, now in German, having ascertained that Marie-Claire, whose mother was Bernese, spoke German, or the Swiss version thereof.

"But that's *schwyzerdütsch*," said Stefanie, with the knowing mockery of the lifelong teacher. "An entirely different animal. The language of goats, not Goethe."

"But *Grossmutter* always made us speak *hochdeutsch* at her dining table," said Marie-Claire. "Especially after church."

"I'm only teasing, *liebling*."

Marie-Claire blushed. There was tenderness in Stefanie's face as she looked at her daughter-in-law; tenderness, thought Ignace, and a kind of spiritual satisfaction that lit her up, for his mother's face was almost unlined, or no more so than before. The wrinkles around her eyes and mouth were the same as he remembered. Now she seemed somehow younger than she had been the last time he saw her, in Paris in the mad, feverish spring of 1940.

She caught him scrutinizing her and smiled. As if reading his mind, she said,

"The last time we were together was a dreadful time, my darling, a dreadful age. I was adrift, alone, at sea, neither here nor there, not one thing or another—only I was always *your mother*. Always. And I am so proud of you, my fine handsome young man, my, just look at you, with your lovely wife." She continued smiling through a fresh upwelling of tears. "And then, like so many in those dreadful days, I disappeared. Poof! And now, suddenly, in a remote corner of Italy, here I am again," she said. "Poof! And I know you think it wasn't fair, the way I didn't get in touch."

"I didn't say that, *Maman*," said Ignace. "I'm not blaming you for anything."

"I know, *mon fils. Je le sais bien.* But I owe you the explanation I'm going to give you . . . because you are mine, and being mine you may well have inherited what has ruled my life, whether gift or curse it is not mine to say . . . by the way, all three of you, it's not for nothing that I'm *Sister* Stefanie, and whatever I tell you today must remain confidential, as confidential as if I were confessing to you. Because in a way that's what I am doing." She raised a hand and touched her wimple, as if intending to adjust her hair; then she sat up straight and went on in a businesslike tone.

"I was sent on a mission by the Most High. And I knew that the risks were great, should I succeed. That my life was certainly over, should I fail. That either way I was entering into great danger from which I would probably never emerge. That is why I never tried to contact you, my dears. *She* would not have allowed it."

Arthur knew who *She* was, and felt suddenly his renewed affection for his wife evaporate in an access of his native skepticism. Ignace suspected he knew, remembering rumors, and he sat forward with the grimness of a scientist conducting a decisive experiment. Marie-Claire, wide-eyed, was simply gazing at the extraordinary old lady who looked so young and who, incredibly, was her *belle-maman*.

Then Stefanie told her tale.

In the early summer of 1942, during the German advances into the Caucasus and the trans-Dniestr region, when the Vichy government in France was at its most slavish, and the Hakenkreuz flew in triumph above the Acropolis and the Eiffel Tower and the parliament buildings of Brussels, Amsterdam, Oslo, Kiev, Belgrade, and Copenhagen, and Germany's art-ist-warlord seemed poised to conquer the world with his unerr-ing military genius, Stefanie, battered and bruised, was taken by a man named Yves Chatillon, codenamed Renard, a resistant who had infiltrated the French Gestapo, from an interrogation cell at Dijon train station to Metz and Strasbourg in annexed Alsace-Lorraine, and from there by special train to the residence of the conqueror of the world.

"To Berchtesgaden?" inquired Arthur, tempted to add "to see your old flame?" but restraining himself; in his wife's eyes there was a stern authority he remembered well that warned him away from such flippancy.

"Yes, to Berchtesgaden. And I went there on a special train. All garlanded in favors, as they say. And two days earlier I had been half drowned in a bathtub by the Gestapo because I was tak-ing documents to Switzerland for the resistance. They're probably still there, those documents," she mused, looking off through the sun-washed windows, "in that tree, outside the window . . . *dans le ciel, si bleu, si calme* . . . no, birds will have used them for their nests by now. Rain has surely washed them away. Even if they survived, they'd be of no use now. Most of the people they were destined for are probably dead. The war's over, the once so vital troop movements and shipments of radio transmitters are all forgotten, all done with. How fleeting everything is! How insignificant tomorrow are the world-altering crises of today!"

Ignace poured water from a carafe on the table into one of six glasses arrayed on a tray and held the glass out to his mother. She took it with a smile, then put it aside and continued.

"We left from Strasbourg, or Strassburg as they called it. It was Goering's train, one of those special trains the Nazis had for their elite. Yves left me at Strasbourg; I later heard he went underground after the murder of Jean Moulin and was himself murdered on the Vercors in '44. His death is in my heart and soul. So many deaths. Daily I mourn for Mutti and Fritz and Sami and so many brave friends. Daily I offer their suffering to my Heavenly Mother, as I offer my own.

"After Yves left, and after we crossed into Germany—the 'interior,' as they called it, to distinguish it from the annexed lands of Alsace and Lorraine—I was occasionally in the company of Hermann Goering. He had been making one of his periodic raids of French art museums, this time in Reims, I think, and he wanted me to see and judge. I wanted to do neither, but in his venal way he was fond of me, not I think for sexual reasons but as someone he felt he could speak to honestly, always a rare thing for a person of power; and he was also interested in me, less honorably, as a person who could be useful to him. He was being pushed out of the limelight by Martin Bormann and he wanted to set up his own little clique of indispensable people. He was intrigued, too, by my visions and experiences, and told me he'd had the same thing, visions of a creature that sounded horribly like the devil I had seen . . . but will see no more, thanks to Her, and to what I did later."

Arthur squirmed uneasily on his chair, and quite desperately longed for a cigar. To his chagrin and surprise, Stefanie shifted her gaze to him from her past and the mountains outside and said,

"My dear, I have no objection if you smoke. I still do, too, at times. These are trivial failings, amounting to nothing in the eyes of God. As long as we remember not to set fire to things. Or people."

Arthur stood and walked over to the single open window and lit a cigar. As Stefanie resumed, he turned and leaned back against the windowsill, watching his smoke stream through the window.

"I must say also that it is because of him, Goering, that I am here," said Stefanie. She was staring at her hands and talking as if to an invisible audience of memories. "He was a perfect man for his time; he was vain, selfish, greedy, conniving, and hypocritical, all qualities highly prized by the Nazis. He was a curious mixture of *condottiere* and sybarite; and of course he conspired in the crimes against humanity committed by the regime he had founded. Indeed, I blame him, more than anyone else, for Kristallnacht. He started the hellish process by despoliating the Jews, then let others take it further—oh it was typical of him to start something off, then stand aside dithering irresolutely when absolute disaster or failure resulted: Look at the bombing of England. But the Anschluss was all his doing, his one undisputed success.

"Yet for every one of his monstrous failings there survived within him the ghost of its opposite. His looting of the art museums is a case in point: he committed an immoral act, one that he knew to be immoral, but for a purpose that was so elevated— his love of art—that he thought the moral purpose canceled out the immoral. In any event, he plainly had no interest in making money from the paintings; he appeared to genuinely love them. When he showed me his Utrillos and Rousseaus he spoke to me of 'depth' and 'perspective' and 'plasticity' as authoritatively as any curator. Of course, his self-indulgent nature was too weak to sustain the rigors of war. Most of the time we were talking he was drunk, or very nearly. He drank champagne exclusively, and exclusively Veuve-Cliquot. And I found out later that he had been on a steady diet of morphine since being shot during the Beer Hall Putsch in '23. Yet for all his grossness and self-infatuation he had more good in him than Hitler. Who by the end had none at all."

At this point she paused and drank some water. Ignace leaned over and refilled her glass. It was a filial gesture, not an ingratiating one, and Stefanie smiled at him in recognition of this fact. He then tried to cover up a sudden bout of self-consciousness by dilating on the character of the Führer, whom he still remembered, dimly, as the energetic playmate "Onkel Wolf," an episode of his childhood he had never confided to Marie-Claire, but which Arthur suddenly remembered, vividly, like a long-forgotten nightmare . . .

"Yes, it's true, he really went out of his mind at the end. Even in his final will and testament he continued pouring vilification on the Jews, the Masons, the doctors."

"No," said Stefanie. "That was in 1945, my dear. That was not the real Hitler."

"Of course, you mean that by then he had become unrecognizable, a monster," interjected Arthur knowingly, through tusks of cigar smoke. "Whatever shred of humanity there was in him had been eradicated. It was around 1943, wasn't it, that he began to totally lose control?"

"No," repeated Stefanie. "I mean the man who killed himself in the bunker *was not Adolf Hitler.*" A frisson of shock rippled through the room, a harbinger of revelation or insanity. Arthur glanced at Ignace; Ignace at Marie-Claire. Stefanie laughed, her old slightly giddy peal of laughter. It reassured them; they smiled sheepishly.

"All right, *Maman*," said Ignace. "Tell your story."

"Maybe I am a fool, my dears. But I am God's fool, and my Mother Mary's. And what happened was what she ordained to happen.

"Goering and I talked for what seemed like days but in reality was only two or three hours. After expounding on his views on art, he was most interested in what I could tell him about Hitler's youth. I told him little, but let him suppose much. Oh, we also chatted about France, and Pétain, whom he admired; and I was introduced briefly to his wife, Emma, who seemed a pleasant, plump person. These wives and mistresses who attach themselves to such monsters of ambition and greed! Ilse Hess, Annelies von Ribbentrop . . . I often thought, there but for the grace of God go I . . . no," she said, with a laugh, "I don't mean you, my dear Arthur . . . "

"Although I am guilty as charged," said Arthur, shrugging. "Except for greed, maybe . . . ambition, yes. But God knows I'm no Reichsmarschall."

Stefanie drank some water and continued.

"That is true. Anyway, it was like a dream at first, and by that I mean it seemed utterly unreal, not that it was wonderful—although I would remind you that, mere days before, I had been in the cells of the Gestapo, reconciled to dying horribly at the hands of monsters. Now I was in a smooth, quiet train, in a comfortable compartment furnished in oak and plush velvet, being served champagne by liveried servants and from time to time chatting amiably with the number two in the Nazi Reich.

"He had a hazy plan to gather around him a rival clique of influential people and of making me—a leftover from the days when I foolishly allowed myself to be used by the Nazis to give speeches—a party seer, some kind of official clairvoyant, the *Reichshellseher*, dressed in a long white robe and brought out at those pseudo-mystical forest gatherings to invoke the spirits of dead Aryans or some such nonsense. My name would lend the cause respectability—the 'von,' you see, it's amazing how many people, especially the semi-educated (as all the Nazis were), are impressed by that one little preposition. Goering spoke of the spear of Longinus and the Turin shroud and the Holy Grail and their protective powers. Gibberish, I thought, and said so, having, after all, nothing to lose. This made him glum and he left me when the train got to, oh I don't know, somewhere in Baden or the Schwarzwald, maybe Karlsruhe, or Freiburg. So for a few hours I was alone with my daydreams and memories and various dishes of caviar and asparagus and baked turbot and of course plenty of champagne. I needed them all. As for Goering, he only reappeared in all his absurd magnificence, quite drunk—wearing a fur-lined cape and boots, I'm sure you've seen the pictures and heard the stories, well it was all true—at the Munich station, where of course there were toadies waiting and a big car and SS guards. Not very discreet, our Hermann, no, no. He liked to be noticed. So we went to Berchtesgaden through the front door, so to speak, me in the second car with Emma, who spoke of nothing, only shopping and the prices of, as I recall, clothes; so, sirens wailing, we went out to the autobahn and averaged a hundred kilometers an hour all the way there, and Hermann's lord and master was waiting at the top of the stairs when we arrived. And the first thing Goering said, as if to put me in my place, was 'Here she is, *mein Führer*—your new *Reichshellseher!*'"

Suddenly she became pensive, troubled, ill at ease. Ignace and

Arthur remembered this mood and forbore to intrude; Marie-Claire, however, by now enthralled and horrified by the narrative in equal measure, blurted out,

"*Mon Dieu*. You visited *Hitler*? At his *Eagle's* Nest?"

Her naïve question eased the atmosphere; Stefanie laughed, and Ignace put his arm around his wife's shoulders.

"Forgive her, *Maman*," he said. "I'm afraid there's a great deal in our family history I haven't told her about."

"With good reason, *mon fils*," Stefanie replied. "Yes, my dear girl, you are quite right. We met at the Berghof but went up to the Eagle's Nest." She explained the difference: that the Berghof was really only an expanded chalet, the Haus Wachenfeld, whereas the other place was a purpose-built retreat atop the towering Kehlstein rock that its owner never called the Eagle's Nest, although such a stirring and pretentious sobriquet would have sat well with him, mused Stefanie, had he known of it . . . she faltered in her narrative then, as she had faltered in her mission that day, sitting with her family then (why had she decided to plunge into this right away, after so long?), sitting with him that day in the great brass lift that rose through the mountain . . .

In the lift nothing was said. She saw herself as she must have appeared to the ruler of the world, as a dim, insignificant creature, yet one possessed of some vague meaning from his life, or *for* his life . . . He was dressed in his wartime feldgrau uniform with the Iron Cross. When they met he kissed her hand with distant dispatch, holding himself in a more monarchical way than before, remote and self-absorbed, like the Kaiser of old; yet he appeared determined to spend time alone with her, an emissary from his boyhood, and he dismissed Bormann, who hovered about from the moment her car arrived and whose blank obsidian stare took in both her and Goering as threats to himself in the lists of the Führer's favored ("welcome *back*, Frau von Rothenberg," had been his ironic greeting; and "ah, Herr Reichsmarschall, your bath is ready"). Goering took himself off to the steam room in the Berghof, sloughing his fur cape on the way and calling over his shoulder half-sober assurances of meeting up again later . . .

"Well, it was the last time he saw his Führer," she said, her
voice trembling, and paused, with a shudder, as if a cold draught
had just blown in. She didn't know how else to introduce the
main topic, the climax of her story, of her life, of history. She
took a long slow breath and clenched her fists, then got up and
went to the window. Standing next to Arthur, who stiffened
slightly as if in the presence of royalty, she continued in a barely
audible voice, staring out the window at the very same Alps.

"The Kehlsteinhaus—the Eagle's Nest—is a quite substantial
building, not the mountain cabin one imagines. It has many
halls and rooms and cellars and a long arcaded sun terrace that
looks out on a drop of about, oh I don't know—about like this,"
she gestured at the precipice below the window, "two thousand
meters?" She looked down. "Yes, about the same. Well, when we
got there, he invited me out there to sit and have a cup of tea.
Did I say invited? Summoned. He never *invited*. We sat and the
servant who brought tea, I noticed, was curtly dismissed. I didn't
recognize her: since my time. So, I sat there with the *Grösster
Feldherr aller Zeiten*, not knowing what was expected of me. At
first we just looked at the mountains. I don't know what he was
thinking, but of course I was thinking of the last time I had
been there, in exactly the same place, the day I had left his life,
as I thought, forever. Finally he broke the silence by asking me
disjointed questions about my job, about Paris, whether I still
lived on Rue Soufflot, and whether I knew he had almost visited
me, but for a scheduling conflict; and I realized he was studying
me, watching but not listening, the way he did, not really paying
attention to the words being spoken, but examining the face, the
eyes, the lips, looking for weakness.

"Then, suddenly, he broke in and asked me if I still had the
painting.

"'What painting?' I asked, taken completely by surprise. This
set him off. What painting? Was I crazy? Was I lying? Why, THE
painting, of course, the one he'd been seeking for years, the one
he'd done of me in Vienna in '09, the one he'd painted in that
old Jew's house, my uncle's palais, I must remember, I fainted
while he was working, had I forgotten that? Had I forgotten how

embarrassing it was for him? How humiliating, to gather up his things and leave that house with the old Jews sniggering behind his back? And did I know that at the time he had nowhere to go but back to that hideous men's dosshouse with those other filthy old Jews lurking about and sniggering at him and stealing his money? And there was that old sneaking Hebrew who . . . and he went off on one of his tangents about the Jews, in the usual very heavy-handed way, in a kind of mock-professorial style with that dreadful leaden Germanic jocularity, wagging his finger and asking me if I'd heard the joke he'd heard from Bormann: Did I realize how many Jews had traveled home by air? *Die Juden haben die Himmelfahrt angetrete!?* If not to Madagascar, then to Heaven?

"Then he laughed, falsely and mockingly, like a stage villain. But he needed no stage."

She slumped against the window. Her family stared in silence at her. She wiped her eyes and cleared her throat, then glanced around with a nervous smile.

"*Himmel Gottl*, I could do with a cigarette," she said. Ignace, with the alacrity of a good headwaiter, produced one and lit it for her. Father, son, and daughter-in-law took fleeting but keen pleasure in the sight of a nun taking deep drags off a cigarette with the practiced ease of a lorry driver.

But when she resumed her tale, all pleasure ceased.

"So I killed him," she said. "I know, of all things I could stand here and say, this is probably the most insane, *nicht wahr?* I killed Adolf Hitler? How is that possible? But it's true, as God is my witness—as He was. And this is how it happened. We were on the sun terrace, as I told you. He was leaning back, half sitting on the balustrade between two columns, with nothing behind and below him. And he was raving, as I said. Making jokes about the deaths of Jews and so on. And as his raving and insults grew louder and more unbearable, I had the most extraordinary feeling—not just of anger, but of exaltation, of something being born inside me, of . . . I don't know how to describe it. It was as if I were changing into someone totally different and being given extra force, almost like an injection of power . . . and of course I was, by my Holy Mother. Her words had been quite clear. And I was at last in the right situation. It was a situation I had been in once before, on the day I had left him, as I thought for good. I was certain there was no one else around; the servants had been dismissed. So I did what she told me to do, what no one else could have done, because I and I alone had a memory of the way he had once been, back in Linz, of the feeble good in him that had long since died, and I needed that momentary insight, like a chink in armor, to strike at him, like a jilted lover. And so I did. I no longer saw the greatest war lord of all times or the Führer of the Greater German Reich but mad Adi, *wappler*, pathetic *schmuck*, venomous *fetznschädl* of a crazy third-rate postcard painter. So it all came together and when he raised his hands in that the studied way he always used, to make a dramatic point, and then leaned back even farther on the balustrade for effect, I got up and rushed over and pushed him hard. Here, on the shoulders," she tapped one shoulder, then the other. "And he grabbed at me but missed and then he just fell and fell, oh how far he fell, turning round and round and round for twenty thousand meters, or kilometers, or into outer space, for it seemed to me he took half an hour to fall till he struck the bottom, and I could see, oh from so far away, his body caught on a rock with his leather coat beside . . . "

She remembered the great wings that spread across the sky, the high distant music she heard, the soft light that spilled from behind the mountains, as she watched his body tumble into nothingness . . .

Greeted and whisked away by the singular personage who had haunted him these many years and ushered directly without preamble into the hottest of his anterooms . . . ach, they say your life flashes before your eyes? Adi's life went by in a second, and the rest of the time en route down the mountain it was the very limited future he saw coming at him and what lay beyond: in place of ever-greater glories and triumphs, the devouring gaze of Beelzebub, whose hot hand he felt gently take his elbow . . . and the saddest thing, just before he hit, was the thought of Linz forever remaining Linz and never having the opportunity to flourish as Der Grösste Haupstadt des Dritte Reichs . . . *and the violent final awareness of not having found that damned portrait . . . and the end was, for that infinitesimal fraction of time, incredibly, blindingly hot . . .*

Ende der geschiste.

The silence was broken by Marie-Claire.

"So who was it, then?"

Stefanie finished her cigarette and tossed it out the window, then walked slowly over to the table and sat down. She adjusted her wimple and folded her arms, her face drawn with weariness. The light dimmed, as if clouds had rolled over the sun; but Arthur, who was still at the window, looked up, and the sky was blue and cloudless, and only an eagle or other great bird with immense wings wheeled slowly overhead.

"*Ma chérie*, do you mean who did the world think was Hitler, from '42 to '45?"

Marie-Claire nodded eagerly, eyes shining like a child's at a birthday party. Stefanie took a deep breath.

"His name was Hartmut Dunkelwein," she said. "Yes, believe it or not. He was a poor relative and hanger-on of Martin Bormann's, a failed university lecturer dismissed for sexual reasons but he was what they call an idiot savant, one of those who are slightly retarded mentally yet capable of the most astonishing feats of memory . . . In Dunkelwein's case, his gift for mimicry, physical and verbal, is what had spared him exile, prison, or worse. Bormann, diabolical Bormann, had spotted his opportunity ages before. So he was on the Eagle's Nest when it happened. Yes, I thought we were alone, I thought Bormann had stayed at the Berghof, but Hitler had instructed him to dispose of me off the side of the mountain . . . using the same methods as, well, as I used on him . . . or that was what Bormann said. It's possible, if the portrait meant so much . . . anyhow, Bormann was there. It was the second greatest shock of my life when, just after it had happened, I heard him come up behind me and say, 'Well, well, Frau von Rothenberg, we certainly have some work to do here, don't we?' I was resigned to being executed, but of course I knew nothing then of the man Dunkelwein, or Bormann's plan. He had hidden Dunkelwein on his estate in Bavaria for several years and had been coaching him in Hitler's mannerisms by showing him news films and even letting him appear in person at Hitler's birthday parties and other functions, dressed as a waiter. Bormann was planning, I believe, to use Dunkelwein as his own puppet after assassinating Hitler in late '42, for no one had the access to Hitler, or the power, that Bormann did, and as the world knows, even if it doesn't know it knows it, the man Dunkelwein bore an uncanny resemblance to Adolf Hitler—or appeared to, from a suitable distance. He sounded the same, if slightly hoarser, with an accent more Bavarian than Austrian (just listen to any of the speeches later in the war, suddenly the Austrian accent's completely gone) and he looked the same, except for a slightly stronger chin."

"Incredible," said Arthur. "Stefanie, you take my breath away."

She smiled.

"Of course. It sounds fantastic. But when you stop to think about it, if you take away the trappings and the mustache and comb the hair back, Hitler was the most nondescript of men; you see half a dozen like him on the streets of Linz or Passau any day of the week. And by '42 the great world-conquering Führer had become such a remote figure that it turned out to be relatively easy to play a trick on the world and keep at arm's length an impostor who had mastered his master's style of speech and mannerisms."

"But surely some must have found out," broke in Ignace. "I mean, it's in*credible*."

"Oh yes, my dear. Many knew. Goebbels—but he didn't want to say anything because he hoped to manipulate the impostor for his own ends. That was true of many at the top. Eva Braun, of course, but she was a pretty fool who wanted only the parties, the cars, the handsome officers. And after the so-called assassination attempt in '44, when high-ranking officers had got wind of Dunkelwein's deception—well, Mussolini, who was no fool, already knew, of course. In fact, he had documents proving it— correspondence between Bormann and Dunkelwein—that *he* was hoping to use to bargain for *his* life when he was arrested by the partisans in '45 just down the road here, at Dongo on Lake Como. But it didn't work, as we know, and in any case it was in no one's interest to reveal the truth, then or now. Back then the longer the charade continued, especially when the Germans were still winning, the better . . . mostly for the German people, who genuinely loved their leader, or the image of their leader. Goering knew the truth, of course, for he was at the Berghof that day, and I had to confide in him in order to escape from Bormann. He and Bormann had long been feuding for control, and sooner or later Bormann outmaneuvered everybody: first Goebbels, then Hess—whom, by the way, *he* had persuaded to fly off to Scotland in '41; then Goering . . . *ja*, Bormann won in the end, before they all lost everything. Goering couldn't compete with his brand of malice. No one could."

Ignace leaned forward.

"And was . . . did this Dunkelwein die in the bunker? In '45?"

"Yes, it was he. Certainly. But not a suicide. Probably executed on the orders of Bormann or Doenitz, the new Führer. No one knows. With no remains ever identified, except mistakenly by a Russian dentist . . . "

"And the portrait?" Marie-Claire was staring, fascinated. "Where is it now? Can we see it?"

Stefanie rubbed her eyes and smiled wearily.

"The portrait, ah, the portrait. Yes, *ma chérie*, you can see it, as long as you have the price of a train ticket to Vienna. The painting of me by Adolf Hitler hangs in the Modern Art Museum there, as a lesser work entitled 'A Portrait of His Mistress,' attributed to an unknown Austrian artist. He never signed it, I suppose, or maybe he used his pseudonym 'Wolf,' which meant nothing to curators. I've only seen it once, you know, and that was very long ago. Please don't ask me how it all happened, exactly. I suspect Goering had a hand in it. And when his collections were turned over to the Americans at the end of the war, the lesser-known works were sent to Vienna's state museums for cataloging. But it's the final irony of ironies, that Hitler, who always lamented his lack of artistic success, should have finally achieved it, to a certain extent, anonymously."

"But how did you escape in the end?" inquired Arthur. "And how did you get here?"

"Goering put me under his protection. Bormann wanted to shoot me at once, of course, while also I think regarding me with a certain awe, as having done on a moment's whim what he had been plotting to do all his life. But in the end he was persuaded that I was needed for a while anyway to coach Dunkelwein. And then Goering appointed me *Reichshellseher* as he'd promised and sent me away to fulfill my spiritual duties at a safe distance, in the South Tirol, and his friend Galeazzo Ciano, the Italian Foreign Minister and Mussolini's son-in-law—a most charming man, oh my dear Arthur I'm afraid he was, you know—anyway, Ciano intervened and placed me here, where I have been happy, and where only Mother Filippa knows this truth I have told you, and even she knows only a part of the whole. The others here know me only as Sister Stefanie, and are kind enough to call me Honored, for my visions of the Holy Mother."

She stared suddenly out the window as if seeing just such a vision, then rubbed her eyes, shook her head and continued in a quiet voice.

"You know, I haven't been back to Germany or Austria since then. It was the late summer of '42, just before Stalingrad, and that was when the combined incompetence of Goering and Bormann and Dunkelwein—oh yes, he started to take himself seriously fairly early on—began to be evident, and of course then the debacle began. For all his faults Hitler was a military genius, you know," she said, almost defiantly, as if determined to cherish some good in the murderer she'd murdered. "Stalingrad would never have happened if he had lived . . . if *I* hadn't killed him. But if he had lived, they would have won the war, no doubt. Where was the American or British military genius to compare with Hitler? Churchill?" She snorted. "Roosevelt? De Gaulle? Consider: The Rhineland; Czechoslovakia; Norway; Poland; Holland and Belgium, in days; my sweet France, in six weeks; the entire Ukraine and half of European Russia, in less time than that; the Balkans; half of North Africa . . . No, my dears, a Germany guided by Hitler would have won, that's a fact. And many more millions would have died, and so many would today be slaves. So who can dispute my deed? Who can contest the judgment of my Mother Mary?"

There was a plaintive note in her voice, like a child making an excuse. She passed a hand across her face. Her shoulders sagged. Awe filled the room, as after a performance by a great pianist.

"*Mes enfants*, my mother used to say 'leave those who hurt you to God' and that's what I've done from the day of my first vision. With one exception, but that was for suffering humanity. And now I am very tired," she said in a near whisper. "Perhaps you can come again later." But she and they knew they would never come again.

Like pilgrims, Ignace, Marie-Claire, and Arthur lined up to pay their respects: Arthur with a kiss on the cheek, Marie-Claire with an embrace, Ignace with both. Sister Stefanie clung longer to her son than to the others.

"When they come to you," she whispered to him, "believe them. For they are real, my darling."

Then they kissed. Her head was bowed when they left in silence, and the darkness seemed to deepen in the room, and there was a great wheeling shadow high in the darkening heavens.

Epilogue

"Is she a saint?" asked Marie-Claire, who thought she probably was, in a way.

"No," said Ignace. "I'm certain she isn't. Read about the saints and somewhere in their characters you'll come across something immoveable, something of solid rock, something that can't be driven by man or nation or Mother Mary. She's a good woman, immeasurably better than most of us, but she's not that strong, and she lived all her life on the very edge of madness. A saint? No, no. She was a self-deceiver, as successful in her line as Hitler was in his, but her deceit had a kind of innocence about it, and his of course was pure malice."

"Do you mean that what she said to us was . . . ?"

"I don't know, *mon chou*. I don't know. But I am sure of this.

Somewhere, on some plane of existence, at some time in her history or the world's, the thing she described *did* happen. But in that way, and to him . . . ? Who can say? After all, where is his grave? No, I don't know, and I never will. And nor will you."

"Your poor *maman*."

"Oh, the last thing she needs is pity. Come. Tomorrow is a busy day."

So they went to bed.

The End

Gustave
Thirteen

COMFORTABLY ENSCONCED IN my old armchair, I watched my future wife on Channel 5, dressed in a bluish-gray suit that set off her auburn hair very nicely, reporting from Police Headquarters on the Boulevard Carl-Vogt on the appointment of Dr. Martin Dürrenmatt to the post of State Psychiatric Supervisor of the Republic and Canton of Geneva with special duties in the Police Department which, by an astonishing coincidence (she said, straight-faced), was under the stern but just aegis of Dr. Dürrenmatt's brother-in-law, Dietrich Fegelein, very busy himself these days with the arrangements for the first terrorist trial the city had seen in many years. The prognosis for the two Pakistanis was excellent, given the universal indifference toward the event enlivened by outbursts of bohemian hostility vis-à-vis the cops: the *Pakis* would no doubt be mildly chastised, served three hot meals a day in Champ-Dollon (the country club laughingly known as a prison, with mountain views and full mod cons), presented with leather-bound Korans, and sent back via first-class jet to Pakistan, where they could grow luxuriant beards and rant at the hated West. Such was our civilization in the initial stages of its inexorable decline.

I turned off the TV, after respectfully allowing Martine's image to disappear first.

A Gianbabuino Camorra double-breasted pinstriped suit, unworn for years and stiff from refitting at the dry cleaners, reclined formally across the foot of my freshly made bed.

437

A brimming cup of espresso steamed at my elbow. Its contents were soon coursing through my veins as a token of the new day.

My lady on Channel 5 was another such token. She was now an official co-resident of No. 135 bis, Boulevard des Philosophes, third floor right. Her belongings were neatly stacked in the corners, pending the arrival of new wardrobes. The Parc de Budé apartment, scorched during the events of November, was deemed uninhabitable by housing authorities; and Martine's mother, now living anonymously in the Vendée, had put it on the market. In any event Martine and Laure didn't care if they never set foot there again. Only I missed it, slightly, for the memory of the archangel. And fainter memories, fading fast.

So: Martine and I had decided to marry.

Yes, I had taken a) a deep breath and b) the plunge. Bachelorhood, the domination of the self, ignoble habits, wandering lusts, unwashed pajamas: goodbye to all that. And why not? I was over halfway to the grave, and she was forty, well preserved but no longer the cynosure of youth's hot desire. Besides, she loved me, I her, a neat equation not always present in the married state. And when the electricity of sexual attraction faltered, we could read to each other from our works and the works of others. And go arm-in-arm for walks along the lakefront, leaning into the wind. And take a slow steamer beyond Chillon to the Dents du Midi, gates of heaven. And go on meandering drives in my cherished car through the wine country of the verdant Champagne. And, like Ignace and Marie-Claire, take the Simplon Express to Domodossola and Milan; and the Settebello overnight from Milan to Rome, and wake up with the poplars of Emilia marching past the window, or the escarpments of the Palatine itself.

The night we'd decided to get hitched we had dinner at the Auberge du Riant-Mont, an old heavy-beamed inn with a stone courtyard and manorial fireplace in the country near Soral, where the wheat fields roll up to the French border hard by the gurgling stream under the frowning Salève. Well oiled after the vinous accompaniment to three courses (*salade verte; soupe à l'oignon; lièvre en croûte*), I challenged her — or Stefanie's—version of Hitler's death.

"Hartmut Dunkelwein? I mean, honestly."

"And, say, *Alois Schicklgruber*? Too ridiculous, eh? But that was his father's name. And almost his."

"Yes, but really."

She raised her hands in mock horror.

"OK, so it's crazy. Any crazier than his life, and where he got to from where he started? And what he did?"

"Well, no."

"Oh and by the way, I know a man who saw the Archangel Michael not once but three times. Crazy, eh?"

"OK. Touché. But still."

She was lit up with merriment and wine. After two or more glasses (a '94 Chateau Bombardier: well aged but still spirited and full-bodied, like Martine), I'd come to notice, she'd tend to talk; but so far I hadn't been bored for a second. (That would no doubt come with marriage.) "You know," she said, "when I think of Hitler and Nazism and Stalinism and all that insanity, sometimes I think that in the 1920s or early '30s we all collectively, the whole planet Earth, tumbled into a wormhole, a time warp, you know, one of Einstein's short cuts to an alternate universe, and that in our own real world, the world we accidentally left, those things, the Nazis and the camps and everything, didn't happen at all, and things went on in a more normal way."

"Normal, eh? So it's your reinterpretation of history."

"Mine? Not at all. It's all what Stefanie said. Or what I say she said. And how do you know it isn't true? Were you up there with them? Or in the bunker in '45?"

"Ah. Of course. As Ignace says, Where is his grave?"

"Absolutely. Oy, professor! There are more things in heaven and on earth. Blah blah blah."

"God knows that's true enough."

Well, we drank to that.

We strolled after dinner to the Citroën, which I'd parked next to an open football field behind the village hall for concealment from passing yobboes and prying eyes. The air was cold and still, with snow coming. I stood and smoked a while. The field undulated toward the Salève, whose looming shape was gradually dissolving into the night. Martine clutched my arm and pointed to the dark field.

"Do you know, Gustave, what that is?"

"A football field."

"Ten out of ten. But did you know that one end of it's in France? Yes, those goalposts there at the far end are in the Département de la Haute-Savoie, whereas the others on this side are in the Canton of Geneva."

"Fancy that."

"Moreover, this is the actual football field where Sami Lebel smuggled his escapees across the border in 1941 and '42. About a dozen escaped that way and made their way back to England."

I gaped in awe, like a Calabrian peasant seeing the Vatican.

"I take your point," I said. "You *did* do your research."

She only chuckled and snuggled up.

So, switching channels as it were . . . later on the same day on which I watched her on Channel 5 in her blue-gray suit, we were married, *mirabile dictu*, in St. Martin's Church at Onex in a Rite Outside Mass, the express version, by Father Benedetto Sanzio. The ritual came after other rituals, a short interview in his office during which Martine, as a protestant, professed such vehement hostility to the faith of her fathers that the priest, beaming, assumed she must be "one of us at heart anyway, eh?" and that if she wasn't she was as good as, and he'd have no problem marrying her in the one true faith. As for me, unrepentant visionary and avowed church non-goer, a few words on the subject of the Archangel Michael were enough to propitiate Father Benedetto's less-than-stringent scruples. We all understood the Seven Sacraments in principle, although Martine as a Prod had to be reminded that the Eucharist to the Papists represented actual flesh and blood, not a mere symbol of same, as her Calvinist pastors would have it.

"I have to admit I find that a bit much," she said. "I mean, really. It's the next thing to cannibalism, begging your pardon, Father."

"Yes," said Father Benedetto. "I hear that a lot from today's nonbelievers. But if your question is, How big must His body be, if so many Eucharists turn into it all over the world all the time?" He quivered with practiced mirth. "Why then, I must say, as big as the world!"

Nonsense, yes, but dear to me as ancient nonsense can sometimes be. And it opened slightly the creaking gates to the corridors of two thousand years of my ancestral culture. I saw as down a long hallway the dim light at the far end through which my angel shone, and I felt freed from the bonds of being mortal.

Mamma was at the wedding, of course. Ignace Lebel, retired Professor of Mechanical Engineering at the University, and his wife of fifty years or more, Marie-Claire, had been invited by Martine and were in the back, studying prayer books. Various friends of Martine's, slick TV types for the most part, but with broad grins and kindly comments, took up the left side of the church. Dr. Dürrenmatt was there, with a pale gray-haired lady who was definitely not Greta. On my end were Paul and Odette Trenet, Paul as my best man. Dr. Petitpoix had appeared, less as a gesture of amends than as a hopeful career move: Once Martine let it be known that she would making a documentary about me and my visions, Petitpoix volunteered his services as a co-star.

"Who knows Termi better, I mean to say? Ha, Gustave?"

"Ha indeed. I'm glad to see you aren't wearing your bicycle clips, Petitpoix."

He fell silent, deflated. Despite my insistent insolence, my job was secure, partly thanks to a "sanity patent" signed by Dürrenmatt (who persisted in claiming, if only to me, that he had seen the angel, too); but I was planning to chuck it anyway and concentrate on a book or two and live off my pension and Martine's better than average earnings . . . and as for Gax? Absent; about ten thousand kilometers absent, actually, as I learned from the Trenets over a quick drink before the ceremony.

"You remember that Brazilian girl Kia something or other," said Trenet, "the ambassador's daughter—?"

"Dos Santos," interjected Odette.

"—who was in one of your classes and two of mine? Pregnant by your friend Gax."

"I'm amazed it was only once," said Odette, cryptically.

"Now he's working in the family publishing firm in Recife. Or is it Belo Horizonte?" He turned to his wife, quizzically. She shrugged. "Serve him right. He doesn't even speak Portuguese. They have him doing the offset, I think. Anyway, she was the one, Termi. She was the 'mole' for the *Procope*."

"And she fed the info to greedy Gax, who wrote it all up."

"But no," he said. "They put their heads together, yes, in more ways than one; but *she* wrote it all. Gax had writer's block, certified by his psychiatrist, the eminent Dr. LeCluyse, who is mine as well by the way (I know, Tavo, you're shocked that I have a shrink) . . . "

"No, I'm shocked that you have *that* shrink. I availed myself once, with scant success."

"Oh? In any case, Gax was excused from fulfilling his contractual obligations to his publisher with a note from his doctor. Not a physical illness, he seems cured of that, if he ever had it. No it's mental. They have an official term for it . . . *constipatio scriptori?* Anyway, last I saw him . . . that was two weeks ago, just before they left . . . he said he'd had enough of that life, and all he wanted was to wear a straw hat and sit on a porch and drink some exotic Brazilian concoction—"

"Caipirinha," said Odette, loftily.

"—and watch the parrots fly about in the trees."

"Parrots, eh?"

"Oh, and he said to say hello to you. That was it. Hello. So: *Hello!* From Gax." Odette gave him a mock-slap on the shoulder for silliness as the image formed itself in my mind—in all our minds, no doubt—of a decaying palace on the Amazon, with Kia's shrewish face barking Brazilian imprecations from the bushes and parrots swooping about overhead and towering tropical cloudbanks and a humbled, harried Gax in a straw hat bent double under the burden of wood pulp and his marriage . . . speaking of which:

Mine then came to pass.

"My dear friends," boomed Father Benedetto, beaming, "you have come together in this church so that the Lord may seal and strengthen your love in the presence of the Church's minister and this community of . . . whatever it is. And Christ abundantly blesses this love, you know. Oh yes. He has already consecrated you in this baptism and now he enriches and strengthens you by a special sacrament so that you may assume the duties of marriage in mutual and lasting, um. Fidelity. And so, in the presence of the Church, I ask you to state your intentions, and make them good." They were stated; they were good. Music chosen by me (Palestrina, Mozart) played, there was the exchange of rings unfumbled by Trenet, Martine and I pleased our audience with a pair of long intense gazes, feet shuffled, then came the grande finale, when Father, reaching toward us with an expansive gesture and looking ceiling- and skyward to Their Place Up There, declared: "You have stated your consent before the Church. May the Lord in his goodness strengthen your consent and fill you both with his blessings. What God has joined, let not Man put asunder, you know. Amen." More music (yes, Mendelssohn's March, I'm afraid: the kitschiness of it raised goose bumps of embarrassment on the back of my neck), kisses, handshakes, a huge sense of relief, a thrill of excitement, a niggle of apprehension—and so into the cars, a rented pair of Mercedes S-classes for them and the good old Citroën for us. I parked next to the Cathedral and we walked down the steep hill to the Place Neuve, illuminated as if for festivities, and across to the Lyrique, the only place in which it was truly fitting for me to bid farewell to my prolonged bachelorhood. It was fully booked for the occasion. We arrived like a party of diplomats, palanquined along a red carpet. A string ensemble played Marguerite's "Jewel Song" from *Faust* (Gounod's). Alphonse, in a tuxedo, stood by the door and offered his compliments. We shook hands.

"Congratulations on the new wife. But make sure she doesn't start sneaking expensive clothes out of the stores," he said, hoarsely, with his usual mock-solemnity. I slipped him a twenty and hastened to the sumptuous table, creamy white tablecloths crowned with blue and white flowers (snowdrops? edelweiss?)

in silver vases. The guests milled about murmuring in admiration, then sat down. In creamy Fendant du Valais, I proposed a toast to my wife. She blushed; applause was general. The mood was high and was heightened further by the excellence of the homely and traditional Geneva dishes that followed: *confit de lapin*, *cassoulet*, *fricassée de porc*, a smooth *gratin de cardons*, the crumbly *omble chevalier* from the deep waters of the lake, and finishing with a tart *tarte aux poires*, all washed down by local wines: Fendant, of course; earthy Chasselas de Russin; a smart Gamay de Satigny; a bolder Cabernet from the borderlands of Dardagny; and, of course, champagne (Veuve-Cliquot) from the legendary golden acres of Champagne itself. Alphonse served, assisted by assistants. I was seated two down from Martine, who had determined the seating arrangements, with Mamma on her right and Father Benedetto on her left. To my right was Odette Trenet, interrupting her dinner with quiet croons of pleasure at nothing in particular. Paul was across from her; next to her, one over from me, sat retired Professor Ignace Lebel, son of the Blessed Stefanie. He was shaking his head and talking to his wife, opposite.

"They had these grand weddings in my mother's day," he grumbled. "I was certain they'd ceased. Or all moved to television."

"But it's wonderful to be invited to one," said Marie-Claire, whom I felt I knew: the bright blue eyes, the rosiness amid the wrinkles, the gentle smile. Both Lebels were in their early seventies, but there was an eternal youthfulness about them such as you find among the devout, or the athletic, or just the ever young. Life in Switzerland is life in aspic, you see, and the old can seem young for want of stress, just as the young can seem old for want of drama. Mamma knew Marie-Claire as a neighbor in Confignon and enthusiastic fellow shopper at the Worldwide Super-Gross Food Mart in the Pink Cha-Cha shopping center at La Praille . . . I mentioned Stefanie von Rothenberg. Stefanie had passed away, she said, with a blissful expression on her face, the day John XXIII was elected Pope, in 1958.

"Her last words were 'Take me now,'" said Marie-Claire.

"I thought they were 'Hold me back,'" said Ignace.

Father Benedetto, warmed by wine and cassoulet and the first wedding he'd presided over in eight years, came over and shook hands with the Lebels.

"Ah, yes, your mamma," he said to Ignace, whose evident discomfiture implied lifelong anticlericalism. "I met her once, you know. Yes, yes, at the beautiful monastery in Italy . . . actually, I said to Professor Termi that when he had finished reading Mademoiselle Jeanrenaud's book . . . silly me, I should say, Madame *Termi's* book, ah ha ha . . . that when he finished, I would tell him of my encounter, because I think he was unsure whether your dear mother ever really existed!"

"Oh, she existed, my dear professor Termi." Ignace grimaced. "Oh yes."

"I'm glad to hear it, I think, my dear professor Lebel," I said. "And by the way, what became of your father?"

The softer expression that thawed Ignace's features told me much about subsequent father-son relations.

"He died in 1968, in Paris, of a cerebral aneurysm."

"Really? Mine died in '68 also," I said. "Of coronary shock. Upon reading about the Russian invasion of Czechoslovakia. He was a communist, you see."

"Was he? Mine was a composer—as you know, of course." He frowned. "From your wife's book." The thought of Martine's book caused him obvious pain. In fact, Martine told me later that when the book came out he had been dissuaded from filing lawsuit only by her assurance, well founded as it turned out, alas, that the book would be a commercial failure. "My father wasn't a very good composer, I'm afraid, not that I know much, but he was very much an artist. His aneurysm was brought on by the noise of the *soixante-huitards* on the barricades outside his apartment—or rather, by the fit of rage that it caused him to fly into. His companion of the moment said he was trying to work on a new opera."

"Yes," said Marie-Claire. "An opera about Hitler."

Would the world and our family never be rid of that name?

"Not *Hitler* again," said Martine. She came over and stood

sipping champagne, with a wife's proprietary hand on my shoulder. Father Benedetto, made expansive by all the good cheer, expanded further and slapped Ignace firmly on the back. The dour professor winced.

"By the way, Professor Lebel, did you know it was the story of your mamma's life that brought these two fine people together?"

Marie-Claire clapped girlishly; Ignace raised his glass to Martine and me in a polite gesture tinged with irony, as were so many of his gestures. In the background, against the soft glow of the globe lamps, Alphonse was marshaling his troops for dessert duty (tiramisu, nougat, *marrons glacés*, etc.) and the quartet was playing airs from Stefanie's old Vienna: "*Traumerei*"; "Roses from the South"; "The Blue Danube"; "*Un Sospiro*" . . .

"I was at the Convent of the Blessed Virgin in the Valle d'Ossola, near Domodossola—ah *professori* it's beautiful," said Father Benedetto, addressing both professors and their wives, "you go from Brig through the Simplon and head up through the highest remoteness—"

"I know. I've been," interposed Ignace. Marie-Claire gave a nervous smile and looked down into her lap. Father Benedetto barreled genially on.

"Ah *bella bella*, then you know, how you come around a corner and there it is, on needle-pointed rocks with a view over half the Alps and nothing around but the sky and eagles and chamois—and now, they tell me, brown bears, thanks to the ecologists who reintroduced the beasts, never mind the locals who must sacrifice their sheep and goats to this misguided foolishness—*Madonna*, you talk about *pazzi, porca miseria*! Anyway. I was leading a retreat of novices—this was when we actually still had a few novices around, when some more or less normal boys really wanted to serve Christ and become priests, sounds quaint today, or suspicious, like they're really all convicts or perverts and want to hide under a soutane, ha?—so I was leading these novices to the convent, where some very severe retreats were held. Too severe for me, but I had the excuse of having to go down to town to organize things while the young people prayed. Sister Stefanie was quite old by then, perhaps my age now or a little older, but she was quite upright, very aristocratic. It was completely by accident that we met. I and my group were coming up a long flight of stairs and she appeared at the top, dressed in the blue-and-white habit of the order, smoking a cigarette. Even in the nun's habit, she looked like a duchess. I introduced myself. 'Stefanie von Rothenberg,' she said, very formally, with a little bow of her head, in excellent French with the slightest German accent. 'I am pleased to meet a good Catholic Italian priest from the great Swiss Protestant city of Geneva.' Very Germanic sense of humor, *molto Tedesco*, so dry you need a drink of water afterward. 'German?' I asked, curious, because it was only, I don't know, '54, and memories were still sharp . . . 'No, Austrian,' she said, 'if there's really any difference'; then she paused and shook her head and said, 'No, no, Father, I am not German, nor Austrian. In my heart I am from Paris. Do you know Paris?' I said yes, I had spent three years there, as a deacon in the Batignolles district, with the immigrants and the peasants from Auvergne. I think she was hardly listening. 'You know,' she said, 'if I could see the Luxembourg just once again, on a June morning . . . ' And I swear to you there were tears in her eyes as she said this. So I left very quietly, *piano piano*, without saying goodbye, or even *au revoir*." And I swear to you there were tears in Father Benedetto's eyes as he said this, but whether they were tears of emotion or of pure champagne was, at that stage in the proceedings, debatable. Ignace leaned forward and patted him on the shoulder.

"I know," he said. "If those bastards had never come into Paris she would never have left. And how different the world would be!" He blurted out a laugh of pure scorn. "*Ha!*"

"Well, that was all there was to it," continued the priest, sniffing. "When we left I looked up and saw her standing at the top of the stairs, watching us like the chatelaine of an antique chateau. You know, I had the distinct impression of a woman *pas comme les autres*. Of course, it was only much later that I heard about her extraordinary association with Hitler and the even more extraordinary theory about why she ended up there . . . "

"Speech!" cried Ignace. "Professor Termi! Speech from the groom!"

I gladly took the bait, sparing both Ignace and Stefanie's memory, and rose to my feet and spoke effusive words of thanks and wellbeing and proposed another toast to Martine and the years that lay ahead, with the grace of God and all His holy angels (especially one), and I offered another tearful toast to my dear dead Papa, *padre mio*, and my dear still-living *mamma mia* . . . who suddenly, loudly, and uncharacteristically burst into tears, vigorously applauded by all and subsequently genially hovered over by Father Benedetto and Alphonse with a restorative bottle of Veuve-Cliquot. Truly, by then we were all quite mellow. Mellow! Autumnal word, graceful and calm, like the barely rippling reflections of tawny leaves in the quiet waters of the Petit Lac. Like the aging swans on the river. Like the soft sighs and muted groans and the slow descent into nothingness of my last stage of life. Now, with a woman to push the wheelchair. A woman to witness the over-ripening of my soul. A woman to survive me.

We sat apart from the others for the rest of the evening, receiving passing compliments like the King and Queen of Geneva: Trenet, failing to get me into focus, and hurried away by Odette; Petitpoix, diffident, unsure what foot he stood on now, but affecting a kind of dignity ("Best of luck to you both" and a curt nod); Dr. and Frau Dürrenmatt, he heavily, Swiss-Germanly, winking at me with the eye he thought was concealed from his ever-bored wife, who of course saw perfectly clearly but cared not, having had long since ceased to care; Mamma and her priestly priest, now merrily infused with the spirits of a thousand grapes; and Professor and Mme. Ignace Lebel, she bright and whimsical, he cordial, yet distant. Before he left, while his wife chatted to mine, he took me aside and fixed me with the steady gaze of the mystic he confessed that he, too, reluctantly was.

"It's hereditary, you know. If you were wondering."

"I was, actually."

"It sometimes skips generations. My grandparents never showed any signs, but there were rumors about my maternal great-grandmother. Anyway, I thought I'd warn you, in case you have children. That's why Marie-Claire and I never did."

"How did you know? About me, I mean?"

"Because," said Ignace wearily, as if forced to repeat something already oft-repeated, "At my age I've learned to read the signs. It's all in the eyes. A certain hesitancy in the gaze, a kind of cloudiness from time to time, a flickering of focus."

"And how often do you, ah . . . ?" I was seized with an odd apprehension.

"See them? Oh, all the time, I'm afraid. Yes, the older you get, as you see less on this side, the more you see on the other. At this very minute, for instance, just behind you, there's one I'd wager you've never seen—yet. But he's at everyone's elbow. Always. He was particularly taken with my mother's friend, as you know. You start seeing him when you get older and he starts looking for . . . shall we say, future tenants?"

A coldness passed through me.

"Ignace, *chéri*," called his wife. "It's late." His name on her lips was still infused with love, even after so many years. Stefanie von Rothenberg's son patted me on the shoulder and forced a smile that didn't reach his hazel eyes.

"God bless you, Gustave. I mean that quite literally. And good luck."

I watched him as Marie-Claire helped him on with his overcoat. He seemed to shrink into himself as they made their deliberate way outside, both walking with precise, tiny steps. Before they disappeared around the corner, he turned and looked back in my direction one last time, shaking his head slowly as he did so.

"*Adieu*, Stefanie," I murmured.

"What are you mumbling, professor? Drunk again, are we?"

My wife was at my side, warm and willing and redolent of wine. Then the stragglers came to make their farewells and they sang and well-wished until the colors and their faces blurred into a single vision of nighttime exhaustion and Martine and I found ourselves outside, tipsily tottering across the broad windiness of the Place Neuve and up the Promenade de la Treille to

the world's longest park bench (I to her: "Didn't you know?";
she to me: "No"; I to her: "Aha, so there's still research to be
done!") from where we glimpsed the bluish-white and honey
golden lamp-necklaces of the Swiss-French metropolis, draped
from Jura escarpment to Salève escarpment, beyond which lies
nothing but the tiny cold mountain villages of the High Savoy
and the eternity of the Alps.

No wonder the Archangel came here; it's a place that mimics
paradise.

And then we shuffled through the rustling carcasses of last
summer's leaves across the cobbles of the Place St. Pierre in the
shadow of Calvin's dark cathedral: Monsieur et Madame Gustave
Termi, somewhat intoxicated, quite well fed, as happy as we'd
ever be, and for all those reasons and many more we were a lasting reproach to the ghost of old John Calvin, who watched in
horror from his sixteenth-century vantage point as we got into
our red beast-carriage and drove away into the realm of the still
living.

FIN

About the Author

Roger Boylan is an American writer who was raised in Ireland, France, and Switzerland and attended the University of Ulster and the University of Edinburgh. His novel Killoyle was published by Dalkey Archive Press in 1997, and was followed by a sequel, The Great Pint-Pulling Olympiad, published by Grove Press in 2003. A frequent contributor to such publications as the Boston Review, the New York Times Book Review, and The Economist, he currently lives near Austin, Texas.

www.dalkeyarchive.com

www.dalkeyarchive.com